MELODY
OF
MANA

MELODY OF MANA

WANDERING AGENT

Podium

For Dr. Bartlett,
who always inspired me to persevere
through hardships to reach the stars

Podium

Melody
of
Mana

CHAPTER 1

✦

I AM AN IDIOT

As I shimmied across the ledge over the little hole, I couldn't believe they'd talked me into this nonsense. I thought I'd be spending a fun day in big caves, playing around with echoes. I did not think we'd spend hours wandering through a tiny maze of little crevices full of that special bat funk.

"Hey, Alex," Steve tried to break in. I ignored him.

"Hey . . ." He looked back.

"Isn't this fun?" Fun!? When we got back to civilization, I was going to strangle him. If this was his idea of fun, then he was never picking activities again.

"Oh yeah, it's great." The sarcasm was palpable.

"Embrace the suck," John broke in from behind. He, his girlfriend, Steph, and her little sister, Julie, had come together for this calamitous adventure. I could hear the laughing as I struggled with crossing the gap, fuming at the collective insanity.

I liked Steph; we'd known each other since kindergarten. Julie was a trip too. John, Steph's new military boyfriend . . . I was less sure about him.

The cave started shaking, and it hit fast. That wasn't supposed to happen in the Blue Ridge. This was the Southeast, not bloody California. The rocks around us rumbled and cracked under the pressure of moving earth, the strain too much for them. Luckily, none fell on me. As it continued, a particularly large wave threw me from the wall I'd been holding on to for dear life. I couldn't keep my balance and fell, right into the crevice I'd been trying to maneuver past.

I freaked, trying to grab on to anything to arrest my fall as the air whizzed past, a rush of dark rock blurring in my headlamp's light. This crevice wasn't that wide, maybe two or three feet. Fingers and arms scraped against rough stone as I fell, only slowing my fall a bit before a floor finished it off.

"Umph! Ow . . . ow, ow, ow," I whimpered from the ground. "Hey! I'm here, I'm . . ." I did a quick self-check for broken bones. I could still move everything without tons of pain, so that was good. "Mostly okay!"

I got no response from yelling up the void I'd fallen down. It couldn't have been that far, could it?

I pulled a small toy ocarina necklace out and began to whistle an SOS. I ran a quick inventory of my current resources while I whistled for help. I had the ocarina, plenty of flashlights, half a bottle of water, and a pack of spearmint gum. Oh, and standard pocket cash and cellphone; I always had those.

I had no idea when I fell asleep, but nothing had changed when I woke up.

"Hey, guys! Little help? I'm still down here!" Still no response. That was odd. I should've been out and curled up on an ambulance tailgate by now. At least that's what all the movies said.

There wasn't much to this cave I was stuck in. I could see a path leading somewhere, but I'd heard that you were supposed to stay put until rescuers found you. I didn't want to imagine what would happen if I wandered off and got lost, only for someone to show up looking for me.

I must have been here for a day or two. I wasn't sure, but my water was all gone. No response though, still no rescue. Even if the others got pulped in that earthquake, shouldn't someone have come looking? I knew we'd left information with people on what cave we were exploring. That was just common sense.

When I woke up again, my head was pounding. I was definitely dehydrated, no way around it, and severely so. I decided to give it one last try.

"Is anyone there!? Can you hear me?" I yelled up into the darkness. The lack of a response sent a chill down my spine.

There was no help on the way? I had to keep going or I would definitely die here. Resolved, I walked toward the path I saw. I was hoping to find a way out, or at least some potable water.

Scabbed hands and knees from my fall protested as I pushed into the cave, deeper and deeper, unsure of my destination. This path was quite long, longer perhaps than the one that had led us in. I knew this was a bad idea: to keep going might lead me to my doom. I couldn't stay still any longer though. Another day and I might be unable to move; if nobody came for me at that point, I would be dead. The caves were cool at least, so I wasn't sweating as I ventured into the darkness.

There was some light up ahead! Rescuers? Maybe a way out or onto a lit cave path?

"Hey! Hey, help! I got lost, please help!" I screamed through my dry throat, begging anyone to aid me.

As I stumbled and struggled forward, I finally turned into a large, open cavern. Nobody was here. There were no happy fluorescent bulbs to greet me either. There were, however, a number of glowing vines all leading to . . . a pool of water! Blessed water!

I ran to the pool and took great gulps of the liquid, not caring that it was untreated and probably full of some nastiness. It was so sweet and cool. I wept as it flowed down my throat before I collapsed at the foot of the pool, laughing like a crazy person until I fell asleep.

When I woke up, I decided to have a good look around. There was some kind of pattern in the stone here. It was natural and flowing but looked oddly like it could have been something graphed out on one of those calculators they had you play with in math class. I had the strange feeling that there was something going on there, but it was just outside of my reach, a hunch poking at the edge of my mind.

The vines were something else though. They were this brilliant blue, shining brightly all over the cave. I had thought they might be lightbulbs, and that seemed reasonable. Their color was quite unnatural. They all led to the water; where were they getting energy from? There was no sun down here, and the only way in or out seemed to be the one I'd used. I even checked in the pool; there didn't seem to be any inlets or outlets there either.

"Weird . . . where did you guys come from?" I ran my hand along one of the vines, brushing the leaves gently.

I piddled around, examining every inch of this cave, but when I got near the path that led out, I felt uneasy. It was like this place was welcoming me, like I was supposed to be here. The idea of leaving sent a cold shiver down my spine and sent me back to the safety of the pool.

Within a day or two though, I was getting hungry, desperately so. My thirst had been abated, so now I wasn't so obsessed with the need for water, but that just left my stomach aching. I briefly considered eating some of the vines. I knew kudzu was edible. But these might be some kind of ivy, which really wasn't. They were also my light source, so munching on them seemed a poor decision.

As long as I stayed far from the exit, I felt strangely calm. I was uncomfortable, yes, but not panicking. I even had enough sense to realize how weird that was. I was sure that even if I knew of a way out, I'd have a hard time wanting to leave this safe little nest I'd found.

Little lights began to form around the vines. Waves of light that shimmered and danced in the air, how lovely. Again, I got that feeling that there was something going on, but I couldn't quite place exactly what it was.

I quickly learned however that the lights would respond to me singing or playing on my ocarina. They moved around in patterns that wouldn't quite come together. It was at the very least beautiful. I even saw a few bubbles forming from my own skin and floating off to join the lights.

There was a non-zero chance that there was something in that water and I was tripping balls right now. I'd have to find out later. If there was, it'd be one hell of a drug. I could think of several uses both for calming people and recreation. If I'd lucked out and found the new weed of the century, I was going to share it with everyone.

After falling asleep a few more times, I woke up to find a flower had grown over where I liked to snooze. It was beautiful, some perfect periwinkle thing. I tried to take a photo, but my cellphone had died. That one last game of sudoku had been too much apparently.

I was still deathly hungry, but other than that, I felt like some kind of nature spirit, lounging in my magical cave of glowing vines and pretty lights. I played more music to lean into that feeling. "A Fig for a Kiss" got a good response from the little glowing waves; I laughed as they danced a bit.

The flower turned into a fruit while I slept. It was big and plump-looking, still periwinkle. I wasn't sure what to make of that and spent the whole day debating. On the one hand, every piece of survival advice I'd ever heard screamed not to eat the unknown fruit. On the other . . . it looked so good, fat and perfect. It also just felt right. This cave grew it right over my sleeping spot; it was like a gift. The cave hadn't done me wrong before; it was safe and good here.

"You wouldn't do me wrong, would you, friend?" I was speaking to plants now. That couldn't be a good sign.

Just before going to bed again, I made my decision and picked the plump little morsel. As I bit into it, I knew it was the right decision. The flesh was so soft and perfectly flavored, and sweet, so very, very sweet. I moaned in pleasure as I devoured it, licking every bit of juice from my fingers and chin. It was too good. I was so exquisitely happy as I lay down to sleep.

"Aaaahhh!" I woke up screaming in agony.

My whole insides were in pain, like I was being rent apart. I looked down to see cracks running along my skin, leaking fire.

"What the . . . !" I was cut off as another pulsing wave of pain flashed over me, unleashing more agony.

This time when I looked down, I saw one of my fingers turn to ash and fall away. I fled to the pool and jumped in, hoping to quell the fire. Much of the pain began to recede as I trembled and twitched in the cooling liquid. I looked around and saw the lights getting brighter, so much brighter. My body was dissolving into the pool, and as I looked up, it all became a single brilliant point.

Gazing toward the ceiling as the lights became a hurricane around me, I felt myself pushed on all sides. Up and forward toward the brightness with inexorable force I went. Waves pushed me ahead as I wondered if this was what dying was like. I was afraid, so very afraid as I got closer and closer to the shining point before me.

CHAPTER 2

✦

REBORN

The pushing turned out to be contractions, bringing me into a new world. Being born is an altogether unpleasant experience for everyone involved. It takes hours, is massively uncomfortable and painful, confusing too. I thoroughly understand why babies cry at their birth.

Finally, I was pushed and pulled out though, and I could breathe again. I screamed for help, not having any clue where I was or what was going on at the time. Someone even smacked my bottom, how terrible.

Soon enough, I was cleaned a bit and passed around. Huge hands took me and strange faces looked down, speaking in some language I'd never heard anything like. They were all women, at least as far as I could tell.

I couldn't see much as I tried to look around, mostly vague shapes; this made me worry I might have damaged my eyes. But all my senses were wonky. Sight and hearing were the most obvious. Sounds were all really weird, on top of the fact that I could only see shades and outlines; it was heavily disorienting. Smells were all weird, too, though most of what I could smell was the result of my birth.

After a spell, I was passed over to what I assumed had to be my mother. She held me gently, rocking me for a bit before bringing me to her breast. Being fed so had to be about the most awkward thing that has ever happened to me. The way she spoke and hummed to me however, had a near infinite kindness buried in it, and it relaxed me immediately.

I tried to move and speak a bit, but this new body was highly uncooperative. My muscles barely responded, unable even to properly support my own weight. My mouth just wouldn't make sounds right either. I couldn't get a single word out at all; it was a real pain.

Soon enough, we were joined by some men. I assumed they were men at least. Their voices were much deeper, and they seemed to have bigger and rougher hands. They were also far less competent at holding me. My scream alerted the women, and after a few sharp-sounding words, I was carefully passed back to my mom.

It was a bit weird thinking about her as that at first, as I already had a mom. After a few days though, it was clear as day. Whoever this woman was, she was my mother in this world, and she did care for me. Once I understood that, I had no issue accepting her or any of the rest as a family as true as any I'd ever known.

Within a few months, my senses improved by leaps and bounds. I could finally see some of the things around me. Our house was a small one-room thing, not unlike an old hut from a history book on the Middle Ages. It wasn't nice, but it was a bit warm. You could tell people lived and were happy here.

My family looked European. There were my parents and two brothers. Dad had black hair with a bit of gray and looked like he was made from taut wires. Mom had pale blond hair and was rather lithe, but graceful. My two brothers were blondes and appeared to be close to ten years old.

One might think that a baby would be bored all the time, but it is not so at all. I was having to retrain my body from the ground up. It was a bit exhausting, but every step brought me that much closer to being myself again, or at least sort of like myself again.

As I progressed, I learned that my name was Alana, which is very pretty. I still wasn't up to speaking. My mouth was getting better; it still felt a bit weird, but I was picking up some of the language. I was now able to understand at least a few words and mostly get what people wanted me to. Phrases like "Come here" and "No, Alana" were very simple.

Mornings in this world started early. Mom tended the fire from some ashes kept under a clay pot while my brothers and Dad fetched eggs and water. Breakfast for them was eggs, bread, and veggies. Everyone quickly ate and began their daily work, leaving only me and Mom at home.

My brothers sometimes brought back things like greens and mushrooms around lunch. Since there were other kids with them, I assumed they were playing and gathering those items. That looked extremely fun so I hoped I could join them soon.

Mom stayed at the house. When it was just us, she did a quick cleaning and put dinner on, mostly soups and the like. Then some of her friends would come by, and they would do handiwork while gossiping about something or other. My guess was that they came here because I was so small. They all seemed really good at spinning and sewing and stuff. I suppose they'd been practicing all their lives.

Dad would come home around dark for dinner, which was decidedly the largest meal of the day here. While there was absolutely more food, there was seldom any meat. Whatever meat there was, was in soups or stews. That felt odd to me, since a meal isn't much without some meat, right?

After dinner, the boys would repair tools and do some handiwork. Mom went over to the corner and worked on a loom as tall as she was. It didn't look like an overly complex machine, but it sure was big. Their whole lifestyle seemed rigid and repetitive, but everyone seemed happy, so who was I to judge?

From what I could tell, my brothers were an absolute handful. It was not uncommon for them to be dragged home by someone, only to have my mother beat them with a large wooden spoon. I never saw Dad get angry though; Mom was certainly the disciplinarian in this house. I will give them this: the boys did seem to rein it in around me. They at least had the good sense to be careful around a baby.

After a couple more months, Mom started taking me to other houses, and I finally got a good look at what was outside. We had a small chicken coop, with a rooster and his tiny flock. He was a proud, colorful little man, who crowed every morning to greet the sun. We appeared to be in a hamlet of about ten houses, surrounded on all sides by fields. They were primarily some form of wheat, with some fruit and veggies mixed in. In one direction, I could see a huge wall of green, which must have been a forest.

Upon seeing other houses, I could say for sure that we were in the middle of the pack. Some of the houses were nicer, some worse, but my family seemed well off enough for this little hamlet. I didn't see all the houses, but Mom was now the visitor, dragging me along to play with other people's children.

I could still see the patterns of light from the cave. I managed to tune them out or bring them forward at will, so I mostly just ignored them. I really wondered if everyone here saw these things; unfortunately, I couldn't ask. They did, however, highlight one house in our hamlet; it was surrounded in little triangles.

The old man who seemed to live there alone was too. He looked like he was being surrounded by the contents of a trig textbook, floating semitransparent in the air all around him. The people of the village seemed to respect him, and he was decidedly the best-off person here.

My days continued much like this until I was about nine months old. Then it got colder, and the seasons led to new work for everyone. I think I must have been born in the winter, since it was now fast approaching again.

One day, I found myself sitting on our rug, playing with my toys. If I didn't want to play, people would come and rattle things in front of me and get all worried until I did. So it was easier to just go along with it. I had a little rattle, but what I really wanted was one of Mom's spindles. I'd seen her using it a lot, and it looked fun. She wouldn't hand it over though, so I just sat there rattling, thinking about how I might get a chance to look over it closer.

As I was going over this in my mind, I saw one of the bubbles start to form around the spindle. Not sure what was going on, I kept at it and saw it begin to move toward me, floating down off the table and closer to me. Keeping my mind on the spindle was hard; each moment, I could feel myself getting more tired, my focus waning. Finally, the spindle landed right in my little hand, and I cheered and burbled in delight.

I can do magic!

It may not have been much, but this was magic! Magic! That's the big one; with that, I might be able to do some things here. I'd have to work and practice for sure.

I cheered and held up the spindle, the sign of my first success, at least until Mom saw me. She rushed over, taking it from my small hand.

"No, Alana, that's not a toy. Be a good girl and play with one of your toys." She pushed a doll I was completely uninterested in at me when I reached for the spindle again.

I cried about it being taken away and grabbed at my prize, but Mom refused to relent. Eventually, I fell asleep, exhausted from my efforts and my bawling to get the spindle, *my* spindle back.

Upon waking, I made a few decisions. I could not allow my family to know what I could do. Who knew how this world would respond to magic? Practice was a must though, and I would be doing that whenever I got the chance.

Secretly, I worked on my first little spell, grabbing the spindle every time Mom turned her back. The progress was slow, painfully slow. She, on the other hand, was unamused by my antics, even popping my bottom a few times. I persisted anyway; soon I would claim it as my trophy, to celebrate my acquisition of magic.

I also managed to figure out how to make both the room and myself a bit warmer or cooler. That new trick was really hard. But as winter approached, I found it immensely helpful. Around the same time, I learned that I didn't need the rattle. Making noise or even moving worked just as well.

My parents seemed to be concerned that I'd not started speaking yet. That was understandable, I guess, since I was about that age. I could say a few words in English, not that anyone thought it was anything other than baby talk. Mom would hold me, looking intently as she spoke.

"Can you say 'Mama,' Alana?" she would ask in the sweetest tone she could manage.

"Won't you say 'Mama' for me?" I was practicing a bit when nobody was around, but I was stubborn, waiting for just the right moment.

One evening at dinner, I decided to show them what I'd been working on all day. Looking across the table, I spoke clearly to my mother. "Mama!" She was thrilled. Everyone smiled, Dad even gave a toast. I followed it up as he was drinking for maximum effect. "Spindle!" I yelled almost accusingly. Dad spat his drink out and across the table; my brothers almost fell out of their chairs. My mother looked more than a bit peeved. After dinner though, the spindle was added to my toys. Success!

As winter fell upon us, I managed to keep the house nice and toasty warm. My family, of course, didn't really know why it was so warm, but they mentioned a couple of times that we weren't having to use as much wood this year.

We spent the whole time cooped up together. There were few chores that required anyone to leave, and when they did, they hurried back to the warmth. During those outings, I got a few quick looks at the outside. Snow had descended in force, leaving everything covered in a thick blanket of white. I was amazingly glad I could stay inside through this mess.

We spent our winter fixing up tools and prepping for spring. Handiwork seemed to be the order of the season and everyone, myself excluded, dove into it with fervor. Mom was weaving like a madwoman as Dad and the boys carved and fixed up everything they would need in the spring.

Our home was lit with lamps for the most part, which was unexpected when I first saw it. There seemed to be several kinds of oil, some of which truly stank. As the months dragged on, the oils, along with some kind of burning rushes, ended up making our house smell horrid.

The normal foods also changed, with cheese and yogurt now making up a sizable portion of our diet. There was less food all around by a huge quantity, too, but without farmwork, that wasn't an issue. My family always drank some kind of ale, never water. I, of course, was given some kind of funny-tasting milk instead. It didn't have a bad flavor, just a very different one.

As spring approached, the boys went back to their gathering. The influx of some fresh greens was quite welcome.

I also saw that the bubbles I'd noticed on myself when I was in the cave came back, floating away harmlessly whenever I tried to do magic. Once or twice, I even started to see them when I wasn't doing magic. It would seem I was forming some kind of aura.

My second year proceeded much as the first, save that I proved myself to my family to be an incorrigible chatterbox, asking them all kinds of questions.

"Mom, what's that?"

"That's the field, where our food is grown."

"What are they growing?"

"Mostly wheat, also some cabbage, some beans, and over there are some grapes."

"Mom, who's that?"

"That's your uncle Barro, he's your dad's brother."

"Mom, who's that?

"Hm? Oh that's Mystien, he's a wizard."

"What's a wizard?"

"He can do magic."

"What do you mean magic?"

"He can make things happen when he wants them to, like he can make fire if he wants fire."

"Can I learn magic?"

"Maybe when you're older; most people can't though."

"Oh, okay."

I guess that it was all a real pain for my family, but how else was I going to learn all these new words? And I really wanted to learn them. The more I could learn about the world, the safer I'd be.

Around the same time, I got to go on my first trip to the village. It was around half an hour from our little hamlet. We're still considered part of it, so it's no big deal, but we were one of five hamlets that spread out around the village proper like the spokes of a wheel. There's around four hundred people in the village, with the same number living in the hamlets. It's nice, but not too busy overall, reminding me of some old role-playing games.

Mom was going to the village for market day, and I finally got to tag along. These were a regular occurrence and served as the chance to stock up and share gossip. We needed salt and ale, the latter of which would be delivered to us, but we came mostly to gossip. Our family had much of what we would need and couldn't really afford much of what we would want.

The gossip was good. Right outside of the village hall, we met with Mom's friends. A nearby empire was having a succession crisis. Some wealthy merchant girl had been found out as the mistress of a duke, to the great trepidation of both families. The local big city was also having some issues with grain output; everyone there blamed their mayor.

The village hall itself was lovely, a huge building big enough to hold the population easily. Mom said it was used for some festivals and dances, things like that.

Near the end of the day, I even got a few candies. They were made of honey and tasted just like it, along with some other fruity flavors on the side. Honey was apparently quite pricey as nobody kept bees. When I asked why, I was told that it wasn't possible.

Beekeeping became one of the things I wanted to invent, right up there with plumbing. We currently used a chamber pot; it was disgusting to an unbelievable level.

That winter was interesting. I learned that most of the dairy, including the weird milk from the previous year, was from some goats one of the villagers kept. I was also given a very small amount of the beer this year, or ale rather, and not a particularly pleasant one. Nobody drank water. I didn't know why, so I just asked, of course.

"Dad, why doesn't anyone drink water?" I inquired one evening.

"Because, Alana, water will make you sick. You must never drink it." He gave an immediate and stern response.

"It does?" I was thoroughly confused by this.

"Mmm-hmm, at least the water around here does. Make sure to drink ale or milk, okay?"

"Okay," I responded. It was weird, but maybe the water around here was dirty or something? Why didn't they just boil it?

Then it occurred to me that I was being dense. They probably didn't know to boil it. Best to stick to milk or ale, it'd make my parents happy at least.

* * *

Things proceeded much the same until I was three. I'd secretly practice magic. I learned to make a little light. I also learned a few new skills, figuring out how to spin some wool into low-grade yarn. My mobility went up, too, and I could now properly walk and run around. This let me spend a lot more time outside.

All things continued like this until "The Incident"—a day that will forever stick with me vividly.

I was playing with a little magical ball of light, trying to adjust its color to periwinkle. It wasn't big, just a small ball I was shifting around in my palm as I worked out the method to change its coloration.

Truthfully, I was supposed to be washing a large old pot my mom had given me. I had all the tools, some ash from our hearth, a little brush. It was an easy thing to teach me about cleaning. Most of my chores were just a bit of light education like this one, not that I was given many chores, perhaps two or three little tasks a day.

Because of my intense focus on that which I wasn't supposed to be doing, I didn't hear the annoying, rude adolescents sneaking up on me. One or both of my brothers thought it would be funny to toss a grasshopper onto their adorable little sister's shoulder to scare her because they could be real jerks when not monitored by more mature people.

They didn't notice the small ball of light fly off to places unknown as I got surprised and spun, struggling while trying to get the bug off of me.

Everyone saw when the insect jumped on to my face and scared me. The spell turned into a blood red flare as I lost control, everything turning deep crimson as it detonated over a nearby field. The noise of it going off was a piercing keening over the whole hamlet, like a scream to accompany the second sunset.

There was dead silence for only a moment before movement exploded. I could hear others running for cover as my oldest brother, Rod, scooped me up and ran for the house. He might have been a stupid git most of the time, but his dedication to protecting me was truly touching.

"Rod!" I called out to him.

"Be quiet," was the only response I got back.

"What was that!?" John asked. My other brother seemed just as surprised as everyone else.

"I don't know, but it's bad." Rod was a bit short with us, but he didn't have time to talk as he ran.

Mom met us at the door and ushered us inside. Slamming it, she began to ask the same questions. When I tried to speak up, I was told to be quiet. Being a little kid really sucked sometimes; nobody ever listened when you had something to say.

Perhaps a minute after the questioning, Dad flashed through the door. I had once compared him to a panther, and how right that was. He was moving so fast; I'd never seen anyone move like that before.

"Is anyone hurt?" he asked. His voice had changed; he sounded like a commander from some war movie.

"No, what's happening?" Mom replied worriedly.

Dad moved to a certain spot and jumped up, grabbing on to the rafters, an impressive feat, being that they were easily ten feet up. Seizing one and holding himself like it was nothing, he tossed down a sack that had been up there, along with grabbing what appeared to be a spear.

"We don't know; we're too close to civilization for monsters to attack. There's nothing in this area that should have done that." He'd emptied the sack to take out a chain shirt and helmet and was getting dressed quickly. "Stay here and be quiet."

I tried to speak up again only to have my mother put her hand over my mouth.

I made one final attempt after my father had left to tell my mom that it was probably me. That ended with not only her hand over, and staying on my mouth, but a number of hard thwacks to my backside with her trusty wooden spoon. A first I might add, as I generally behaved well.

"No talking, understand?" was her whispered threat. The spoon was still in hand.

My parents on Earth hadn't believed in corporal punishment, so this was an extreme first. I tearfully nodded; if they wanted to chase after shadows, I wouldn't try to stop them any further.

It took a couple of hours for Dad to return. When he did, he was still wearing his war gear, looking like something out of a movie. Mom looked at him with worry as he led us out, taking us to meet with all the other families near the road to town.

"The old man's still out there checking; we're going to the village," Dad announced to everyone, before turning to lead us.

All the adult men of the hamlet were here and well-armed. Most just had some farming implement, but a few like Dad had proper weapons. Only one other was in armor, and he took the rear while Dad took the lead. Everyone's eyes scanned the area around as we went, nearly in a panic.

Once we got inside the palisade of the village, everyone calmed down. Quickly, we made our way to the village hall and got inside. As soon as the men left, the talking began. It was sunset, and everyone was now on complete edge.

I was sat down and given a very firm scolding. Mom was livid that I had kept trying to talk when told to be quiet, particularly in such a dangerous situation. She particularly emphasized that I was being far too disobedient, then threatened to spank me again if I said another word. Her exact words were, "Be quiet until an adult tells you otherwise." I had every intention of obeying.

As night crept in, more and more people showed up. From what I could gather, all the spokes were being summoned in a panic. Their conversations just sounded like "doom doom" from where I sat silent. I could only imagine how livid these people were going to be when they found out that I was the one who caused the explosion.

The theories were completely out there. One said that it was the kickoff signal for a war with the empire, whoever they were. Another postulated that a goblin tribe had moved in and tried something, only to be shot down by a neighbor who pointed out that there'd been no goblins in this region for well over a century. My personal favorite was the old man who swore he'd seen something just like it, when a wizard tried to make a teleportation gate and it malfunctioned, turning him into a fine red mist.

The one thing that everyone agreed on was that Mystien would figure out whatever it was. He was apparently the only wizard in the region. From what I could gather, those who could focus magic were quite rare. When he entered the room, all eyes went immediately to him, the focus sharp.

"I've determined that what we saw was most likely a spell failure of some kind. While the effect was dramatic, the damage and trace left in the area was almost nonexistent. Therefore, it was probably a fairly weak effect that failed," he announced to the crowd.

"Are we in any danger?" asked one person.

"Does that mean they have wizards ready to attack us?" another interrupted.

"Do you know where this came from?" a worried mother jumped in.

"Were they trying to burn our fields? Poison us?" one farmer interjected.

A man I would later learn was the mayor moved to the front. The wizard thumped his staff loudly on the floor, and silence descended once again.

"Now, I want everyone who saw the blast directly to come forward and tell us exactly what they saw. Maybe then we'll figure this out."

Several men came forward; my brothers did too. They were at the back of the line. Each man described the fieldwork or whatnot he was involved in when they saw the flash. A couple said they saw something moving away. One claimed he saw a giant bird just before.

When it got to my brothers, the mayor looked down at them. "All right, boys, what were you doing when this all happened?"

"We were . . . um, playing with our little sister," Rod offered.

"Yeah, just going to see her, she was washing some dishes or something . . ." John added.

They both then agreed that they hadn't seen the source of the light. The mayor looked a bit more sternly at them. "Where's your sister?" he asked. No girls had been brought forward for the little questioning.

Mom helpfully brought me up and set me down beside them.

I looked at the wizard, his aura still messing with the magic in the air around him.

The wizard looked down at me, even I could see one or two little bubbles drifting off of my skin.

He knew.

I knew he knew.

He knew I knew he knew.

Busted.

"What were you doing when all this happened? Your brothers seem to think you were doing chores. Is that so?" Mystien asked. His expression was clear; he'd take no nonsense from me.

"I-I was playing, and a-a grasshopper jumped up on my face." I didn't have to try to look afraid, I was.

"Oh? What were you playing?" he responded. The mayor looked a bit confused, several townspeople seemed to be questioning why that mattered.

"I was . . . um, I was playing with a light," I offered helpfully, tugging on the hem of the tunic I was wearing and looking down.

"Show me." His tone left no opening for wriggling out of this.

"I don't see why this matters," the mayor piped up.

"Show me," Mystien said again.

I hummed a short song, and my little ball of light appeared in my hand, pretty and blue. The wizard looked like he was trying to maintain as firm a face as he could. The mayor rubbed his eyebrow ridges like he was getting a headache. The crowd took about five seconds to get angry, and another five to quiet down as the old man beat his staff on the floor.

"Why didn't you tell anyone earlier, girl?" the mayor looked truly miffed.

"I-I tried to; people kept telling me to be quiet." That one actually got a chuckle from the old man.

"It's just a newly blooming bard playing with and losing control of her powers. Everyone can go home." He was still trying to suppress his mirth.

"Oy, we lost half a day of work, and all this time for this nonsense, come on!" One irritated man shouted. I flinched at that.

"Aye, you did, but we found something well worth it," Mystien offered.

"And what the hell would that be?!"

"You might not know this, but bards can learn basic healing magics, and once I get her trained a bit, and I will, this village will have a basic level of magical healing." That shut everyone up. There were several murmurs of how that would be great, and while a few were still a bit miffed, they started filing home. The mayor on the other hand . . . well, the mayor looked like it was Christmas, and I was the biggest present under the tree.

Looking at him, the old wizard, and my parents, I could quickly feel my life getting harder.

CHAPTER 3

✦

THE BASICS OF MAGIC

After returning home from the little town-wide excursion to the village hall, I was ready to pass out. It'd been a long and busy day for all of us. My father, on the other hand, had something he wanted first. He picked me up, setting me down on one of our chairs.

"Master Mystien has been kind enough to agree to start training you tomorrow. You're going to listen to everything he says, and do exactly what he tells you to, understand?" his voice was firm.

"Yes, Papa." I looked up at him, meeting his tired eyes. It was because of me that he'd been running around all afternoon.

"And you're not going to use magic at all unless he tells you it's okay to, got it?" he continued, setting out his ground rules.

On this point, I didn't want to give it up. I'd been using my one little trick to keep the house a comfy temperature for a good long while now, and I waffled, looking away.

"Um . . . I've been using magic to keep the house warm or cool for a little bit . . ." I really didn't want to give up my magical HVAC.

He gave me a light bonk on the head for that, "You'll not be doing that until he gives his permission either. Magic is dangerous, Alana."

"Umph, okay, I won't, promise," I pouted about that, but there was no winning here, not tonight at least. When winter was in full force, we'd see who wanted a heater and who didn't.

"I mean it, sweetheart," he leaned down to look me in the eyes, "I've seen men killed by spell slingers who were more smart than they were wise." My dad hadn't talked to me much up till now, but he was painfully sincere here.

"Okay . . ." I mumbled.

"Good." he perked up, "Now, everyone to bed, it's late enough already."

I scampered off to the corner of the house where we kids slept; my brothers made some complaining noises about it but joined after a fashion.

The next morning, I was awoken early, as was everyone else. We collectively had breakfast shoved down our throats by Mom, and the boys were told to make themselves busy till the afternoon.

After they'd left, she brought me over to the hearth, where the biggest of our few pots was warming. It was a massive clay monstrosity.

"Soup?" I inquired, looking at the vessel used mostly for making a couple of days' worth of stew at a time. It wasn't hot yet, and likely wouldn't be for a while, but it was nicely warming.

"No, you're starting training today, yes? And we're going to make sure you're nice and clean." She gave me a smile that was somehow more threatening than anything I'd ever seen. Her voice was sweet as she pulled out a rag and a bit of soap, something we seldom used.

I may have significantly underestimated how irritated about the previous day's events she was, because I was thoroughly, roughly scrubbed clean. I struggled and complained in vain as she, rather more forcefully than was necessary, washed me head to toe.

We did not bathe very often here in this world. I'd been able to wipe myself down a little bit here and there, but an actual, proper bath was not something I'd yet experienced. This mockery of that most relaxing of rituals did get me clean, even if I felt like I'd been scoured that way.

I did make the mistake of using one of the many words my brothers were so fond of using when my parents weren't around and found that my mouth became the soap holder for the rest of the "bath."

And so, after being cleansed and shoved into the nicer of my two outfits, my mother took me over to the old magus's house. I was thoroughly exhausted by the time we arrived.

"All right," Mystien said as we stood in what looked to be the main room of his home. He had two others off to the side. I didn't know their purpose but could assume at least one was a bedroom from the lack of sleeping arrangements here. "I know you've been messing around with magic, what can you do so far?" he inquired.

"Umm, I can do the ball of light thing. I can heat or cool a room or myself a little bit and I can move small objects." I listed the things I could reliably manage.

"Let's see them, one by one. How you heat and cool yourself and the room are separate bits of magic, so show each of those." He seemed contemplative as he watched me run through my tricks.

"That's not a bad start; we'll polish those first and work on the light today, since it's been the one to cause the most trouble."

I blushed a bit in embarrassment at his reminder, and we began the process of ironing it out. I made small corrections to the flow of the magic and the way I was focusing it at his instruction until I began to wear myself out.

"That's enough; it looks like you're running out of mana," he declared after about an hour of work.

"Mana?" I asked.

"Mana is the energy of magic; it's all around us, you can see it, no?"

I nodded in confirmation.

"To use magic, you must use a small amount of the mana in your body, putting it out into the world and using it to shape the mana around you. If you were like me, then we'd have to spend a good bit of time teaching you how, but you're no wizard, that's certain." He moved into a lecturing position, scholar's cradle and all.

"Not like you?" I wasn't certain how to parse that bit.

"Indeed, you're a bard . . . there are, four rough categories of magic use, three of which are spellcasters," he began.

"Wizards like myself work with forces outside the body; we can also summon simple substances. I specialize in water-type magic particularly, but that's not important for now. That's knowledge-type magic, and it's based on the user's understanding of the forces and things they're altering or creating." I nodded along.

"Then there is belief magic; its practitioners are often called clerics or priests, though sometimes they go by other things, depending on what they, in particular, believe and do with their abilities. They work exclusively with living or sometimes dead things. They are the best healers; they can also make plants and the like grow if they work in that direction. Their magic is based on their belief that what they're doing is right or proper."

That sounded weird, but okay.

"Finally there are bards like you, who use instinctual magic. You can work both with living things and with forces. You can even do some summoning; though it'll be hard, you'll be able to summon more complex things. Bardic magic is much, much slower and quite a fair bit weaker than the other two, but it is very versatile and is based on instinct. It's normally focused through song or dance, something like that."

It sounded like I'd be a "Jack of all, master of none" kind of mage, but that was cool with me.

"You said four, that's only three," I said.

"The last is physical magic; it sometimes develops in people who use their bodies a lot. It affects only the self, making you stronger, faster, and more resilient. I'm not sure how it works exactly; nobody is. It's some kind of battle aura, what your father uses. And it's by far the most common."

"Okay, I think I understand. Can I ask a question?"

"You just did, but feel free, I encourage as many questions as you have."

I groaned internally at the idea that he might be like an elementary school teacher.

"Why did everyone seem happy when you pointed out I would be able to learn to heal?"

"Oh, that's a good one," he said, nodding.

"Well, it's like this, spellcasters are quite rare. Of them, most are wizards, by a large majority. Of the types capable of healing, few would be in a small village like this, and even though your healing abilities won't be anything like having a priest-type caster around, it could easily save lives. It's quite rare to be able to find a healer reliably outside of a fairly sizable city, so you'll be a boon to the town."

He was smiling at that.

"Really?" I was a bit incredulous at this idea. I looked at my hands, frowning a bit.

"Well, you won't be able to heal injuries instantly like a priest could. But before long, we'll have you able to fix up a broken bone in an hour or so. Same with poison or disease. If someone breaks a leg around harvest, it's real bad for their family, and reducing their time down will be a huge value to everyone."

I pouted. "People are going to bug me a lot, aren't they?"

"Yeah," he chuckled. "Yeah, they are, but it'll help out your family, and everyone else, too, and you'll make good money off of it."

He talked for a bit longer about the nuances. Turns out that only about one in a thousand could learn to cast magic, of those around four in five were wizards of some kind. Priests and bards were the only healers outside of some rather backward medicine, and they were a pain to contact. Mostly because priests had to feel like they were doing the right thing, so they spent a lot of their time going here and there trying to help people.

Bards, on the other hand, had a reputation for being flakes, troublemakers, and the like, and often lived a nomadic life to keep ahead of whatever problems they may have caused.

Around lunch, my mother came to take me home. This would be the set schedule for the foreseeable future, breakfast early, followed by magic training till lunch, and chores in early afternoon, then I could play around the house till dinner.

I should note that due to my age "chores" did not imply doing any actual useful work. Mostly, I'd be shown how to do things around the house that I could reasonably achieve, sweeping and the like, or cleaning old pots. My mother could do these in a fraction of the time, but the whole point was to teach me how. Even the pot I was cleaning during "The Incident" didn't really need it, it was just an exercise to teach me about doing dishes.

The house itself was circular. With a construction similar to wattle and daub, a frame of thick wooden logs with a mesh was made. The mesh was then covered in a mud and straw mixture that was painted over with a whitewash and a thatch roof. The floors were hard, pounded-down dirt, which stayed cleaner than you'd think. Furniture was sparse, a table and chairs and a central hearth, which served as a kitchen. On the walls were various tools and storage containers and a sleeping area, with several small mattresses that were just big bags stuffed with straw and husks. These were covered with a couple of warm blankets.

About a month in, Mystien had some words for me after some particularly mind-numbing training.

"Alana," he began after finishing a lecture on some of the more in depth bits of shaping mana for use.

"Yes?"

"I've decided that you've gotten to the point you can safely use the spells you've designed yourself," he declared.

"Hooray!" Finally, I was able to get back to messing around on my own.

He frowned. "Just because you're allowed to does not mean I'm encouraging you to start floating half the stuff in your house. Those you were using were fairly harmless, and this is a test to see whether you can be responsible. Don't fail it."

I nodded with as firm a face as I could, which was not particularly firm at all. "Mm-hmm."

"There is something else too," he began after sighing at what appeared to be poor childish resolve. "I've called in a favor from an old friend. He'll be coming by in a few days to teach you some healing theory. I've not got much of that, but it'll mean you should spend your afternoons with me as well. We won't have him for long."

I eagerly accepted, and more importantly my parents did too. Three days later, I was cleaned up and ready to meet this new teacher. I'd even managed to convince my mother to let me wash myself this time, avoiding another harrowing experience. She was feeling a bit ill that morning at any rate.

I walked myself over to my teacher's home, to find two men who could not have been more different chatting right beside his door: my mentor, the calm, old gentleman in his sedate blue robe, short white beard, and silver hair shining in the morning sunlight; the much younger man beside him was, in a word, loud—his clothes were a mix of vibrant red and yellow, and covered in medium-quality embroidery. Their quality was middling from what I could tell, but the statement was extreme. It was a big, bright sign screaming "Hey! Look at me!" His face was clean-shaven, and he wore a feathered hat that could only be described as jaunty.

"So," the newcomer began as I approached, "where's this new apprentice of yours? Not late is he? I don't believe you'd pick up someone who wasn't worth their salt, but I also don't want to believe that there's anyone in this town worth training."

"You'll meet her in just a second, Jackson." The magus saw me approaching but didn't say anything; he seemed he was enjoying watching his junior ramble.

"Her? HER?! Don't tell me you dragged me out here to talk to some girl you've picked up to give a few"—and he made finger quotations—"'private lessons,' have you?"

"No, that sounds like something you would do," came his flat reply.

"Fair point, is she cute at least?" the bard asked.

"I think she is, though probably not in the way you're thinking."

"And you haven't." At this point, he made a lewd thrusting motion with his hips, and I realized he was wearing an enormous codpiece.

"Uh!" It was a bit disturbing to watch.

"Decidedly not, nor do I plan to," Mystien chuckled.

"Well then, do you mind if I . . . you know."

"You'll need to wait for a while on that account I think," was his good-humored response.

I was getting a bit tired of this.

"Why's that?" Jackson inquired.

"Hi," I spoke up from just a bit back.

"Hey, kid," was the response I got. He barely even looked at me. "So? You got an answer for why?" he asked again.

"Hi," I said again, prompting him to look at me fully. For just a moment, it looked like he was about to tell me to scram, then his eyes focused.

"Her?"

"Yup."

"Seriously?"

"Yup."

"What are you, kid? Two?" He bent down to look at me incredulously.

"Three and a half!" I spoke with all the anger of a child who was older than described. That got me a laugh.

"All right, kiddo. I don't believe you can cast jack or squat. Show me one spell, and I'll think about helping you out."

So I showed him my whole lineup, one right after the other, as by the book as we'd practiced.

"Well, all right then," he said after seeing what I could do. "Yeah, I guess we can work with that."

Mystien was wearing a shit-eating grin as he watched the impressed bard agree.

And so began a few days of training under Jackson, who showed me firsthand why bards were often thought of poorly.

Jackson was rude, big-headed, and had a propensity for lewdness, which just went beyond the pale at times. That said, he also had an understanding of magic that meshed greatly with mine. We jumped in straightaway, after a quick overview of what I needed to do for a basic healing spell, which mostly consisted of focusing on what you wanted the magic to do, visualizing the mana as a calming, repairing light.

The practice was simple enough. I'd cut my finger lightly with a sharp knife then cast while going through the visualization. I placed the light into one of the bubbles that constantly came off of me, wrapping it around the wound and letting it seep in. He also taught me the song he used to focus while doing this, but I found it not much to my liking. So I used one of my own, a calming theme from an old TV show, very violin-y and good to hum.

It took me a few times to get it to work, and when it did, it wasn't all that fast. This got me approving nods from both men.

"Not bad, kid. You'll need to practice that one a lot to speed it up a bit, and while I don't recommend live practice, for bigger wounds you may want to envelop the whole body. That'll be hard where you are at right now, but it's something you should try to pick up."

We continued like this till lunch, which I ate with them. Jackson giving small comments here and there about pulling the mana in closer, and focusing it to be brighter and sharper. By the end of the day, I could heal my cut finger in only a second or two.

I was given a few bits of advice on how to deal with poisons just before my dad came to pick me up. Jackson told to think over them, but not practice. We'd do that tomorrow.

The next day, I was greeted with a bundle of leaves, which I was told to rub my hands in when I first came in.

"All right, kiddo, you remember what I told you about poisons yesterday?"

"Mmm, you have to focus on pulling out what doesn't belong and add in a little healing on top of it to help with whatever damage the poison has done in the first place." At that moment, my hands were beginning to itch terribly.

"Right you are. Now you're going to do that one finger at a time to fix the poison ivy you just rubbed your hands in." He smiled as he said that, the jerk.

That day proceeded much like the previous one, ending with some notes on diseases and the methodology for their repair. In comparison to the training I received before, this was hard and made it seem as if I was cramming for a test. Though I was told that each of these techniques was groundwork on very minor injuries, anything more serious would be monumentally harder.

I dreaded going back on the final day my temporary tutor would be around. If Jackson was going to demonstrate each technique on me . . . I hated feeling sick. I would just complain the whole time.

"Ready to give curing sickness a shot, kiddo?" I was asked as I came in. I frowned.

"Well, I got a surprise for you. Look here." He brought out a cage with some field mice in it. They were green, literally green.

"These here mice have a special disease in them, something some priest cooked up just for training. They'll stay green as long as they've got it in them, so it's easy to see when they're cured. Also the sickness won't jump to people and it isn't even that bad for the mice. Wins all around. I brought these here from my own personal practice group."

I looked on at his explanation, a bit stunned.

"What, you didn't think I'd make you sick or something, did you?" he asked with a mischievous grin.

"I-I kind of did, actually," I replied honestly.

"Tut-tut-tut, after all I've done for you." He shook his head.

I couldn't think of how to even respond to that, so I just mumbled some thanks.

"All right then, let's get cracking!" and so it began.

Curing diseases was a bit odd as well. You have to focus on finding the bit that doesn't belong and then ripping it apart. Pulling it like poison doesn't work. You add a bit of healing to it, too, because sickness can cause the body lots of damage.

I was ready to collapse by the end of the day. This was by far the hardest of my three new techniques, but I still had a few questions.

"What about summoning? If I wanted to make dirt or something, Jackson?" I perked up a bit. This was one I really wanted to know about.

"Oh, creation magic? Well, you have to visualize the mana coming together into the form you want it in. The more familiar the concept of something is, the easier that will be. Stuff like water is the easiest. Everyone knows what water is like, but you can also do things like food. Bread creation got me through some bad times, and it's always useful on the road."

He gave me a very basic explanation.

"But, and I mean this, you'll need to grow a lot before you can do much of that. You're still just a kid, and that's some mana-intense magic, so don't rush it," he warned.

We bid Jackson goodbye the next morning and were not an hour later interrupted by an irate villager from the main village. It would seem someone had spotted Jackson attempting to, and succeeding in, seducing his girlfriend, and he'd come by to give him a good beating.

The man left, disappointed that he'd missed the interloping bard, cursing and venting as he tried to chase him down the road.

"I've never been able to figure out how he does that," said Mystien. "He always manages to skip town just before the heat hits."

CHAPTER 4

AN AFTERNOON
WITH MY BROTHERS

The days droned into weeks, and before long the harvest arrived and went. I'd like to say that I became significantly proficient at healing, but I was mediocre at best. Progress was certainly made in that department, but the going was painfully slow.

Just after our fields had been harvested, dinner brought with it an interesting conversation.

"Got a message from Creekrun this afternoon. They think they've got a monster in one of their caves," Dad declared. I knew Creekrun was one of the nearby villages, but this was the first I'd heard of an actual monster in the area.

"Wow! What kind? Are we going to go kill it?" John perked up, excited by the idea.

"You're not going anywhere, but I'm headed that way with a few others tomorrow morning, and we don't know, probably just overgrown coyotes or something, but those can be nasty to tangle with." He talked like this was something normal.

"Well, I'm heading into town in the morning," Mom declared, "You boys'll have to keep an eye on your sister."

"I'm going to practice though," I piped up.

"Nah, we're taking old Mystien with us," Dad explained.

"Why?" In retrospect a foolish question.

"Because if it's something nasty, he can cook it before it gets near. Wizards are cool like that," Rod popped in.

"Aye, that's the plan. Some of the guys wanted you to come, too, Alana, but they're idiots." I shook at the idea of fighting monsters, or even being near them.

"Maybe you could call someone to deal with it, like a monster hunter or something?" I asked.

"Adventurers might come if we asked, but they're more of a problem than a solution to something like this. They'd drink the town dry, burn half of it to the ground, kill the monster, take everyone's money, sleep with the mayor's wife, then flee before the lord could come deal with them. Soldiers might come out, but the lord would charge the town, and it would take weeks for them to do so, particularly now; they're all out gathering up his taxes." Father seemed to harbor a bit of resentment for both groups.

"Oh, um . . . I could look after myself," I offered, both parents ignored that idea completely.

"I'm hurt, sister. You don't want to spend time with us?" Rod leaned in, smiling like a fox.

"That's just mean, and we could've taken you out to the woods to gather; it's tons of fun," John joined in. "Even some berries just coming in."

"No, no, you just want to sit around the house like a baby though, huh?" The teasing was already getting old.

"No, I'll go." I glared at the two of them.

"Great, we'll head out early then," Rod declared.

"Make sure you're back before sunset," Dad instructed them with a harsh look.

So the next morning after breakfast, my brothers took me with them, and we headed toward the forest, a few baskets carried for our haul.

The walk there was quite a bit further than I was expecting. Having seen the trees from my house, I didn't think much of it. But it turns out that when you're short, everything is much further away, and the constant complaints of my brothers about how slow I was didn't help at all.

As we approached the woods, I began to smell something lovely, the familiar scent wafting around as I looked for the flowers. "Come here and try this." John led me over to the big bush of honeysuckle, showing me how to pull out the stem and suck out the little drops of nectar. "These are the best," he added as he ate a few.

Rod laughed from a bit behind us, "Teaching her to suck things, John? What'll you do to the family's reputation?"

I thought to tell him off, but realized a three-year-old wouldn't likely understand that, so I just glared.

"You're saying dirty things, aren't you?" I accused over a frown, "I'll tell Mom." I threatened the most dangerous thing I could think of easily, and at it he blanched.

"Ah . . . no, just saying we don't want you to get known for being too greedy about sweets, is all." His stammered explanation was almost funny.

"Well, okay then, let's go." With that declaration, I began walking into the woods, only to be caught and pulled back to the spots they knew better.

I quickly learned that there were a few very strict rules. The most important being that we weren't allowed to take any animals. It was bad to even look too closely at them, as they belonged to the local lord. This was a major crime, and you could be badly punished for even a rabbit. Secondly, was not to mess up the trees, for the same reason. We could take from the bushes and mushrooms, and anything near the ground, but not damage the trees. We'd pick up wood on our way out I was told, sticks and the like from the ground. Finally, we were not to take too much from any plant; we could always come back and get more. Nobody shared their gathering spots outside of family and a few close friends, who'd only go to the well-known ones.

Our first stop led us to a small gully, and behind a curtain of overgrown bushes, there was a cave. It was so well hidden I could have walked past a hundred times and never seen it.

"A cave?" I stood near the entrance nervously, having had bad experiences with these before.

"Yup, this is where the best mushrooms grow. Dad showed us. Now come in, it's perfectly safe." Rod practically dragged me into the little hole.

Inside was a room around thirty feet in diameter. The light was low, with an extra bit coming from some of the mosses, a light greenish glow flowing around them. I could see a bit of mana flowing about them as well and stopped to study them for a while.

"What about these?" I asked my brothers, pointing the illuminating growths out.

"Glow moss? Grows in all the caves around here, but if you pick it, it stops making light, so it's not useful and it tastes bad too," John said. "Not interesting, but these are, see the mushrooms here? Pick the white ones, the red ones will make you sick, the blue ones, very sick." He pulled out and showed me the three that grew there. I recognized the white ones from much of our food.

"We come here all the time"—Rod came over to check on what I was picking, pointing to the larger fungi—"cause these things grow like crazy. Also it's a good place to hide out if you ever make Mom mad," he chuckled.

After we grabbed a healthy quantity of fungi, my brothers showed me a number of small herbaceous plants and ferns. We focused on the easy to identify ones as we walked through the woods, even managing a few handfuls of nuts here and there, until we found an old path.

The path led us down to a tiny creek, little more than a bubble of water over some rocks.

"Fish?" I asked, looking at the water.

"No, no fish in this one, or none big enough to eat," said John.

"What we're after is that." Rod pointed to a tallish tree beside the bank of the stream. I could see a few fruit hanging from the upper branches, but it was probably too small to climb.

"What is it?" I looked toward the fruit; they were something I'd not had before.

"Pawpaw," responded my brothers. "We normally don't get much. Everyone grabs the low ones too fast . . . but think you can get a few, Alana?" Rod looked down, smiling. It seemed like he'd planned to bring me there for a while now.

"Mmm, sure." I sang a brief tune and managed to pop a few off of the branches I couldn't reach. We got maybe ten before I stopped.

Rod cheered at the haul. John brought one over to me and cut it open with his belt knife. It was green, had a rough skin, and was just smaller than a banana, I hesitated at first, but after a taste dug in, it was sweet, so sweet, and I'd had almost nothing with any sugar since coming here. The whole thing tasted almost tropical. It'd probably make a magnificent smoothie and if I had a blender, or ice.

"Wow!" was all I managed.

"Yeah, I know." Rod shoved a few pieces in his mouth as well. "Delicious."

We each ate one. I was tempted to go for another, but the thought of having one after dinner proved just tempting enough to hold me back.

We spent a bit more time slowly making our way home, picking out a few more edibles and finally some sticks for firewood to top off. Our baskets bursting full, we cheerfully exited the forest laughing about the obscenely good haul.

As we exited the tree line, I saw a cart coming down the road. Some of the men in it recognizable. We three waved to them and called out, but they seemed off. Something was wrong about their gait, the way they were looking toward the trees.

I saw my father begin hurrying toward us as soon as one of the others pointed us out, and his look froze me in place. There was blood dripping down his face from a head wound, more stains on his shirt and pants bearing the dark, brownish-red that only came from one thing. He took the basket from me, quickly shoving it over to Rod and lifted me into his arms, power walking back to the cart.

"A couple of people got hurt. I need you to heal them. I don't expect it to be perfect. Do the best you can." His words were curt, strained as he spoke. Normally, his tone was kind, but today . . . today he sounded like a soldier.

I nearly puked when I saw the men in the cart. Two men, soaked in their own blood, one had his stomach chewed open, his organs held in place by a pressed-down cloth. He was shaking in pain, a friend holding on to his hand for comfort as he ground his teeth to not scream. The other not much better, his shoulder looked like it was barely still attached, pulped meat replacing what should have been ordered muscle and bone. He'd been lain on his side, a few seconds revealed why as he coughed up a spurt of blood.

I was stunned into inaction until my father lightly shook me. "Heal them," was his command and I shakily began casting, trying to focus, but I'd never seen anything like this in either of my lives and just trying to bring it all together was throwing me.

Mystien came over and calmly placed his hand on my dad's shoulder. He leaned in and began to speak gently to me. "Breathe, you need to focus, first on the man coughing. Work on his lungs first; you know exactly what to do here. Bring your mana into place slowly and use it to repair him." His voice was enough to bring me back to my senses fully, and I began as he instructed.

Following my mentor's instructions, I worked first on the damaged lungs. It was harder than any of my practice sessions by an order of magnitude, and I could feel my mana draining from me. My head was pounding when I finally got the lungs into a state where I could not worry about the man dying immediately.

I moved to the other man's belly, and it was even worse, as my mana flowed over the wounds, trying to knit and piece them back together I could tell that this wasn't working, I was too drained, his organs were shreds, most of the blood dripping along the cart, and through its boards was his, refocusing I pushed on, until blackness seeped into my vision and took me.

I awoke in Mystien's house, a couple of women were there tending to the two injured men, along with my father and the homeowner.

"Oof," I said as I came to. Based on the lights and the darkness in the window, I could guess it was night.

One of the women, a friend of my mother's named Theara, came over and spoke softly to me when she saw that I'd awakened. "They still need help, particularly Leon. Can you help them?"

She indicated the man whose stomach was still in a bad shape. I could still see a bit of blood leaking out, his breath barely there and ragged. I tried again to help him, but if anything, he was worse. Some of the bleeding had stopped, but some was building inside. I'd have to move to disease removal to know for sure, but I was guessing some infections were already beginning.

I did what I could, attempting to find the worst spots. But a few minutes in, something went weird, like my mana was having trouble latching on. I looked up to hear Leon's breath hitch a few times, followed by a gasp as air escaped him. The healing failed. It seemed as if I was trying to fix a piece of wood. I could feel it, almost taste it as he died, my mana still wrapped around his body as it became a corpse. The sensation was . . .

I fell to my knees and emptied my stomach, shaking and crying as the man's death hit me. It was all real, all too real, and I knew I could do nothing for him. The sensation was visceral. I knew, for a fact that nothing would bring him back, and it struck me like lead.

My dad came over and took me to a chair, sitting me there on his lap. "What happened? Why'd you stop?" the woman tending to Leon asked, still holding a cloth to wipe his sweat.

"He's . . . dead," I managed to say between sobs, holding on to my father's shirt and looking away. I wasn't sure what happened to the woman, but it was quiet. I could hear nothing but my own crying, feel nothing but my dad rubbing my back to calm me. It took several minutes to calm down enough to stop. Eventually, I did, and I lay there for a while as it all washed over me.

After a bit, Mystien came over, putting down a small bowl of stew and crust of bread. "Eat," he instructed.

"But . . . the other man . . ." I began.

"Orlen," he said, "is resting and stable. You'll need to do a bit more before he'll be okay, but for now, eat."

"But . . ." I tried again.

"You are still shaking and haven't eaten. When you're done, you'll be ready to go work on his wounds." He would brook no argument. "It'll be fine, now eat."

It was annoying, but the old man was right. I was trembling a bit as I began to munch on the stew. But as I mopped up the last bits with the bread, I'd calmed down considerably. I still felt horrible, but it was better.

Orlen's shoulder was a disaster, so I started there. Whatever happened to him had crushed the bones and muscles. While the outside looked bad for being cut up, it was nothing compared to the internal damage. By the time I had most of that sorted, I was nearly out of mana again and needed to go rest.

Dawn greeted me the next day, and I was still a bit woozy as John greeted me, holding me out a basket, "Mom made you breakfast, eat up." I grumbled about people shoving food at me, but did as I was told, finding a generous egg-and-cheese omelet, and even one of the pawpaw we'd gotten the day before.

I couldn't help but think about how much mana I'd wasted getting the fruit down as I ate it. I'd like to say it tasted like ash in my mouth, but it was delicious, which only made the guilt I was feeling over not being able to save both men that much worse.

I spent that morning fixing up Orlen though. By the time I was done, he wasn't in perfect condition. His ribs would still need a week or two before fully healing, and his shoulder was still raw, but he'd be fine on his own soon. He was a nice-enough guy, chatting a bit as I worked.

"That was a total disaster. What was that thing anyway? Not anything I've seen before," he asked as I was putting the last touches on his ribs.

"Mountain lizard, and you shouldn't have seen it. It shouldn't be within a hundred miles of here," the old mage answered him. "Not sure why it was, but we'll need to let Lord Hazelwood know, it's too strange," he said thoughtfully. "At least its body will be able to pay for all the damage. A half dozen or so different parts are useful."

"Okay, that's about as good as I can do, for right now at least," I broke in as I finished up what I was working on.

"All right." Mystien looked me over a bit. "It should be more than enough. You'll have to manage on your own from here, Orlen." He smirked a bit as the man reached up and ruffled my hair, with a loud objection on my part.

"Thank you, Alana. One day, you'll make some man really happy." I stuck my tongue out at him at that. I didn't need to make anyone happy except myself.

"And one day, you'll not get half eaten by a beastie," I retorted before I turned to leave, gaining me a few chuckles.

A couple of days later, I returned to my lessons. Though I couldn't stop looking at the place on the floor where Leon had died, my mood sinking every time I did.

"You can't save everyone, girl." The comment shook me out of my thoughts a bit.

"I wasted a bunch of mana picking fruit. If I hadn't, then maybe I could have . . ." I began.

"Oh? Did you know how dangerous that monster would be?" my teacher asked.

"No . . . Dad said it was probably no big . . ."

"And you went to get your fruit after knowing we were coming back with injured?"

"Well, I didn't know . . ."

"Ah, are you the one who brought the mountain lizard here then?" he prodded.

"Of course not!" I snapped at him.

"Well, it was brought here. We found out just this morning. None of this was your fault, not even a little, and it's no small thing that you managed to save one."

That gave me something to think about.

"Now, listen up, you won't be able to save everyone, and if you try, you'll just run yourself to death, so don't. Save who you can, help who you can, and those you can't . . . well, it happens. It's sad, but it happens."

I chewed on his lecture, finding one thing that stood out.

"It was brought here? Who would do that?" I asked, disgusted once I understood it.

"Not someone you need to get involved with if you can help it, so don't say anything. I thought your father was going to put a fist through a wall when we got the news. On a happier note, Creekrun sent over a bunch of smoked and salted fish, which will be quite nice." It was obvious he was trying to distract me from questions I was better not knowing the answer to.

"Hooray! Meat's expensive too!" I cheered, hoping I was being convincing, but I did like fish . . .

JACKSON IN TOWN

Waking up this morning was magnificent, a comfortable bed, a bottle of good wine—a rarity in these parts—within easy reach, and most importantly, a redhead who was plump in all the right places curled up next to me.

She woke just after I did, and to my joyous surprise, was feeling quite randy. Our tongues were working around each other. Each trying to find its way into the other's throat as I ran my fingers down her silken skin, reaching for the moist warmth between her legs. Already she had started moaning in anticipation . . . when some bastard started beating on my door.

And that was the moment my day started getting worse.

"Busy," I yelled at whoever had the absolute gall to interrupt this.

The beating continued. "Urgent message for you, sir!" he yelled through my door, obviously unwilling to kindly fuck off.

I planted a kiss on the lovely woman's lips, giving her chin a light shake. "One moment, my sweet. I'll be right back with you," I whispered to her, and rose, turning and opening the inn room door with a smile on my face, in my full and exceptional stature.

"So, tell me what brings you to my inn room on what was an excellent beginning to a day?" I asked the shocked-looking young man, "You don't look the kind to join us, and frankly, I don't like to share."

He held out a rolled piece of parchment.

I unrolled it, noting the seal of the local lord as I broke through it and cursed, "Well, shit." I looked to the woman behind me. "I'm afraid my dear I've been summoned. We'll have to continue at a later date."

Not twenty minutes later, I strolled into the lord's manor with his messenger, greeted by one of the stewards, a sharp-featured man I'd met several times before. "You know, my friend, I was greatly enjoying my morning before His Excellency summoned me here. I assume there's been some emergency?" I inquired.

"Quite so, sir. I've been instructed to take you to his office straight-away," he spoke as we walked.

The manor really was something to look at, the walls pure white and decorated with tasteful portraits, a lush red carpet covering the marble floors. The whole thing was obscenely lavish compared to the rest of the city, not to mention the surrounding lands.

"I hope you weren't interrupted in the middle of anything too important?" the steward inquired, seeming to read my slightly cold mood.

"A lovely woman, with skin like fresh cream, hips wider than a river after spring rain, and hair the color of an inferno . . .. Julie, or Juney, or was it Juline . . . something like that," I explained.

"Ah, well, quite a shame then . . ."

I could see the door to the office we were going to now. The steward rapped upon it several times, and I heard the gasp of a woman. A few moments later, a maid, disheveled and obviously a bit flushed with heat, which was doing nothing to offset her stunning proportions, opened the door for us, bowing and closing it as she quickly made herself scarce.

The jerk is here getting it on after ruining my perfectly good breakfast, what an absolute bastard, I said to myself.

The baron saw me looking over the woman ever so briefly, speaking after she left, "Ah, Sasha is quite the girl, yes? You could have her this evening if you like, a thank-you for your quick response."

"Your generosity is greatly appreciated, my lord, but I've an appointment with a young woman already, perhaps another time," I responded as I hardened the fake face I used with nobles. "I like girls who can actually tell me no; there's no joy in it if they've no option."

The man shrugged. "Very well. At any rate, several of my best men were injured earlier, a mountain lizard they were transporting got loose, and I'd like them healed."

I quirked an eyebrow. "Certainly, but I'm not nearly as good as Father Mannory, surely?"

"The whoreson left," spat the baron in disgust, "As if I didn't give him plenty."

"A shame." I bowed placatingly.

"Probably because you kept trying to have your way with the female temple staff, I may need to follow his example . . ."

"Hmph, upon his whole order, at any rate, I'll pay you what I'd have paid him. I just need those men up and ready as soon as possible, need to get my monster back." He was licking his lips at the thought.

"Certainly, my lord, I'm sure the villagers are panicking about its escape."

"Bah, they don't even know. If any are stupid enough to fight it, they deserve what they get."

It was a frankly cold response, but not unexpected.

"Very well. Then, shall I begin immediately?" I asked, wanting to leave this place as quickly as possible.

The nobleman waved me off, and I happily set to my work.

Some hours later, and more than a bit of complaining from the knights about how I was too slow at healing them, I walked back to my inn, considering the options should I decide to move on.

"I'd worry for him trying to bring in the kid, but with the Roaring Torrent and Panther of Kelson's Hill there, nobody in their right mind is going to harass that hamlet . . . if he even finds out about her."

As I came in the door, I spotted a familiar redhead, and she'd acquired a friend, a raven-haired girl who was, in my humble opinion, quite bouncy.

"Well, well, well, today might have been a bust, but perhaps tonight can be salvaged."

✦

CHAPTER 5

WINTER, AND HELPING
THE TOWN

Creekrun did indeed send over a massive amount of fish, too much for any one family. All the men who went on the extermination got a good share. My family got three shares, for the help and healing afterward. I was told my dad performed heroically in the fight by a few men when the fish was handed out. It was a huge help to our winter supplies.

As time went by, I learned more and more about what went into prepping for the end of the year. This year, I was in the thick of it, now able to reliably work at piling up wood and food, and aiding in the preservation that Mom did, pickling, drying, and otherwise putting the fruits of our labors away so we could survive winter.

It was one evening, as we were preparing the last of the oil for our lamps, that my mother informed us children that she was pregnant. Her smile at the announcement gentle and calm.

"Really?" asked Rod, looking a bit surprised.

"Mmm, the day the men went to Creekrun, I went to talk to one of the midwives in town. Based on that and other things, I'm quite sure. I think it'll come around early summer." She nodded; based on Dad's expression, I could tell he'd known for a bit now.

"We'll have a lot of things to prepare," I piped in, "clothes, a crib, and all kinds of stuff, won't we?"

"Not too much, there are several women with babies in town right now. There'll be no need to make new clothes when we can buy some cheaply, and baby clothes are simple to make. We will need to make one or two small things, but it should be fine," my father responded. He'd been through this a few times before, too, and seemed unconcerned.

I blinked at how nonchalant they were being about this, but I'd never had a child, nor any little siblings, in either life, so I guess I wasn't really an expert on this.

Upon seeing my concern, my mother just patted my head. "It'll be fine, I've been through this before dear," she said, smiling.

My brothers also looked unconcerned, almost uninterested, which made me want to kick them, something I'd reserve for when I was bigger, for now I just glared. "At least act like you're worried," I said, as I poked Rod and frowned.

They all just laughed at me, but Mom did end up having me practice working on spinning and even showed me how to use her loom. I was too small to do it at any real pace, but when she wasn't using the loom, I'd be put to weaving some simple sackcloth.

My teacher gave me some direction on a simple spell to make water, nothing fantastically difficult, but the basis for more complex summoning magic. I was told to practice it as often as possible since we'd be putting lessons aside until spring. It seemed almost everything went on hiatus for winter.

Mystien also told me to learn to read. Something I viewed with great trepidation, until he showed me the basics of it. I'd been told that you could learn to read Korean in an afternoon, and this was similar in nature. The alphabet was phonetic: if you could say it, you could write it. The symbols were also all clearly related, the patterns designed to be easy to recognize. Learning to read was just a matter of practice.

I was informed that a king from a nearby country had ordered this setup made several centuries ago. The wisest men of his land designed it; the system only ten vowels and twenty-five consonants. It was so easy that it spread like wildfire, bringing the language with it. Therefore, almost everyone could read and write, and while most peasants felt no need to most of the time, almost all of them could.

When informed of my assignments, my dad made some comments about how I was a bit young to be learning to read. My brothers hadn't started until they were five, apparently. But Dad ceased his objections when Mystien pointed out that I'd been making several of the characters on the ground as they talked, whispering their names to myself. For my part, I didn't know this until I heard the old wizard laughing.

So winter began in earnest after the first snowfall, and we retreated into our home, only coming out for the most necessary of work before returning. I got to spend my days with Mom, learning about making cloth, and writing things on the floor for her to check. It was altogether relaxing.

Several weeks into our winter break, someone knocked on our door. It was early afternoon, and we were all busy with our various crafts, but this was such a weird happening that it took a moment for my father to get up and let our visitor in.

"Ah, hello, everyone, good day, I hope everything is well?" the mayor asked, he seemed a bit nervous.

"Quite," my dad answered him. "Bit unusual for you to come by in the middle of winter, something wrong?"

"Well, sadly I must say there is." The mayor began to slowly explain, "It seems the kingdom is moving a number of men to the East, to our border with the empire, and many of them were, ah, not properly prepared. We've been receiving far too many who won't be able to continue without having rather severe frostbite healed . . ."

"What about their healers, the army should have more than enough to fix some frostbite, should they not?" Dad didn't seem to be at all interested in what the man was suggesting.

"They were sped along to the border. Some are stopping for a day or two to fix up a few of the men, but they're still piling up, and it's beginning to cause problems. Not enough food, nowhere for them to stay . . . if we could just get them moving through the town . . ." The mayor looked downright pitiful.

"And Lord Hazelwood? Why hasn't he sent someone to fix this?" My dad was getting more irritated by the moment.

"Nobody to send, Verren. The priest working for him left months ago, and it would seem the bard he had picking up the slack jumped town just before the first snow. We're on our own here. He even rerouted the army around Hazelwood so that he wouldn't have to deal with this anymore."

I felt bad for the mayor. He was stuck here and screwed by all the authorities who should have been able to help him.

I noticed something I hadn't ever before. My father had an aura. I'd never seen it, but now, when he was getting angry, truly angry, I could see it start to rise. It wasn't shapes like Mystien and I had, but rather more subtle: a light blackness, growing as it moved about him. I wondered how he'd hidden it, and I wondered more if the mayor knew how much danger he was in.

"And you want me to send my daughter down into their midst to patch them up and send them on their way?"

"No, no, I don't, but if nothing changes, they'll pick the village clean of food in a month. We're holding as it is, but the numbers can't keep growing like this. Soon . . . soon I'll have nothing to offer the hungry soldiers, and not long after that, they'll start taking from the citizens. They'll tear the place apart looking for food."

The mayor had his eyes down. It was an awful sight, a man powerless to fix a problem, asking for help he knew he had no right to.

It took a few moments for my father to consider, his eyes boring into the mayor, but eventually I could see him calm a bit. "Very well, but I'm going with her, and someone is going to pay the same wages that a middle-ranked healer working for the army would be getting. I don't care if it's you. I don't care if it's Lord Hazelwood. I don't care if it's whatever poor bastard they left in charge of their men in town. Make it happen."

The mayor visibly relaxed, letting out a breath he'd held as my father made his demands. "I'll take care of it. It'll take a couple of days to arrange it, but it'll be done." And after some hurried goodbyes, he took his leave.

It was two days later that we got word that all was ready. Dad had packed supplies and made arrangements with his brother who lived in the town proper for us to stay. I think I'd only met my uncle once or twice in passing, so this would be an interesting change.

That day, Dad carried me to town. The snow was easily up to his knees, and it would have been impossible for me to walk in at any reasonable pace. He also had on a pack, which had to weigh two hundred pounds, from what I'd seen him putting in it, but it didn't seem to hinder him in the least.

I spent a good long time looking for his aura. I only saw one or two small flashes as we went, and it was easy to understand how I'd missed it. I'd seen him move in superhuman ways before, but it hadn't registered properly.

"How do you hide your aura?" I finally asked.

He laughed. "Finally noticed it, huh? There's a couple of tricks, but they don't work well for casters and are pretty frowned upon by most. It's considered rude, like wearing a mask."

"Then why do you do it?" I was a bit confused why he'd do something rude.

"Old habit, it's fine though. Most of the people around here who could see it already know it's there." He adjusted his hold on me, and I shivered against his coat. It was really terribly cold.

"Will you teach me how?" It sounded like a good thing to know at any rate.

"Perhaps when you're older, though, like I said, it doesn't work well for casters. Mystien doesn't bother most of the time. You can still see his even when he's trying, though it is a bit less pronounced, or so I'm told. I can't see them." He decided to change the subject, "Are you excited to see your uncle Barro?" he asked me.

"He's the big guy in town, with the beard, right?"

Dad nodded.

"I don't think I've ever talked to him. You and Mom don't take me to town much."

"Hmm, fair enough, we'll have to bring you more often. He's good people." Dad scratched his short beard a bit as he thought about it, and I smiled at the promise to come see something new more often.

I told him about all the things in town I wanted to look at for the rest of the short trip, making him laugh. Apparently, most of it was thought of as rather boring.

The door of my uncle's house was on the second floor of a building just off of the main street. From what I could see, he lived right over a black-smith's shop. We were hurried in by an older, lithe little woman.

"Oy, is that my little brother then, come to find a place to stay, have you?" a good-natured booming sounded just after we entered.

"No, just making sure some old man hasn't died on me," Dad jibed back.

Uncle Barro appeared shortly thereafter. If my father was a prowling cat, he was a bear of a man, his beard and hair dark but beginning to gray with age, arms thick as telephone poles and muscles bulging, as opposed to the taut wires of my own father's frame. He wasn't much taller, but his build and movements belied that.

"Come and sit for a bit, we'll talk," my uncle offered.

"We need to get down to fix up those soldiers, after dinner though, aye?" Dad responded.

It was clear Barro had something he wanted to say, but it could wait. We'd be there for weeks at least, perhaps the rest of winter. Instead, Dad put down his pack and took me down the street to the tavern, where I gathered at least some of the men in need of healing were.

As we went down the street, he spoke to me, "I'm going to do something that is going to make everything a lot easier, but it might bug you a bit, okay?"

"Okay," I nodded, not sure what he was talking about.

Every hair on my body stood as his aura poured out. It surrounded him like a mist, black as night, it was like looking upon death. I almost began to tremble. Nobody else noticed. It was as if death walked the street, holding a little girl in his arms. The image was terrifying.

"O-oh," I managed.

He kissed me on the head. "It'll make things easier, trust me."

I nodded. "Yes, Father." I was feeling a bit more respectful than normal, almost like I was in trouble and wanted to look sorry.

He chuckled a bit as he opened the door and we stepped in, going right up to a man in a slightly nicer uniform than the others in the main room. A few others bustled about while most were in chairs or hastily made bedrolls, their injuries obvious.

"Sergeant," Dad began, causing the man to look up at us. "I'm Verren; this is my daughter, Alana. We're here to help the injured men." He spoke this all quickly and with finality.

The man nodded, quirking his brow a bit at me, "Glad to have you. I've had the least serious cases that we need dealt with brought down here. You can begin as soon as you're ready."

I was put down and walked over to the nearest man, who had his foot propped out and was watching the proceedings, "Let's see what's wrong," I piped.

The man looked to the sergeant, who gave him a firm nod, before unwrapping his foot. His toes were blackening from where they'd gotten frostbit. I began casting once I had an idea where it was going, and while the damage was certainly there, it didn't appear too deep or bad. Within about ten minutes, he was patched up enough for me to move on.

After the first, none of the men gave me weird looks. Several even smiled and thanked me as I looked after them; none of this damage was all that deep. It took some time to work the magic, but it was nothing like the men from Creekrun. These would be in great pain from walking, but beyond that, nothing much. It took about two hours to clear the tavern's main hall, after which I was given a quick lunch before moving to the rooms.

Those cases were slightly worse, but nothing too bad. I was on the third one when I heard a man down the hall shouting.

"Now where's this girl I'm paying so damn much to be here?" came a rather irritating voice. It sounded like a middle manager, the kind of person who reveled in their own tiny pond of power, making those around them miserable.

A man appeared in the door of the room, his face in a grimace. I registered him briefly as he started to scoff, then we both realized a few things. First, his aura was weak. It was weaker than Mystien's. Heck, it was weaker than mine, and it was certainly weaker than my irritated-looking parent's aura, from where he stood in the corner. Secondly, said parent was shooting daggers at him, like he was nothing.

"I believe you've found her," Dad practically growled. "Now, do you have any other need of my daughter?"

The man blanched, all his pompousness fleeing from him like a rabbit. "Ah, just checking on things, good work with the other men, Miss," He was a bit stiff, but still managed to hold his composure. He seemed to have been well trained on that account.

"Thank you," I said, having little else to add to the conversation, being too busy as it was anyway.

"Well then, keep up the good work." The man left in a hurry. I heard him go quickly down the steps. The sergeant was left by the door; he just looked confused for a few seconds before nodding and heading to his own work.

"What was that?" I asked after I'd finished with the healing, for that room at least.

"That was the second or third son of a nobleman, or perhaps the son of a second son, realizing that causing you problems would be a losing proposition for everyone" was the only answer I got. I spent another hour healing before finally finishing up for the day.

I practiced my other spells for a bit after we got back to Uncle Barro's, after which we had a good dinner made by my aunt, whose name it turned out was Elna. She was a lovely woman, if a bit quiet, and her cooking was a refreshing change from my mother's.

Dad talked to Uncle Barro while we cleaned up and then we all chatted for a while. I sat on a bench with my father, opposite another with my aunt and uncle. I curled up and closed my eyes, letting myself relax a bit after the long day.

"Verren." Barro lowered his voice, likely assuming I was asleep. I wasn't yet of course, but . . . "This isn't some border skirmish, not how they're moving troops. They're even calling up some of our lads."

"They call for men every year, and every year a few hotheads enlist," Dad replied.

"Aye, aye, that they do, I know one hothead that joined the call as soon as he could," Barro chuckled, "But this is different; it isn't just a call. Come spring, they're going to draft some of the lads who don't sign up. The mayor got wind; he wanted me to let you know."

"An actual war? Are they nuts? We're not on the border, but we're certainly close enough for it to spill over here if it goes wrong." Dad sounded unhappy at the information.

"Ermath may not be giving them a choice. You may not hear it from out in the boonies where you are, but from the sound of it, they're massing troops. Your lads are too young, and mine are all moved out, but it's bad news, little brother, bad news indeed." My uncle sighed, sounding tired. I knew Ermath was the proper name of the empire, but not much else about them, same as I knew our kingdom was called Bergond, but that kind of thing just didn't come up much.

"I left the army to get away from that nonsense, Barro, nobles who only care who was whose kid, the blaring incompetence of their mess, and the constant fights. Even this far out, are they still going to keep pushing? Where does it end?" Dad sounded some mix of tired and angry. "I hate to say it, but what if the kingdom lost? Do you think . . . ?"

"Don't finish that thought, Verren, you know where that line of thinking leads. We've both seen it." There was sadness in that, though I didn't understand it.

"I'll have to teach the boys to fight come spring," Dad mused. "As for Alana, well, we'll see if Mystien has any ideas on how she can defend herself. But I hope she never needs it." He petted my hair. "Regardless though, as long as the army doesn't drag them in, they should be fine." He laid back for a few moments, before he returned to more mundane conversation. I continued to feign sleep until he picked me up and took me off to a proper bedroll to sleep.

Our days continued much like that, more frostbitten men were always showing up; however, once I worked my way through the backlog, it wasn't too bad. We even had a few more spellcasters come by now and again. They seemed to approve of my work. There were also a few knights who popped in. This group gave Dad some weird looks, almost as if they could nearly see something off about him. I could tell that most of them had auras, too, mostly weaker ones. I assumed those who had any of note wouldn't be stopping in our out-of-the-way little town.

After a bit of practice, I managed to get my water spell to make ice, too, and learned that I could in fact fix missing digits. I assumed that meant I could fix limbs as well, but even a pinky toe was so mana-intensive to regrow that I shuddered at the thought.

After learning to make ice and learning that I was being paid a good clip for this work, I did make a request of my father: to order an ice cream churn from Uncle Barro. He didn't know what it was, but after a bit of pestering and telling him I thought I had an idea that would be good eating, he finally relented. The plans were simple enough for a hand churn, and with my ice-making spell, the spring and summer would surely improve. I also got him to order me a beehive, another thing he didn't really understand, but the woodworking was cheap. After making a lot of money for the family and mercilessly pestering him about it, he finally caved.

Once winter slipped away and we were no longer needed in town, we went home. The snow was mostly gone by this point, and I got to skip along as my dad carried the churn. He was picking up my hive in a few days, and I was in a cheery mood.

Mom even let me take some of her extra thread and weave it into a loose mesh. Well, let me is a bit of an exaggeration, I did it and pretended like it was a mistake. She was a bit cross, but I told her that we could still use it. I'd think of something.

"You had better. Spinning all that wasn't easy," she glared at me, obviously suspecting foul play on my part.

"I've got an idea. Don't be mad," I answered placatingly.

"Looks useless to me," Rod offered.

"Nope, nothing for that," John said.

I gave them a grin. I knew two young men who would be helping me. Bee stings hurt.

CHAPTER 6

✦

HONEY, ICE CREAM,
AND FALLING NIGHT

Spring came, and I managed to convince Dad to let me set up my hive in an unused corner of one of our fields. That area was a bit too rocky to be useful, and clearing it out would not have been worth the effort in my family's opinion.

There were no bees in it as of yet, a problem I was currently working on. I started by building an appropriate outfit for my brother, Rod, and he volunteered to help me a bit. The main part he'd need was a face shield. Using mesh, and with a bit of haphazard straw weaving, I would be able to construct something that at least looked like it'd keep bees off of his face.

I was only allowed to work on my side project in the evenings. Chores waited for no girl, and between that and lessons, I was swamped. It would take me a few weeks at the very least to prepare the hood and gloves.

It was a few days after returning home that those lessons began with a checkup from my now mentor, Mystien.

"All right, welcome back, let's cut to it." With that, he handed me a book, a first for me. It was already opened to a particular page. "Let's see if you actually did what you were told," he said as he smiled.

"The basic structure of water-type magic is the triangle. Visualizing it while imagining the properties of water will increase the effectiveness of your water magic," I read. Suddenly, the shape of Mystien's aura began to make a bit more sense, along with the feeling that the magic he used was based on trig.

"Very good, I never taught you that, but using it, let's see what you can do with water magic now, shall we?" he asked, pulling over a pot. "Fill this up as much as you can."

I began to do as he asked, filling the pot up about halfway with the normal amount of mana I'd been using for a practice spell, a marked improvement.

"Um, can I try again? I think I can do better," I asked him as he emptied the pot. He nodded and brought it back over.

This time, rather than just triangles, I pictured things as I'd learned they were in science class. Oxygen, covalently bonded to hydrogen in a bent angle. I even tossed in the hydrogen bonds that made water so much like it was. I almost blinked, the mana usage plummeted. It was still slow, but I easily filled the pot with the same amount of mana. Doing water like this hadn't occurred to me before.

"Very good. What did you do?" he inquired as he looked over my work.

"Umm, I sort of changed it a bit." *How could I explain my knowledge of chemistry to a wizard? I may have made a mistake here*, I said to myself.

"Well, I learned a bit about making ice over the winter," I admitted, which got me a stern look. "And how I did ice was just water with a hard hexagon shape." That got me a startled look.

"Putting aside that you were experimenting with magic without my supervision, something you are not supposed to be doing, how did you know that hexagons worked well with ice?"

"It just seemed right," I lied. Explaining that ice crystals were hexagonal at standard temperature and pressure was a bit too much for a four-year-old. "But if you take a hexagon and divide it up like this"—I drew a diagram out, showing where the oxygen and hydrogens would go, cutting off to make a standard water molecule shape—"next you just make the edges grab to the center pieces like this." I drew several angles representing water, with dotted connections between what would be the oxygen and hydrogen atoms. "And then I imagined it all moving around a lot, because water moves a lot," I finished.

He blinked at my words. "Stay here for a moment," he said before stepping outside. I assumed to cast something. When he returned a few minutes later, he gave me a very hard look. "You are not to tell anyone else about your technique; it's too strong. You don't want to be known to know that." His words had both a harshness and concern in them.

"Wh-what?"

Mystien looked a bit scary and seemed to be implying something important.

"The army will want this, and they won't want anyone else to know about it. They will go after anyone they think knows." His statement chilled my blood, the way he said it didn't help.

I nodded, "Okay, I won't tell anyone." Of that much at least, I was sure.

He ran me through the rest of my spells afterward. My comments on repairing more serious injuries only got a small comment. "Yes, almost anything can be healed, even missing parts, but the mana goes up by quite a bit if parts are missing." He shrugged.

When my father got home that night, he actually used his belt on me. I almost never got punished, being a pretty well-behaved kid, and never before by Dad. Apparently, Mystien told him about my unauthorized experimentation with magic, and the clarity of how not allowed that was became clear.

Upon finishing my brother's improvised bee suit, we began Operation Acquire Bees. Rod thought I was insane; John couldn't stop laughing. First things first, we needed the basic tools, knives, which every child over the age of eight carried, a smoker, improvised out of a small clay pot we used to hold coals at night, and a small cup and board on which to capture a bee.

I had never kept a beehive before, but my uncle had, and had explained far more than I thought I'd ever cared to know about bees when I showed even the slightest interest. He was a really nice man, even bought me a book on the subject, but my interest stopped after the first time I went to watch him and got stung like ten times. I briefly wondered how he was, and I knew I'd probably never know, but I hoped he was well.

I began by catching a bee on one of the afternoons I had off, a bit of honeysuckle nectar as bait, and holding it for around a quarter of an hour, following it once I had released it, a process I repeated for around four hours. After a good amount of trying and some luck, I managed to locate a hive, ten feet up a tree.

The next part had to be done at dinner. My father had taken to training the boys in fighting during the afternoon, and they were both tired when I struck.

I poked Rod while we were eating. "Big brother, will you come help me catch some bees?" I asked pleadingly.

"It's spring; you don't get honey until summer," Rod said, leaning back in his chair.

"I want to catch the whole hive though," I continued.

"For what?" he quirked an eyebrow at me.

"So that we can harvest honey from it many times." I could tell I had his interest.

"That won't work, Alana," he responded, "at least I don't think it will." He scratched his chin.

"I'll make you ice for your bruises," I offered, knowing I needed some immediate incentive, "if you help me with my project." He looked at me full on now. "You can use it for drinks too. I could just heal you, but I think ice would be better, wouldn't it?" I kept pushing.

Dad had started their training, and while John had taken to fighting like a fish to water, Rod had not. He still managed to hold his own just through size and reach, but that gap was closing quickly upon him. Every day, he looked more like he'd taken a sound beating.

"You should help your sister, if nothing else, it'll make her stop pestering everyone about it," Dad offered from the side. "If and when she finds a hive, you two take a day to put it in her weird little box." His blessing, along with the added benefit of a day without training was the final push I needed.

"Okay, little sis, you find a hive and I'll help you." Rod patted my head. He seemed to think I never would.

"Found one earlier today, Rod. We can do it tomorrow if you want." I gave him a big grin.

"Devious," John laughed as all involved agreed on what our plan for tomorrow was.

I spent the rest of the night making a small wicker cage for the queen.

"Okay, there'll be a bigger bee, right, and you need to get it. If you don't get that one, we failed," I explained as we brought all of our tools near the hive. "John and I will be way back. We'll get the ladder and stuff after all the bees are gone."

"You've explained your whole plan here several times, I know," Rod retorted.

"Okay then, it's all on you," I went and stood with John.

We watched as he carefully pried open the hive and began putting comb into frames with string, each then loaded into the box.

"He doesn't seem bothered by the idea of opening up a beehive," I commented to my other brother as we watched.

"Why would he be? After ten or so, all us boys hunt them in the summer," he responded. "Wish I could draw though . . . I'd love to have a picture of this," he quipped. He seemed to think the whole operation was the funniest thing he'd ever seen.

"You go after bees?" This was news to me.

"Yeah, honey is tasty; you can sell it in town if you like. Also it's the thing to give to a girl you like; girls really like sweet things." He nodded. He wasn't wrong, my pushing for this whole operation was some evidence.

Rod finished up and waved at us. The bees looked peeved, and he held up the little queen cage, giving a gesture that he'd succeeded. I made cheering motions as he packed up and took the hive off to its new home, the cloud of bees following along.

After a solid wait, John and I cleaned up the tools. We both got one or two stings doing so, but managed without too much hassle. I also grabbed up a few dead bees, for future use. The next day, I came back to scrape all the extra wax I could from the now defunct hive; it was useful stuff.

The bees, to my great relief, actually stayed, and after a few more bits of instruction, Rod became quite the beekeeper. I was surprised at how well he took to it, but it seemed he'd developed a soft spot for the little bugs. I also kept paying him with ice and the occasional healing, which probably helped.

My hive had come with two extra boxes, what would have been called "supers" on Earth. These I loaded up with frames and filled the wood backing with a layer of wax.

I also did some measurements on the bees, and a bit of testing with a couple of boards and a box to come up with a size for a queen excluder. Getting it was a mess, involving cajoling, and the healing of several villagers before my dad would order it for me. Uncle Barro made it to exact specifications, and my little wire mesh was ready in time for summer, to my great joy. The box and my supers were installed immediately as per my requests.

Midsummer rolled around, and life continued as it was, the peace of all of it only broken by a dinner conversation.

"Sorren reckons his ox has about had it. He's planning on slaughtering it in ten days," Dad declared.

Sorren was one of our neighbors; he was nice enough, "That's going to be a lot of meat," I said, nodding.

"Aye, it is; he's invited everyone to have a big feast of it. We'll salt most of it, but there should be a good bit for cooking too. We'll need to take something with us for the feast, like honey." Dad looked at me squarely.

"Not from my hive," I pouted.

"Don't be greedy, Alana," Mom chastised me.

"It'll make more honey over time, if we take it now, we won't get any more from it," I argued. "What if I find another we can get honey from?" Compromise was often a winning solution.

"If you can find another that can give four jars of honey, we'll leave yours." Dad was nothing but reasonable.

I had to give it to him, even on Earth, most parents would just say no to their kid. I knew he expected me to fail, but still. The jars he indicated were of a standard size; full I could guess he wanted around two gallons of honey, twenty-five or so pounds. That that was almost assuredly more than my hive would have was not lost on me.

"Okay," I agreed, knowing that this was the best deal I could get. "Can I borrow Rod for a few days?"

Dad nodded, "You can. But if you don't get that honey, I don't want to hear any whining about taking it from your hive."

With that, it was settled.

The next day, Rod and I went to the forest. We had to go a good ways in so that we didn't just find my hive again, and from there I showed him my technique.

"I like it." He nodded as he watched me following the bees. "How long will it take?"

It was his only question.

"As long as it takes," I replied, a frustrating, if not incorrect answer.

It took half the day, at the end of which we were both quite tired, but we found one. The hole was around twenty feet up in a tree and amazingly busy.

"I'm going to check it out," my big brother declared as he began to climb.

He made it about halfway up before stopping, tapping the tree and climbing back down.

I looked at him, my question obvious.

"It's big," he responded. "That thing is big. Let's come back tomorrow and we need to bring John."

I didn't really understand, but nodded; he seemed to know his stuff.

Rod and I returned the next day with all our tools, and what even seemed to me like an obscene number of baskets. John and I watched as Rod began to crack open the hive.

I understood why he'd stopped halfway up. It looked like the bees had hollowed out this whole tree, which was, I finally saw, quite dead. This thing was a monster of a hive.

I began that day to realize that while my oldest brother might not be much of a fighter, he was undoubtedly skilled with his hands. He pulled comb after comb from the tree, deftly cutting and separating the honeycomb from the brood, tossing them in different baskets.

We wanted both the honey and the wax from the brood comb. Both were quite valuable, though the honey more so for us.

Rod had to put the raid on hold twice as we retreated, for me to heal some of the stings. He was getting dozens, just from the time and quantity. I made sure to take the extra time to deal with the poison too. It was slow, but important. While he continued, John and I would head home to deliver our bounty and eventually get more baskets.

The whole process took the entire day, at the end of which I had to divide our spoils, the boys deciding that they'd helped more than their share.

Mom joined me for this, chatting as we worked to set up the lot.

"How many jars do you reckon this is?" I asked. I was arm deep in crushed and cut-up honeycomb.

"I don't know, dear, more than enough I'd say. How big was the hive?" She looked at the baskets that I was working on.

"Huge. Are we going to make the honey into anything, or are we just going to take pots of it with us?" The whole idea of a big feast was something new to me, large animals were almost never killed, and if they were they were sold at market.

"Some of it. I've got some nuts we can toss in, too, and maybe we can find something else to take." Mom had crushed up several cones, setting them to drain their contents into my ice cream churn, a device she had been glaring at, since it sat unused at an increasing interval.

"I've got an idea." I then proceeded to explain the use of that churn. Pretending it was something one of the soldiers over the winter had told me about when asked. The ingredients for ice cream were all close at hand, or easy to get, with the honey as sugar, we were set.

The morning of the would-be feast, we awoke early and gathered with the rest of the local families in an open area near Sorren's home.

It was a party atmosphere as the men slaughtered the old ox and began the process of cutting the meat into cuts, several of them also setting up tables and the like for when all was readied. The women and girls started the long process of communal cooking, chatting idly as pots of meat and vegetables simmered happily.

I was paired with two girls named Sara and Lena, both about a year older than me. I'd met them a few times, and we'd played a bit when we were still toddlers, but as of late I hadn't had much to do with them, I was too busy with everything. It was a bit odd talking to those around my physical age, being so much older mentally, but I decided that I needed some friends, and this would be a good place to start.

"Are you excited about the food?" I asked, this got fervent nods.

"Yeah, I've never had beef," Sara said.

"Oh, I had it once, it was yummy, kind of tough though," Lena added in.

"I think it is kind of tough, but it looks like we're roasting most of it with sauce. That should help."

Indeed, most of the meat being cooked today was going in large vessels with a sweet sauce, a mix of honey, vinegar, tomato, and herbs, what one might expect from a standard barbecue sauce. Guess that might be universal.

We alternated with tending the two pots we'd been assigned and playing a game not unlike hopscotch, save that the board was circular.

Throughout the day, people came by to talk. Even my brothers came together a few times. Rod seemed determined to awkwardly flirt with Sara's older sister, Sandra. They made a cute couple.

Several other girls came by to gossip with Sandra after the boys had left, asking for opinions and the like on my brother, as well as a few more boys his age. The discussion on who was best was intense. Sandra's mother and my own were off in a corner, too, huddled together in conversation. I couldn't hear much from them, but it would seem they approved of the pairing, or at least thought it was adorable.

These might have seemed like games to me when I first came here, but it was quite important. Our little hamlet was tiny; even the whole village wasn't that big, and the list of potential spouses was short. All that considered, it was quite possible that my big brother would be marrying the girl he was trying to chat up when they both came of age at eighteen.

Lunch consisted of mostly quick-cooking foods, the only meat being some that had been shaved thin, but even then it was still a bit tough.

The old beast had been ancient. It was short, but rather enjoyable on the whole, we even had some meat sandwiches. I thought they were a hit, but most passed.

After lunch, Rod dragged John with him to continue his flirtations several more times. Eventually, it became a distraction. Mom solved this by filling up the ice cream churn and setting the two to work. I provided the ice, and with a bit of salt added to it, the two could use their overabundant energy productively.

The whole event could only be described as a miniature festival and continued on until dinner, which started with a series of toasts to Sorren's generosity, and his toasts to the others who'd brought food as well. The food that night was the best I'd had since coming to this world. Slow cooking the meat was absolutely the winning choice, and whoever had made the sauce was an artist. My ice cream was the after-dinner hit; Mom got someone from every family asking how to make it, even old Mystien came by to check out the churn.

The sky was darkening as we cleaned up, our bellies full and joy on every face. It was as a few last jokes were being told that we saw him coming, a rider in some kind of official-looking getup. All conversation stopped as he came; he didn't even get off of his horse.

"Is this everyone who lives here?" asked the rider.

My father looked around. "Yes, it appears to be, something has happened?"

The rider nodded to my dad, pulling out a scroll as he did so, "Good, it'll make this easier."

"Oyez, oyez," he intoned, his voice loud enough for everyone to hear.

"By decree of His Majesty Erik the Third, King of Bergond and Master of the Great Cities.

"War is henceforth declared upon the Empire of Ermath. To suit our great nation on this righteous endeavor toward their destruction, every man between the ages of eighteen and thirty, excluding those with three or more children below the age of fifteen, is henceforth ordered to report to the appropriate officials for registration in the kingdom's military."

With that, he rolled up the scroll.

"Thus ends the official decree. You should report to the mayor, who will be sending you off to Lord Hazelwood once that is done. That's who you should see. Volunteers outside of the required men will, of course, also be accepted."

The messenger looked out over us, our whole group stunned to silence. "Be well."

With those last words, he rode off, leaving us standing there as night fell upon our happy little home.

CHAPTER 7

✦

BIRTH, DEATH, AND GATHERING SHADOWS

It took a few minutes for the shock of it to sink in; once it did, all the children, myself included, were hurried off to bed. Some of the older boys were pulled away by their fathers though, Rod among them. I had some idea of what war meant, but there were a number of questions.

First of all, the age range of the men called up was huge. Most of the adult men in the village fell in that range, even if there was an exception for those with lots of young children. Secondly, the timing: it was late summer; harvest would come by soon, without those men . . . I almost shuddered at the implication. Finally, this was a royal decree; there was no getting around it. If you were in the called group, you *would* show up, or you *would* be charged with a crime that might well end in your death. That was not normal.

I could guess why the older boys were at the men's meeting. If so many were leaving, someone would have to work the otherwise empty fields, at least through the harvest. Not to do so would be a disaster of impossible proportions. The idea of all that food wasted almost made me sick.

"John," I whispered over from where we were laying on our little mattresses.

"Yeah," he leaned over, looking at me.

"This is really bad, isn't it?" I asked.

"Worse than I think either of us know, little sister," he said, looking worried. "But it'll be okay."

I wished I could believe that.

"I'm scared." There was no point trying to hide it now.

"Pull your mattress over here then. I won't let anything happen to you." When I did so, he wrapped an arm over me protectively. My brothers could be real flakes sometimes, but I knew they were both on the way to becoming great men.

I looked over to where my mother was beside the door. She looked as if she could pop any day; the stress was apparent on her face as she waited for my father to come home. It was the last thing I saw before I fell asleep.

The next morning, everything happened in a bit of a rush. As soon as breakfast was eaten, my father looked across the table to me. There were bags under both his and Mom's eyes. I had no clue when he'd returned last night, but it must have been late, for I hadn't heard him come home.

"Alana, you're going to learn some new things from Mystien in the next few weeks. You need to make sure you master them, as quickly as possible, no excuses." I nodded at Dad's firm words.

"You'll also be doing much of the work around the house come fall, so learn as much of that as you can." That was an odd one, but not a big deal.

"John, you and your mother will be helping Rod take over a couple of fields. It'll be harder work than you're used to, and you'll still be having training in the evenings. Some of the older boys will be joining us too."

Mom nodded along. It seems she'd talked with him earlier, perhaps last night.

"The other boys?" That made John blink a bit.

"Yes, there are some who are still underage, but not by much, everyone of age is, of course, leaving, but others will likely have to go soon too. We talked last night, giving them a bit of training now may save their lives later." Dad sounded like a military commander right now. I knew he was some kind of former soldier, so that made sense.

"A few of the men just above age may join as well. Just in case . . . they decide to call up more."

He seemed bothered by that idea but was hiding it.

I hurried off to my magic lesson right after breakfast, quite nervous as to what would happen.

"All right," began Mystien. He already had several books pulled out and opened.

"You know that there are things that bards can do that others cannot already." I nodded.

"We will be focusing on two abilities, also I'll be trying to teach you some attack magic." My eyes widened. "How serious is this? How bad is this whole thing?" I asked.

He gave me an appraising look. "You are smarter and wiser than any child has any right to be, Alana. It's disturbing sometimes," he said, then sighed. "I've never seen it this bad. Taking men just before harvest is a move of desperation. It means they don't expect many of them to come back, because if they do, there'll be no food. Even if they don't, many will starve." I just stared for a few moments, processing.

"Two abilities, then attack magic. First, Jackson explained to you that bards can summon complex things, like bread. We're going to work on that, as we may well need it." He took me over and had me start reading the books he'd set out. They described the process and visualization, as well as how hard it was.

The standard for bread was to visualize its structure, the holes, and the feel of it. This was exhausting. I managed to make a roll not much bigger than my small hand using this before I had to stop and let my mana regenerate. The taste of that first roll could barely be described as bread.

I tried something a bit different my second attempt. I visualized the process as I understood it—the kneading to bring the gluten together, the yeast that made bubbles of carbon dioxide when it rose, the heat of the oven—bringing all the parts together. This worked much better. I got a roll that was twice as large and quite a bit more tasty. It even had a slight sweet note. That aside, my mana was still tapped out from that, leaving me wiped out.

Learning new spells was draining to an insane degree. Mystien had explained when we first started that it was best to master a few abilities that had strong use at my age, then to move on slowly. Apparently, many were the spellcasters who tried to learn lots of things fast and ended up never developing an ounce of power. I could tell from all my own practice that he was right: repeated practice of a few things made them much stronger, whereas new things were painfully weak.

We continued all morning. I'd practice until I was pooped. Then he'd read me descriptions from other bards on how they did this same spell, running me through the processes and visualization. The size of my little roll only increased slightly, but it did increase. By the time we finished, I felt hollowed out, using so much mana was exhausting in its own way. The rolls became our lunch, I even had a couple to take home for dinner.

* * *

About a week later, my mother went into labor. It happened in the middle of the night; several women from our town came over to help. The men were kicked out of the house with little ceremony as the women worked, prepping everything, including one bringing a weird-looking chair. Once it was in place, it became obvious what it was, and that it was normal in this world for women to give birth from a seated position, rather than a laying one. That was a bit surprising. But I'd heard of some places doing that, so it wasn't alarming or anything.

The whole process took until the sun was beginning to rise. I spent most of it fetching things and watching closely, so that I could learn what to do. That was considered important.

It was a girl, and to everyone's heart-crushing despair, stillborn. There was nothing that could be done, nothing anyone could do. Both of my parents wept. Mom was inconsolable. After a time, Dad and the boys went to bury the baby. It was a simple grave in the hamlet's communal grave-yard. The marker read "Beera," the name they'd chosen if the child was a girl. Mom just held me for the rest of the day, refusing to let go.

After that, my little sister was never mentioned again in our house; it became an unspoken rule. I would every now and then see my moth-er's face change, the memory flashing by, but she never said a word about it. For the next several weeks, Dad, too, would sometimes just hold Mom. I learned by actually visiting the grave that there had been many such deaths. But by some unwritten agreement, babies who died at birth were not talked about by anyone. The culture shock of that left me reeling.

So it became almost a footnote, the uncounted lost children of a world, those who never knew life.

My whole family was slowly overburdened for the next couple of weeks. With so many of our men leaving, the women had to take up their tasks. Everyone in town was working flat out. Most of the jobs was hard, heavy labor, and while they'd done some in the past, the increase was just too much.

Within three weeks though, I was reliably producing enough food to give my mom a break on some cooking. That was when Mystien intro-duced the second new lesson.

"Jackson didn't tell you, and I hesitate to at your age. I wouldn't if you were any other child," he began. "Do you know why bards are so often found in taverns?"

"Because the average bard is a bit of a drunken womanizing flake?" I replied. That got me a hearty laugh.

"No," he continued, "one of the quirks of bardic magic is that if a participating crowd is present, the effects can be improved for a given spell. It's a minor effect, and each new person helping gives just a bit less of a boost then the previous, but it can be a good boost, particularly with enough people."

"That sounds powerful," I said, blinking at what certainly had to be some kind of hack.

"It does, but it's not as much as you'd think," he explained. "The difficulty of controlling it increases far faster than the power boost. Try to draw on too many at once, and you'll lose control completely. Even absolute master bards can only control around fifty additions at once. Twenty is, in fact, what most can do when fully trained. If we can get you up to five for now, I'll be happy." He pulled out some books on this technique as well, showing me.

Over the next few days, the method of using others was explained thoroughly between my castings of the bread spell. It alternated with stories of bards who'd overreached and the horrible things that had happened to them.

The most telling of these was some foolish man who, in a bid of desperation to end a war, tried to focus an entire stadium of people. His spell had worked, protecting his city, but the backlash was so great that he blew up, taking a fair chunk of the stadium with him. I shuddered to think the kind of magic that could have been worked with some of the concerts on Earth.

Of note is that the additional participants didn't have to know anything about what you were trying to do. They didn't have to have any mana either. What was needed was for them to willingly join in your performance, lending their voice, or whatever performance you were using, to your own.

After several days, Mystien and I started singing together as I cast. We used a simple children's tune. Using this technique was weird. Having others join you created a sort of reverb. The best way I could describe it was like being aware of an additional speaker being added to my magic. I had to manage this additional boost as I cast. The whole thing was a bit distracting, like adjusting the levels of it mid-song without stopping, but the power boost was real, almost half again as much juice.

The additional bread was, at this point, more than we needed. So it was given to some of the families in town who were having a hard time.

It took a few weeks before we started adding more singers to our lessons. Mystien elected to use children whose fathers had left. This had many benefits: it acted as free babysitting, the children got fed while with us, and those who came went home with some bread for lunch and dinner. It was so popular we had to start a rotation of the kids who needed it, as I couldn't manage many at once.

Being taught attack magic didn't begin until the harvest started, which was notably earlier than in previous years. The theory was introduced a few days before while my mana was recharging.

Mystien went back to his lecture mode: "Bardic magic is poor for almost all attacks, even those it has are not particularly strong. What we'll be focusing on is a type of directed sonic attack that can cause minor damage, but will mostly be painful and disorienting. It's something to use as a last resort, so you can escape."

Then I was given a rundown of what was basically a sonic scream. It even required a quick, harsh movement, a scream being the standard form for most bards.

I had to practice this one after all our helpers had gone home, and more often than not, alone. It was directed, but even those not in the line of attack still got a bit of a taste. I had to use it on Mystien every few days to show him how I was progressing. By the time harvest was finishing up, he declared it good enough that I could practice on my own. I supposed I'd reached a level where he no longer wanted to expose himself without reason.

The harvest exhausted my family. I barely saw them except at dinner, which was a quiet restful affair. We'd all worked hard, since after my magic training I'd had to do most of the cooking and cleaning for the household. Without magic, it would have been impossible; with it, it was barely possible, stretching my body and mana to their absolute limits. Once harvest was in though, we knew it would all be better. Winter was a much more restful time.

I was there when the tax man came; this world's version of the IRS was significantly simpler, but no less hated. I didn't understand at first why he'd come with so many guards, or why they were all armed to the teeth. When he announced that Lord Hazelwood would be requiring the same amount from our little hamlet as in years past, I understood. Number of guards notwithstanding, he almost had a riot. The crowd roared in rage hurling insults at the men.

"You greedy bastards, we lost a third of our harvest!" one man shouted.

"You take our men and now this, screw off!" came a woman.

"Lord Hazelwood wants this much," Sorren yelled. "Tell him to bring his fat ass down here and get it himself!"

"If my husband were here, he'd rip off your arm and beat you to death with it!" another shrill voice added.

The crowd was about to burst, but farmers against soldiers was a losing position. Dad hadn't said anything and was moving to the side. He'd already sent my two livid brothers back to where I was, well away from the main crowd.

"ENOUGH!" The roar was almost loud enough for me to feel it, and the twenty-foot high wall of water that sprang between the two sides left no doubt as to who was responsible. I'd never seen magic like that. I'd never seen the old wizard actually be serious, and the sight of it shook me.

Mystien strode forward. It would appear he'd scared the soldiers, too, as they visibly shrank from his approach. He pulled a bag from his robe and threw it to the official.

"That's my share, and an additional fifth of what the rest of the town owes. You may count it if you like." He spoke loud enough for everyone to hear him. He paid his taxes in coin; that or grain were the most common means of payment.

"We can take care of the rest," Dad said to the crowd, trying to calm them. "And if anyone needs help afterward, they'll have it." His words carried some weight, and with him and Mystien together, the crowd backed down. It was tense as everyone paid, mostly in goods, but nobody tried to attack the official or his guards.

When it was all said and done, I sighed in relief.

"Well, at least nobody got hurt," I said.

"They will in other places though," Rod pointed out.

The town could have thrown a parade for my teacher, who, to my surprise came back to my house with the family.

"If they keep this up, there'll be a full-scale rebellion," he said to my father as we all set down to talk.

"I shudder to think of what the riots in any major town will look like if they try it there," Dad offered. "Blood in the streets for sure."

"That was a lot of money, are you sure it's okay?" I asked Mystien.

"Most of it came from the mayor or the army in town," he informed me.

"What? Why?" That was a bit confusing.

"Mayor came to see me the other day, begged on his knees for you to be available this year to do the same as you did last year. The three of us discussed it, as the old man didn't want you to lose practice on what you'd learned," Dad replied.

"The money was the main part of my demands. It'll take some of the pressure off locally," Mystien explained.

"I got a few other things," Dad said, then paused as he thought.

"You'll have to keep up with some of the work you've been doing, making bread; something he doesn't know about, so don't tell him. A few local boys will be stopping by the village every few days to pick it up. They'll get some equipment, along with some perks in the town for us."

I nodded as each task was explained to me. It was nothing too much, but enough to take a lot of the pressure down to manageable levels.

So my winter was spent much as it had been the year before, with a few exceptions. My uncle Barro had acquired a few new pieces of furniture, to make his house just a bit nicer. Every other day, runners came to take baskets of bread back to the hamlet; nobody outside of it knew I could make bread, so it was no big issue. The number of soldiers I was healing a day was also capped; this had been part of my father's demands, which the mayor had no choice but to accept.

Spring brought with it another season of painful drudgery for everyone. The labor shortage was still an undeniable problem, and try as everyone might, there just wasn't any way to plant all the fields. This was compounded by the fact that several other of the little outposts of our village had lost a few more men to the tax official's guards, in a pointless loss of life.

It was a couple of weeks after the planting finished, during one of the lulls in the farming cycle of labor that something odd happened. Late that night, after dinner, but before we'd gone to bed, a knocking came at the door.

"Verren, it's me," Mystien's voice came through.

Dad cautiously opened the door. "What is it? You wouldn't come for anything that could wait."

"We need to have a discussion. We've a visitor," my teacher told him. "It'll take a while."

Dad nodded. After the wizard had stepped away, he came over to Mom and said, "When I come back, I'll knock in three groups of five. Don't open the door for anyone else." With that, he left.

It was more than an hour before he returned, knocking exactly as he had described.

"What was that about, Dad?" Rod asked.

"Not something you kids need to worry about."

He didn't elaborate more than that.

VERREN'S LATE-NIGHT MEETING

It was rough, but we were making it. I looked over my family with pride, knowing that as long as we could keep going, we'd get through this. Everything was going to be okay.

The knocking at the door surprised me. There weren't many who'd come by this late at night, and none without cause. Upon opening it, I saw who might be my oldest friend aside from Barro; his face was impassive. With a few quick words, we departed from my home.

"You going to tell me what this is about, Mystien? It must be major for all the cloak and dagger," I asked as we walked.

"You'll see when we get there; talking about it now would be improper." Mystien did like his mysteries. Wizards, what can you do with them?

"All right then, can you at least tell me where we're going?" We hadn't left our little hamlet. If I had to guess, I'd say we were heading to his place.

"My home, of course," he laughed.

The old bugger pulled out a bit in front of me as we got there, opening his front door and leading me in. I felt a bit of a push as I crossed the threshold, some sort of defensive spell. He laughed at my cocked eye.

"Can't be too careful these days, my friend," he said as I shook off the charm. It wasn't there to repel me.

Inside was a single figure, his back was to us, staring into Mystien's fireplace. Upon hearing us enter, he turned, and I recognized him at once, the man I knew as Commander Durin. The man cut a regal figure, his bearing that of the true nobility, with sharp, straight features that made almost anyone look up to him.

I saw much of the man who'd once been my superior officer, but several things about him had changed. He was older, his once pure black hair was now speckled with gray, a few wrinkles had grown too. He also had put on armor that I'd never seen before: pure black metal plates overlapped to give him strong, if flexible protection, a symbol of a raven on his breast, and all topped by an ebony mantle upon his shoulders.

"Verren, my old friend." His voice was rough, as it'd always been, but you could hear the smile in it.

"Commander, what are you doing here?" This man in this place was more than a bit unusual.

"I've come to make the two of you an offer. I'm hoping you'll take me up on it," he replied with a grin. "You see, I'm recruiting the best men I know of, and you two are certainly on that list."

"Trying to bring us back into the army?"

I was sure he knew how I felt about it after I'd left. We'd had a few words just after my retirement, and the taste of ash the kingdom's armed forces had left in my mouth still lingered.

"Yes and no," he responded, "the current war with Ermath is not the one I'm interested in." He shrugged.

"Nor do I work for the kingdom anymore."

"If not this war, then what?"

I knew the commander had always been planning. His orders often seemed a bit unusual, but almost never failed.

"This kingdom has failed, Verren, the empire is not much better," he said, sighing. "You could make arguments about where, perhaps it's the rigidity of the nobility. In any just land, men like you two would be offered positions of power for your years of dedicated service. Perhaps it's corruption, for we certainly have that as well." His speech was almost sad.

"If we gathered up our old unit, perhaps we could have some effect on this war, but then what? In another decade, another will happen, and the same problems bringing disaster now, might bring it then," Commander Durin explained. "No, my friend, I propose we tear the system down, right to the ground so we can rebuild it, better, more just then it was before."

"You're suggesting a rebellion?" I asked, stunned.

"I suppose you could call it that," he replied, nodding.

"I . . . have a family. I can't leave them, not now, not with all that's going on." Asking me to join up for this was madness.

"Mystien said something similar," Durin said, clapping me on the shoulder. "I understand, my old friend, but you may not have the option to stay with them forever. If you decide to join me, you, and whatever men you trust can come anytime. There's a way station about a day's walk north of Hazelwood, you know the one?" He looked at me.

"Yeah, only one out that way," I confirmed.

"Go there if you do want to join me, or must, ask for a room downstairs and you'll get what you need." He then thought for a moment.

"Your family too. If you think they will have no choice, tell them where to go. I'll treat them as if they were my own." With that, he bid us both well, shaking our hands firmly as he did so.

"I hope we never need that information," I said to Mystien after Commander Durin left.

"Whenever have you known him to give you direction without a point?" Mystien asked me.

I almost glared at the old wizard before returning home, having much to think over.

CHAPTER 8

✦

SUBTERFUGE AND TRAVEL

As I neared the summer of my fifth year on this world, my lessons continued with Mystien, though they did change somewhat. We no longer focused entirely on control, but on more mundane things as well. He had a number of books and maps showing things like geography, grammar, manners, and the like, which he used to teach me. This was not like a formal education on Earth, as it focused much more on how to interact with people based on their social standing, and knowing the important things about the bigger players.

Every day at the start of lessons, I would be given instructions. These would explain how to treat Mystien, as well as the status I was supposed to assume. From my side, I would need to act somewhere between a pauper and a minor noble, boy or girl. I would then treat Mystien as someone between a pauper and a high-ranked noble, though our ranks would only differ by one or two degrees.

"Mystien," I asked one day after we'd finished, "why are you training me in all these different mannerisms?"

He looked me over for a few moments. "You will probably not always stay here. You will need to know how to act around people of every status."

I nodded. "Okay, that makes sense, but why are you having me learn how to act as people of a different status or a boy?" I had some theories, but I wanted him to confirm.

He gave a sly smile, "You're too dang quick for a five-year-old. It's like talking to an adult, you know that, right?"

I just kept looking at him. "That's not an answer, is it?" That got an actual laugh.

"No, it wasn't. Well, in a couple of years, you might have to hide. Casters being rare around here. If that happens, I want you to be able to blend in anywhere."

"Oh," I said. It would seem he was giving me a basic course on . . . spy craft? Escape? What would I even call this?

I spent a few moments considering this. I could already make food and drink anywhere, anytime, along with some quantity of gathering. With my magic backing me up, I might be able to disappear into any environment like a ghost. I had a few concerns though.

"That makes sense. Are you going to teach me to hide my aura?" I inquired, making a few notes for later. "Oh, and can you tell me my role the day before that happens?"

"We'll get there," he promised. "Anything else?"

"Oh, I should probably learn about clothes, and begin carrying things that might be important, for practice," I said.

Our lessons got much more in depth after that. I even started dressing up a bit and changing my hair, mostly because it was fun, and fun was short on the ground these days.

My guess was that whatever had happened at their midnight meeting had spooked my teacher something ferocious, though I knew he'd never tell me. I did get my parents to give me a small belt knife. I was a little young by their thoughts, but when I told them I thought it would help with lessons, they agreed.

I started picking up a few more things here and there as well. I made a real effort to be friends with Sara, which my family approved of as an alternative to some chores. We ended up doing things that mostly consisted of work anyway. Her family did a kind of weaving to make small straps, which my mother didn't. The straps were used for all kinds of things, but Mom was just bad at it, so she traded for them instead. I wouldn't say I was good, but I could manage the simpler patterns.

I also worked on some of the other handcrafts that girls of every level of society practiced, things like sewing and embroidery. It was a struggle to learn, but practical, and I could at least claim they were useful lessons. I didn't bother with learning the crafts most boys knew. My brothers were already doing a ton of that, and it would take too long to get passably good.

I also noticed some changes in John. He was starting to develop the barest hints of an aura. It would flare up sometimes to something impressive, then fade to almost nonexistent at other times. Its shape was much like Dad's, but steel gray instead of black. My dad seemed to notice John was changing, too, and was giving him more training in combat than anyone else. When I asked Mystien about the aura, I was told that some people took a while to come into their own, but eventually it would stabilize. Poor Rod still struggled.

My oldest brother kept working the hive, and even added another with some of the petty cash he had. He claimed that he thought it was a good investment, but I suspected he just liked working with bees. The day came when he told me that one of the things I'd asked him to keep an eye on had happened.

"Hey, you said we'd gather the honey up when four fifths of it was capped off, right, Alana?" he said to me one night.

"Yup, that sounds about right," I responded.

"I'm going to do that tomorrow then."

I blinked at his words.

"Done already?" I asked, then thought for a while. It was getting warmer; maybe that was about right.

"Well, you should try to not cut the comb off completely; maybe the bees will rebuild faster."

I shrugged as if I didn't know they would.

He nodded and continued about his after-dinner work.

The next afternoon, he and several other boys were at our house working on the combs. Each one of them seemed interested in putting up his own hive. The work was so little, and the payoff in valuable product so high, that they were chomping at the bit to get started. I decided to get my share from my hive from Rod partially in money this time, rather than keeping the wax.

Rod moaned and complained about me not needing actual coinage, but I had some ideas. If I was to be ready to flee at any time, I would need some, and coins were the best way to carry value easily. He handed me two silver coins, each about an inch in diameter several days later, and I realized I had another problem.

"Dad," I asked my father that night, "can you explain money to me?" I heard Rod laugh in the background.

"It's a way to carry something valuable but small . . ." he began.

"I understand that much, but what equals what?" I clarified.

"Oh, sure, well, there are thirty coppers in a silver, and twenty silvers in a gold. Though you don't see gold much around here," he explained.

"Those are weird numbers, why those?" I asked after hearing that. I was expecting orders of ten, like you saw in most games.

"Well, it's two times three times five for copper to silver, and silver is only worth about one twentieth of gold by weight. The silver and gold coins weigh the same; coppers are a bit off, but fairly close." I almost dropped my jaw at how good of sense that made.

"Makes it easy to divide things up," he finished.

"Okay." I was a bit speechless . . . I suppose life wasn't like a game.

One day after our practice session, Mystien asked me an unusual question.

"I've got business in Hazelwood in about a month. How would you feel about tagging along?"

"I'd love to!" I'd never left our sleepy little town since coming to this world, and going to the nearest major city seemed like an exciting adventure.

He held up a hand, "There are conditions: first, your parents have to agree; second, we'll be putting on a bit of a charade." These seemed important.

"A charade?" I asked.

"Yes," he explained, "you will be playing the part of my new apprentice, a boy of merchant stock."

I laughed at that, "Okay, I'll get my parents to agree, but I'll need clothes to look like a boy."

"I'll get the clothes. Anything else you think you'll need?"

"A hat," I told him.

With that, we settled it.

My father agreed with some argument, but ultimately he trusted Mystien enough to let me go. In the intervening time, my brother harvested honey again. It was later in summer, and this time he had several who came by to watch and ask lots of questions. Most were from other little hamlets or the main village; one was from Creekrun. I got one of my two silvers in copper this time, so I could have some pocket money for my own town run.

That morning, Mystien came by with the clothes for me, which I changed into while listening to him and my father talk outside.

"Why exactly are you having my daughter cross-dress?" I heard Dad asking.

"I've already explained that to both you and her," the old wizard said, giving a rather curt response.

"Well, I know, but . . ."

"But nothing, you and I both know a boy will attract far less attention than a girl, particularly if the time should come when we're not around to protect her." His voice was a bit harsher than normal. "Besides, there are already too many people who know about a young girl in our town who's a bard. I don't know how many yet, but if word spreads, the lord might send someone to sniff around for a new personal healer. Muddying the water can only help that."

"Then wouldn't it be better to just not have her go?"

Dad seemed a bit prickly about being lectured.

"No, she needs the experience. Hazelwood's not a huge town, but learning about how they work will be good."

I agreed with Mystien, mostly because I wanted to go though.

I came outside to join them once I'd finished. My new outfit was a loose-fitting blue tunic and trousers, with a brown vest, along with a toboggan-style hat. I took the time to do up my hair so it looked short under the cap. Once ready, I came out and spun.

"How do I look?" I asked.

"Like a boy," Dad said.

"Yup, quite good," Mystien replied.

"Well, sir, I'm quite ready to leave when you are," I told my teacher in my best "merchant boy" accent.

"That's just creepy." Dad shuddered.

"All right then, let's be on our way." And with that, the older man turned, leading me out the door.

As we walked, we began to discuss our planned route.

"First we'll head east to Creekrun; we'll arrive there sometime in the afternoon and spend the night in their tavern. From there, we'll head to Khole's Hill, again spending a night. We'll arrive in Hazelwood early the next afternoon. Any questions?"

Mystien rattled off the locations and general plan.

"Should I keep up the accent for the entire duration, Teacher?" It seemed like the first thing to ask about.

"Yes," he said, nodding.

"Very well then, are we expecting any trouble, and should we encounter any what is the plan?" Since this was part of his training regime, it seemed the best to ask.

"Good questions," he responded, "we are not expecting any issues. This is a well-traveled and peaceful route. If we should encounter anything, stay behind me. If I tell you to run, flee to the previous town and lie low in the tavern where we stayed."

I nodded at his instructions.

"If all else fails, use your attack magic, but that's a last resort, as would be fleeing into the wilderness."

"Understood, sir. Is there anything else I should know about this trip?" It didn't hurt to try.

"I doubt the other towns are doing as well as ours. You are not to use magic without my express permission outside of emergencies. Also, stay close to me. Your father might just kill me if something happens to you." Then he listed off a few more things.

"Yes, sir," I replied.

We stopped for a quick lunch just before noon at the halfway point. It was a simple affair of bread (summoned), water (summoned), and a bit of dried fruit. While sitting, I was asked a question.

"How would you like to make this slightly more difficult?" my teacher said, grinning.

"I don't mind, sir. How so?"

I was genuinely curious.

"Suppressing your aura is a fairly simple trick; all you do is try to remove the outward sign. In my case, I take apart the shapes mine forms," he said. "Try it while we're on our way; it'll make you concentrate a bit on another action."

So I went about popping my bubbles. I imagined using a pin to poke each one. It didn't seem all that hard.

"Like this then?" I asked.

"Not bad. I can still see it, it's just smaller. Now, see if you can keep that up for our whole trip." He had an evil expression on his face. I suspected this would be harder than I thought.

It was much harder, even just as we were walking. Dividing my attention almost made me trip several times.

As we approached Creekrun, I could see a few of the fields. Almost half were laying empty of crops, or getting overgrown with weeds.

The people we saw as we passed through the village's walls were even worse. Orsken was holding up well enough. For us, it was a bit tight. But here, several villagers had obviously lost a bit of weight.

"Things are not going well, are they, sir?" I asked, nearly slipping from my act.

"No, no, they are not," came the reply. From the tone, I would guess it was worse than even he expected.

We found the town's tavern easily enough. The burly old man working it told us that there were no meals served right now, though he did still have some ale. After having a couple of glasses of the lightly alcoholic drink, we headed up to a rented room. There were two beds, and when we closed the door, I breathed a sigh of relief.

"Aura," Mystien reminded me. Apparently, I had to manage it even when in private.

"There are no meals being served in the tavern, what does that mean?" I asked as I went back to popping bubbles.

"It means that there's almost no food left in town. Or at least, no extra food. Creekrun is a major fishing area. I'd wager most everyone here is eating almost only fish."

"Why aren't they having the young men and women work the fields?" It made no sense to me as a farmer's daughter.

"Watch your accent. And because they don't have many fields. Fishing is their main industry."

"Ah, I see, that's a bit distressing," I remarked.

I summoned us a bit of dinner, and we took a quick walk around town before returning to our room around sunset. At Mystien's direction, an early night was declared, so we could be out of town at dawn.

Khole's Hill was quite honestly much the same as Creekrun. It was, as the name suggested, situated on a hill. The people here looked worse than those I'd seen before. Nobody was at the level of starving yet, but there was a distinct lack of men of all ages. A quick inquiry with the barman, who was quite old, indicated that the riots here over the taxes had been quite bad. He spoke to us quietly about it, as it was a bit sensitive.

"Aye, they went on for two days, eventually the lord sent out a detach-ment. It wasn't pretty." He sounded a bit broken by all of it.

Our stay there was not particularly interesting, though their tavern did have a bit of porridge to offer as food. It was a definite improvement, only in that I didn't have to use more mana.

By the time we arrived at the gates to Hazelwood, I downright hated this trip. The dress-up game had lost all its shine because it never ended, the food was bad, and the new clothes were both hot and uncomfortable.

As an aside, keeping my aura contained at all times was giving me a constant headache. I had no idea how Dad did it.

As we approached, I realized something. Hazelwood was a city, not a town, nor a village, but a full-on city. The walls were probably twenty feet high, stone, and judging by the men walking on them, fairly thick. I could see the crenellations from afar, but once we got near, the machicolations became obvious as well. Judging by the size, I would guess around ten thousand people lived here most of the time. There were perhaps less right now. It even had guards at the gates, seeing who was coming in and out.

"Names, occupation, and business in the city," one of said guards asked as we got close.

"I'm Mystien; this is my apprentice, Kale." I could have hit myself. I forgot to ask the fake name he wanted me to use. "I'm a wizard, and my business is seeing an old merchant acquaintance." He spoke as if he'd been through this a hundred times.

The guard stood up a bit straighter when he heard Mystien was a mage and called over another guard to look us over.

The new man was dressed in lighter armor, and it was easy to tell from his aura that he, too, was a caster and not a powerful one.

"I see no strange auras or anything of note. The boy's not that strong; his master on the other hand . . . may I ask your name, sir?"

"Mystien," the first guard told him.

The second guard stiffened for a moment, then nodded. "That concludes our check, please have a good day, sir."

After he let us through, I looked over at my companion. "His reaction was a bit unusual, wasn't it, sir?" I asked.

"Not too much," he responded. "About ten years ago, I was involved in a war. Made a good name for myself with the locals."

He didn't elaborate.

"Oh, you've never spoken of it before," I said, prying a little.

"Because I don't like to; war is not enjoyable, lad. I hope you never have to understand that firsthand."

That was a clear dismissal to the conversation, so I went somewhere else.

"I see a number of taverns near the gate, sir. Which one will we be staying in?"

It was a harmless enough inquiry.

"We won't be staying near the gate. There are several that are for the average traveler, but as spellcasters, we'll need to head a bit further in. In this city, there are only two taverns nice enough for us: The Golden Lion and The Scarlet Harlot. We'll be staying in The Scarlet Harlot."

"Could you explain why we need to stay in a very nice tavern, sir? Also, is the harlot a brothel?"

"Spellcasters exist in an unusual place in the social hierarchy. We are not commoners by law, and while many are nobles, many are not. That and the prices we can demand for our services means that if we stay somewhere cheap, it will reflect badly upon us and raise suspicions."

At the next part, he laughed. "And no, The Scarlet Harlot is not a brothel. One does not normally sleep in a bordello."

"Good to know, sir," I deadpanned.

"Also," he continued, "I know the owner and would love to see her again."

As we walked through town, I noticed the changes. The area around the gate was most definitely aimed at travelers, though just past it was a very poor section. Once you got past that, things went up, first merchants, getting slowly higher class, then finally where we ended up. The last street we came to was distinctly high-class: clean, paved, and with more guards. The people were also well-dressed, a few in what might be called finery. I felt we stuck out, but the number of auras told me we'd be fine.

I was a bit put off as we arrived at The Scarlet Harlot. For one, the building was red, naturally; secondly, it was a bit much. The doors were enormous and were opened for us by an attendant. The inside was bustling; the smell was amazing in here. Obviously, there was no lack of food at this level. Mystien led us forward to one of the serving girls, of which there were three, picked for their looks if I had to guess.

"Greetings, sirs, and welcome to The Scarlet Harlot." The woman was wearing a rather low-cut red dress, as per the theme, and winked at us as we came near.

"Good day," Mystien returned.

"A pleasure to meet you, miss."

I thought I would be ill.

"My, what a polite young man," she said, smiling at me. "How can we serve you today? Food and drink? A room perhaps? Or should I make arrangements for something else?" She gave my teacher a very wide smile at that. I was fairly sure I heard him say this wasn't a brothel.

"Two meals, whatever the special is, and a double room. And please tell Veska I've come to visit," he rattled off, seemingly uninterested in her advances.

"Who should I say her visitor is, sir?" the woman asked as she led us over to a rather private table.

"Mystien," he said, and she hurried off counting the coins he'd passed her.

The meal was magnificent, roasted chicken with herbs and vegetables, finished off with a cobbler.

No sooner had we finished, then we were led down a side hall, ending in a gilded double door.

/ CHAPTER 9

◆

GAINING KNOWLEDGE

We were led through the doors, our guide leaving us and closing the door. As it clicked, a woman approached the large desk there. She was around as old as my mother and was a stunning redhead. What almost threw me was that she was dressed in what could only be described as a nightie. It was crimson, barely covering her, and . . . silk? I hadn't seen any silk since coming to this world.

"Well, well, well, look what we have here," she crooned, giving Mystien a suggestive smirk.

"Veska, could you not put on proper clothes to meet people?"

Mystien seemed a bit tired by her appearance.

"Why would I do that?" she asked. "Anyway, who's the kid?"

"My new apprentice, Kale," the old mage explained.

"It's . . . quite nice to meet you, miss." I was a bit flustered.

She looked me over for a few moments. We were examining each other's auras. Hers was almost like tentacles, spreading out and caressing everything around her. She walked over, kneeling in front of me with her chin resting on one hand. From this angle, I couldn't help but notice the small circular tattoo on her right breast, something complex . . . and definitely magical.

"Oh, is that so? Well, there is a problem, young master Kale." She was smiling as she spoke.

"Whatever would that be?" I asked innocently.

Her free hand snapped out quicker than I could react, yanking off my hat and sending my hair flowing down.

"You, my dear, are far too pretty to be a boy."

The laugh that went along with this was like tinkling bells.

I flushed crimson as she spoke, covering my face a bit. I didn't realize I'd lost control of my aura till she stood up and spoke again.

"That's a pretty strong aura for a kid so young," she said as I was wrangling it back down.

Mystien sighed.

"This must be the young bard girl from Orsken I've heard about then?" she asked, handing me back my hat.

"What have you heard?" Mystien asked in a deadly serious tone.

"Not much, truthfully. That there was a young bard girl, and that she was healing a lot of soldiers over the winter. Mind if we're properly introduced?"

"Fine, Alana, this is Veska, Veska, Alana," he rattled off quickly.

"Um . . . hi," I stammered.

"Training a little girl for espionage, Mystien, how devious. I love it." She gave the old man a sly grin.

"Don't go spreading information about her. If the wrong people get hold of it, you could make an enemy of both her father and myself."

"Her father?"

"Verren."

"Well, shit, won't go sticking my head in that wasp's nest," she said as she backed off a bit, went over to her desk, and sat down.

"So, to what do I owe the honor of your visit?" Veska asked, all business now as she looked us over.

"I'd like information on what's going on with the populace and general info locally," Mystien said. Seemed that the woman was an information broker.

"In return, I get?"

He held up a small envelope, "Information on a dessert, supposedly from halfway across the nation. Must be something local because I've never had it, and it beats out almost anything I've ever had. Better even than the stuff from the capital." He had her attention now.

"What's it called?" She looked curious.

"Ice cream," he told her.

I was just a bit miffed about my recipe being sold. Of course, I'd told them it wasn't mine, so I couldn't be all that mad, but still.

"I'll trust you with your assessment. What you want isn't too important at any rate." She leaned back in her chair.

"Local info goes about like this. Most villages got hit hard by so many men leaving, Hazelwood's insistence on keeping the taxes normal hit even harder. Two or three had major riots over the tax fiasco. I'm sure you went through Khole's Hill on your way. They were one."

"How bad were the riots?" the wizard chimed in.

"Bad enough. Soldiers had to be dispatched to two, in those far too many died. If the war doesn't end soon, those towns might not make it. On a more disturbing note, I've also heard that some towns have begun stockpiling weapons. If Lord Hazelwood tries to collect full taxes again, I doubt anything less than using the actual army will make it happen." That got Mystien's attention.

"Will he?" he asked.

"That's still unclear; he's sort of an idiot. I've also heard rumors that they might expand the draft to include some older men, but that's unconfirmed." She seemed a bit miffed that these answers weren't any more substantial.

"What about the food situation? What's that looking like?" Mystien was going to get his money's worth it would seem.

"Not great, on average it's about what you'd expect from a draft this big. Worse by a bit because of the timing of it, of course. We're not at critical levels, but depending on where things go, we could be in a year or two." Veska poured herself a glass of juice from a pitcher on her desk. "If they expand the draft it'll be bad, but for now, things are holding."

Mystien nodded. "I don't suppose you'll tell me how the war is going?" He seemed hopeful.

"Poorly, Ermath caught us off guard, and tons of resources are being poured into it. I think the border may get pushed back a good bit. We may even be in Ermath soon enough, but if I had to wager on it, I'd say they won't take the whole kingdom. They're taking heavy losses too."

"You seem unconcerned," I pointed out.

"My sweet, I'll have to move or hide my assets, but I'll make it through either way," crooned the woman. "Only thing that them moving in changes too much on my side is that all the brothels in town will be flush with new clients."

My teacher indicated that he'd heard all he needed, and the two of them chatted about some other light business while I put my hair back under my hat. Veska had some items and the like that she wanted filled up with mana and negotiated a price. From the sound of it, she could do it herself but didn't like being too drained of power—something I well understood.

* * *

The room we stayed in that night was posh. It had two great beds, stuffed with down or something, and clean linen sheets. There were also a few pieces of furniture, a desk and chairs, and a small nightstand, things not present in our other rooms. The dinner that night was equally on par with the lunch.

Mystien went off after dinner to "handle the other business with Veska." He came back quite late that night and turned a bright red when I pointed out that he smelled like perfume and had lipstick stains on his mouth. I'd never seen anything like that from him, but it seemed he'd had a thing for her. That also explained why we were staying here.

The next morning, he took me out into the town.

"All right, we're going to go over the basics of how to find things in a town this size," he said.

He took me around, this city, like almost every other one in the nation, was divided into districts.

The nobles' district was mainly housing and shops catering specifically to the nobility. It was tiny in this city and always located at the very center, normally nestled within or beside the entertainment district. Next came the entertainment district, where you would find the nicer inns and taverns along with the areas for festivals and the town's brothels. Then came the residential and craftsmen's districts, which were together and surrounded by a small gap. Mystien informed me that if there was a fire, most often it started in these two areas. The merchants' district was an area around the main street, between the entertainment district and the main gate. The poor district was called "low town"; it was a smattering of areas located near the wall between the gates.

The gates were a special case. All of them would have some amount of taverns and the like near them, but one was designated the main gate, which was different in that it was the only gate where anyone other than a pedestrian could normally enter. As such, the main gate had stables and areas for caravans to be processed around it. It also had a much more substantial number of taverns and general goods shops.

He also told me that most wizards would work in the nobles' district. Bards, of course, more often work in the entertainment district. Veska, of course, was a bard, and it wasn't unusual for one to run a tavern. The happy, generally-given-to-singing patrons made a great focus for bard-type magic.

* * *

After he gave me a brief primer on haggling, Mystien took me over to the merchants' district. I took a bit of time looking around at all the wares being hawked before stopping at one stall, the woman running it sold hairpins of various types. I went up and indicated a small box of bronze-looking bobby pins.

"My big sister has been complaining about wanting something to use so she could put up her hair up. How much are these?" I lied fluently to the woman.

"Oh, good eye, young man, but wouldn't you want something a bit fancier?" The saleswoman pointed out some decorated pieces, with enameled designs on them.

"No thank you, those look a bit out of budget, and I don't know which she would like best." I deflected her. I really did just want something simple.

She sighed, giving me a quick once over. "Those are ten coppers." Her price was high, not a complete rip-off, but more than would be fair.

I wanted these for around seven. "They're very simple; I could give you four."

"Four?" She seemed a bit insulted; it was a good act. "I could come down a bit, but certainly not below eight."

I picked one up, looking it over and thinking for a moment and offered, "Six."

She gave me a hard look and said, "I could meet you in the middle, how about seven?"

"Fair enough," I stated, then counted out seven coppers for her. I was quite happy with how it'd gone.

After I went back over to Mystien, he looked at me. "That was not bad."

"I have two older brothers, I know how to negotiate," I chuckled, "Seven is what I wanted to pay in the first place."

After that, I went by several more shops. I checked prices on general goods, as well as secondhand clothing. It might be useful later. Clothing was far more expensive than I'd thought it'd be, even secondhand. I consulted with Mystien about those prices, and he confirmed they were within a normal level. Upon further consideration, it did take a lot of work to make clothes, so that made sense.

Our day was, in my opinion, quite productive, and once we got back to The Scarlet Harlot, we went over everything once more. Mystien seemed pleased with the mix of information he'd gathered and training he'd given me. We rested early, prepping to head home at dawn.

Summer began to close after we returned. The bright warmth of what had to be my favorite season gave way to the coolness of fall. It also led to much more work for everyone as the harvest had to be brought in. I was even brought into the fieldwork this year, a new first. I didn't like working in the field, it was hot, itchy, and otherwise miserable, but I still did my part. By the end of fall, I'd come to the conclusion that one day I would make sure to move, so I didn't have to be a farmer when I grew up.

It was just after the harvest that the tax collector returned. This time, he told us that our taxes had been drastically reduced by Lord Hazelwood. We were only expected to pay about half of the normal rate, much to our relief. I couldn't help but notice that he had significantly more guards this time, and they were all much better armed.

My lessons on espionage training continued. This mostly consisted of hammering out my accents. I will say that Mystien was suitably impressed with how well I could change up my hair with only some string and the bobby pins I'd bought. One day after lessons, I brought up what I thought was a rather good point.

"Mystien, if the taxes are too bad, why don't people just move to another place?" I asked.

"The majority of people in villages like this can't." His response was a bit weird.

"Why not? You'd lose all your land and stuff, but if it got too bad, it'd be an option."

"You misunderstand. Most of the people in this village, and most others are peasants." He said it like it was obvious.

"How does that change things?" I asked.

"Peasants are commoners, bound to their land. It would be highly illegal for them to leave without the local noble's permission."

"I don't like that. I want to be able to leave." I was adamant on that point. I'd be nobody's slave, and if they tried to keep me here when I grew up . . . I'd think of some way to fight.

"I told you when we were in Hazelwood, spellcasters aren't commoners. In fact, no one who can do magic is."

"Oh," I said. "That's some special treatment."

"It's for good reason," he replied. "Someone capable of magic is both a commodity and a dangerous enemy. I could go anywhere. Even if it was illegal, most nobles would be happy to welcome me to their lands. The same would apply to you. Some have even tried to entice me to join them, but I like it here."

"So, because you would be welcome elsewhere, they don't try to keep you?" That made a sort of sense.

"Also, if I decided to fight to leave, I could cause great destruction. It would take many, many normal men to fight me if I knew about them. The same applies to most spellcasters."

"I don't think I could fight that many people," I admitted.

"You are a child, Alana. If someone tried to hold an adult bard and said bard got angry enough, they might get a dozen or so assistants and begin doing things like making storms or releasing diseases. While few bards develop the spells to cause destruction like that, it is quite possible."

"Oh, wow, I never thought of something like that." I had to take a few moments to process that.

"It applies to physical magic users too. If someone like your father wanted to, they could fight a dozen armed men with just their bare hands, well at least he could in his prime," Mystien continued. "We'll add to that that magical talent tends to run in families. So you're not often fighting one, but many families, and they often have children to protect. Only a suicidal man would take those odds."

"Don't nobles have magic users too?" That seemed another point to address.

"Of course, to be considered a noble, one must *be* a magic user of some form. They won't have many though, and those are valuable resources as well. Why waste them over a fight you can avoid?"

"Yeah, that would be dumb. I didn't know that all the nobles were magic users. I guess it makes sense," I said, contemplating the ramifications of being weak when such powerhouses were running around.

Mystien nodded. "Magic is weird, it can be inherited, though that depends on a variety of factors. One can also undertake certain rituals in an attempt to unlock knowledge magic, but they are more often than not fatal. Even if you do succeed, if it's unnatural it can ravage your body and drastically shorten your lifespan."

This was all news to me. I had no idea you could actually force yourself into becoming a wizard. It sounded deadly nevertheless.

"Do people try to unlock other types of magic?" I asked.

"There are no known ways to do so. Even those who unlock knowledge magic are extremely rare, mostly because the attempt is generally considered suicidal." He thought about something for a few moments before continuing. "The only time I've heard of it succeeding was a young man from a noble house who couldn't manifest his own. In desperation, he bought the reagents and did the rituals. It worked, and he gained the ability to do magic, but he died not five years later. I've heard of many similar cases where the person in question blew up or caught on fire when the magic was forced into them."

I wondered for a bit if that was what had happened to me in my previous life. If the fruit had tried to force magic into me and that had been the end. I stared at my hand and shuddered. The pain was something I never wanted to experience again.

"All right. That's enough for today, off you go." And with that, Mystien shooed me off to my other chores.

As was his tradition, the mayor came by just before the first snowfall. He found us at the little area our hamlet was using for training. I'd come by to watch; it was a good place to sit around with Sara and talk. It was such a good place that almost all of the older girls had made it their usual habit to sit out of the way and chat while they did a bit of handiwork. With only pure intentions, I'm sure.

The mayor came up to my father and began to speak, "Verren, as I'm sure you know, things haven't really improved . . ."

Dad cut him off with a wave of his hand. "Malke, you've had years to come up with a solution to this, or at least plan something earlier. You're not getting it from us this year."

Huh, I guess the mayor's name was Malke. Everybody always just called him "the mayor" as far as I'd heard.

The mayor paled. "Now wait a moment, please be reasonable . . ."

"I have, and I have thought about it enough, we cannot spare her this year, and that is final." Dad's tone was hard.

The mayor looked to me for only a moment, almost like he wanted to ask me. He then thought better of himself. "What am I to do then?" he asked.

"You are the mayor; it is your duty to figure that out." Dad was being a bit harsh in my opinion, but he did have a point.

And so it was decided that I would stay at home for the winter this year, and hopefully for the years to come. Going to town for the whole season was frankly a bit grating.

* * *

"Dad, why did you tell the mayor we wouldn't help him this winter?" I asked at dinner. I was happy, but I still thought there were things I was missing.

"I told him, he's not worked to come up with a solution yet, it's irritating," he said, then continued. "I've also heard that people are starting to learn about you, and we need to put a stop to that, not going this year will help."

"Did you actually want to go?" Rod asked from the side. He was ever the peanut gallery.

"No, it's a pain," I told him. "I'd prefer to stick around here."

"That's good," John added as peanut gallery number two. "It's a lot less running for us."

"You boys are missing the point," Mom piped in. "The whole operation will be easier on your sister, us, and all our neighbors."

"What do our neighbors have to do with it?" Rod asked. "I get Alana and us, since she can keep the house warm, but how them?"

Mom flicked him on the forehead; he was getting a bit big for a spanking now. "If she's not using all her mana to heal up those soldiers for the idiot mayor, she can make more bread to feed them. You can also do group magic, can't you, dear?" she asked me, to which I nodded.

"Oh! we can invite a couple of the girls over to join in, and it'll be a great time!" I was excited to actually enjoy my winter for once.

"Hey, I have a friend or two who could help; you don't have to only invite girls," Rod boldly jumped in again.

It was my turn to flick him on the forehead. As I did so, I had to appreciate that my brothers were truly growing; he had to be pushing six feet. "Girls are more fun to talk to. I was going to invite Sara and Sandra, but I'll just tell them you don't want them around."

"Oy, oy! I never said that!" he panicked.

Dad leaned over, clamping him on the shoulder, "Son, you've lost this one, it's important to know when to give up." That got a few laughs.

Winter was a wonderful affair. A couple of the local girls would join us every day for a singing craft circle, with breaks to talk about whatever local gossip was flying around, which mostly concerned how much of a wreck the village was at the moment, and discuss our projects. Sara came almost every day, and in that time I managed to make myself a nice little woven belt. It was long and double thickness, so I could use it for years, and had little pockets for things like hidden coins and spare bobby pins. I privately named it my utility belt, a joke that nobody in this world would get.

Sandra ended up coming by quite a bit too. Her excuse was to spend time with her sister, but from where I sat it looked like she just wanted to make puppy eyes at Rod. She even volunteered to mend one of his shirts when he ripped it. Mom nodded her approval. Rod, for his part, became a clumsy, absolute mess when Sandra was too near and had to be monitored by more responsible adults—a list that included everyone.

It wasn't all wonderful; my main complaint was our diet. It consisted of bread, bread, cheese, bread, yogurt, bread, bread, and bread. Winter had always been a bit tight, but this was getting out of hand. There was also the fact that we had less lamp oil; most people were converting any edible fat into food, so it was a no-go this year. I could have used a light spell to fix our lamp problem, but doing that all the time was not really feasible.

As the winter wore on, there were a few arguments about who was allowed to come over to our house every day, and how much food everyone got from me. It was tense, but it boiled down to the fact that my close friends were getting some real preferential treatment. A couple of the families without kids who could come play with us got a bit cross about being left out, and a deal had to be brokered to keep everyone happy. It boiled down to a series of food deliveries from those who did visit us often, all monitored for fairness by my father. I'm sure some of the people didn't really trust him to see to it that things were distributed fairly, but all seemed to agree that accusing him of not doing so was a stupid act.

Relief washed over me as the snow finally started to melt and the first green sprigs poked out their heads. Variety in my diet became a possibility.

CHAPTER 10

◆

DESPERATION

The melting snow brought a flurry of activity. Our last couple of years had been bad, so we knew that we had to get going quickly. Every child was put to work on food collection immediately. The adults hit the hard labor running. Nobody was relaxed.

All the children in our little hamlet scoured our section of the forest. We even met up with groups from a few other hamlets. They were ranging far, but it was well within the unwritten rules we followed for them to do so. What struck me most was how much worse they looked. Our children looked a bit thin, to be sure, but the ones from the other hamlets had sunken cheeks and looked desperate.

About a month in, we encountered something I'd never seen before. Sara and her sister had joined my brothers and me for a run to one of the better-known spots for ferns. The spring was an ideal time for these, as they grew fresh new leaves and shoots, which were quite desirable. Two men were in the forest, who were moving in a way that indicated they didn't really know their way around.

"Sirs," Rod spoke up. As the oldest, he was our nominal leader.

"Ah, hello there," one of the men said, the other had something behind his back, but I couldn't see what. "How are you today? Out gathering?" His tone was too sweet; it was off.

"We are, and you?"

"Oh well, we're well enough." The newcomer nodded. "From the looks of you, you must be doing quite well. Mind sharing a few spots?" he asked as he came closer.

"Not at all, though the best spot for a given area would be nearer to home, right? Where do you two live?" I'm glad my brother was at least a bit sharp; we could all tell something was fishy here.

The man approaching us moved quick, drawing a fighting knife from his side and lunging for my older brother. Rod wasn't good at fighting, but he'd been training for some time now, and you could only be so bad with that much under your belt. With a quick movement, he avoided being hurt.

John stepped in, pulled the small belt knife he carried, and slashed the first man's side. Since my two brothers were together, I had no real worries about their defeating the first newcomer.

What worried me was the second one, who dropped something behind him before he made a move. He, too, had pulled a knife and began charging. I knew he'd get close before John and Rod had finished dealing with the first newcomer, and he could possibly taking down one of them.

I had just enough time to gather my mana like Mystien had taught me and screamed. I aimed the spell directly at man number two's face, and the air shook as it flowed out in a stream. Everyone got hit by it at some level. The other girls dropped to the ground, covering their ears; my brothers' fight took a momentary pause as well. Man number two fell to the ground in the fetal position, grabbing his head. I had practiced this spell, but hadn't aimed it at another human in quite some time. I was a bit stunned by the effect.

My brothers recovered first; they understood at some level what had happened at least. In the corner of my eye, I saw Rod take the fighting knife from the first man, turning it around, and burying it in his neck.

It took less than five seconds for man number two to look up. His face was a horror, blood leaking out of every orifice as he focused on me and charged, seeming to find me his biggest threat. He made it three strides before the blur that was John hit him from the side. Both of my brother's hands were on his belt knife, one pushing the pommel as he deftly slid it between the man's ribs, savagely twisting and pulling it away. A bright crimson spray covered both me and John as the man fell, one of his hands only a few inches from me.

I stood, frozen in abject terror as the two men's lifeblood was soaking out into the ground. A small part of me thought that I should heal them, for a trial or something. My common sense smacked that small part and told it to go sit in the corner and think about what had just happened: these men had tried to kill us. I don't know for how long I stood there in shock.

John shook me a bit to bring me back to my senses.

"It's okay," he said, "Come. We have to go back home now, tell people what happened."

"Why did they . . . ?" I didn't finish.

Rod pointed to the thing the second man had dropped, "Rabbit, they were poachers, or bandits; either way, it'd be a death sentence if they were caught."

Nobody even approached the discarded rabbit. The ground was muddy enough to show that we'd not yet come near it, but if we touched it, or got caught with it . . .

We fled back to our hamlet. Sandra pulled her sister and me while the boys took up defensive positions. It didn't occur to me until later that they didn't know if there were more potential threats.

As we approached, several of the working men rushed over to us. Three youths covered in blood tended to get that reaction.

Sorren reached us first. "What happened?! Are you okay? Why are you covered in blood?"

"Two men attacked us in the forest. We're fine; they're dead." John said. He was the quickest to respond, and his brevity was ideal for this.

"Where?" Sorren asked, his eyes scanning the forest edge.

"The path to the field where the ferns grow," Rod answered, this time.

"You." Sorren pointed to one of the men. "Get the mayor and whatever men he thinks appropriate." He then pointed to another. "You, go get these kids' parents. We'll take them to my house, it's closest."

We were at Sorren's for a couple of hours. He was generous enough to offer us some drinks and water to wash off the worst of the blood, our clothes were still covered though. During this interval, we had to explain in detail what had happened a number of times: first to our parents, both sets; then to a few of the other men of the town; finally, to the mayor, who had brought along several of the soldiers to deal with those passing through town. Each of these groups wanted an in-depth play-by-play of the action.

Upon the official investigation, it was found that the two men were known. They had deserted shortly after arriving at Orsken. There was no official reward, but the army officer who had come with the mayor complimented us on taking the men who'd eluded him. The men of the town did a sweep of our area of the woods, finding no others. In the end, it was decided that the kids from our hamlet wouldn't be foraging for the foreseeable future. There might be others who'd turned bandit, and it was deemed not worth it.

I actually didn't mind; the whole incident had made me a bit more leery of the woods, and bandits joining the fray was something I was not interested in dealing with at all.

There was at least one positive. Sandra seemed to have claimed Rod as her own completely; they'd been a bit flirty for a while now, but she could probably have reclassified herself as a growth. I suspected they were running off a bit due to his going missing a few times. I didn't know if they'd just gone somewhere to make out or if it'd lapsed into full "romp in the hay," but I supposed I'd find out if Sandra became knocked-up.

When next we met, Mystien had a few things to say.

"I saw the results of your attack spell, good job."

"Er . . . thanks, it didn't really do much, but it bought some time I guess," I responded.

"It did enough, and you've now gained some experience in combat, so what did you learn?" he asked calmly, still sounding like a teacher going over a simple lesson.

"I've learned that I don't want to be in combat again," was the answer I gave. It was true to a fault.

"Not a bad lesson, seeking it out is generally foolish, but not what we're going for."

"Okay, what are we going for?" I asked, a bit confused.

"Think about what you did in that fight, what you did well, and what needs improvement." He sat waiting as I chewed over that for a bit, running the whole thing through my head again.

"I responded well by taking out the second fighter, giving my brothers a chance to deal with the first." He nodded.

"I failed to follow up my attack though. My first strike was reaction, but I need to keep thinking after the initial reaction." I looked around, trying to process it all.

"If John hadn't been there, I would be dead," I finished. Mystien nodded at that assessment as well.

"That's around par for what you should be learning at this point. Your training took over for the first bit, but you hadn't trained for the second." He looked at me with his important information face. "Most people will only do what they've trained to; it can be both good and bad. You want some reactions that will happen without you thinking about it, but you must also maintain your head in a fight, make sure you don't freeze up."

I nodded. "How do I do that?"

"For now just think about how you need to respond; you're too young for any real combat training." He seemed to be planning again. "I hope to cover that in depth in a few years though, once you've developed enough for it to be useful."

I didn't like the sound of that, but there was no point in arguing it now. He didn't have any immediate plans to start beating me with a stick or whatever, and trying to go against it would just cause me more problems.

As spring neared its end, I had a chance to go to town with my dad. He wanted to visit his brother and check in. I was glad for a chance to get out and gleefully tagged along. When we got to the village, that all evaporated.

The village was in desperate straits. Most of the people were now looking quite a bit thinner than they should; some could have been in ads about starving kids. This was in contrast to the few soldiers who were in the town, still passing through. They seemed a bit thin, but not on the same level. It struck me how much worse things were here.

I did some quick mental math on how our hamlet was doing, and I concluded: we'd lost a lot of men, but as I gained power and Rod's hives took off, a lot of the slack was taken up. In normal times, I'd be doing very little food making, but under current conditions it easily consumed 90 percent of my mana. I practiced everything a couple of times daily before going back to making bread, but that was still the brunt of what I was doing.

Even my training was making room for this. I hadn't realized it, but Mystien was absolutely focusing on things that didn't have high mana use. He'd taught me almost no new spells recently, instead concentrating on honing what I could do and non-magical education. I knew now that I needed to pay more attention to these things.

None of this changed the state of the village, of course; there was nothing I could do for that. If I let them know what I could do, I'd be a walking bakery for my foreseeable future, and that was a no-go.

Barro greeted us warmly. Unlike the rest of the town, he seemed to be doing okay. Turns out being a blacksmith during a war meant you had endless work and could get what you needed, no problems. I still took the time to get him a basket of baked goods after our chat; family takes care of family after all.

He sent us off with a bunch of things some of our neighbors had made. He also gave Dad a fairly sizable box, but notably didn't say who it was for. It was a bit odd.

After we got home, Dad went to deliver the goods, except his box. Curiosity indeed got the better of me, and I had to take a peek. I was sure that he wouldn't be too mad. I froze and slowly lowered the lid after I saw the contents. I got away from this box; it could only bode ill.

It contained spear tips, a solid mass of spear tips, several dozen. Why did Dad need these? Who were they for? Was he planning something? Veska had said something about people hoarding weapons, and I felt fear. Would a civil war soon take our home? I knew my father; he wouldn't do anything wrong, would he? My head raced; it took me a long time to calm myself. I knew one thing for certain: whatever Dad was doing, he thought it was the right thing, and I should trust him.

Summer was more of the same. We eventually had to restart foraging groups, though they increased in size substantially, and each had several older boys or men armed and alert with them. Beehives became everyone's favorite new yard ornament, popping up all around our whole village like pink flamingos. Things were still rough, but it seemed that people were finally starting to get a handle on it. There wasn't full-on recovery. Life was still hard. But the number of starving-looking people shrank to almost zero, so the signs of improvement were there.

We even had a priestess visit our village, a true rarity. She stayed for about a week and was loaned a full house. There were several empty ones now. I saw Sandra coming out of the priestess's home one day when Dad and I were picking up more things from Uncle Barro. He made us do many deliveries. I personally think he just liked that I would always leave him some bread when we left.

Several weeks later, I got curious and had to ask.

"Mystien, why does Sandra keep coming by after my lessons?"

"Don't go getting involved in other people's business, Alana. It's a very unattractive trait."

"Veska gets involved in other people's business, and you don't seem to mind." For that remark, Mystien bonked on the head with a nearby book.

"Veska has years of practice, and knows the meaning of the word *discretion*, you do not."

That comment stung, and I pouted off. Who needs to know if it's secret anyway?

CHAPTER 11

BACK TO HAZELWOOD

Fall had just begun, and we were harvesting a few bits here and there. It was still a bit too early for an actual harvest, even if we were ahead of schedule, but that flurry of activity was yet a week or two away.

My family was having a bit of a lazy day, working our way through a small tomato field. There were a few that had become ready for us, and we plucked them gingerly. The work was calming and easy enough, a good rest from the insanity that would shortly begin.

The rumbling of hooves disturbed our whole hamlet. Turning in the direction of the sound, I could see a small carriage with two riders making its way up the dirt road that led here. It was a well-made coach, wood with some apparatus to soften the vibrations I'm sure any occupant would feel. The riders, for their part, were lightly armored, but on very nice-looking horses. Our mayor appeared to be hanging off the back of the carriage for some reason, looking completely out of place.

Dad went up to meet them while I hid behind a particularly bushy vine. Neither of the riders had an aura I could see, but I was a bit scared, nonetheless. I could barely hear their conversation when the mayor came near.

"Verren, Lord Hazelwood sent for the priestess; apparently, his daughter was severely injured in a training accident." The mayor looked nervous, and well he should be. Dad looked like he might take the man's head off.

"Well, she's been gone for weeks now, and she's certainly not staying up here," he snapped.

"I . . . w-w-well one of the soldiers in town m-m-mentioned . . ." Malke was stuttering.

"We heard there was a bard in this hamlet; time is short and we're here to take her to help the young mistress." One of the two riders spoke up. He did not share the mayor's nervousness; to him, this was an order.

The other rider responded to this. "Watch your tone. We've no orders to bring the bard girl, and any mage will be able to refuse without them. You piss people off and you'll have to explain why we couldn't bring back a healer." He seemed the senior of the two and nodded to my father.

"Our apologies, but we are in a rush. If you could kindly bring the young woman in question, we'd like to speak with her."

"I'm her father; you'll speak to me," Dad turned his gaze to the senior, dismissing the younger guard.

"Greetings," the man began. He seemed to know this would be an uphill battle. "As was already said, Lord Hazelwood's daughter was injured in an accident. We were sent to request assistance from a priestess we'd heard was staying here, not knowing she'd left. If you would consent to render aid, I'm sure you would be well rewarded."

"How has he failed to yet hire a new healer?" Dad fixed the man with a hard look.

"They are short on the ground right now, as I'm sure you know." There was almost a sigh in that response.

Dad looked over them, considering for a moment before calling me. "Alana, come, we're going to go assist Lord Hazelwood."

I exited my hiding place and walked over to them. The mayor was polite enough to open the door for us as the carriage turned and sped off, carrying us toward Hazelwood. I was a bit of a nervous wreck. If only because I'd been told numberless times not to attract that particular man's attention.

This method of travel was night and day to walking. For one thing, it was much, much faster. It had taken days of walking from Orsken to reach Hazelwood. Traveling this way, it might only take a couple of hours—how fun! The ride itself though was a bit rough. I was constantly bounced around, hitting the walls and seat roughly a handful of times before latching on to my father's arm.

The roads, such as they were in this part of the world, were mostly dirt paths pounded down with perhaps a bit of gravel on them. The city had some paved streets, as was the main thoroughfare leading to it, but those between towns were not.

There were only two small windows on this particular carriage and, try as I might, I couldn't get a good view of the outside, so I decided to talk to my father instead.

"Doesn't this count as drawing Lord Hazelwood's attention to me?" I asked him, since we were alone.

"I don't like doing this, Alana, but if we refused and his daughter died, not only would he know about you, he might blame you for it."

"Why hasn't he hired a new healer yet, do you think?" I mostly wanted something to take my mind off the shaking.

"Because this is a rather rural area; he's a prat, and as the guards said, healers are short on the ground right now."

"Okay, is there anything I should know?"

"Don't agree to help him in the future. Outright refuse any offer he gives you. Even if it's something small seeming, just say 'no thank you' to anything. I'll do most of the talking; it would be nice if you'd pretend to be shy." Dad rattled off his instructions. Seems he knew a thing or two about dealing with the nobility.

Before long, we arrived at the city. I knew because we slowed, and I heard our guards talk to the gate guards. We went straight up the main road toward the manor, and I finally had a good chance to get a look. Hazelwood was not in the best form. The passing people looked better fed than the peasants outside, but only marginally so. From what I could tell, the market was almost empty of food as well, though there was a bit here and there.

The manor itself was a fortified building within a secondary wall. I would have called it a castle, but it was just too fancy-looking. This was a place built with a mind to displaying wealth first and actually providing defense second. The walls were plastered white, and there was a decidedly grand-looking entrance, even if the door was rather small.

The carriage came to a stop as a hawkish man in formal dress came forward to us. He opened the door, looked in, and stopped.

"We were expecting a priestess, what exactly is the meaning of this?" He gave the guards a sharp look.

"The priestess had left the area already, sir, but we did manage to find this young lady, the mayor of Orsken reports she's a bard of some skill." One of the guards was polite enough to respond for us.

I pretended to hide behind my father as the man's attention returned to us.

"Well, this is most unexpected, but I would like to welcome you. I'm Lord Hazelwood's head steward. If you would, please come with me." With that, he led us up to the door and inside, chatting as he walked.

"Young lady, can you heal wounds? Potentially poison as well?" He turned his head to address me as we were led along.

"I . . . um . . . yes, I should be able to do that." I put on my best "cutesy shy girl" voice. "Er . . . are there no other bards or priests in Hazelwood?" There was no time like the present to gain information.

"I know of one other bard," he responded, probably thinking of Veska. "But she claims to not know or have an interest in learning healing magic." His tone indicated he believed that as much as I did. "It's also difficult to get in contact with her most of the time." This man was a wealth of information, I was so glad he chose to share it with me.

I did make a note of the tactic Veska was using. If I ended up somewhere else, I might consider using that trick to remain unmolested by people. She was not only lying through her teeth, she had also set up a way to hide. I guessed that she had people warn her of any incoming messengers so that she could go elsewhere, and arrive hours late for any meeting where her presence was expected. If I ever had enough people answering to me, I'd definitely do that.

As the steward opened a door, he gave me a nervous glance before showing us inside.

He spoke as we entered to a man seated beside a bed who was middle-aged and a bit larger than most. He had an aura around him, one of moderate power.

"Your Excellency, it would seem the priestess has moved on, but the guards sent for her found a young bard girl. It seems she might be able to help." He spoke softly to the nobleman.

Lord Hazelwood turned, his eyes widening visibly as he saw my father, then flicking down to me hiding behind Dad's arm as if afraid.

"I do not care that you were hiding from me. I will not ask any questions of you today. If you can heal my daughter, you will have my gratitude." His voice was wooden.

I was given a slight push by my father and came over to the bedside. There was a girl in the bed, somewhere in her mid-teens. There was an aura about her, barely. She had horrid burns covering the left side of her body and was shaking slightly in her sleep.

After a very short examination, I began to cast, spreading the healing mana over her. The burns were fairly deep, some even going past the skin and into the underlying tissues. I was glad that the damage was similar enough to frostbite. That fact would make it more straightforward.

It took a long time to deal with the burns, during which time her father left us. I took my time trying to keep any scarring from appearing, which I was quite successful in doing. Once I had dealt with all of the burns, I looked for poison. The steward had mentioned it, and it seemed a good idea to pull any out before it caused any more damage. This led to a secondary problem.

"Could you call for someone?" I asked my dad.

A few minutes later, the steward returned. It seemed he intended to handle this personally. When he saw the state of the young lady, he smiled, looking very relieved. "Oh, wonderful," he said.

"You talked about potential poison," I asked, stirring him from his musings. "There are multiple foreign mixtures in her body, but I can't tell what's what. I'm assuming some are medicine of some kind, but I won't be able to pull any poison out without taking it too. Will that hurt her?"

He thought for a second before going to consult with the nurse who'd been tending her. Most medicines are just weak poison. I was guessing they gave her one to make her sleep, but as I had told him, I had no clue what was what.

When he returned, the head steward looked at me.

"It should be fine. Though she may be in some distress when she awakens. Is it all right if I stay?"

"Um . . . that's fine, sure." I tried to look like I was trying to look like his presence didn't bother me.

I pulled the poison and medicines from her, drawing them away and out of her body.

She awoke with a start, gasping as if in pain for a moment before looking down at herself.

"What? Where am I? Who are you?"

The steward stepped forward, speaking gently, "My lady, you were in an accident, and this girl came to heal you. Please be calm."

"You're, um . . . not quite done yet. Could you please lay still for just a few more moments?" I asked.

"Very well," she said, sounding a bit irritated about the whole situation.

I took a few moments to check for any infections that might have been the result of the burns, but she was lucky on that account.

"There, all done." I smiled at her as I declared that I was finished. I was also thoroughly exhausted, so being done was a blessing.

"Excellent, you may leave now," she said, making a shooing motion with her hand.

All right, you snooty bitch! I liked you way better when you were asleep! I said to myself. Oh, how I longed I had said that out loud, or been able to knock her stupid ass back out. Sadly, I did not and could not.

We left her as I felt a vein on my head pound and were shown to an extravagant room where we could rest for the night.

"What a cunt," was the first thing I said as soon as I knew we were alone.

My father did a double-take at his six-year-old making such a statement.

"I don't know where you learned that, but if your mother hears you saying that word again, she'll wash your mouth with soap," he warned.

"My brothers. And maybe, but she'd agree with me while she was doing it." That got a laugh from him.

We had a chance to clean ourselves before we were brought dinner.

I had a steak, an actual steak! There was a tiny bit of melting butter on the top, dripping off of it. It was delicious, heavenly, and perfectly tender. The vegetables and mushrooms served with the meat were roasted until soft and sweet, their juices popping as I bit into them. At the end of the meal, a maid brought us a small bowl, a new dessert that had been making the rounds. "Even Lord Hazelwood is fond of it!" Ending on ice cream was a great choice in my opinion.

After dinner, I went into a practical food coma. I laid on the bed thinking, *That meal might have made all the work, hassle, and irritation worth it.*

"That was amazing," I said as I slipped off to sleep.

"Yeah," was the last thing I heard. I was glad Dad agreed.

The next morning, we were given a tasty, if light breakfast. I ignored most of the bread and dug into the fruit, greedily eating those things that I didn't have at home. After which, the steward came to see us again, this time, presenting Dad with a sizable bag of coins.

"Lord Hazelwood offers you his utmost thanks for your aid in this matter and has arranged for a carriage to return you home." I personally suspected that the steward had made those arrangements, but whatever. We were getting paid.

The ride home was slower, and therefore exponentially more comfortable. I claimed one gold and a couple of silvers from the money we made. Dad complained about children not needing to handle so many coins, but

I'd done the work so I got a claim. I had no clue what he was doing with the money I got from healing people and the like. I assumed it went into the house finances, and we didn't want for much, at least the things we could buy. I also guessed a good clip was going to the rest of the hamlet. Dad did stuff for that reason alone a lot.

Our little trip and job had made me completely forget about harvest. I was reminded harshly when we got home and resumed our normal chores.

This year, I ended up working a small field with Mystien, so that we could practice magic when my mana was replenished. Rather than his normal lectures, he regaled me with stories of his youth in the capital to pass the time as we worked. He and a young bard by the name of Lucien had gotten into endless shenanigans.

"And he jumped out of the woman's window, pants around his ankles, and landed face first in a cart of manure. I had a hard time running away from that one, because I couldn't breathe."

"Whatever happened to him?" I asked.

"Oh? Well, we both got older. A little while after I joined the army, he opened a tavern called the Starlit Sky. So far as I know, he's still there. Lucien's the one who trained Jackson. They're much alike."

"I'll have to go there one day; the capital sounds like somewhere to see," I said.

"It is. A city that big is something on its own level," Mystien looked out at the fields, breathing deeply. "But you know, there's something special about living out here in the countryside too. I truly love it here."

"Yeah, it's beautiful. If there only wasn't a mountain of work to do all the time, it might be perfect." That got me a laugh.

After harvest, we had a small celebratory meal together with the rest of the hamlet. Simply making it through this year had been cause enough for us to party. Our harvest had been good, all things considered, and a few of the foods needed to be eaten anyway since they didn't store well. A number of older chickens were slaughtered. They added much needed meat to our diet and made way for fresh stock.

Word arrived not long after harvest that the age of men required to serve in the army had been expanded to now include almost every adult man able to hold a spear. Some like Barro were exempt, as their work was vital to keeping everything running. Those under the age of adulthood were not called; there seemed to be some kind of taboo there about those too young going to war. This was not altogether unexpected, but it was still a heart-wrenching event for everyone.

That day, my father took the boys aside to have a conversation with them. He had some instructions for them should anything go wrong, ones that he chose not to share with me. He did tell me that I was to trust them to take care of me.

I wept as both Dad and Mystien left, sad to see those that I cared about so much going off to fight. Mystien was kind enough to leave me with a number of his books and strong admonitions to keep studying.

What was unexpected was that three days after they'd left a mass of soldiers moved into the village, gathering up everyone from it and all the hamlets to the village hall.

A man in elaborate armor walked before all of us, looking harshly out at the gathered crowd.

"Where are they?" he loudly questioned, nearly yelling.

"Every single one of the men from this town called to join the army disappeared, all of them. Do not expect me to believe that none of you knows anything about it, either, that would be impossible. So tell me where they are, and do it now." Stunned silence greeted him.

"I will find them. Right now every home, every barn, every shed, field, and scrap of woods are being combed for those men. If you tell me where they are, only the leaders will need to be executed. The rest will be spared so long as they agree to serve their duty."

Nobody said anything. The silence stretched on for minutes as he looked out at us. It actually seemed that nobody knew.

CHAPTER 12

LOCKDOWN AND THE ORDER OF THE SHIELD

Nobody was allowed to leave after the military commander had made his announcement. There were discussions among the people, but everyone was kept in the village hall while we waited. Our population had plummeted with almost every adult man leaving, so we could all comfortably remain there while the soldiers searched everything.

There were perhaps ten guards in the hall, and they allowed some ale to be brought in, along with some chamber pots from the local tavern. There was no food, and we were not allowed to take from any of the nearby homes. For the first few hours, that was not an issue. But once night fell, the people were getting progressively angry.

The anger receded only a small bit when the military commander, whose name I was told was Orin returned and announced, "We have searched the central village and determined that none of the deserters are hiding here. Those of you who are able may go home, or may go to friends' or relatives' homes. You will not be permitted to leave the palisade."

He delivered this message as the sun was setting. There were a few complaints, but most of those were only murmured.

My whole family, of course, went to Barro's house. He had enough room and knew I would happily provide a bit of dinner. We sat around the small fireplace and talked a bit about that day's events.

"I'm worried about Dad" was my opener.

"Don't be." This response was chorused from everyone in the room.

"But . . . but he's missing, and we don't know what happened. He could have gotten hurt or something." The others looked at one another for a few moments, before Uncle Barro motioned me to come sit by him.

"Your dad's tougher than nails, Alana, and he's got Mystien with him," Barro explained.

"Maybe they got attacked by bandits, or a monster," I complained.

"They were in a group of more than thirty men, old men mostly, but armed men. There isn't any bandit who's going to go after that, nor any monster, not around here at least. More than that, there was no sign of fighting, if there was, the army wouldn't be reacting like this," he told me.

"Then what happened?" I asked.

"What happened is they wanted to go. Who knows where they got off to, but they went on their own," Barro patted my head reassuringly.

"You boys don't know where they went, do you?" Barro asked

"No, sir," Rod and John said, shaking their heads. "I kind of had a suspicion that something was going to happen, but Dad didn't tell us they were all going to desert," Rod said.

"Don't go repeating that, none of you," warned Uncle Barro. "That might get a bit of trouble for all of us stirred up." Then he looked at me, like I couldn't keep a secret. That was just rude. I was full-on from another world and nobody knew. I could keep my mouth shut about important stuff. Mystien had even given me basic spy training. Okay, I was still six, but I was a very competent six-year-old.

"I won't," I pouted.

Around noon the next day, we were all called back to the village hall.

A few of the soldiers there looked downright pissed.

"We have begun the searches of the hamlets," declared Commander Orin. "If these are unsuccessful, and nobody steps forward, you will be allowed to return to your homes to gather your things. After which, every-one will be restricted to the village until told otherwise." This announce-ment caused an angry wave through the crowd, one silenced by the group of angry, armed men who looked monumentally pissed.

"There were some incidents this morning while we began our search." That got everyone's attention. "And so I have a question for the lot of you. Why exactly, in the name of all good sense are there large boxes of bees spread throughout the hamlets?"

I immediately understood the angry-looking soldiers. I'd be cross, too, if I were doing a search and upon throwing open the suspicious box in the middle of the field found it full of angry bees.

I told myself not to laugh. I said to myself, *No laughing, no laughing, don't imagine these jerks having a suddenly bees moment.* That didn't work. I buried my face in my mother's dress, hoping that my loss of composure might be taken as bawling. Being six had a few advantages.

My oldest brother, Rod, bless him, stepped forward. "The hives are kept for honey production, sir, makes it easy to get honey during the summer."

"Explain that to me, lad," came the response.

"It's like keeping a chicken, only you don't have to feed them, and instead of eggs, you get honey." Rod seemed to feel that that was explanation enough.

"That's . . . insane, but . . . okay," Orin said, rubbing his temples.

After that, we all returned to our respective places of shelter. Many of the people from the hamlets had family in Orsken they could stay with; the rest remained at the village hall for the moment.

As anyone could have predicted, the soldiers found nothing. Nobody talked because nobody actually knew where the men had gone, or at least as far as I could tell they didn't. It came to pass that we were all going to be kept in the village proper for now. This was not the end of the world, as it was coming into winter, and almost everyone just holed into their houses for several months, but there were problems.

It became apparent when we were allowed, under guard, to go and retrieve our things that the soldiers had left our homes in a mess. Some houses were left open for a full day and things were ruined. About one beehive per hamlet was knocked over. There was also no way to take all of our stuff with us; there wouldn't be enough room. We took what we needed and locked up the house. I grabbed the old spindle I had first cast magic on, adding it to my belt, a bit of nostalgia was okay now and again. The livestock issue became apparent when we got back to the village.

There was nowhere to put all of them. There was no way to feed all of them. Arrangements had to be made for chickens, pigs, and a handful of large stock animals. The fact that we were going through a minor famine and had a drastically reduced population were the only reasons it was even close to possible. Even then, a fair number of the livestock so vital to our way of life had to be slaughtered and preserved for food.

Since our little village would still be playing host to soldiers over the winter, the townspeople were moved into vacant homes, or squished in with friends and relatives. It was highly uncomfortable for everyone. This led to an all-time low in the goodwill of our citizens to the twenty soldiers who had been assigned to deal with our village.

Several days after we were all moved in, Sara and Sandra showed up, along with several of the other children from our village.

"I really hate to impose upon you, but . . ." Sandra began, talking to my uncle who'd come to see why there were so many kids at his house.

"Out with it, girl." Barro was a nice-enough man, but he was very straightforward.

"Several of the families were getting a good bit of food from Alana. That situation has, if anything, worsened, but we're no longer receiving that aid. We've come to ask for help." I liked Sandra; she was a polite girl and my brother's girlfriend.

"I have no issue with it," I said when my uncle looked toward me.

He left the arrangements to us, and it was decided that every day some people would come by to help me with my group casting, and I'd give them the bread made from it for their troubles.

This went on for eight days before we were disturbed. My family, along with four of the children we knew were sitting around, bringing food into existence, when harsh knocks came from the door. We stopped and my uncle went to open it, revealing a line of men, led by Commander Orin and our mayor.

"Greetings," Orin said as he entered. "I've received some reports that an unusual number of different children come by every day." He looked at my uncle. "I'm sure I don't need to tell you that this unusual activity has led to a number of questions, ones that I'd like answered."

I had a personal dislike for both Orin and all of his men. They hadn't actually been deliberately harming anyone in town, but they represented everything wrong with the system. Their actions did not hurt those they disliked, and yet, they caused incredible suffering and damage to innocent bystanders.

"Well, ask your questions then," said Barro. My lovely uncle was nothing if not curt.

"Straight to the point, I like it," the soldier stated as he moved in, looking us all over.

"We've noticed everyone who leaves seems to take bundles with them, bundles they didn't bring. What's in them?"

"Bread," Barro stated plainly.

Orin raised an eyebrow at that statement, "Interesting, and where are you getting so much bread?"

"Alana, show him."

I grumbled internally a bit, then obediently sang a short tune, conjuring a small roll as he watched.

"Wait just a second, I didn't know you could do that!" the previously quiet mayor angrily interjected.

"That was by design, Mayor Malke." If he was going to join those keeping us locked up, he was getting both barrels of rudeness.

He was shushed by the military man, who came over to regard me. "That's a good trick, and the children coming by every day are for . . . Ah, using them to increase your power?"

I nodded.

He seemed to be running some numbers in his head. "How many additional can you handle at once?" he asked.

"Around twenty, but I can't keep that going for long, I get better long-term results with just under ten." If we were going to be telling him about me, it seemed proper to at least be honest.

"And you're Alana, right? I've heard so much about you from the mayor. I was hoping you might help us out when the snow starts to fall, being able to make food is just another good thing you could do." He smiled at me, almost like he was trying to be friends.

"You and your men have kept us locked up here, and you're causing irreparable damage to our village. I have no intention of helping you."

He frowned a bit at that, "My men and I are just following our orders."

My old world had prepped me for that excuse to an insane degree. "Many men have done evil things because they were just following orders."

He sighed. "What the men of this town did, it can't go unanswered. If nothing was done, it would be repeated everywhere. Our country would fall apart. Surely, you understand this?"

"I do, but that does not mean I am happy about it."

The commander thought for a few moments. "What about the men traveling to the front? Surely, you wouldn't begrudge them?"

"I wouldn't, but the mayor and army have had years to sort out these issues. If I continue to help them, it will just encourage them to never fix them."

Every winter brought another surge. Men were gathered at the end of fall, just after their harvest. It was mostly those traveling long distances who ended up in trouble.

"Do you plan on continuing to make food for the townspeople?" I was actually surprised that this man hadn't gotten angry with me. The mayor, on the other hand, was fuming in the corner, looking ready to spit blood.

"I do." I did plan to, so there was no issue answering this one, and didn't see how it could hurt anything.

"If you were to move to the tavern, you could more easily and fairly distribute it. You would also have volunteers to join your song at any time you wished." His suggestion was sensible, but I couldn't see his angle.

"I'll order my men not to enter if you do so, nor to take any of the bread you make." I narrowed my eyes,

"Why are you offering those terms?" He certainly knew they were suspicious.

"Because it will ultimately make my job easier. If the people are starving, they will cause more problems. My men could be hurt if that happens. I am also from a town not unlike this and do not wish to see the people come to harm." It seemed good reasoning. "Your cooperation will help the villagers. And while I would prefer your direct aid, you will also be aiding me. Everyone wins this way."

That was an astoundingly good argument. I looked to my uncle for his thoughts. Barro considered for a bit then said, "I'll make arrangements with the tavern owner. I imagine he'll be thrilled. If that's what you want."

I nodded. Orin smiled and made his way to the door.

"That's it?!" the mayor burst out as he came to the threshold.

"What's it?"

"She's been hiding her abilities from me, intentionally refusing aid, to both of us, certainly . . ." he sputtered.

"She is a child. Even if she was obligated to tell us what she could do, which she isn't, the only ones who have the right to command her to labor are her parents and guardians. That aside, providing food is rendering aid. I am satisfied that there is no illegal action here, and as the one placed in charge of the military men in this village, my decision is final."

The mayor was apoplectic while I reevaluated my opinions of Orin.

The tavern owner's name was Perry, and he was absolutely thrilled to have me. He was a very old man, but genial. Barro set us up so that people could come by in groups based on where they lived. A schedule was posted on the door, and bread would be provided based on that. We ran six half-hour sessions over a six-hour period. When the session was going on, there was a strict access list as to who could come in and how much bread they could take. But during the breaks, all were allowed to come and enjoy themselves. I had a generous amount of time to recharge, and while my neighbors got less, it was at least very equal.

I gained insight into why the push to get me to heal people was not too hard either. Just a couple of days before the snows began, a priest arrived in town. It would seem both the mayor and Orin had called in every favor they could to bring the man, named Rosk, to stay with us for the winter.

Rosk was in an interesting situation. Even though he was helping the army, an action that had made the mayor astoundingly unpopular, he seemed welcome everywhere. He was even allowed in the tavern at all times. He always raised his voice to help me summon more bread, but pointedly never took so much as a bite of it. He often gave me kind smiles while there too.

These things eventually led me to speak to the man.

"I like your necklace," I finally called out one day. It was a weak excuse for trying to start a conversation.

He looked down, fingering the medallion that hung to his chest, bearing the symbol of a shield. "Ah, the symbol of my order. It does bring me some comfort as well."

"My teacher mentioned orders a few times but didn't tell me much." That much was true. Mystien had mentioned the order in passing a few times, but never given any real info. I'd assumed it was either unimportant, or he was waiting until later.

"I would imagine you don't interact with any of the orders too much in a town this small, so that's not overly surprising. Did you have some questions?"

Giving me a blank check on asking questions was just too much, "Oh, tons! So . . . what does your order believe?"

"That's an excellent place to start. We believe in protecting the weak and providing them what shelter we can."

"How so?"

"Well, for example, we run most hospitals, orphanages, and the like, and also promote some rules and laws."

"So your order has lots of healers?" That was news to me.

"Every order has lots of healers; mine is just more willing to put ourselves in danger to aid others."

"Huh."

"The military uses our services extensively, and the armies of most nations won't attack us or our patients."

"Really? Why?"

"Firstly, because while we stay out of the fighting, if they did, our priests would turn their magic against any attackers." That was no joke. I knew priest-type magic specialized in dealing with living things. I didn't know exactly what it could do when turned to combat, but I imagined it would be nasty. "Secondly, because we refuse to work with any army that makes flagrant violations of certain rules."

"What kind of rules?"

"We have rules about the treatment of prisoners and conquered people, hospitals, and child soldiers."

"Child soldiers?" I asked. That seemed weird.

"Yes, we believe that those under the age of majority shouldn't be forced into wars or hard labor."

"Orin said something about only my parents being able to make me work." I thought that had been a weird statement at the time, if a very forward-thinking one.

"He is not a priest, but he holds tightly to our beliefs. That would fall in line with them; your parents might assign you chores or work to help, but having a government force you to do so would be unacceptable." He gave me a pat on the head.

"In war as well?"

"Quite forbidden by our rules," he stated gruffly. I now understood why the young men had been passed over while the old ones were taken.

"Those are quite good rules," I mused out loud.

"I think so. Do you have any other questions?" he asked with a hint of amusement.

"Um . . . this might seem a bit odd, but why did you come here, rather than Hazelwood? They need a healer badly too."

"We had a small enclave in Hazelwood, but the baron there harassed some of the young women under our protection, so he will do without." That was harsh; they were not making idle threats about leaving people high and dry. I made a mental note not to cross them without good reason.

"Similarly," he continued, "this village might be considered either prisoners due to war, or conquered people. By being here, I can assure there is no misbehavior. I doubt Orin would do anything, but my being here protects him from accusations of it."

"Should I know what the rules regarding us are?" I asked.

"Mostly, that he cannot actively cause harm without reason, and that he must make and allow reasonable attempts to fulfill the needs of those in his post."

"So that's why he's allowing . . ." I waved a hand to indicate the tavern at large.

"Yes, of course, may I ask one in return?"

I nodded; he'd been amazingly nice to answer me so thoroughly.

"Were you forced or pressured into doing this? It's a very large amount for one so young. I was initially concerned when I heard about it, but you seem in good spirits and well taken care of."

So that's why he spent so much time in here; he was keeping an eye on me.

"No, I was doing about the same for my neighbors before we were all ordered into the village. It seems the right thing to do."

That got me another pat on the head.

For the rest of the winter, the priest and I would have light conversation whenever he came by. It was nice to have someone who I knew would not try to work me to the bone to wring out every benefit they could.

CHAPTER 13

✦

COLD SHOULDERS AND FREEDOM

The days marched on, and winter approached its inevitable end. I didn't know the exact day I was born. That's not how most villages measured time, much more important was the changing of seasons. As I approached the turning to spring that would mark me as a seven-year-old, I stood at the back of the tavern. Something about the view from behind the bar made me smile. It would have made a perfect painting.

Well, almost perfect, at this time everything was being moved around by the departing group. Tables were pushed to one side as the chairs were formed into rough circles, and an enormous pot, loaned by the tavern owner Perry was being set on the fire to heat. I myself was doing a bit of preparation, putting away everything that was out for the daily distribution of bread.

Around the time I finished, a great number of women began to join me. Some carried large tubs in groups, others had washboards and cleaning utensils. Many carried large sacks or baskets of soiled clothing. Today was a laundry day, something that had been decided on early into our confinement.

By getting together and doing our laundry collectively, we had a much needed chance to socialize. The gossip, news, and good humor spread at this event brightened this otherwise quite dismal time for us, and so a couple of times a week we held laundry day. Because the water was heated and disposed of in a communal fashion, it was also massively more efficient to work all at the same time. Anyone could go to any such day they pleased, but friend groups tended to come together.

Today was one of the days most of our hamlet had selected, and I looked up as I saw Mom coming in, bringing some of our things. I skipped over to help her, and we set up in our normal place.

Sara's family joined us, her mother looking up at mine.

"We're going to slaughter one of the pigs tomorrow, would you and Alana like to help prep the meat?"

"Of course," Mom heartily agreed. "What time?"

"Bit after lunch, I'm going to go and see if I can get a trade on some herbs and salt."

"I've got a bit. How much do you need?" I hoped Mom could get a good trade here. I'd love pork for dinner.

"It's about an older one, so we'd need a small sack of salt and about as many herbs as can be spared." That was a fair amount.

"You're making sausages from the organs? Or are you doing soap this time?" Mom inquired, both options had their merits.

"I'm thinking sausage this time. I'm all settled up on soap for the moment."

"Would you trade half of those for the salt and herbs?" Mom was being pretty generous here. Both of the things we'd be trading away were "premium goods," and while meat fell into that category as well, sausage was considered one of the cheapest of meats.

"Done," Sara's mother agreed with a smile.

A woman leaned in to discuss buying the blood. She had a dog, and it could be used in some puppy chow.

Sara and I got close and started going over our favorite mixes for spicing sausage, since we'd almost certainly end up assigned that job. She liked one with rosemary and fennel, which I thought was a bit odd tasting. I put forth a strong argument in defense of sage, which I would use as much of as I was allowed.

"Two spoonfuls of sage, tossed in with half a spoonful of rosemary and pepper, to add a back flavor. There is no mixture better."

"Well, at least you got the rosemary right, but it should be one each of it and fennel, one half of pepper, one quarter of sage." We would never see eye to eye on this point. The discussion was fun though.

There was an odd couple in the generally happy group: a man and woman, both washing a small mountain of clothes.

The man was one of the soldiers passing through. It had been decided that one soldier would be allowed to sit in and use the communal water on each washing day, so that he could clean some of the clothing for those men who were leaving.

None of Orin's men were permitted in the tavern, a rule that had only been violated one time. I had not been present for that incident, but it had nearly led to a riot. That had been narrowly avoided when his commanding officer, upon learning the problem, had publicly berated him in the street, followed by assigning him all the unit's most unpleasant work for a solid month.

The woman was Anta, Mayor Malke's wife. I didn't know her and had no intention of getting to know her. As one who'd been aiding the soldiers, Malke, and his wife by extension, were declared persona non grata by the rest of the town collectively. She knew this and kept her distance. I suspected that as soon as the war was over they would be forced to move.

When we'd first been confined here, a couple of the more hotheaded lads had gone about causing trouble. This had ended with little more than them getting flogged in the town square for their foolishness. That period had continued for only a week or two before one of the older grannies proposed an altogether more elegant solution.

The soldier had stopped working and walked over to our group. As he approached, the room went dead silent, every head turned to face him.

"Ah, excuse me, ladies. It seems I've run out of soap. I don't suppose you've any you might be willing to part with? I could pay or trade with you . . ."

"If that's okay . . ." He was getting far more hesitant now.

Nobody said a word. Nobody moved. Every pair of eyes, from the youngest girl's to the oldest granny's, rested upon this man, and all were silent. There were no glares, only blank faces. Everywhere he looked, he was greeted by silence and staring eyes.

It took only a few minutes for the man to lose his nerve and return to the corner, visibly shaken. Once he sat back down we resumed our talks as if nothing had happened.

This was why the soldiers had to do their own laundry. Nobody in the town would speak a word to anything less than formal business. Even with those things that necessitated a response, there would be no discussion, no chatter, only cold movements and short concise sentences. Most of the time, soldiers staying in a village like this would find one or two women who'd be willing to do their washing and the like for them for a price. Here, on the other hand, every time they asked, nobody would respond—not that any would have right now.

If, of course, that man went to a shop with an order to fill, the shop would do so, if they had any. But none of the few merchants who were still open would offer any assistance beyond the most basic. Nobody would give any answer as to who might have what, or who might be able to trade. Most of the soldiers understood by the time they left and were thoroughly creeped out by it.

The mayor, on the other hand, did not get silence; he got vitriol. Old men would spit on the ground as he passed. There were a number of jokes that girls would loudly whisper to one another about him wherever he went, making sure he knew they were laughing at him. A number of boys, in a fit of creativity, had come up with insulting songs to sing when they saw him. I liked using several of these while I was doing magic; it brought me a small joy. Everywhere he went he was followed by words like "betrayer" and other insults.

Anta was not treated quite as harshly but was still made as welcome as a cesspit.

There was almost no dissent on our treatment of the soldiers or the mayor. Peer pressure was fucking terrifying.

As we processed meat the next day, I idly wondered how spring planting would be handled. Surely, they would have to do something. I had no idea what would happen, but I'd heard Rosk had agreed to stick around from Sandra, so I knew it wouldn't be violent.

It was as the snows thawed and spring broke that the announcement was made. We would be permitted to return to our homes. This was not over-all surprising. Refusal to allow us to plant would have led to people knowing they were going to starve and having a direction to point their anger. We were still mad, but this gave us just enough hope to continue.

The soldiers were staying though, and would be conducting peri-odic checks and patrols to harshly stomp out any perceived insurrection. Behind closed doors, this led to a lot of grumbling. We still shunned them, so they didn't know, there was much discussion on how they were wasting time. Everyone seemed to agree that they had spent more time and effort trying to punish us then it was worth—all they'd really done was cement our village against them.

Of note, they were also fortifying the village. The rumor mill said the war was not going well, and the Ermathi troops were moving closer by the day. That was concerning, but I was divided on my opinion of it.

Regardless of what might come, we knew what would come if the fields were not worked. It was for that reason that we packed our things and set out to return home. As a parting gift—even though we'd be only a short walk away—Barro gave my brothers chain-mail shirts and eighteen-inch blades. He reasoned that with the bandit incident in the forest, it'd be wise to have them.

Mom opened the door to the house and groaned.

"Should have come up and done a bit of cleaning before we packed up everything."

We were carrying most of our stuff with us. Nobody had really thought about it and just jumped at the permission to leave, but our house was a disaster.

I looked in. "Wow" summed it up fairly well. Dust caked every surface, wind had blown the contents of the chimney into the house, and spiders and the like had claimed the open territory.

"Alana, fill up a bucket with water and grab . . . let's start with the hearth. After that, we'll need to do the beds so we can sleep."

"So what should we . . ." Rod began.

"Go check the tools, fields, and hives. You two are more of a hindrance than a help when it comes to cleaning." Mom cut him off. That was kind of cold, but really true. Men didn't do a lot of household cleaning in this world, and those two were particularly inept.

I made a small light, which I had float in the middle of the room. It made everything clearer, which didn't help the appearance at all.

"I'll start up top; it'll be easier for me to clean the places we can't get to easily," I told Mom, firing up the trusty old, "move stuff" spell and grabbing a wet rag.

The boys were bogged down with the disaster that was unkempt farmland. Had it been anything other than over a winter, it might have been too much for them. That kept them away from the frenzy that gave new meaning to the words *spring cleaning*, repeated in every house in our hamlet.

It took two days, at the end of which I was ready to collapse. I did revel at the fact that our house was once again clean though. When we'd got the last bit done, Mom and I lay together and took a nap. It was a wonderful sensation of warmth that rolled over me as I settled into sleep.

The fields were planted a few weeks too late; it was a struggle for everyone. Some of the seeds would probably not yield much because of the timing, which would not make for a good harvest.

Part of our struggle was that we'd lost so much stock. With fewer oxen to pull the plows and equipment, we struggled. We resorted to using hand tools on several fields, just so that we could get something into the ground before it was too late.

The other part was that nobody had had enough food, and our stores were tapped. I don't know if they planned it, but Orin and his men had thoroughly screwed this town. Too many things had been left behind and too many animals had to be killed because of their stupid lockdown. We'd already been running on fumes as it was, with just enough to keep going.

The losses might have seemed minor from the outside, but every chicken lost cost us many times its weight in eggs. Every pig killed didn't get the chance to fatten on the roots and forage, turning waste into valuable food and fertilizer. Each cow gone lost us both a plow animal and a source of dairy. The list went on and on, and it was compounded by the fact that they would no longer multiply, hitting both the present and the future.

When this war was over, there would be a reckoning. I couldn't imagine that men coming back from the front lines would look at what had been done to their homes and do anything except rebel. They already had the training, weapons, and experience. They also had an inkling of what the nobility had been hoarding; while we went hungry, fat, rich men in their little castles feasted. Perhaps the fact that many nobles were spellcasters would hold the tide of rage, perhaps it wouldn't.

With all that in mind it was good to be back home again. We were once more able to come and go as we pleased, once more able to roam the forest for fresh foods. Sure, we were borderline starving, but we were free and that alone gave us new life.

MYSTIEN GOES TO
THE WAY STATION

I walked beside Verren as we left the village. We put a bit of distance between ourselves and the rest of the group.

"I am not returning to the king's service." I spoke with a finality on this, because there was one.

"Nor I, my friend," Verren said to me.

"So the first question is, do we take Durin up on his offer? Or do we go another way?"

"That's a hard one," he answered. "If we do join him, we will end up fighting against the kingdom's armies at some point. At the same time, I'd trust him with my life, I even told my boys where to go if it should ever come to that."

"Sounds like you've already decided then," I told him.

"Suppose I have, should we go back for them?"

"That's the real hard one. I don't think so, wherever we're going my money is on it being a military installation. If things go wrong where we are, they might get killed in the crossfire."

Verren bristled a bit at that. "They might get killed if they stay in the town, too, Mystien."

"That's true, but it's a farming village. No army would attack them; they'd just come in and take over. I would be more worried about the fact that we're heading into a famine if Alana wasn't more than capable of keeping them fed."

"I worry about her most of all. The mayor's been holding himself back because I was there. He may try to force her to work for him."

I shook my head. "You worry too much. Did you see what she did to that poacher?"

"No, can't say I did. I was out looking for others that day," Verren quirked a brow.

"Well, let's just say if Malke pushes her too hard, he's going to sorely regret it. John is close to unlocking physical type magic too."

"I noticed, if he had already I'd be able to sleep soundly."

"What about the other men? Do we take them with us or slip away tonight?"

"If all of us go, it'll draw less attention to the two of us individually." Verren rubbed his chin as he considered the positives and negatives.

"True, I think they'd join us if we asked. Where are you on that?"

"They'd join us, and I'd trust them. They're not the cream of the crop, but they're good men. Durin said to bring men we trust if we wanted, so I say we take them."

"I agree. So, Verren, where do we tell them and when?"

"We'll ask to have lunch where the road from Khole's Hill meets the main one. We can tell them there and slip up to the way station. That way, nobody has a long time to get afraid and cause problems. That road's paved, too, so no footprints."

"That's a solid plan, few places it could fail," I looked around, keeping an eye on our surroundings.

It was only a couple of days waiting until we reached the spot where the roads joined, just after where we ate lunch. I waited till the men were fed and walked out before them. Verren and I had discussed how to do this a few times, and it was decided that I would be our mascot.

I could feel my nerves pricking as I stood. "I've known you all for years and I served in the king's army once. The way I see it, I don't owe the kingdom a thing, and I'm not fighting in this foolish war." The men froze and looked at me.

"Mystien, if you desert, they'll come after you, they'll hang your corpse on the roadside as a warning," one of them said nervously. He was not wrong; they would try to do just that.

"I've got a place I can go. The one who told me about it has my trust. Furthermore, he told me that any men I trusted could come as well; I trust all you men. Will any come with me?"

"I will." It was Sorren, that was quite unexpected, but welcome.

"Me too." Another man from our hamlet spoke. His daughter had been coming to me asking me to charge a tattoo she'd gotten. I doubt he knew that or would approve.

"And I."

"I as well."

"You've never done me wrong, I'll come, Mystien."

It started with the men of our hamlet, spreading to those who knew me. Before I knew it, every one of them had agreed.

I could tell from the look of them that they were nervous. I had very little time to show them some results, or we might lose a few. Losing any could bring the might of the army down upon us, ending with us losing all.

"All right then, let's go." I turned and led the way, going north once we hit the main road.

The thing about so many soldiers moving around was that nobody even blinked at us walking down the road.

The way stations were a series of stopping locations, situated in areas where there were fewer villages so that travelers could have a place to rest and resupply. This was a program designed to encourage merchants and messengers, and its effectiveness was middling at best. The main problem was that many of these simple affairs were just not maintained well. Nobles viewed them as a waste because they didn't need them, and who cared if their lessers could travel easily.

This way station had a series of covered shelters and a central building. It was roughly standard for its kind, probably hosting one family to maintain it. I could see a small garden in the back and a warm yellow glow coming from the windows on the office.

A bored-looking woman in her twenties manned the desk. She was some kind of mage, not powerful, but strong enough to take on anyone likely to harass her. The woman did a double take when she saw me. Casters were thin on the ground here.

I gave her a warm smile. "Greetings, I'm traveling with some friends of mine and we'd like somewhere to rest. I'd like a room downstairs."

Her back went straight and she nodded, "How many, sir?"

"Around thirty,"

"Of course, if you'll go get your men, I can take you to your room immediately."

Once we'd brought everyone in, she gave a quick look over us before moving to a door. "This way please, gentlemen."

She led us to a basement. Once there a small catch opened the floor, leading the way to a lower room, this filled with what could only be contraband, I noticed a few things here and there that were decidedly illegal. That room had a second hatch, one that worked on a tiny bit of mana being pushed into a certain brick. It was hard to see, but a well-trained mage would catch it if they were looking. The third room was larger and full to the brim with weapons. It looked like someone's armory. If this was found, either an impossibly well-provisioned secret society or rebellion would be suspected.

I was stunned, almost physically so when our guide went to the back wall. I could tell she was pulling mana through it. That was a rather advanced technique. Any normal person would think the contraband room was what was hidden. A skilled mage or someone paranoid would likely suspect this was where the real action was. Another level of subterfuge seemed excessive.

The wall slid open to a rough cave. "If you'll follow me this way, sirs." That was all she said to us. The farmers were getting nervous; they'd never seen anything like this. I was shaken, nobody would use this level of security for anything below the level of a state secret.

At the end of the hallway, we came to a door bound in iron. Two attentive guards stood in front of it. A few lamps had been distributed; I was just behind our guide. At her word, the door was opened, and we were led into the final room of this facility.

It was large, perhaps forty feet on each side, and made of stone.

"What is that?" asked one of those we'd brought with us.

I was a bit busy trying to process what I was seeing. "It's a gate."

"Um . . ." Verren's response was not unexpected.

"It connects two points in space. They're incredibly rare, I know of perhaps a half dozen in the world. They were made by some ancient sage or order; nobody quite knows how."

"This is where I must leave you." The woman looked pleased. I think she enjoyed seeing jaws drop. "If you'll just step through, someone will tend to you on the other side."

I stepped forward to the archway, glittering blue and covered in runes. Durin had implied that he was going to take the kingdom and any who opposed him. If he could set up this, I believed it.

CHAPTER 14

✦

DROUGHT AND
ONCOMING FAMINE

We were struggling. There was no way around it as the first day of summer hit. The food was . . . me for the most part. Several had killed dairy animals and even a portion of their breeding stock. The forest was being picked clean. Even our cave was empty of mushrooms; someone else had found it and picked it dry.

By this time, I'd been forbidden by my mother, something backed by both brothers and every adult in town, to join the foraging parties. If something happened in the forest and I couldn't make any more food, the hamlet might fall.

Every day I woke up, cast until I had only enough mana for an emergency, rested, then cast again. This was repeated as many times as it could be any given day, and Mother had asked me not to cast anything except my bread spell. I did a bit of studying between castings and some spinning, but my heart wasn't in it. I needed breathing room, and there was none.

Worse still, spring had been low on rain. Our crops were surviving, but we were still going to be under production. When I looked out, the fields were too sparse and too brown.

My brothers had taken to leading the foraging parties. Said parties were getting more armed and territorial. That, too, was a powder keg from what John was telling me. Though there had been no spotting of bandits in a good while. Seems they had the good sense to evade the forest constantly patrolled by soldiers and bands of angry, ravenous, armed youths.

* * *

It was about ten days into summer that I had visitors. I recognized some of the older men. There were four, along with Orin, Rosk, and Mayor Malke. They asked to speak with me; my mother, of course, joined in, along with an old man who was as I understood it, the eldest in our hamlet.

"I had hoped we might speak to young miss Alana's mother privately," the mayor began.

"And I've been hoping you'd find a cliff and throw yourself off of it." I cut him off. I had had a horrid couple of weeks, and quite honestly he could fuck off.

Everyone else frowned at me, though a few only halfheartedly.

It was Rosk who spoke. A wise decision, of those here, my opinion of him was the highest. "Alana, this is a formal meeting, kindly remain civil."

I grumbled my consent to his request.

"The situation stands like this. The village, and all of its hamlets are on the brink of starvation," Orin began. "I know it is a lot to ask of you, but the amount of food shared from this hamlet has decreased substantially. If some of your bread could be diverted, it would be a great help."

"That is not an unreasonable request," I replied. There were several smiles from our visitors. "Unfortunately, it is not a feasible one."

"Why not?" Orin asked. Rosk looked curious as well. The elders gave tired looks.

"You are not a farmer, nor was your family, I would guess," I told the officer.

"I don't see what that has to do with anything. Please explain."

"In the winter, we are mostly idle. One can't farm in snow as far as I know. During this time, little food is needed. A lamp that is kept low needs little oil, yes? But if it is kept bright, it requires more."

Rosk was the one to try this time. "That may be true, but you were providing enough for two or three of the hamlets. Certainly, you could provide some aid."

I sighed. "A man idle requires around a third of what a man engaged in hard work needs. There aren't many men, but it holds true for our workers here."

The priest considered this point for a few moments. "Can you find any leeway? Perhaps if you managed your casting carefully?"

"I am already doing so, Rosk. I'm currently stretched to the limits on what I can do, and there is no leeway."

"You can't just refuse to help us!" one of the old men shouted, standing.

"Our people are starving, too, you can't do nothing!" another agreed.

"Nothing!" I roared, "NOTHING?! You came here to ask for aid. The situation is simple. I cannot divert my magic toward you or my hamlet will starve. If they decide to divert a portion of their bread, that is fine with me, but I will *not* force them to do so." I took a breath, letting my aura flare, much to Rosk's surprise. "You asked if there was spare, there is not. You asked if I could cast more I cannot. What you haven't done is give a single idea within those bounds. Do that and I'll help all I can." I was raging. "And while you ungrateful bastards try to come up with some idea, remember that I fed you and your families over the winter and asked for no payment in return."

"Calm down, dear, and sit back down." Mom pushed lightly on my shoulder to return me to the seat I hadn't realized I'd left. It took me a few moments to get my hands to stop shaking.

The mayor, in a great act of foolishness, began to speak. "Tantrums such as these . . . " Commander Orin's hand locked on the mayor's shoulder like a vise and said, "She's not wrong here. Let's see if a proposal can be made." It was a polite way of telling him to stop talking.

Both Orin and Rosk kept their eyes locked on me. The smart men in the room knew the kind of things an incensed mage could do.

"Then let's brainstorm something. What do we have?" Rosk asked, looking toward the other men.

"The funds and stores of the town are for most practical purposes empty, tax revenue has been almost nothing for a couple of years now, and the cost of hiring a priest drained us down to less than five gold coins," the mayor said first, offering nothing.

Several of the village elders listed off what few assets had survived the years of bad times; it wasn't much.

"What about the honey?" one of them asked.

"That could keep us going for a while, but it won't be enough to make it through to harvest," our elder responded.

"What if we sold it?" I asked.

"Nobody around has spare money for sweets," the mayor replied, looking condescending.

"There are nobles in Hazelwood; they might."

"That much food in one shipment will be a target."

"A few of our boys could go; we'll get them spears," one offered.

It was echoed by all, even the mayor.

The old men talked like this for a while. They came to the conclusion that they just needed to make it until they could sell that one good, and it might be enough.

"We just have to make it until the honey is ready then. Alana, is there truly nothing?" our old man asked.

"I am at my limit; no more can be made. You can ask some of our neighbors to give a portion of their food if you want. I'd be willing to give a bit of mine."

"No, you will not." Mom nixed that offer. "You'll eat every bite of your allotted amount."

That got a bit of grumbling, which was silenced by a single glare.

"You ask too much of a child. If you continue to ask, you will receive nothing more. I will see to that." Mom wasn't as strong as my father was, but she could be quite scary.

"Amara, please be understanding . . ." the mayor tried again, and again quickly understood his input was unwelcome with only a glance.

"Mayor Malke, the only reason the men left in this town haven't torn you to pieces and hung you from the palisade is that there are too many soldiers around. This war will end though, and when it does, sons and husbands will return to see what a mess Orsken has become. Were I you, I would flee before that happens."

The mayor paled. He'd always been a bit incompetent, sniveling to those stronger than him, a bully to those weaker. His true crime though had been siding with those that had locked us in. Not one member of this village would overlook that; it had caused too much pain and fear. I doubted he'd thought of that when he did it, but he had committed that betrayal. He had failed to fight for us when we were our weakest.

I don't know if any man could come home to find his mother, sisters, his wife, or children starving, all telling him who was responsible, and let that man live.

Orin would need to flee too. He was not as malicious, and he had some traits I admired. All that was irrelevant when he became an enemy.

Mom stood, taking me by the shoulder. "It sounds as if you have things worked out. Since you've no further need of my daughter, we are going home."

I left with her. Nobody tried to stop us, or even call out as we went.

* * *

It was several weeks until the honey was ready to be taken. Several men and women—Mom included—opted to give a portion of their bread to other people in town. They had also absolutely forbade their children from doing the same. I was even watched while I was eating, to make sure that I didn't short myself any.

Rod was told that he would be going with the shipment, and hopefully return with supplies because he was the older and bigger of my two brothers.

John was told that he would stay with me for the duration in case our idiot mayor tried anything else because he was the better fighter.

Both felt that they had gotten the better end of the deal due to stroked egos. Teenage boys could be wonderfully easy to manipulate sometimes.

None of Orin's men, nor the soldiers passing through, would be going. It would go against their orders, and they wouldn't get anything from it anyway. For the same reason, Rosk stayed. He, at least, would have been welcomed.

I slept poorly while they were away. There was simply too much going on, too many needs pulling at me for me to rest properly. The whole trip took nearly a week, and when they returned, we saw their results.

They were good. The honey had managed to bring a good price on the market, and the men negotiating had managed to find someone who was willing to sell them some grain and fish. It was not great in that we still got far less than we would have from a normal run. But it was enough. If we kept doing it throughout the summer, we'd at least make it to winter.

I did not envy the people who'd have to deal with distribution of the grain, or the endless arguments over who got what and who contributed more. Those discussions could only end in more anger.

I counted myself lucky that I had no place in those arguments. I didn't want any anger directed at me or my family. I also regretted that I was not part of those arguments, because I was of the firm opinion that our best leaders had all been called off to war.

While our food situation was presently manageable, we had other pressing problems. Namely, that by midsummer, the rain was still well below where it ought to be. This was a slow-burning issue. There was enough so that the crops weren't outright dead, but they were certainly suffering. The water levels in the wells were also suffering. The little creek in the forest was dry according to my brothers.

In any other year, this would have been something difficult to overcome. This was not a normal year. Our stockpiles were gone; too many years had passed where too many workers were missing. There was no safety net, no backup of stored food or funds with which to purchase it.

If the harvest failed, this village was doomed. No amount of pushing on me or anyone else would solve it.

A few people had the straight audacity to ask me if there was anything I could do about the lack of rain. I barely resisted the desire to throw things at these people. I then had to admit that it was "possible" to make a rainstorm, in theory. I crushed their building hope by explaining how much of my time and mana would go into trying to just learn to do that properly. The real questions were: If I stopped making food to learn to make rain could I learn to make rain before half of the village died of starvation? Even if I did, did I have enough mana to keep people from starving to death while watering our fields? The answers were a resounding no.

Even with what we were getting from the city runs, it wouldn't be enough. Added to that was that every indication that the Ermathi armies were moving to the eastern borders of our region. It was all too much. One day just a couple of weeks before harvest, I broke. I'd just made a load of bread, and it was being carried off to its intended recipients. I was cleaning a pot, just a stupid pot, and I began to weep. I fell and leaned up against the wall of the house and just bawled. I cried and cried until eventually Rod found me and picked me up.

"What's wrong!? Are you hurt?"

"It's . . . not . . . enough." I spat out between sobs.

"What isn't?"

"The food . . . this harvest is too small . . . I can't do enough . . . the village will starve over winter . . . it'll be slow, and there's nothing I can do about it!" It all came out at once. It was all sadly true.

"Shh, it's going to be okay," he said as he carried me over to my bed and held me, rocking me back and forth. "It's going to be okay, Alana. Just hold out a little longer and your big brother will take care of everything."

I didn't see how that was possible, and just kept crying, curled up in his arms.

He held me until I'd cried myself to sleep, then put me to bed. At breakfast, Mom told me he'd let the last group of delivery people know I'd passed out and couldn't make anything for them. John came to join us, followed shortly after by Rod, once they'd finished their morning chores.

"I'm going to forage today, got a new spot that I think will give some good stuff," Rod declared.

"Great, I'll come with you," John said, perking up.

"Actually, I'd like you to head over to Creekrun and pick us up some fish. I think we could all do with a good dinner."

He passed over a handful of coins to his younger brother.

"You're a bit faster than I am, so you should be home for dinner, no problem," Rod added, smirking.

He wasn't wrong; John was faster. He would be faster still soon. The flashes of aura popping out were almost constant now. I was expecting it all to push its way out any day now.

"All right, sure," John agreed easily. I wondered if he'd run the whole way there and back.

John headed out with haste to his task as Mom left on her morning chores.

"Thank you, Rod." I hugged him. I knew he was going through all of this nonsense just to make me feel better.

He ruffled my hair and kissed the top of my head. "Okay, I have to go. Behave yourself now, okay?"

"Okay!"

With that, he ran off.

My day after that was quiet and relaxed. I was still really worried, but having something to look forward to give me what I needed to keep going. I worked through my daily tasks with vigor, feeling more energized than I had in months.

It was late afternoon when someone came to get me. There was some commotion and apparently I was being called for.

What I saw when I got there took all words away from me. I dropped to my knees as I looked upon it.

CHAPTER 15

✦

ROD'S PROMISE

After bidding my little sister goodbye, I walked out, heading to the barn that was our meeting place. I found Sandra there, laying atop the hay and climbed up beside her wrapping her tight in my arms.

"Hello, my love," I said softly as she pressed against me.

"Mmm, good morning. Now, will you tell me why you needed to borrow Dad's bow?" She gestured to the leather pouch laying a bit away from us.

"I'm going after meat today. A rabbit, or if I can get it, a deer."

"What!? You know what'll happen if you're caught!" she hissed at me angrily.

"I do, that's why I sent John away, but I need something to keep my sister going. I need her to keep it together until harvest is over." I looked at the rafters, going over things in my head. "I found her yesterday completely broken down. She cried herself straight to sleep. If we can just keep her going a bit longer . . ."

"I'd be more worried about winter," Sandra said, with anguish in her eyes. "It's going to be brutal and everyone knows it."

"I will not be here for winter, and I want to talk to you about that too." She froze in my arms, tensed as tight as she could.

"I'm of age now, Sandra. After harvest, they'll make another call for men to go fight, you know that." I could feel her shaking, but this was a conversation that had to happen.

"I'll be leaving before that happens. I've already discussed it with John. We're taking Mom and Alana and, we've got a place I think we'll be safe."

She looked betrayed. "You're leaving? Now? We need all the help we can get and you're taking your family and running?" She was clearly starting to get angry, so I put a finger to her lips

"I . . . I want you to come with me, as, um . . ." I was so nervous I could hardly think straight. "As my wife. That's why I'm telling you now."

She looked a bit shocked, "What about my mom and my sister? Can they come too?"

I hesitated, "I was told to bring the family. Even if we marry, I don't think they'd count. That's why I want to wait until harvest is in; I plan to hide everything we bring in for your mom and sister so they can survive too. John wanted to leave today but agreed to wait so we could help them."

She leaned up against me, burying her head into my chest. "What do you think? It's the best I could come up with. We'll be able to be together, and your family will have the best chance I can give them." I rested one hand on her hip, letting my thumb stroke her gently there.

It took her a few moments. She finally looked up and kissed me, our lips locked together as I pulled her soft body against mine. "Promise me you aren't going to do anything this stupid again."

"I promise I'll come back from this little hunting trip and we'll be careful as careful can be. What about um . . . my other offer?"

She smirked and said, "We'll talk about that after my future husband comes back from his little trip, now go."

I gave her one last kiss before grabbing the bow and hopping down. I looked at her there, propped up on one arm. She was so beautiful, she'd lost weight, we all had, but it would come right back.

I quickly made my way to the forest. I knew just the spot, a high hill, covered in game trails. The foragers never came here, since there were almost no edibles on this little grassy spot. It was the perfect place.

I spent hours there. I picked some plants so that I could have an excuse in case I was found. Normally, a bow would have been suspect, but with how things were now, not going in armed to the teeth was madness. I was even wearing the mail and blade Uncle Barro had given me.

It was getting late, too late for my comfort when I saw it. A rabbit, tucked into a little spot in the grass. It wasn't a deer, but it would certainly do. I only needed one shot to take it. The poor beast didn't quite die, but a yank on its neck solved that problem with ease.

Something grabbed my attention and I turned, looking toward the village. A large group was moving in that direction. It looked like part of it was breaking off and coming more toward the woods. Behind them another large group was following. I could only just see the second patch of people. Whatever it was, it was bad, that much I could tell.

I was still a bit lost in thought when I heard it.

"Why, hello there, Rod. You're out far." I turned to see Mayor Malke. He had several soldiers with him, one of the patrols. Quick head count said three crossbowmen, three halberds, one asshole.

They hadn't seen the rabbit yet, but they would. There was still blood on my hands and the ground. I wouldn't give them the chance. I drew and fired as one of the crossbowmen flinched, seeming to sense something was wrong. The arrow buried itself in his gut.

I knew I'd have to kill all of these men, or at least most of them. We'd have to flee tonight I reckoned.

The mayor froze up; he didn't know what had just happened. His eyes went wide in fear.

The soldiers took a beat to process, but not very long. Within a second, two crossbow quarrels were already sailing at me.

I hadn't stood still. Ducking and charging as one went wide and the other scored my shoulder, a few rings popping with a *ping* as they flew away. The wound was minor, only a slight scratch.

The men with halberds tried to form up and bring their weapons to bear. I drew my blade as I dodged past the points and into their group. Dad had always said that was the weakness of a pole arm, hard to defend once your enemy is too close.

I scored a light cut on one man's shoulder, narrowly missing his head. As he stumbled, I turned on the other two. I stabbed, hoping to take down one of them so I had a bit of breathing room. As he parried the blow, I heard the *twang*, then I felt the third crossbowman's quarrel bury itself in my thigh.

I stumbled, the force of the leg wound throwing me off balance.

I looked up to see the final halberd flashing in the sunlight and thought, *I'm so sorry for breaking my promise, my love.*

CHAPTER 16

THE DAM BREAKS

Rod was dead, his head and body on the ground, separated by about a foot. Someone had dropped him there. I couldn't think. I couldn't process what was happening. There was a crowd gathering around; it was abuzz.

There were some soldiers. One was on the ground being talked to by the mayor. The others looked nervous. They formed a defensive line, their weapons at the ready.

I saw John come up beside me, package in hand, Mom was just behind him.

"Hey, Alana, what's . . ." They both froze. Mom looked like she was in shock, her breathing hitched. John took only a second; he dropped the package as surprise took him. Then I saw his jaw clench, fists too.

John's aura exploded. It was no longer wisps here and there, but a raging fire, a silver blaze that surrounded him head to toe.

The mayor turned and saw me, coming forward. "Something's going on in town. I need you to heal these men . . ."

I never heard the last bit as it was interrupted by a scream. A keening wail of pure anguish washed over us. The agony in it hollowed out everyone it touched as it pressed in like a wave.

I saw Sandra push her way forward. Someone tried to grab her and failed. She roared again in pain and anger, drawing her knife to charge those who'd taken my brother's life.

It was cut short by two thunks as the crossbowmen buried quarrels in her chest. I couldn't have healed those fast enough to save her.

That noise as the metal-tipped wood buried itself in the girl's body was the signal.

I screamed, pushing mana into it as hard as I could, a flashbang in the face of the mayor and his little soldiers.

John became a blur in the direction of the soldiers, moving like nothing I'd ever seen.

The buzz of the crowd, cut short for only a second, returned as a roar of fury. Together we charged forward, pulling belt knives or work tools. Some ran to battle with only their hands.

The intruders never stood a chance as we fell upon them like a horde.

I buried my knife in the mayor's thigh, aiming for his femoral artery. My mother and a half dozen other women and girls grabbed him, holding him down as small hands pushed steel into him again and again. No longer would we wait for this traitorous bully to get his due; the women of the town had had enough.

The boys and old men ran at the soldiers, ripping their halberds away as they pulled them down.

"Under the armpit, boy, where the armor is thin . . . Aye, there's a good lad!" I heard our elder shouting his encouragement as he grabbed a man's leg.

Sandra's mother held one of the unarmored crossbowmen by the neck as Sara gutted him like a pig, one long cut, sternum to crotch.

John was absolutely savaging one of the halberd wielders. Two of the man's limbs lay nearby as the boy repeatedly smashed his face into the ground.

It was quickly over. We stood covered in blood and shaking in rage as we looked toward each other, not sure what came next.

It was John who spoke. "Mom, take the women and children and get to Creekrun. We have friends there, and you'll be safe while we deal with this." Then he faced the older boys and elders and announced, "Men, we are cleansing our town tonight, and damn the consequences."

"I am staying," I declared.

"No." He turned, looking like he wanted no argument.

"You'll need healers when it's all done. I'm staying."

He looked at Mom, and she nodded.

"Find somewhere to hide, Alana, and stay hidden. If your brother doesn't get you by dawn, come to Creekrun." Mom seemed nervous about it, but knew healers would be needed.

I looked at John. "Dad's cave, the one with the mushrooms." It was a good spot, well hidden and far from the action. We both knew it well, so I had no worries.

"Fine," he conceded through gritted teeth.

* * *

We broke as it had been decided. I did take a few moments to put on my other dress and grab a couple of things. I made sure I had my favorite belt, with the pockets. I'd put in one gold, ten silver, and eight copper coins, as well as some of my hairpins by this point. I hung a waterskin of ale from it in case I got thirsty. I also grabbed my spindle and a bit of wool, so I'd have something to do while I waited.

That sorted, I ran to the woods. I knew the path by memory and reached the cave quickly. Once there, I ducked in, finding a secluded corner where nobody could see me from the entrance.

An hour or two in, I heard movement by the entrance. I froze where I was, as it just as quickly disappeared. I made a couple of rolls for a quick dinner and began spinning. I liked this idea because it was mindless work that required enough attention so I couldn't think about the day's events or worry about what was happening now.

I'm not sure how long after I started spinning that it happened, but a number of voices came. Several people entered the cave, trying to be quiet. I put my spinning away silently and shrank down as much as I could, listening intently.

"Are you sure it's safe here?" It was a man's voice.

"Absolutely. I found this place years ago while hunting with his excellency. It's practically invisible from the outside. You lot didn't even notice until we were upon the entrance," another man retorted.

"How deep does it go?" Unlike the other two, this voice sounded calm, the accent almost academic.

"Not too deep, I checked it out before, and it's only the one room."

"As long as we are safe until this blows over, I do not care." That voice was female and vaguely familiar.

Five men and a girl entered the cave. Four of the men were dressed in armor of various kinds. Of these, one seemed injured, he was limping. The last was in a robe. The girl, just on the cusp of adulthood was in a rather fancy traveling dress. All six had an aura, though of them, only the robed man's was stronger than mine. I nearly peed myself when I saw that, this was not a group I could fight.

I kept hidden, trying not to draw their attention. I wasn't sure how they'd respond, but I didn't want to find out.

"Hawkins, go outside and keep an eye out. If anything happens, let us know immediately." That sounded like one of the armored men. I assumed he was the leader.

One of the other armored men left.

"Sorrin, what are those bubbles?" I heard the girl ask. I saw her face and was almost sure I knew who it was.

Shit, I'd forgotten to tamp down my aura. As the wizard turned and raised his hand, I leapt behind a rock.

The force of the impact on my shelter made me scream a bit in panic. Once it stopped, I heard blades being unsheathed. I made a gambit I hoped would work.

"That's not a very nice way to treat someone who's saved your life!" I yelled.

"What?" It sounded like the robed man asking. *Good, keep talking. Talking is better than cutting, or spell throwing.*

"That's Lord Hazelwood's daughter, right? A couple of years ago, she got hurt in a training accident; they brought me in to fix her up."

There was a moment of silence before the girl spoke. "There were two people who were there when I was healed, describe the other." She sounded a bit curious.

"My father? A man with dark hair. Has an aura like black mist."

"She is correct," the woman told them, to my great relief.

"Come out slowly, do not try anything." This was the leader's voice.

Very, very slowly, I came out from behind the rock. I could see that the man, Hawkins, who'd been sent out was now in the entrance, a blade in his hand.

"Can you prove that you are a bard?" the wizard Sorrin asked.

"I can summon a bread roll?" I offered.

He nodded. "Do so."

It took only a few moments before I was holding a small roll, which I munched.

"What is a bard girl doing hiding in a cave?" their leader asked as I ate.

"Hiding," I answered truthfully. "There's a big fight going on in the village."

He nodded to that. "All right, fair enough. Can you heal?"

"I can." I had a feeling that he was going to ask me to patch up his friend.

"Fix up Dallon then." I slowly went over and cast healing on the injured man's leg. An arrow had hit him in the shin. It was just inches from his knee.

The wound was nasty. Arrows were like that, but not too terribly bad to heal.

"Thank you," their leader said, right before he punched me in the face.

* * *

I woke up some time the next day, with a monster of a headache. Added to that, my hands were tied and I'd been gagged. It would appear that someone had thrown me over their shoulder like a sack of potatoes and was carrying me along.

A quick look around told me that we were in the forest somewhere, instead of on a road. The air smelled slightly of smoke as well, though all I could see was trees.

"Mgh, mugh, mrr." I couldn't get anything reasonably sensible out from the stupid gag.

"Ah you're awake, that's good," came the voice of Dallon. He seemed to be carrying me. "Hey, Captain, the girl's up."

Said captain made his way over to me and began talking. "Good, you're up. Here is the situation. A contingent of the Ermathi army attacked your village last night. So far as we can tell they burnt most of it, along with the forest. Now, most of my men wanted to leave you behind to die there. Heck, even I wanted to leave you behind. Sorrin though pointed out that someone who can summon food and heal us could prove vitally useful, so you'll be joining us for our trip. Once we get there, we'll let you go. Any questions?"

"Mrr, murr, mrr, murgh, murr."

He took out the gag.

"Can you not just let me go now?" I asked.

"I'm quite afraid not. You know our unit composition, size, and anyone who caught you would know our general direction," he answered. His tone was at least polite.

"I don't suppose you'll believe it if I say I won't tell anyone?" I inquired hopefully.

"I can think of about a half dozen ways to make you tell me anything I want to know." Okay, that's a scary response.

After agreeing not to cause any trouble, I was at least ungagged and allowed to walk. They kept my hands tied, with a lead going toward one of the men in the group at all times.

We walked for a couple of days through the forest. One of the men, Hawkins, would come and go frequently; he seemed to be some kind of scout.

Most of the men were annoyingly quiet. None of them wanted to talk to me, or tell me anything about where we were going. The young lady and Sorrin spoke a good bit, but I was told in no uncertain terms that if I tried to start a conversation with her, I would be gagged again.

I didn't learn much about all this, but I did pick up a few tidbits of information. We were heading west. The men's names were Sorrin, Dallon, Hawkins, Crusher—I suspected a nickname, no mother would name her child Crusher—and Captain Jones. The young lady's name was Lady Gwenna Hazelwood a-bunch-of-increasingly-ostentatious-titles, or something like that. Also, they were all jerks.

Okay, they weren't that bad. I was royally pissed that I was being dragged along for whatever their mission was, but they weren't overly mean to me. I didn't even have to do much work. I provided some bread for every meal, a pittance compared to my past couple of years.

About four days after we had begun our trek, we came to a road. This had been expected apparently as nobody but me seemed in the slightest bit surprised.

That night, we stopped at a way station. I'd never been to one before, but I was familiar with the concept. These were situated between villages and cities on well-traveled routes. My hands were untied before we got too close, and the captain decided to have a conversation with me.

"While at the way station, you are to pretend to be my daughter." That grated; this man was nothing like my father. "You are not to speak to anyone first, and anything you say is to be only the most basic. Am I understood?"

"Understood."

THE FURY OF
THE DOWNTRODDEN

I looked around as the girls went off; there were a few things that needed settling. I took my brother's blade, adding the scabbard to my belt as the other men picked up the weapons from the fallen. I call them men, but most were old, far too old. The others were close to my age.

"So, we just all initiated a revolt. I'm sure we all understand what that means," I started.

"We know, lad, we're all dead men," the elder spoke, looking around at all of us. "But the women didn't touch any of those we killed, did they? If any gets caught, he ought to at least be able to remember not seeing them do that."

All of us nodded.

"We might be all dead men, the . . . Malke, he said something about a commotion in town?"

"Yeah, he was going on about an attack," one of my friends, Malcom, chimed in.

"Then maybe we're not dead men. I say we kill all these bastards and let whoever is attacking take credit. Let's kill them too. I'm damn tired of people invading my home." My proposal got a round of nods.

"We should ask the other hamlets to help," our elder decreed, to some consternation.

"You think they will?" Malcom asked.

"They will," came his response. "We've got about fifty spears stuffed away in Mystien's house for something just like this."

"Won't be enough for everyone, but it'll help. I propose two groups; we circle around opposite sides and meet up once we've got everyone who wants to come. We may even figure out what's going on." This was my best idea at least; nobody else had any counter points.

The run from hamlet to hamlet gave me a chance to work a few things out. Dad had told me that I would probably manifest physical magic, but he didn't know exactly how. So I made a list of what I noticed had changed. I was much, much faster than I'd been this morning. I could now sprint forward like a thunderbolt, surreal. I was also far stronger. A few experimental jumps, and one pull on a tree trunk, and that was clear. I thought my body felt . . . tougher, but I couldn't quite test that right before a fight. My senses and reactions were also cranked up. If I focused, I could see the wings on a fly fifty feet away.

We managed to get a glimpse of what was going on in the village. This information was added to what we could see. There were men at the main gate, perhaps a hundred or so Ermathi soldiers. This group seemed to be trying to break into the village. They had other, small groups stationed around the walls in fives and tens. It seemed like they didn't want anyone to escape. One of the hamlets near the main road had seen around thirty of the kingdom's finest blaze past before the opposing unit had appeared. So the village had been reinforced.

We had perhaps fifty volunteers, few of which could fight worth anything. What we did have was knowledge of the land, and that both sides were currently ignoring us. It was good that they were ignoring us of course, as either would almost instantly crush this gathering of peasants.

"So, are our goals to aid the village?" That question from one of the elders got mixed reviews.

"I think our goals are to kill the outsiders. Or better yet have them kill themselves," I pointed out.

"All right, so how do we deal with them?" another man asked, scratching his chin.

"Hmm, we hit the surrounding groups, pick off as many as we can," our elder proposed. His motion was accepted.

Less than half an hour later, I found myself crouched in the grass beside three others. One was an older man with a crossbow he'd "retrieved" from a soldier back home. One was around thirteen; he had a weird staff weapon with a sling on the end. Something his dad had taught him he said. He also claimed he could put a fist-sized rock into a man-sized target at three hundred paces. I was dubious on his claims, but even if he failed he had a big stick. The third was just older than myself, dressed in mail, and even had a shield to go with his spear. I was hoping man number three knew how to fight; he'd be our defender.

Before us were five men looking toward the village. They didn't worry about peasants, not with their numbers and training.

I slipped off to the side, ready to flank when it went to melee.

The slinger and crossbowman loosed simultaneously, both hits. My concerns about the weird staff were gone. Now I just wanted one; he'd completely pulped a man's spine. Four of the five were still functioning; the quarrel had missed by inches.

They took a moment to orient themselves before finding the direction of the attack and charging, shields up, swords out.

Our slinger aimed for the left side. He got one more shot off, a miss, before both got behind the heavy. Everyone readied for the incoming melee . . . well, everyone except our opponents.

I flew out from my hiding spot as they passed, meeting their right flank by slicing through the closest man's neck. His neighbor didn't have a chance to respond before I'd savagely buried a blade into his gut. As their last two met our front line, I met their back. It was over in an instant. With that, I was beginning to realize just how much I'd gained.

We continued on like that a few more times before all the groups began to pull back, forming two groups of twenty. We'd managed to take a good few and gain some more actual weapons from it. Even if we all went in at once, twenty would still be too many. Even if we won, they'd have reinforcements before we could take them all. With that in mind, those with ranged weapons continued to harass them as best they could.

From the loud noises coming from the gate, I took a guess that they would soon be inside. That palisade had been built to keep out bandits and small monsters. It would slow organized soldiers, but not stop them for long.

Of greater concern was what they were doing outside. It appeared they were tired of us taking shots at them and had decided to send out fire arrows, setting the fields aflame. I froze when I saw that; the fields were too dry. They wouldn't just drive us back; they would burn everything.

Within minutes, the wildfire had begun to rage. It spread through the dry wheat like nothing I'd ever seen. Billows of smoke drove everyone to retreat. Our enemies were pushed against the palisade by smoke and heat, eventually gathering all together at the gate.

I had to stand back and look as the lands turned into an inferno. I'd resolved to leave this town some time ago, but I didn't hate it. There was a very slight bit of guilt as I realized that our actions had doomed Orsken. Even if it would have survived the starvation that was coming, it wouldn't now.

Some of the other men gathered with me to watch. There was no point in trying to stop a fire of this magnitude. I heard one old man weeping, overcome with the sight of his lifelong home going up in flames.

I walked toward a nearby field where I knew some goats were normally kept, taking off my swords. The boy from my group followed.

"Hey, where are you going?" he asked.

I walked over to the trough used to water the goats. It was huge and full of disgusting water.

"Through the fire, to kill them." I didn't hesitate as I began to soak myself with the muck. "To kill them all."

"What's the point?" The kid was persistent, I'd give him that.

"The point? The point? They drove away my father. They murdered my brother. Those two groups of bastards all deserve to die! That is the point!" I saw him shrink away as I yelled at him, good.

As I dripped, wet as I could be I started to make a plan. Going in through the main gate was not going to be possible. While I could now jump pretty high, but not that high, my only hope was to climb.

"Hey, kid, you got a belt knife?" I looked at the boy whose eyes were still wide. He pulled one out and handed it to me. "Thanks."

I went far from the gate, far from the fighting. I was fast now; I'd run through the flames and use the knives to hold me to the wood as I climbed. That seemed like something that was possible.

So I found the place where the fire looked thinnest and bolted, my knife and the boy's in my hands. As I hit the fire, I could see the water steaming off of me. Even speeding as I was, it took a few seconds to pass through the blaze. My skin stung as wisps of fire brushed along it. I took one breath only and almost coughed, barely managing to keep it in as I moved. As the wall approached, I jumped with all my might and made it about fifteen feet up. The knives held true into the wood as I planted them.

The problems were many though. I coughed, and the hot, stinging air only made me choke. My knives had driven into the wood deeply. I tried to pry one out, but the blade was stuck. Eventually, I managed to free it, and after nearly a minute of coughing and pulling, I managed to drag myself over the edge.

I lay down behind the wooden wall, sputtering for air. What I had done was foolish, insanely so. I'd nearly died from overestimating myself.

I could never do that again. I felt like I'd been out in the sun too long without a hat, my face and hands stinging. There were angry red patches on the backs of them just forming.

As I stood, a man came running up to me, one of Orin's.

"Hey, you're one of the kids from town." He laughed for a second. "Thought you were an enemy soldier there for a second. Looks like you're dressed for battle though, boy. If you're ready to serve the king, head to the ga—" He looked down to where I'd shoved the boy's belt knife into his chest, gasping.

"Fuck the king," I whispered as I pushed him over the edge of the wall.

Part of my mind was screaming. I'd just killed a man who'd greeted me as a friend. He was no threat. He didn't even know what had happened. Another showed me images of the hungry villagers, poor fields, and my brother, lying on the ground, beheaded, at the feet of men just like that man. It slowed me for a moment, but only a moment.

When I arrived at the gate, I found that the fighting had already moved to the streets. I waded through them, taking any man I found in either army's regalia. I was swift and brutal, slicing limbs and stabbing deep. I didn't count how many I took, letting my anger drive me on and on, toward the center of town.

There, at the village hall, I was truly surprised. It had been surrounded by torches, twenty feet out, and haphazardly painted large on the walls was a circle containing a shield. Dad had told us of the sign. The priest had designated this location a sanctuary. He stood at the door in a suit of armor, in one hand a shield, in the other nothing.

As I blinked at the sight, I saw a girl perhaps fourteen fleeing a soldier of Ermath, screaming as she ran past the torches. She ran toward the door and tripped, landing hard. As the soldier crossed the line of torches, Rosk said nothing. He only lifted his hand, allowing an angry red light to fly toward the intruder.

The man died screaming. I had no idea what had killed him as he fell to the ground, but it shook me.

Rosk looked down at her, speaking gently. "Go inside. The helpless are safe beneath the Shield." The girl stumbled again as she obeyed, looking back.

He looked to me next, his face conflicted. "Were you forced to fight?"

"No." I spoke the truth loud and clear.

"Then you may not enter until it is done, or you are unable to fight." I could tell he was sad, seemingly disappointed that I'd made my choice.

"I understand." With that, I turned, heading toward my uncle's shop.

* * *

By the time I arrived, there were few left fighting, but I found my uncle locked in combat with a man in full-plate armor. A few dead from either side told me these two were the last of a skirmish.

Barro fought with an ax, a huge two-handed affair he swung with aplomb. His opponent though was too fast and too strong. With a two-handed sword, he pushed back the larger man. Each blow jolted him until a savage kick slammed him into the wall of his own shop, crumpling him to the ground.

Before he could line up a killing blow, I ran in, aiming to put a blade under his armpit. He turned in time, deflecting the strike away. He was fast, not quite as quick as me, but very fast.

"Physical magic? I'm impressed, boy," he spoke as we fought, with him deflecting a handful of my strikes. I barely managed to parry his first return. It came in like a thunderbolt, screeching as my blade pushed it away.

"You're strong," I remarked as we circled each other. He would advance as I dodged or parried, then fall back as I struck at his joints. I scored a hit on the back of one knee as I jumped past a slash that would have easily bisected me. It was shallow, an irritant, but not enough to impair.

The problem was obvious. I couldn't get past his armor. Perhaps in a hundred blows I could hurt something deeply enough to disable him. He only needed one on me though.

"If you surrender, I'll spare you. I would hate to kill such a promising young man, for you'd do well in the empire's armies," he said, making his pitch.

"I'll pass." I had no intention of fighting for them or the kingdom.

"Very well. I am Aiden, of the third imperial legion."

"John, of Orsken."

Our introductions done, he attacked in earnest. Before he'd merely been testing me, but now he fought to kill. I still could not injure him, his armor deflecting anything he allowed to get through. His skill made up for any lack of speed as he pushed me back again and again. I realized a second too late as I blocked the same blow my uncle had, and the same follow-up kick sent me flying into the open front of his shop.

It hurt as I tried to suck in the air that had been driven out of me, both my blades tossed to the floor.

I saw my death as he walked through the door. "I did not come here to kill you, boy, but I must. Goodbye."

The loud *clang* as something struck him from behind rang out through the shop. He turned as the quarrel fell. It was enough. I grabbed the one thing that lined every surface in a smith's shop and flew at him. A blade would have skimmed harmlessly off of his armor, but the hammer I planted in his temple struck true.

Even after he fell, I struck again and again, unwilling to risk not killing him. I stopped only when his helmet was caved in and brain fluid and blood began to flow out.

The ancient tavern keeper limped over to me, crossbow in his hands. "You looked like you needed some help. Reckon you'll make it?"

I laughed for a few moments from the sheer relief. "Yeah, suppose I will."

It would have been wonderful if that had been the end. It was not; armies do not surrender or flee when an officer dies. The fighting went on all night. Half the village burned to the ground, corpses littered the streets, and injured men groaned in pain everywhere.

The empire had won the field, slaughtering the kingdom's soldiers. In turn, they'd lost so many in the fight that what few remained had fled.

Just before dawn, it was finally over and I stumbled toward the woods to retrieve my sister. She would indeed be needed. A few drops of water fell on me as I struggled up the road.

It was like an icicle was pushed into my heart as I came to the woods. All that had been green and brown was now charcoal or angry red. The bottom truly dropped out as I worked my way forward, trying to find trees and landmarks as the deluge that might have saved our fields a day early poured down on me.

When I found the cave and saw that it was empty, I fell to my knees and wept. How could I have been such a fool? I should have taken my family and fled, but instead I got caught up in my desire for vengeance. Now my sister was gone, too, lost because of my own madness.

There was a pang of hope. Perhaps she'd fled to my mother in Creekrun. Perhaps she was safe.

We searched for a week finding no trace before we finally gave up, my mother forcing the issue. I had to accept since I took her and my uncle to the place Dad had described. My spirit was crushed. I knew that they wouldn't blame me, but I had failed all the same.

The village was done. What people there were left went elsewhere to seek shelter. Some went to Hazelwood to beg for aid, some to other villages and their relatives. The priest and tavern keeper stayed until everyone else had left, sharing one last drink for the place. As Perry closed his doors for the last time, he and Rosk parted ways, each going to seek a new place, one thing was clear to all. Orsken on the Forest was done.

CHAPTER 17

✦

ESCAPE AND SANCTUARY

I was lost in thought as we entered the way station. There was no way they were going to let me go. I had to get away and soon. I spent some time looking around as we entered. There was one worker at the desk when we came in. He was a man, no aura; even if I shouted for help and he believed me, he'd just die, right before I did. There was a map though, and that was certainly useful.

This way station was at a crossroads, each road heading very roughly in one of the cardinal directions, the north one went a bit east, the south a bit west. If I had to guess by the size of the dots, the nearest decent-sized cities would be north or west. That was a bit useful to know too. We were also quite far from my home, a week or two depending on conditions.

"Hello there, sweetheart, how are you today?" The clerk had gotten the orders for the rooms and turned when he saw me looking at the map.

"I'm all right I guess," I lied. I'd fixed up my face where I'd been punched, but if he could see under my sleeves, he'd notice the rope burns that stood out bright and angry there. I could have easily healed those at any time, but they might be useful.

"First time staying at a way station?" He could obviously tell I was a bit nervous, so I nodded. I didn't want to get this man's skull crushed.

The clerk patted my head before I left with the troop.

Lady Gwenna had a room to herself, of course, and a rotating guard through the night. The rest of us stayed in twos. I was placed with Jones, as he was supposed to be my father, but as he was attending "Her Ladyship," Crusher and I were unpacking the room. I was glad to have a chance to talk to him. He wasn't particularly bright and might tell me something useful.

"Where are we going anyway?" I asked. I didn't really expect lots of info, but let's fish and see what we catch.

"Lady Gwenna's got a cousin or someone a bit west. Going to stay with him." Now that was great to know. I knew where they were heading, and where I didn't want to go.

"How long till we get there?" I tried to make my best impression of "Are we there yet?" to see if he'd tell me.

"Don't know, few days? Week? Captain will tell us when we get there." That was less useful information.

I pouted, quietly grabbing a few extra pillows and blankets as I formed up my plan.

Jones joined us a bit later, just as it was getting dark.

"Go to bed. I'll be just outside and the door will be locked. Knock if there's an emergency." He always took first watch. I guess he liked his beauty sleep.

"Yes, sir," I said as I hopped into the bed, turning to the wall and pulling the covers up over me like a shawl.

I waited for a few minutes after I heard him close and lock the door before beginning.

Now, the thing about a cliché is, that it's only a cliché to someone who's seen a hundred movies and TV shows. Would stuffing a bed with pillows and blankets have worked on anyone from Earth? Probably not, no. What about a knight from a magic fantasy land? I'd give it 75, 80 percent tops. Those odds I'd take far better than mine if I stuck with them for even another day.

After a few minutes, my bed stuffing looked . . . eh, passable, and I moved over to the window. Once I got it open, I was forced to look down. Oof, it was going to be a ten-or twelve-foot fall easy. Stuffing my mouth with my hair so I didn't yell when I inevitably broke something I lowered myself out, dropping.

My ankle twisted sideways with a jolt. Note to self, do not try to land in future, let your legs buckle. It took me a few moments to stop breathing hard and hum a little tune to fix that up. Then I took a few more to use my old friend the movement spell to close the window.

Once I'd recovered a bit and caught my breath, I began to run. The ground was soft and a bit muddy here from recent rain, and I went straight for the southern path, pumping my legs as hard as I could against the smooth cobbled street. I went this way for a couple of minutes before stopping and looking back. I checked to see if I had left any footprints.

There were none. I sighed in relief and removed my slightly muddy shoes, chuckling a bit. Then I began to jog north. I could keep up a jog much, much longer than a flat-out run and hoped that those jerks would either take the bait, or not care enough to try and find me. I was a bit jumpy as I passed the way station again, but there was nothing for it. I just had to hope that nobody saw me fleeing.

After about fifteen minutes, I got my shoes back on. If they found me this far away, I'd take the extra speed from having shoes over any semblance of stealth. I fled for the whole night, alternating jogging and walking, not sure how far I could make it.

I could tell that I was getting close to a village from the worked land. Much like that at home, it was not being sowed to its full potential. It was nearing dawn, and I wanted to sleep. I also wanted not to encounter any people, just in case. I saw what looked like a hay barn and decided it wasn't getting better than that.

Hidden as best as I could manage, I began to take stock. I still had most of my stuff, save my belt knife. I was another day, perhaps two, depending on the time I made from the city I'd seen. Would the noble girl's guards come after me? I doubted it. They might look a bit, but I just wasn't much of a threat. Sure, they'd have killed me to keep me from causing any future problems, but they had a job to do.

Reassured, I drifted off to sleep.

Blood. There was blood everywhere. It was all over me, all over my hands. I could feel it, smell it. I looked up and saw the corpses strewn everywhere. A man with a sword loomed, raising the blade to strike.

I awoke with a gasp. I could feel my heart pounding in my chest as I sucked in air. Trembling, I reached up to wipe the tears from my face as I tried to calm myself.

For the first time in a while now, I had time to mull over my actions in Orsken. We had killed those men. Had we been provoked, certainly, but was there a better way to respond . . . I was unsure. I had taken a life for the first time. I could not undo that. There was no bringing them back; no returning to the past to try and find a new path.

I thought on that for a long, long time, but found little peace. It disturbed me to my core, and I never again wanted to walk down that path.

* * *

While I sat and thought, I worked a few stitches out of my belt to free a few of my coins. I did this until the sun was fully set, then pulled myself up and returned to my run. All through the night, I traveled. It was easy to follow the road, and I had all the supplies I needed through magic.

I made decent time, and as the dawn broke, I saw the walls of the city. As I walked toward it, I had a few other questions to answer. I needed to decide what to do now. It was likely I could find work here and stay the winter. Or I could try to return home. What if I got home and there was nothing there though, or if our village was declared in revolt and I had to flee again?

By the time I made it to the gate, I'd decided that I would spend the winter here. I could send a letter when the roads opened up in spring. At least I could get news of what had happened to my home.

The guard at the gate looked at me strangely; his eyes went up the road as I walked up. It was still early, and the gates had apparently just opened.

"You alone, kid?" That didn't seem like the standard question on who I was and what my business was.

"Um . . . yes."

"Where are your parents?" He seemed worried; that was nice at least.

"My dad got called by the kingdom to the war. My mom and I got separated."

He nodded. "You got family in the city then? Come to stay with an aunt or something?"

I shook my head. "No, sir, but I need to find some shelter before the snows start."

He sighed. "Come with me." I was motioned into the gatehouse as the other guards took up his position.

I was a bit nervous as I was led in. The room was small but had a table and some simple chairs.

"I'm not in trouble, am I?" I asked.

The guard chuckled a bit at that, "No kid, we just have to sort you out. Normally, I'd offer you a bit of soup while you wait for me to get somebody, but things are a bit tight right now."

"Oh . . . okay." I had not considered this possibility.

I was unsure what was going to happen, but there were too many guards outside for me to just run off easily. I did face-plant into the table a few times. This would certainly be a massive headache.

It took a bit before a new guard led a robed woman in. I easily recognized the medallion she was wearing. We both blinked as we recognized the auras surrounding each other.

"Greetings," she said. "I'm Abigail, what's your name?" She spoke so kindly, just like someone used to dealing with frightened children. Had I been a frightened child, I imagine I would have been very relieved. Guess I'd just have to act a bit.

"Um . . . Alana, it's nice to meet you." I gave a nervous reply.

"Well, Alana, I'm going to take you somewhere where you'll be safe until we can find your family okay?" She reached out a hand.

"I was . . . going to go and try to find some work in a tavern or something." I explained the gist of my plan to her, keeping my hands back.

"We can discuss that later." That sounded suspiciously like a no.

I considered for a few moments the potential repercussions of telling her to take a hike. Then I got up and followed. I knew that at the very least I'd be safe if I went with her, and safe was something I'd not been too much recently. I pointedly didn't take her hand, which got me a scolding frown.

She took me through the city; it was called Istlan. It was very much like Hazelwood. We went up toward what I guessed would be the edge of the merchants' district, near the entertainment district, until we came to a large gray building.

Unlike many of the temples and churches on Earth, this place was almost austere. It could have been any public works building, save for the Shield icons on the doors and a small sign near the entrance. Once inside, she took me over to a smallish hall and gave me a little bowl of thin soup.

"So, how did you come to Istlan, Alana?" That seemed an innocuous question. It also gave me a good chance to badmouth the people who'd taken me from my home.

"I was kidnapped and escaped."

"I don't suppose you've any proof?"

I undid the buttons keeping my sleeves in place and rolled them up. Her eyes furrowed deeply when she saw the rope burns from where I'd been bound for around a week.

"I would like to know who did this to you." Her voice sounded as if she were trying to contain her anger at this point.

"A group of soldiers. They wanted someone to heal them in case they got hurt."

"Were these men soldiers of the kingdom?"

"It sounded like they were in personal service to a noble." That much was the truth. I could tell it wasn't a truth that would make this woman happy though.

"Will you behave and eat your soup while I go and speak to some people?" Her voice was sickly sweet. Even I could tell that this was more of a command.

"I-I can do that." Something about the way she went from looking mad to looking almost saccharine made every hair on my neck stand up.

I did munch on the soup after she left, staying where I was as I'd been bid. It was some kind of light broth with barley and small chunks of vegetables. For a meal, it would be considered quite poor, but there was a food shortage. I really liked it as it was a refreshing change from bread.

Abigail returned not too long after with two others. A male caster, who I assumed was another priest, and a woman. The woman was not a magic user but had a matronly look about her. I had little doubt that she could organize any group to within an inch of their lives.

"This is Father Mannory and Gabbi. They work with me here, and we'd like to hear your story from the beginning."

CHAPTER 18

◆

THE ORPHANAGE

The priests and their helper wanted the full rundown, and I was all too happy to give it to them. Well, mostly, I did leave out the part where I helped kill a whole bunch of the kingdom's soldiers and our mayor. Instead, I simply described that there had been a bunch of fighting.

I was asked about the names of the major people in town. I happily gave them, including Rosk, the priest who was staying there. I could easily describe him and his aura. I knew they were getting all of this so they could check and see if I was who I said I was.

When we got to my kidnapping was when they really leaned in. Father Mannory, who I supposed was higher ranked than the other two, was particularly interested. He grilled me. He wanted to know each soldier's name, a description of their aura as best I could, along with their person. I even had to repeat out as many of Gwenna's titles as I could. I had to admit to them that I'd not really paid attention, and we hadn't talked except for her to confirm that I'd been the one to heal her.

"So you were treated like that even after you'd helped her before?" Father Mannory was tapping his fingers. They came down in a wave *ta-ta-ta-tap*, his nails were loud against the table.

I nodded.

"Did you meet anyone else when you went to heal her? Anyone of her house?"

"I saw her father briefly and a steward. The steward was nice enough."

"Can you give me a description of the steward?"

"No . . . that was a couple of years ago, I remember that he was nice, but not much else."

He nodded. Then he had me go over everything that happened while I was being held. Gabbi was making a few notes on the people, places, and the like. The other two just listened, asking for details that they could confirm.

Eventually, we'd finished. It had taken the better part of the morning. I was exhausted at this point and had other things I wanted to do before I went to sleep. At the end, the priest healed my hands with a wave of his own. It would have taken me a few moments to do that, but he made it look effortless.

"I hate to tell you this, but they will not be prosecuted by the law for what they did to you." Father Mannory seemed a bit irritated by that fact.

"I didn't really expect it." It was a depressing fact that nobles could get away with almost anything.

"If we'd caught them in the act . . . That would be a very different situation. Without that though, there is little that can be done within the law."

"Within the law?" That seemed a strange turn of phrase.

"Oh yes, there's not much the courts will do. I can, however, see to it that every order, every priest, and every bard around knows that the Hazelwood family condones the kidnapping of healers, even child ones, after I confirm your story of course."

"Of course. It is true though." I had given him more than enough to figure that out.

"I completely believe you. Once it is confirmed, I doubt they'll be able to find anyone to fix so much as a scratch for them." His smile was vicious, almost enough to make my hair stand up. He gave me an appraising look. "Lord Hazelwood has caused problems for our order before with his poor behavior. This, however, is beyond the pale. If he and his house cannot behave in a manner fitting their station, they will not have any aid in keeping it."

I already knew not to tick off these guys, but I now mentally underlined and bolded that statement.

He saw my look and let his face soften, patting me on the head. "Now go with Gabbi to get a bed set up for your stay. Lunch is not far off."

"Um, I was going to go and find a place to work at for the winter, so I could rent a room."

Father Mannory gave me a questioning look. "Would you not stay here? The orphanage will take care of you, at least until we can find your family."

I shook my head. "I need some money to send a messenger back home. I also want to buy a few things here and there."

"You are an unattended child, with no family here in the city. I'm afraid I must insist that you remain under our protection. Even if you could make some money, with food prices and availability right now, it might very well not be enough."

"I can make my own food, and that is what I would be hired to do. While doing that, I am certain I could make enough to survive the winter." This conversation was not going where I wanted at all. I knew if I didn't change his mind I would be treated as just another orphan. If that came to pass, I might abandon the city, a daunting prospect.

He had to think about this. "The children here are allowed to do much as they please in the afternoons, provided their chores are done. If you can make food, it should be acceptable to replace cleaning duties with supplementing our supplies. I will not let you stay at a tavern, but if you wish to work at one after your morning lessons, I will permit it. Though I would like you to pick one close to our temple, and you must return before time for bed."

Now I had to be the one to think. I was sure there were a number of rules hidden in the fine print of staying here, but I was reasonably sure that they would treat me well.

"What is bedtime?" I asked.

"The eighth evening hour for a child of your age."

The day was divided into twenty hours, ten morning, and ten evening. That time was actually later than I'd want to be out.

"Okay, I can do that."

Afterward, I was led to a room I would be sharing with two other girls. As soon as Gabbi showed me my bed and the small trunk for any personal items, I promptly passed out.

I was awakened just before dinner by a girl poking me. I started and turned toward her, bolting upright.

"Where am I?" I asked, remembering just seconds later.

"The orphanage, are you new?" The girl speaking to me was about my height, her hair was jet black and fairly straight.

"Um . . . yeah, I'm Alana."

"I'm Gigi. You looked tired, but it's almost time for dinner. If you don't show up, you don't eat." She gave me a smile, reaching out her hand. "Come on, I'll show you to the dining hall."

Gigi dragged me along with her. She didn't talk much as she led me back to the room where I'd been given some soup before. Instead she led me to a seat with another girl a bit older than either of us.

"Hey, Susie, this is our new roommate, her name's Alana."

The new girl, Susie, was blond. She sat at the table with perhaps two dozen other kids. We were all packed in here like sardines. It was obvious extra benches had been added to accommodate all the children, and as more filed in, I was glad we'd gotten here well on time.

"Hi there, Alana, I'm Susie. If you need anything, or any advice, just come to me. Oh, and I'll help you trade chores for better chores in the morning, all right? Don't accept any offers until I check them over. Some of those are hard to do, and you'll want an easy one." The way she rattled that off made me sure that if I were being given normal chores and I did follow her advice, only she would be having easier chores.

"Sorry, Father Mannory already gave me mine. I don't think I'm allowed to trade."

Susie blinked. "Wait what?"

"I'll tell you later, anything else?" If she was going to be giving bad advice, I'd like to hear it now.

"Um . . . most of the girls meet up in the older girls' dorm after dinner. There's some rules, but they're not bad. Oh, we'll get some extras at the beginning of the week, cleaning supplies and the like. That's about all you need to know for the moment."

We chatted about our interests and the like over dinner. My roommates wanted to get to know me understandably, and the feeling was mutual. Nobody asked me how I'd gotten here, or what my story was. I was grateful for that and reciprocated.

Our dinner, as it was, consisted of a nice veggie soup and an apple. It was nice, even if it wasn't much. I knew this was better than many village children were getting right now.

After dinner, a few of the kids gathered up the dishes and took them off to an adjacent kitchen.

"Kitchen duty is the best. It's easy and it's short." Susie looked after them jealously. "Well, let's get off. The temple staff eat after us, so no sitting around and chatting here."

The older girls' room was close by and significantly different from our own. For one, it was way bigger, there had to be six girls staying in here. There were a few chairs and a small table. It also had a small stove on one side, wood stacked beside it. As I came in, the beds were being moved away and some blankets set out to sit on.

An older girl came up to us as we entered. "New girl, have you been told the rules yet?" She looked strict and was probably sixteen or seventeen.

I shook my head. "No, I haven't."

"It's fairly simple. Don't sit on anyone's bed or mess with their stuff. Don't make a mess. You're too young to go messing around with boys, but when you get older, there's rules for that too. Last is that everyone puts four spoonfuls of oil in the communal jar so we can run lamps at night. You won't have been given any yet, so you'll need to put eight in next week. Any questions?"

"Oil?" I was familiar enough with lamps. My family ran oil lamps, but I felt I'd need to know about the situation here.

"Yup, at the beginning of the week, you'll get a little jar that they'll put a ladle full of nut oil in. You can put it on your food for taste or use it to run lamps in your room at night. The priests like to give us some choices like that. Since we're all here together, we end up using less, but everyone who's not in the little kids' room has to put some in."

So it was a communal lighting fund. That made good sense.

"Okay, I can follow those, no problem." I agreed to the terms set. If it would make it easier to get along with people, I could manage little stuff like that.

Once that was settled, I went with my roommates to a spot they liked and started spinning some while we talked. All the girls here were doing something. A couple were making baskets. There was also a smattering of sewing, spinning, embroidery, and other handcrafts going on. One girl was even using the card-weaving thing my friend Sara had used to teach me how to make some straps.

From our conversation, I learned that all of these crafts were ways for the girls to make a bit of money at night. They had some time in the afternoon where the girls who could get one would work jobs, but these things helped supplement that income. Most of the jobs were laundry or cleaning, but two of the older girls had jobs as waitresses near the gate.

As I relaxed on the bed I was given that night, I made plans about all the things I'd need to do the next day.

CHAPTER 19

✦

RUNNING AROUND IN ISTLAN

I awoke earlier than my roommates, though not by much. Morning was a bit frantic around here. We rose early to draw water and empty chamber pots, and do a bit of basic self and room cleaning. Breakfast came next; it was similar to dinner the night before, but lighter, barely a snack. Then came lessons.

The lessons we were given were practical in nature. First came basic math and reading, simple stuff that I'd mastered quite a while ago. There was nothing more complicated than multiplication in this section, problems that everyone could do without much effort. Then the girls and boys were divided into groups and taught the basic skills that they would need for day-to-day life. For us, this covered fiber-based arts (sewing, weaving, etc.) followed by basic household budgeting and management.

This was a subject that interested me a lot. The girls here were given the responsibility of coming up with how much of any given good the temple would need for the winter for our care. Then prices for goods were provided, and we had to devise a budget. This was done by individual, dorm, and finally orphanage quantity. The teachers would look over our work and correct any mistakes they found before sending a few of the older girls out to negotiate with merchants for the goods.

It was strange to think that we were the ones in charge of the day-to-day operations. Of course, the staff was keeping an eye on our work and would step in if anything got out of hand. Still though, this was a strangely practical education.

The boys were being taught quite different things. Since there was no money to pay for apprenticeships, they were instead being taught mostly the craft of being city guards. The priests liked the idea of the children they raised going on to protect others. Everyone else liked the idea that these youths would be raised to serve the public; it was a win-win.

The boys over ten were also given combat instruction. It was deemed useful since they would be entering either the army or guard. A retired soldier had been hired to this effort, and he drilled them in the common formations and methods of fighting. It seemed common practice to begin teaching these things no earlier than ten, though this was just social convention.

I was informed that the orphanage had a few fields that we could work to learn the basics of farming. I was very glad I seemed to have missed that; harvest was a ton of work.

Most of our teachers were not priests, but rather temple staff like Gabbi. They numbered in the handful and all were quite devoted to the precepts of the order. By asking questions, I ascertained that such people were viewed well since their efforts allowed the priests to focus on the magic that helped society function. They were called acolytes, and while it was rare, some would manifest priestly magic due to the strength of their belief. That was a rarity though; most priests developed their powers while small children.

Before lunch was served, the staff ran down a list. One girl had skipped out on her chores the previous day and was taken to the front where she was given ten strikes with a cane. Her previous day's task was then added to what she'd be given today, and she was forbidden from leaving the temple until tomorrow. This was quite rare I was told, since the tasks were easy enough to do and everyone knew the punishment.

Lunch was similar in nature to the other meals. It was a slightly thicker vegetable stew, yummy, but not enough. At lunch, chores were distributed based on age on some form of a rotation. We were allowed to trade if we wanted. To do so, all parties involved simply had to tell a member of the staff after lunch. Turning them in was the same; just have a staff member check.

I took the time after lunch to do and turn in my chore. Those on cleaning duty were a bit grumpy when I asked them to sing with me, but they obliged. It was only a few moments before I'd filled up the two large baskets that were my mandated amount. It took most of my mana to do so, but other than that it wasn't too bad. Jaws dropped as I turned to Gabbi, who'd stayed behind to supervise.

"So, if I wanted to work at a tavern, which one would you recommend?" I asked.

"Was it seriously that easy for you?" She was still not quite believing what I'd done. The kids assigned to cleaning looked as if they were having a similar reaction.

"It took the majority of my mana to do that, Gabbi. It was close to the max I'll be able to do for the next hour or so, I do not consider it 'easy' at all." I glared at her. I didn't want her to increase my workload as I'd had quite enough of my nose being pushed to the grindstone, thank you.

"Right, right, The Silver Fish is just across the street. If you went down the road a little, you'd come to Haven's House; they're both pretty good."

She had recovered nicely.

"When you go to speak to someone, please take me or one of the others with you. It would be bad if you were taken advantage of."

"Okay, I'm going to go do that in a couple of hours. Would you care to join me then?" I intended to check and see some things in the market first.

"Certainly, I'll be in the girls' workroom around that time." The room she indicated was one where a few optional after-lunch lessons were held. It was also where we could go to practice things like weaving, as it had some looms.

"See you!" I waved to her as I left, hoping to escape before I was given another task.

First I went to near the gate to find a message service. It was fairly easy to locate the biggest one. They were happy to relay my letter to my family, telling them I'd been kidnapped and where I was. Unfortunately, the clerk told me there was a fair chance that it wouldn't get there in time for a response to reach me before spring. Only high priority and very expensive letters were delivered during the winter. The roads were just too cold and covered in snow. Since that service would put me straight to broke, I decided to just use the regular rate.

In the market, I used a small amount of my hidden funds to check the price of bread and replace my belt knife. A frankly pathetic-looking loaf was currently running around six copper coins. I did take the time to inquire from the merchants about the good taverns in town. Two names came up most often: Haven's House and The Tipped Bottle. The last one was out, as it seemed to be close to where the nobles lived, too far for the priests to let me go there.

"Someone told me about a place called The Silver Fish, what are they like?" I asked the smith who'd sold me my new knife.

"The food is fine, but the ale is watered a bit. The decor is also just a bit cheap. I'd go there for a meal if I wanted something quick, but I wouldn't stay there." That was a harsh review, but it told me quite a lot about the place.

"Thanks, have a nice day!" I gave the burly man a big smile as I turned to return to the temple.

Finding Gabbi was easy. She was doing some repairs on a few garments for the smaller kids when I came in.

"I've decided to give getting a place at Haven's House a go."

"The Silver Fish is closer." She obviously disagreed with my choice.

"So it is, but the owner has a reputation for being cheap. It will be better to go somewhere where the owner isn't." I honestly didn't feel like dealing with someone who didn't want to pay the proper price for things.

"Hmm, if that is your choice. Let me finish up this shirt and we'll go." It didn't take her long to fix the small rip in it. I had to stop for a moment and admire her perfect tiny stitches.

The building we approached was three stories high. Its edifice was calming, all gray stone with a small garden out front gave a good feeling of homeyness. At the same time, the high level of maintenance spoke that it was a nicer establishment. Whoever ran this place had a good eye.

Once we got inside, we were greeted by an expansive dining room with a high ceiling so that you could see some of the second story. A roaring fireplace was in one corner and it, along with a few hanging lamps, provided a warm, moderate level of lighting.

One of the waitresses came up to see us. She was in a high-cut dress whose colors were velvet brown and deep blue. It wasn't sexy like The Scarlet Harlot's staff had been, but rather looked a bit girl-next-doorish.

"Welcome to Haven's House, how can I help you today?" There was a board with a menu; it read about like I was expecting.

"I'm a bard, and I'm hoping to find a job for the afternoons, could we speak to the owner?" I would handle the negotiations, regardless of what Gabbi or anyone else thought about that.

It took a few moments before the waitress returned and led us off to a back room. There we found an older man sitting behind a large, polished desk. A few reports were scattered here and there, and ledgers sat upon the shelves behind him in neat rows.

"Welcome, I hear you're looking for a job?" The man waved us in with a smile. He had no aura that I could sense.

"Yes, I'm hoping to find a bit of work."

"I've been told you're a bard, what can you do exactly? I don't really need a healer. And as for charging magical items, that's not one we do much around here." He was at least willing to hear me out. Though from the sound of it, he didn't think he'd need me.

"I can do a few different things. For now, the most important is that I can summon bread, with the food shortages surely there's some need for that?"

"Perhaps, show me." He was clearly interested.

I conjured up a loaf about the same size as that I'd seen in the market. I will say my work was generally of a much better quality.

The owner picked it up and examined it with a keen eye. Eventually, he broke off a small piece and ate it.

"Okay, I'm interested. How much to bring you onto my staff?"

"Ten coppers a day, another six per loaf of that size you want me to make for you." The daily rate was something near what a low-cost laborer would make.

"Four per loaf, I can get basic bread other ways." His counteroffer was not too bad, but it was too low.

"Six. Six is how much a poor-quality loaf is currently costing in the market. Mine is not only better, but as winter creeps in, the cost of buying ingredients or finished products is going to increase. Add to that that, this is a restaurant, and you'll sell it for ten easily and the price it should be is six. You'll make four-copper profit for negligible effort on each one."

He looked taken aback for a few moments, then began to laugh. "You drive a hard bargain, girl. How about five?"

"Should I go to one of your competitors instead?" I asked as sweetly as I could.

"Fine, fine, six, anything else?"

Gabbi looked as if she was going to say something, but I got on that first.

"I can only work from just after lunch until dinner. Also I'd like three days a week off."

He asked for clarification, and I gave him more exact times, one that would bring me back home well before my appointed curfew. I could even squeeze into getting dinner at the orphanage if I kept to that one. The second part was slightly less than what a normal worker would do. I was a child though, so that was probably fine.

He agreed, but told me I'd have to stay in the back until I got a proper outfit. My current dress was worn and getting a bit small on me. He also wanted me to work the days he had the heaviest traffic. Both of these worked fine for me.

I was set to start the next day. When I left, I had a big smile on my face and was almost skipping down the road.

Dinner that night had an extra bit added to it, something that made everyone happy. It seemed my chore would be enough to at least help out around here, and that made me feel as if I was earning my keep.

Once I got to the after dinner meeting though, the grilling began.

"So . . . rumor has it that you can make bread with your magic?" one of the slightly older girls, a teen named Kalie came over and asked. She got a bit closer than I would have liked.

"Um . . . yeah." There was no real point in trying to hide the truth.

"You will make a bit for us after dinner right? Since we're all here working together?" she asked, eagerly pulling me against her. "I mean, we're practically family, aren't we?"

"Actually, I was going to work on something else." This did not get a positive response from Kalie.

"What could possibly be important enough to work on otherwise?" she asked as she began to squeeze my shoulders, her voice lowering dangerously.

"I wanted to learn to make cheese. Don't worry, I'll share with everyone. Once it starts to get cold, I also want to keep the room warm, that'll take a bit of my mana too."

She brightened right up. "I knew you were going to be nice to us. We'll be like sisters!"

That wasn't going to happen.

"Hey, she's our roommate! You can't go grabbing her away!" Gigi and Susie both got hold of me, seemingly determined that I should help them the most as they tried to pull me away, resulting in a tugging contest.

This winter was going to be exhausting.

CHAPTER 20

✦

MY FIRST WINTER
WITHOUT FAMILY

Working at Haven's House was wonderful, mostly because it gave me an excuse to go out during the winter and see people other than those in the orphanage. Though I will admit the pay was quite nice. I was saving it all for when I actually needed to buy something.

I ended up doing dishes for two weeks before I could order myself a new dress, then another two after that as it was made. All in all, the outfit was lovely. The cloth was a deep purple. It fit more comfortably than anything I'd owned in this world, and I loved it. I ordered a second in dark blue once the first was delivered, resolved to have some nice clothes.

I knew that back on Earth dye colors had been restricted in the past, but it didn't seem so here. Some colors certainly were more expensive, but anyone could buy and wear them. I had thought that a bit strange, but magic existing certainly did change a number of things. I would have loved some pure black outfits, but a good, solid black was the most expensive thing sold.

Around the time that my clothes arrived, snow had started to fall. My constant pestering of the messenger service I'd hired had to end then, as I knew that I wouldn't be getting anything back until spring. I was still worried about my family and about Orsken. I knew that whoever was left after the fighting was done was going to have a brutal winter. Unfortunately, I had no choice but to accept that there was nothing I could do.

Each day of winter began early. After being awakened, I'd begin by doing a bit of cleanup in our room and using my mana to get my chore done nice and early. My roommates would always badger me to make a bit more so they could have a snack, and I obliged.

After that, we had breakfast and lessons. These were much the same as they had been. Though due to the season, there was more emphasis on doing handiwork than preparation, since that was what was needed now. I was still rather enjoying these, as they were calming and quite practical in nature.

After lunch, I would often go to work. On my days off, however, I'd make some extra snacks for the boys who were training. I didn't have to do this. I was making some food for the girls at night though, so it seemed fair to me, well, close enough. After that, I'd sit around and do some spinning, or make belts like Sara had shown me.

Our post-dinner girls' hangout was about my favorite part of the day. It took me more than a week to get an edible form of cheese to summon. I had almost given up when I got something that was at least similar to a Parmesan. Getting it all to work right was an absolute nightmare. There were multiple flavors and sub-flavors, texture, water content, and all manner of other factors that had to be right on the mark for the cheese to taste right. It was also brutally mana-intensive. I could summon loaf after loaf of bread, no problem, but one or two pounds of cheese and I was spent. I suspected this had to do with how much practice I had.

I dreaded going to bed though. My sleep was plagued with nightmares of Orsken. Some nights I dreamed of the people I knew slowly starving to death. Other nights, I would see us killing the mayor and his guards over and over again. I couldn't shake the feeling of monstrous guilt for what we had done to those men, and as I saw their deaths repeated in my mind, I was horrified at my own actions. I had nobody I could talk to about this either. I didn't dare admit to anyone that we'd revolted against the king and killed his soldier; it would be a death sentence for sure. On the worst nights, all I could do was sit there and silently cry, begging for the day to come, so that I could have something, anything to occupy my mind.

Many days I had work though. I'd alternate between summoning loaves of bread and tending the tables. Our visitors were mostly locals, with a few who were staying at the tavern over the winter mixed in. Shortly after beginning to work the floor, I started to learn the regulars' names and orders. My cute appearance elicited a good amount of tips from all those who thought of me as nothing more than a very hardworking child.

I did not take advantage of the fact that I was considered an "orphan," as that seemed just too sleazy to me. The couple of times I was asked about my parents, I told people that my dad had been drafted and my mother was busy, which was the truth as far as I knew.

One day at work, I was called into the back by Mr. Haven, the owner. That was a bit odd, while he sometimes did come to the front I'd never been called to his office before. I immediately began to go over everything that had happened in the past few days, looking for something I'd done wrong.

"Ah, Alana, come in. I've got a bit of a request for you." He opened his door and motioned me to a chair. I was really glad that he didn't seem mad in the slightest. I wasn't sure if I could deal with explaining why I'd gotten fired to the temple staff. In fact, he seemed a bit nervous.

"A request?" I looked around the room for anything that seemed out of place. The only thing of note was a wooden box on his desk, about medium-sized.

"Yes, yes, bit unexpected. A business owner in town needs some tools recharged for her. Normally, she has a wizard friend who does this, but unforeseen circumstances have arisen where he's currently unavailable." He was quite vague about all of this.

"And you want me to recharge them?"

"If you can, my dear, that would be lovely. You'll get paid for this, of course. I'll see to it that you don't lose any of what you would have made because of it."

"Um . . . okay, what do they do?"

"They maintain a field around an area that keeps out the cold and keeps everyone nicely warm. You don't see such things often, but my friend's eatery caters almost exclusively to nobles. I think they find such things quaint. One can sit in the middle of a snowstorm and still feel toasty warm. Huge waste of mana if you ask me."

He took several cubes out of the box, setting them down in front of me. I hadn't seen any magical items before. The cost was just too high for most people to afford, so I studied them.

I felt myself quite irked by this use of mana. So many of the people were suffering right now because of a famine our inept leadership had caused, and they were concerned about being warm in a snowstorm? I was even more put off because they couldn't at least be bothered to recharge the damn things themselves.

I had to wonder for a moment how this country hadn't had some version of the French Revolution yet.

"So . . . do I just, shove mana into them? I've never done this before." I had a spell that did the same thing, but they were certainly convenient if they could act like a battery for that.

"That is my understanding, yes."

Experimentally, I picked one up and pushed a bit of mana into it. A few of the runes near the bottom lit up as I did so. The light crept up toward the top as more was added. I could tell when it had finished. It also left the room significantly warmer.

"Turn it off if you don't mind; just press the top there." As I did so, the central rune on the item went dark, though the others remained lit.

There were four in total, after I'd finished up the last I looked at Mr. Haven.

"There are a lot of people suffering in villages right now. Why isn't anybody doing something about it? If they can waste mana for this, they can certainly help people." Some heat had worked its way into my tone as I spoke, more than was strictly necessary.

"Girl, you have to understand. So far as nobles and the really rich are concerned, the only useful exports of those villages are food for city folk and disposable soldiers."

"What?"

He sat down, motioning that I should do the same. "Most of their food is grown on specialty farms. Most of the goods they use on a daily basis are made in cities, by expert craftsmen, not in villages."

"So what? If the villagers die, no big deal?"

"Not so far as they're thinking, no. They need numbers for their wars. Even a mage can fall to enough men, but it takes a whole lot. So they want the men for soldiers. They also know that the grain and the like flows to a lot of the city dwellers, and those city folk have to be kept happy to an extent."

"But that's insane! The taxes and everything have so many just starving to death!"

"I know it is, girl, but the villagers can't do anything about it. Most of the city folk won't do a thing about it either. Why go against a system that's working for you?"

"Won't they eventually revolt?"

"Perhaps, but what happens when they do? It's hard to bust a city without a pretty well-trained army. Even if you did, you'd have to get up to the nobles' district, and then fight all the minor nobles living there. That's a pretty daunting task for farmers. The amount of magic that could be thrown at them would cause impossible losses."

I pondered that for a bit. A region would have only one ruling family. Only one man would own the city and the lands around it, but several families of nobility might live there. These were minor nobles, one or two generations out from being married into one of these more powerful families. Those with real skill would marry back into the leading groups, while those without would slowly drift into marrying merchants, craftsmen, and the like. I'd picked up that much from conversation. I didn't know just how many there were, though it wasn't many. Nor did I know the specifics of how all this worked. It seemed that all these people could do something about the suffering around them however. They just didn't, because it didn't affect their lives.

Eventually, Mr. Haven came over and patted my head. "No need to worry about it too much. It don't help nothing anyways." He then gave me a smile. "Now! Back off to work with you, food isn't going to serve itself." I laughed as I left. He was surprisingly good at improving people's moods.

I was eight now as spring broke, bringing with it the birds and new sprigs of growth, and taking the snow away. It also meant new messages were being delivered! Several weeks in, the messenger service finally had something for me.

I was bouncing as I ran back to my room at the temple. My mood dropped like a stone as soon as I had the envelope open though. My own had been placed inside, with a letter attached.

We regret to inform you that this letter is undeliverable as the village in question has been destroyed. Inquiries at nearby towns and the city of Hazelwood do not indicate the presence of the intended recipients nor any known relatives.

I sat there completely numb, unable to process what I was going to do.

CHAPTER 21

✦

THE RETURN OF
AN OLD ACQUAINTANCE

Both Gigi and Susie were alarmed when they found me unmoving, staring out into space.

"Hey . . . Alana, you okay?" Gigi spoke hesitantly, seeming to sense something was wrong.

"A-ah, I just . . . need a bit . . ." I had no idea how long I had sat there trying to think of anything.

"Want us to come get you at dinner?" Susie was peering at me nervously.

"Yeah, sure." I went back to reading the letter over and over again. I was trying to find something to bring me some hope, to tell me what had happened or where my family was. There was nothing.

I was still a bit numb when they came to get me. I ate dinner mechanically, rebuffing all attempts at conversation. That night, I skipped our normal evening gathering, instead returning to my room to be alone and think.

My family weren't confirmed dead. That was important. Similarly, my dad was out there, somewhere. I needed to find out if Mom and John had made it, or alternatively find Dad and Mystien. If I could do neither of these things . . . I didn't know. I was hesitant to stay here at the orphanage, but there was something important.

They needed help here. Frankly, I couldn't abandon them, not after everything. I had some people here who I could at least nominally call friends. This famine was also getting worse the longer the war dragged on. It just didn't feel right to go until I knew that that at least was sorted. I already had dreams of starving villagers; nightmares of starving orphans would only make it worse.

I also needed to consider if my family would be able to find me. The odds on that weren't good, but I didn't know what to do about that right now. Perhaps I could contact someone who knew them well and tell them to let my family know if they ran into them? Would that work? Maybe, but the list of people who might know that I knew of was short.

Jackson perhaps, he'd trained me for a bit and if I could find him he might run into them somewhere, but he was a flight risk anywhere he went. I had no contact with Veska. I could go see her, but that would take me back into Hazelwood, not a great prospect. She'd also absolutely demand some form of payment, who knows what? Mystien mentioned a friend of his in the capital too . . . What was his name? Lucien, yeah he owned a tavern or something. He might have a way to contact someone. They weren't great leads, but they were leads.

Perhaps the priests could help. I might guess that the village priest Rosk knew something, if he was alive. I could go ask Father Mannory to try and contact him, but I wasn't sure how that would go down. The worst he could say was no, and it was the easiest lead. That sounded good, I'd speak to him after dinner.

Making it through the next day was a real struggle. All I wanted to do was finish so that I could get back to the temple and accost a priest. Was that too much to ask? You'd think not, but with spring, the taverns were getting absolutely swamped, and I was run ragged the whole afternoon. By the end of my shift, I hated customers vehemently. I angrily grumbled to myself about their irritating demands as I walked back to the temple, even if they hadn't done anything that bad.

Cornering the man was a bit harder than I'd thought it would be. He was a wily sort, and seeming to know that I was looking for him and hid in his office through dinner. Or he was just as busy as I was, one of the two. Eventually though, I tracked him down and beat on the wooden door.

He popped it open, looking down at me with a quirked eyebrow.

"What brings you to see me? Hopefully, nothing bad."

"I tried to send a letter to my family back in Orsken."

"Oh? Did you manage to get hold of your family then? That's wonderful news!" He seemed genuinely happy for me. Until he saw my face at least.

"No . . . actually, the village has been destroyed. The messenger couldn't find any lead either. I was hoping . . . Um, there was a priest in the town, Rosk, is there any way you could contact him? He might know something." I looked at him hopefully, unsure of what he might be able to accomplish with his magic.

Father Mannory opened the door fully. "Come in and sit. Do you have the letter from your messenger service?"

I slipped in as he was pouring tea for us, handing over the slip of paper I'd gotten once he'd passed me the cup. He took a few moments to look over it, frowning.

"I sent someone out to get his information on your story, but my messenger hasn't quite returned yet. I'll have to look into what happened, but I imagine that Rosk is making his way back here. We are the main temple in the region, so once his assignment is done he should return."

"Why hasn't he come back then?" I asked. This was all too much. I just needed to know, needed to know if my mom and brother were all right.

"Be calm, Alana, it often takes a priest a bit of time to travel. Most towns we stop in have some need of aid, and unless we are rushing off to some emergency, we will try to provide it."

I knew I was being selfish, but I wanted to go home. Even if there was no house left, I could at least be with my family. I was desperate, almost ready to cry. If that stupid priest could just hurry up and get here, maybe I could be with Mom and John again, or at least find out if they were all right.

Father Mannory interrupted my spat of self-loathing. "Is there anyone they might have told where they went? Perhaps a cousin in a nearby town, or a friend?"

"Well, Mystien has a . . . friend, in Hazelwood, and she seemed to know Dad. I don't know if Mom or John knew her though."

He blinked. "Mystien?"

"Oh, he was a wizard who lived in our village; he trained me to do magic when I was first learning."

"You've never mentioned him before. Is there anyone else who taught you?"

"There was a bard named Jackson; he helped me learn basic healing." I hoped I wasn't giving away any secrets here.

"I see, and you said Mystien had a friend who might know something. Is there a way to contact her?"

"Oh, she owns a tavern in Hazelwood. I don't know if she'll tell me anything without payment though." I let that sentence slowly drop off. There was no chance of getting free information there.

"That would be Veska then, wouldn't it?" he asked, quirking an eyebrow.

I was legitimately surprised by that response, and my face must have shown it.

"I used to live in Hazelwood, Alana. I do know the larger business owners, at least some of them. As it stands, I've already sent a message to her asking for some details as well. If she knows anything, she might let us know."

"Oh . . . I um . . . thank you." I knew he was doing some of this for his own reasons and beliefs, but if he was willing to help me find my family, I didn't care.

Father Mannory gave me a kind smile over his tea. "I know that it is hard when people tell you to be patient. In this case though, it is best to just wait a bit. Things will come as they will, and we have more than enough problems without struggling to find something that is likely already coming to us."

"Yes, Father Mannory." I wasn't much for platitudes, but I had to admit he was probably right here.

"Now, run along. I'm sure the other girls are eagerly waiting for you to bring them some extra snacks."

I flushed red. I hadn't been hiding it precisely, but I was being quiet about making extra food for us. "Um . . ."

"I'm not angry, Alana, but the boys might be a bit cross if they find out. So do try to keep it quiet." He waved me out and I skedaddled. We both had a bit of work to do before morning apparently.

That night, in our normal after-dinner gathering, I got promises from the girls to not tell the boys about the extra food. Adding threats that it might dry up if they found out.

One day as the spring went on, slowly making its way toward the heat of summer, I was working the counter when a familiar figure walked into the door of Haven's House. The owner had joined me at the counter that day, and he looked up too, smiling.

"Jackson! How wonderful to see you again. Welcome to Haven's House." My slightly energetic greeting made Mr. Haven turn to me and cock an eyebrow.

"You two know each other?" he asked, seemingly surprised.

"Nope, no idea who the kid is," Jackson replied smoothly.

"We met a couple of years ago. You came to give me some 'special training.'"

"Wait what!?" Mr. Haven's face immediately turned to the new-coming bard, hardening like stone.

"Whoa, kid, no, no, that never happened!" Jackson stammered, looking a bit afraid at the tavern owner's glare.

"What? Yeah it did, in Orsken, you were there with me for three days." I was probably playing this up a bit more than was totally proper, but . . .

At this point, my boss was pulling out the overly large stick he kept beneath the counter to deal with rowdy customers. "I knew you were a bad egg you little pervert, but a kid?"

"Hey, wait, you know me, Haven, I would never." He was almost to the door at this point.

"Yup, Mystien called you in to teach me to heal people, don't you remember? You stayed with him and helped with his lessons."

Both men stopped at this point and looked over at me. It was obvious from my mischievous grin that I'd been messing with both.

"He's a nice guy, Mr. Haven. His techniques even helped save some people."

They were both now giving me unamused looks.

"Wait . . ." said Jackson, looking at me intently. "I remember you; you're that kid the old man wanted me to train."

"Seriously," my boss said. I couldn't help but laugh at his deadpan delivery. "Go do some dishes, kid, before I decide to tan your hide." Giggling as I retreated, I fled to the kitchen.

Jackson ended up taking a room here. There was plenty of work for him in town, so he didn't really need a job. It was a few days before I managed to get a chance for a conversation with him. I was quite eager, but giving him a bit of time to cool off seemed the wise choice.

"Hi again!" I plopped down beside him where he sat eating an early lunch.

"Here to accuse me of more impropriety?" Jackson glared at me. It would seem he was still a bit sore about that.

"Not at all. I just wondered if you'd mind answering some questions for me."

He sighed. "Are you going to pester me until I do?"

"Most probably yes."

"Fine, ask away then." He seemed a bit tired already.

"Do you know where Mystien went?"

"If I had to guess, he's at home in your village. What in the world are you doing out here anyway?"

"Nope, Orsken's gone. Before you ask, no I don't know exactly what happened, I got kidnapped."

He froze and looked at me, blinking.

"Gone? What do you mean gone? How could a village be gone?"

"Gone as in destroyed. From the sounds of things, someone burned it to the ground."

"With that old codger and your pops there? Who would burn it? An army?"

"Nope, my dad and Mystien disappeared when they got called up for the draft. Do you really not know where they ran off to?"

"I'm . . . sorry, kid, but I don't. I've been staying off of Hazelwood land for a while now. The lord was getting pushier and pushier about wanting healers after the Shield left." He leaned back and stretched, looking a bit put off by that fact.

"I'm aware; his daughter's guards were the ones who kidnapped me." I got the chance to deadpan this time.

"Bold choice on them, most priests would go absolutely crazy if they saw that."

"Yup, it was a bad plan on their part, but that's not important. What is important is me finding my people, any ideas?"

"Can't say I do, kiddo. You could put out some feelers, but other than that, just go find some of their old friends. They might get a letter or something one day. You want anything else?"

"In fact, I do. I need to learn to fight. Being a bard, I'm guessing you know all the best tricks we can do in combat, and I'd like you to teach me."

That got him laughing again. "Now that might be the most interesting thing I've heard all week."

CHAPTER 22

✦

WORK AND TRAINING

Jackson agreed to teach me a bit about fighting as a bard, on the condition that I help him with his work. We decided that half of my days off would be helping him, and on the other half, he would help me. Though he argued that since helping him might act as training, it was all helping me.

Our first day working together was simple enough. We met at the tavern at my normal work time to go about his business.

"You're late," he said as I walked in.

"I'm perfectly on time. This is when I start work."

"Really? Huh, I thought it was earlier; no matter though. Let's be off." With that, he rose and led me off into the streets.

"So . . . what are we doing? Making food? Or healing people?"

"Hm? No, no nothing like that. We'll be filling up some magic items. With the Shield having such a large presence here, we're not currently needed as healers. While food isn't a bad idea, I'll get paid a lot more for using mana to recharge items."

"Really? I mean, what kind of items do people use? Nobody in my village ever had stuff like that."

"Larger businesses and nobles use magical items to some extent. There are a great number of different kinds, but most of what we'll be doing is household items. On a noble estate, these would often be recharged by the lesser members of the house. As the number of people called off to war has culled that down, we'll be doing it instead."

"Are you sure this will be the best way to make money? I make pretty good at the tavern."

"Very sure. Working at a tavern is a good job, but nobles pay big money to not be inconvenienced."

"So . . . okay." I wasn't actually sure what to say to that, at least without badmouthing the nobility in the middle of the street. "You just need me to push mana into them then, that's it?"

"It would be nice if you could act all polite and stuff, too, but basically yes. Oh, and don't get too involved. They're always looking to pick up potential spouses for the children of branch families, or lesser sons. You want no part of that, so don't talk too much about yourself. Tell them I'm your teacher and leave it at that."

"Oh, so maybe I could go and join up with a noble family and be all fancy and stuff." You could practically feel the sarcasm in the air.

"Don't even joke, kid. In your position, they'd treat you like a battery that could pump out babies and nothing else. You'd be treated like garbage, and if you ever weren't useful enough, you'd be tossed out like it too." For once, he looked serious. There was something to that look; if he wore it more often, he might seem like a decent guy.

"Message received; I'll not make any overtones to it."

He stopped as we arrived at a big mansion, giving me a few pointers about etiquette as we walked. I'd covered most all of this in my training with Mystien, so no big deal so far.

A maid greeted us at the door, giving us a wide smile.

"How can I help you today?"

"I'm Jackson, and this is my student. We're here to top off some items."

The woman seemed to be expecting us. "Oh yes, right this way please."

She showed us to a large entryway where we recharged magical lights. This was our first task, and it was a simple one. These little sconces looked like crystals set into the walls, and the amount of mana they used was apparently just tiny. Working together, we had them done in only a few minutes.

Afterward, we were escorted to various places around the house. Heaters like those I'd filled with mana before were common in parts of the house, as were water heaters for the bathrooms and a large walk-in fridge. The kitchen even had a small item that would purify water for drinking.

All of these had to be refilled on a weekly basis I was told. While they were certainly useful, none of these were really necessary for anything. I would have guessed that there were more and more powerful items around, but we had no business with those.

When we were finishing up, another maid came to join us. She brought a bag of money for Jackson, which she slipped into his hand with a salacious smile. I could see just the barest hint of aura about her. It was properly formed, just extraordinarily weak.

"Thank you so much for your help. My lady wished me to tell you that you were welcomed to come back anytime. I would so like to see you return, since you've been such a big help."

She was practically cooing. I thought I was going to barf.

"Well, it is good to be found useful. Unfortunately, I've other duties to attend to today, so I must bid you farewell." I realized quickly that he was being careful not to agree to anything.

The maid led us out without another word, giving only a small wave at the door.

On our way to the next house, I had to ask. "Did she just . . ."

"Oh yes, that maid is probably a few generations out from anyone with real ability. She's hanging on to the barest thread of mana. You saw that, didn't you?"

"Yeah, I've never seen an aura that weak."

"She was trained to use magic. If I had to guess trained quite hard, but she has no talent for it at all. That's why she's a maid now; she can use what paltry mana she has to recharge items like we were, or, I don't know, draw a bath. That's going to be about her limit though, and it's one she won't ever surpass."

"That's sad. So she was trying to get all friendly with you because what? She wants a husband with stronger mana?"

"She wants children with stronger mana," he corrected. "I, on the other hand, want nothing to do with the politics."

Jackson had a good aura. He was stronger than me, but not by much.

"So you'll turn her down?"

"That depends on what she wants, Alana. I won't be taking her as a wife, that much is for sure. I am quite sure that I've fathered a number of bastards though, making another won't bother me in the least."

"That seems a bit . . . immoral." My face made clear my opinion on the matter.

"Don't look at me like that. The children are all well taken care of. I do make sure that I'm not dumping them on poor commoner girls. The mothers also know exactly what the arrangement is. For something like that, everyone needs to agree, and they need to know what they're agreeing to."

"I suppose that's not too bad then. It's just kind of wrong that you don't take care of them, isn't it?"

"A large number of men have little to nothing to do with raising their children. Having a father around is ideal, but that woman doesn't really want me. She wants my mana, and perhaps my kids. I don't like being where I'm not wanted."

The morals here were just too different. I'd been fairly against things like that in my last life, so the idea of a father intending to make a kid and bolt just sat wrong with me. Even in our village, the idea of a father not wanting to take care of his kids would have been heavily frowned upon. At the same time, Jackson had a point. If he wasn't wanted or needed, why stick around? I did know at least that that wasn't the arrangement that I'd ever want. So I decided to drop the subject.

Our process repeated itself twice more. One more woman hit on him. One wanted to introduce me to her son. I was quite thankful when my companion deftly pulled me away.

I fell into bed that night, exhausted from the day's activities. It wasn't hard work exactly, but dealing with the nobility and their personal staff was tiring to no end. I looked forward to when I could get my training, when I would finally be able to protect myself. Those were my thoughts as I drifted off to sleep.

It was a few days later that Jackson and I met at the courtyard behind the inn. It was out of the way enough that we could easily train without having to leave the city.

"Okay, kid, what do you know about fighting?" He had a few things in a bag, but wasn't telling me what all they were.

"Um, not much. Hit the opponent with a scream spell then stab them with a knife. That's what I've been doing up till now."

"That's not a terrible plan to be honest. What other spells do you have?"

I ran through the list of my spells, bread, cheese, water/ice summoning, the light spell, the warming one, the scream one, of course, the movement spell, and finally, the healing magic he taught me.

"You could use ice to set up traps, but your main attack is the scream. As for a knife, it's only good against opponents who aren't armored, ones who require something a bit different," he said as he pulled what looked like a stick with a lump of cloth on the end out.

"Um?"

"A mace is easy to carry, easy to use, and hurts like a monster when hit by one. It's also good against people in armor." He passed me the mace and took another out of his bag to show me some swings.

"First though, I want you to point your scream spell at the wall over there and show me what it's got." He pointed to a spot about ten feet away.

I let loose hard against the piece of stone; the grass even moved a bit as it struck. Jackson took a few moments to let his ears stop ringing.

"You need to focus that, hitting your allies is not acceptable. You've got plenty of power in it, but it's way too wide. Nobody outside of your target should hear more than a yell."

First he showed me. Setting up a little cloth standard that he made fly back as he yelled at it. I heard nothing but him hollering. Then he came in and made a few adjustments to my visualization and targeting. It turned out that I needed not just to focus on adding power to my voice, but also pulling all of it into a direction, like a spotlight. Once I had that down, it came together without too much trouble.

From there, he had me practice with the mace. We went back and forth, with him pushing hard the idea of combinations of strikes and changing rhythm. I was sweating hard by the time my mana had recovered.

He ran me back and forth through these two drills until I just about dropped.

"The most important thing to remember is that you are not the front-line fighter. It's good to have a few well practiced strikes, but against some-one who's skilled those won't help. Your scream should be able to pull a knight down for long enough for you to hit him, but a wizard or priest will always out range you, and their attacks are deadly."

"Okay, so . . . try to avoid fights?"

"Of course, you should avoid fights; that's a given. You're learning this so that you can protect yourself in a worst case, or while traveling. You belong nowhere on a battlefield."

"All right, I don't want to get into fights anyway. So about the mace, do I summon one or something?"

"You've never tried to summon rocks or metal before, have you?"

I shook my head. I had been focused on food.

"For whatever reason, minerals, metals in particular, are unbeliev-ably hard to summon. The rarer metals are the hardest. I don't know why. Some sages have suggested that it's something to do with their structure; others say that it's because of their relative rarity. For us though, it doesn't matter."

"What about a wooden one?" That seemed like a viable option.

"You could do that, and it would cost lots of time and mana to make. It would be useless in battle, and there are easier ways to get firewood."

"So just buy one?"

"Yup, if it really comes to that, you could probably make something out of ice that would hurt. We're going to use that one a little different though."

After a few more rounds of practice, he sent me off. I was physically beat this time as well as mentally. It seemed I'd signed up for a very hard course in combat. I hoped that would mean I would be useful at it.

We went through the summer, practicing various techniques. Once I had those basic elements, I had to scream at a target, then run in and hit it with a series of strikes. His next tactic was to make a thin sheet of ice on the ground while my opponent was distracted by being blind and deaf. He even went over some basic knife-fighting moves. He was clear, however, that that wasn't really his forte.

During the last few weeks of summer, he went over what he felt was the most destructive idea he'd had: group casting the scream. According to Jackson, he'd had to actually use this once or twice. Even with just the two of us, the results were shocking. It went from a stun only to a mid-range spell that could send out a shock wave, throwing our cloth target into a wall hard enough to bust open the fabric.

"It still won't kill a man, but it'll really hurt."

"You don't have to tell me. I can imagine it."

"With that now down, it is my opinion that you know enough for the time being. I will be heading somewhere else now, to seek a new fortune. Keep practicing and one day you'll be strong, or at least strong for a bard."

He left that afternoon, walking off into the sunset.

The next day at work was when the angry men started showing up. We had three after his hide by the time I left to go home.

VESKA EMERGENCY MEETING

An urgent knocking woke me from what was a rather lovely dream.

"Who is it?"

"It's me, ma'am, urgent report for you."

I could hear the stress in the familiar tones.

That was interesting. It was seldom that Sean, my hired hand, woke me. It was far more odd for him to actually have any note of urgency to his voice. With a wave and a bit of power, I released the lock on the door, allowing him entry.

"Now, now, what's gotten you so worked up?" I held out my hand for the report. It wasn't long, a single sheet that took me less than a minute to read.

Then I reread it, three times. I couldn't believe what I was seeing here. I blinked and rose, heading to the closet. If this was true, then I needed to move now.

"When did this come in, Sean?" I asked as I opened the closet doors. The dozens of outfits lining the walls shook as I hastily flipped through them.

"When the gate opened. Looks like the messenger was waiting for it so he could get to you first thing."

The aide followed me. He was one of the few who might be allowed into one of my most private domains.

"Good for him. Do we have confirmation on the source?"

"No doubt, ma'am, the Shield is certainly spreading it."

"I can hardly believe it. Does anyone else know?"

"I doubt it. What should we do?"

"Send out a request for a meeting with all the major businesses. Make it a lunch and mark it as urgent. Also, pull our asset out of Hazelwood's manor; have her sent out of the region if need be."

My aide bowed and left as I put on a rather more conservative dress. It was a lovely black one with red embellishments. While almost no skin was showing, it still hugged me tightly from the high collar to the waist.

I let my hand linger on a personal favorite outfit that hung nearby. That tiny red silk number had never failed to get the desired result. Sadly, this day was not a day for pleasure, but a day to prepare for war.

Leaving my quarters, I headed toward my office. There was an immense amount of paperwork in the various drawers that had to be pulled out and prepared for my upcoming meeting, as well as a few files that I'd be bringing along for additional purposes.

One of the back rooms of The Scarlet Harlot was a place set aside for large gatherings. Business, weddings, the odd orgy, all had occurred in this room. It was well appointed with lush red carpets around a sizable table.

The last to arrive was the representative of the magical item shops. There were only a few in town, and their leader was an aged man with a beard. He looked almost stereotypical for a wizard, but it fit his profession.

"Now that we're all here, Veska, can you tell us what was so urgent?" The first to barge in was the leader of the merchants, Joy, a thin, severe woman.

"Certainly. The Order of the Shield has begun spreading rumors that the Hazelwood family is so desperate for healers that they're kidnapping those they find, including children."

The silence was absolute, stretching on for several moments. Everyone looked stunned, a few had to take a moment to rub their temples.

"Is it true?" A portly man, Sal, one responsible for food distribution, was the first to recover.

"It does not matter if it is true." That came from the nominal representative of the artisans. The man was a smith and looked as if he could bend metal with his bare hands.

"Of course, it matters!" responded the merchant.

"No, it really doesn't. If you care though, I believe they've done the checks on this. They don't act without a solid foundation, not for this." I knew for a fact that they'd been asking about Hazelwood's movements. The requests on when his daughter had left to flee back from the advancing front, and the composition of her personal retinue probably related to this incident.

"Do forgive me, but what effects will this have? The Shield hasn't sent anyone to the city in a couple of years now, and we've made it through that." The one who piped up this time was a reserved-looking middle-aged woman. You would never know from the look of her that she ran the city's gambling halls.

I could answer this one in a way she would understand best. "They have not, but this will keep all priests out. It will also drive bards to avoid the region like a plague. There are few healers here now, and those anywhere on Hazelwood's lands will likely disappear when they hear of this. It will mean that getting magical healing will be impossible or very nearly so."

"So they're ordering our city abandoned of healers? Isn't that an act of war or something?"

"No, because it's not an order. Even more so, while we can 'know' it's them spreading the information, you'll have a hard time proving it. Even if you could prove it, nobody would care."

"Perhaps we could hire freelancers? There must be some who would go against them," Sal asked.

"Normally, there would be. But with the current circumstances, they were already at a premium. I can get perhaps two. In a city this size . . ."

I had nothing to help that, not at this point at least.

"Can we get them to rescind this? To stop declaring the city as an enemy?" It was the artisan's turn.

"Not so long as the current baron or any of his immediate family rules," Joy answered for me.

"So this will be long-term then?" the smith asked, looking around at the rest of us. There were nods everywhere. "Should we worry about the men in the army? Will this fall on them too?"

"It might," I answered. "Save for the fact that the war will be over before fall hits fully. It's proven too costly as it is. One more harvest that can't be brought in would push both sides too far economically. Negotiations have likely already begun on that front."

"That's the best news I've heard this year. So if there's no undoing this until Lord Hazelwood and his men are gone, do you think he'll just kidnap healers now? If he's already being punished, there's no reason he shouldn't." The man really should just stick to working metal.

"I would wager that if more reports like this reached the priests our esteemed baron would die of some fast-acting illness within a month."

The big man looked stunned. "Now, I know those lads don't take much in the way of violations of their sanctuaries, but are you telling me they'd just kill the man?"

Joy looked at him with pity. "There have been a number of times where leaders have openly flaunted their rules. The fact that leaders tend to die of illnesses easily cured by magic not long after violating a major order's mandates is why the different orders hold so much power. The second part, if true, is also important. There might be some pushback if he were using a criminal, or some drafted soldier, but a child? Nobody would lift a finger to save him."

There was a little bit of back and forth on options. Truthfully, there was little that could be done, other than abandon the city or move assets out of it. The only reason I'd told them was to minimize the damage when it all got out to the general public. I'd worked too hard to build up my home in this place to just throw it all away, so I at least would be staying. Several of those at this meeting though, and a number of the lesser nobles in town, would definitely not.

Back in my office that night, I went over the last of my work. There were still a few reports that were bothering me a bit.

I was guessing that the kidnapped healer was Mystien's apprentice. She'd been reported missing right after that group of guards had passed through her doomed little village. I also felt that even where she was when I met her, she might have been able to give some meathead knights the slip.

Far more bothersome were the other reports of missing people. From here and there, people had been vanishing into thin air. This was from both our country and the Ermathi side. A few whole units had turned into mist as far as I could tell. The number of magic users among the missing was also far too high, and almost all of them were from villages. These people were almost certainly targeted. I was at a complete loss as to why or how this was all being done, but the numbers looked to be in the low thousands. Something unusual was on the horizon, that much was sure.

By the time I found my bed that night, I was thoroughly exhausted. Hopefully, the days when the worst thing going on was a small argument between rich families would return soon.

CHAPTER 23

◆

PEACE AND THE OPEN ROAD

It was on a bright and sunny day as summer faded to autumn that the word was sent out. Messengers had run all through the city declaring the fact; the war was over. I was working this day and many came by the tavern to drink in celebration of this occasion.

They were not celebrating because we had won. From all reports, it had been practically a stalemate; the borders barely changed. Rather, everyone knew that with the end of this fight, that much of the suffering of the past few years would fade. Their sons, husbands, fathers, and brothers would soon be returning. I saw old men weep tears of joy that their beloved sons would be coming home. Women jumped and danced in the streets because their husbands would soon again embrace them.

Haven frantically tried to purchase as much food and alcohol as he could from any merchant that would answer him. Istlan was a bit back from the front lines, but we were situated on a main road that many would be taking to return to their homes further west. We had little time to prepare before the first wave of returning soldiers would pass by. Knowing such a group would desire food, drink, and women, every business involved in such things was trying to gather all the resources they could for the inevitable horde.

Even in the temple, there was some amount of celebration. Around a third of the children here had some relative who was in the army and would certainly come get them when it was all over. Susie purchased a bit of honey with her saved pocket change and shared it with Gigi and me that night. It was a bit nostalgic since I'd had none in Istlan, and the taste of honey on toast was a refreshing change.

As I munched on the sweet treat, I thought of my own kin. I had no idea where my family had gone, so there would be no happy reunion for me. I'd only known a few relatives here anyway, but the fact that they were all now missing was rough. I longed to see my mom and dad, to eat around a table with them as a happy family once more. I briefly even thought of what would happen to the men of Orsken. Did they know? Had anyone told them the village was gone and the people scattered? There was nothing I could do at present, so I tried to put it from my mind.

It took a couple of weeks for the first group of men to come by. That day, every tavern in the city filled within hours; fortunately, I had the day off. I stood by the gate as they approached, some thousand men passing through before heading west to their homes.

They looked a bit strange to me. Some were obviously in good spirits, laughing and cheering with their friends and the small crowd that had gathered upon hearing of their approach. Others though looked tired and sad. More than a few looked broken, their eyes like something I'd seen in photos of soldiers on Earth. These were not glorious victors, returning home to cheers. Rather they were men who'd been in a war they never wanted, eager to be home and done with all of it.

"Meline?" I heard one of the men call out, apparently recognizing someone.

I yelped as an arm wrapped around me from the side, pulling me in close to someone I didn't know. It took me only a second to turn around and let loose a harsh scream onto the person, an act that seemed to alarm those around me.

"What was that?"

"An attack?"

Several men turned to look at the two of us as I hopped back and drew my knife, looking toward the soldier who'd nearly picked me up. A few came close, looking between the two of us.

"What happened?" A man who seemed to be a leader among this group stepped forward. He seemed to be the one in charge of this unit.

"He grabbed me." I pointed to the man who was still trying to recover from my point-blank attack.

After several moments, he could finally stand up and process again. The leader stepped forward and looked at him harshly.

"What's with grabbing the kid?"

The man who'd took hold of me looked at me for a few seconds before he blushed red. "I . . . I thought she was my Meline for a moment, I'm sorry."

Several of his friends looked at him with a mix of irritation and pity. "Your kid has to be three years older than this girl and is back home," one of them pointed out.

"I'm really sorry for that."

He bowed his head, and I nodded back as his friends drug him off.

Their leader came over to me after the others had left. "I'm really sorry, kid. Poor guy's been worried sick about his daughter, and you really do look a bit like her."

"He still shouldn't go grabbing people," I pouted.

The man chuckled a bit. "True, true, I'll talk to him later. Nice shot on him though, you dropped him like a stone."

"Mmm." I truthfully hadn't had time to go all out, so the power was lacking. I was not about to let this guy know that had I not been so surprised I would have likely rendered his friend at least partially deaf.

He patted me on the head, much to my chagrin, before turning to join his companions.

It took several weeks for the men of Istlan to be sent home. While there were a few nights of celebration as the different groups came in, there just wasn't time for too much of that. The men immediately jumped into helping with the harvest, making sure that it got brought in properly and without any issues for the first time in years.

When Susie was picked up by her dad and I could finally see the prices of bread going down, I knew that the famine was finally ending. That led me back to my previous decision though. I liked the priests here, but I had no intention of remaining in the orphanage until I was of age. I considered these things one day while working. Even my work here would soon change; bread was no longer such a prime good, and I would wager I had less than a month before Mr. Haven wanted to renegotiate the terms of my employment.

"You look like someone who's got a lot on their mind," a man at the bar said as I got around to cleaning that part.

"Yeah, the famine is finally ending here, isn't it?" I pointed out.

"Sure is, but that's not a bad thing. With everyone coming home, we finally get a break."

"I know, but it'll mean things change."

"Things are always changing, kid. Some are for the better, some for the worse, but always do things change."

"I wonder what will come next," I mused.

"Winter," he said, "after that spring, as the whole cycle starts again. Though everything will be locked down for winter first."

I nodded. Winter was indeed coming, only a few weeks out now. With that, I made my decision, I'd be leaving, just after I got my preparations done.

It didn't take me long to buy basic traveling provisions, I also grabbed a set of boy's clothing in my size. People would be less prone to worrying about a boy in my experience than a girl, and it would help to throw off any attempts from the priests to follow me.

I made up two letters. The first was to Mr. Haven, to tell him I was leaving. Then one to Father Mannory, saying basically the same, and that I was sorry but I wanted to be on my way. I hoped that the priest would understand, even if he was pissed about it. As I wrote those letters, I came to the realization that I was really leaning into the bad reputation that bards had for being complete flakes.

The merchant areas near the gate were the place to go. They would post notices of where they were headed, and if they wanted any passengers. That was not an uncommon thing; it gave the merchants a bit of extra cash and filled up any empty cargo space.

A merchant caravan was leaving to the capital not three days after I'd made my decision. They were allowing some passengers to travel with them. So after breakfast that morning, I made my way over to them. I had my bag stuffed with some dried meat and fruits, with my dresses stuffed into the bottom to make it look very full of provisions. I'd finally purchased a small mace, which hung from my belt by a leather strap.

The proprietor was easy to find; a few questions to workers led me right to him.

"Excuse me, sir, I understand you're headed to the capital?" I was going to go with a slightly higher-class accent than I normally used in the hope it would make things easier.

"Sure am, kid, we're leaving in an hour. Why?"

"I'd like to get a spot as a passenger if that's at all possible."

"Just you? Where are your folks?" He was suspicious, which was fair I suppose. A kid traveling alone was odd.

"Just got word my dad's not coming back from the war, but I've an uncle in the capital. I'd rather stay with him than be alone." It was a simple enough story, if not a true one. I'd wanted to see the capital for a long time, and I knew that Mystien's friend lived there. If I couldn't find him, then I'd be about in the same place I was now, so that seemed the best bet.

The man gave me a hard look. I couldn't tell if he believed it or not, but he nodded. "Sorry to hear it, kid. Price is fifteen silver coins, for a full gold one, we'll throw in ale and one meal a day. You're on your own for the rest of the food though."

I considered for a moment. I could easily make it without the extra food and drink. On the other hand, not taking it might be suspicious, and a bit of variety might be nice anyway. I handed over the full gold. I had a bit of leeway on my finances now. That was a large cost, but it would not be too bad.

"All right, kid, you'll be in the wagon third from the back. Like I said, we leave in an hour, if you're not here, you forfeit your spot."

"Understood, I'll be there."

It only took me a few minutes to go to a messenger service and have the letters delivered. I knew they wouldn't be out until tomorrow morning, as I hadn't put a rush on them, and that suited me just fine.

Having done that, I returned to the caravan and took up a spot in the third wagon from the back. It wasn't super spacious, and there were already a few people here. I nodded to them as I got in, setting myself up in a vacant spot along the right side.

It wasn't too long until the wagons started moving. Nobody in here with me had an aura, so I felt fairly safe. Though when the guards did their inspection of the cargo, I was careful to repress my own as hard as I could. I wanted to look like nothing more than an ordinary passenger. They were quick, comparing faces to a number of known criminals before they waved us through.

As the wagon rattled down the road, a woman across from me looked at me. She had a small child sitting on her lap, cooing up at her as the soft rocking of the slow cart lulled him to sleep.

"This is my first time traveling, how about you?" She seemed to just be making small talk.

"Hmm? No, I've been between a few cities before, first time with a caravan though."

"Aren't you nervous? I always heard that there are monsters and bandits outside of the cities, waiting to eat you up."

I tried not to giggle but made a small smile. "Not many monsters around here, not many bandits either. At least that's what my dad always said."

One of the men in the cart laughed as he heard that. "The boy's right, lass." He then turned to me. "Can't say I've seen many kids your age hauling around weapons though."

I shrugged. "A family friend who liked to travel showed me how to use it in case I got in any trouble. I'm not too worried about bandits or monsters, but I don't want to be completely helpless either."

"Oh? Going to protect us from any bad guys then, lad?" He was on the verge of a full belly laugh at that one.

"Nah, but if someone comes after me, I'll happily kneecap them before I run." Now about half the cart was snickering.

"Good! At least you're not a complete fool then. If anything does happen, let the caravan guards deal with it, lad, like you will only get in the way."

I nodded, and he patted my shoulder. As we talked a bit more about the goings-on, I looked out the back of the wagon. I got one last look at Istlan as we rounded a corner. It had been my home for a good while, but the idea of staying was stifling. I couldn't live under the rules of the priests. If it had been my family, I wouldn't have minded. They weren't the same though, while I respected them, there was no love there. Without that bond, and without obligation to help those who'd protected me . . . I had to leave, there was simply no other choice. Perhaps that's what made bards. Without strong enough bonds of love, we just wouldn't stick around. Sooner or later, the obligations and pressures would drive us to find something different.

CHAPTER 24

✦

THE CARAVAN

s our caravan crossed through the local forests, I learned that the man who'd teased me on the first day was named Sorn. He was in his mid-twenties, with long black hair and a bushy beard. Sorn was a bit of a joker, but I got the feeling that he at least meant well. He told me that he was headed to the capital in a bid to start up a new business, since the war had caused so much destruction around his home. While I never told him all the details, I did understand that to an extent. His village, much like my own, had been destroyed, but because of bandits in search of food in his case.

"I didn't think bandits were that bad though? We had a few around us, but not nearly enough to take down a village," I told him when I heard how his home had been destroyed. We were walking with the caravan for a bit. The fresh air was nice, and stretching your legs every now and then was an absolute must because of the cramped wagon.

"Normally no, they aren't, but this looked to be about fifty men who'd deserted from the army. I wasn't there, but I'm told they hit hard."

"Did they get caught?" I hated to think that such men would be wandering around still.

"Yeah, an army contingent came and hanged the lot of them. Scum like that don't stand up to much once they're against a real fighting force. Wish I'd been sent to help."

I nodded; once a group went bandit, there wasn't much else to be done with them. They couldn't really go home, as they were wanted men. I hoped my dad hadn't gone that way.

"So, you said you're going to join up with an uncle, lad?" He changed the subject rather than continue to talk about his own home.

"Yeah, Dad got called out to go to the war, and he's not come back."

"Capital's a far way to go though; no friends or the like closer?"

"One, but a neighbor tried to contact her about a year ago, and I've heard nothing. So I'm guessing that there's nothing there for me. I'd go see her, but she lives out in Hazelwood, and I'm not going there."

The story was close enough to the truth for me. I certainly wasn't planning to return to Hazelwood anytime soon.

He sucked in air at the mention of Hazelwood. "Aye, I've heard some nasty rumors about that place here recently. Sounds like the nobility there has gone nuts and is kidnapping people, so I'd not want to go that way either."

I was really impressed at how the bad rumors about them were spreading. Even the non-casters were hearing about it; that was something. "At any rate, what are you planning to do once you get up that way? You said you were starting a business?"

"Aye, lad. I'm a cobbler, best you'll ever meet. If your uncle won't take you in when we get there, you come find me. You seem a good lad, and I wouldn't have a problem taking you as an apprentice."

I smiled at his offer. I'd never need it, but he seemed genuine. "Thank you for the offer, I'll keep it in mind."

I did take a moment to look at his shoes. They certainly were nice.

"Even if I don't, I'll have to come find you for some boots at some point."

That got me a laugh, and before long we returned to the cart. This was not an enjoyable proposition for me. It was too cramped, and with too many people around for me to cast anything.

Nobody here knew I was a bard, at least as far as I knew, and I wasn't planning on telling them. There was too much mess to go with it. People would ask me to do stuff for them, expect it even, and frankly, I didn't want to. Was I being selfish and childish? Yes, I was. I would, of course, help them if they needed it, but I was just about fed up with being everyone's pocket spellcaster.

There were only a few small villages on our route between Istlan and the capital. I suspected that the leader of this crew knew he'd end up spending too much time if he went to many large cities. Regardless of his reasoning, our route steered around every other city of size until we got nearer to the capital.

Once we got too close though, that wouldn't be much of an option. The capital was huge, its lands quite a bit larger than the others. Around the capital's lands were the so-called central duchies. These were larger than the barony where I'd come from, and apparently had a lot of power in the kingdom. The dukes and duchesses who ruled there were far enough up the social ladder that I didn't need to worry about them, because we'd probably never meet.

There were several types of titled nobility in the kingdom, who all served pretty much the same role. Barons were in charge of small fiefs, perhaps one medium-to-large city, with a number of villages attached. Above barons were counts, who held a larger domain, including perhaps three cities with attendant villages. Highest were dukes, who'd be in charge of at least one major city. Dukes were generally only found at major hubs, or in the area around the capital, and were quite rare. There were a few others who had outdated titles, or had retained their titles from other lands, but these were the exception rather than the rule.

There were also a number of nobility who lived in, and mainly attended to, the capital and its immediate lands. These were generally given the title Court Baron since they held no lands of their own. Their placement in the hierarchy was unusual since they did not rule anything but were often very close to the royal family.

I knew almost nothing about the royal family. There was a king. His name was Erik III. He had at least a few children, but I had no clue who they were. I assumed he had a wife, or did have at some point, but I was unsure. Most of this also seemed unimportant for me to learn. I'd had to learn far too much about politics in my previous life, and I was frankly happy that as a non-noble, nobody cared if I knew anything about them at all.

We were still around a week out from the central duchies when I found myself one night sitting around a fire with Sorn. I'd taken to hanging around him a bit. He would often tease me, but he kept a smile on his face. Regardless of how bad things had been for him, he somehow managed to stay at least a bit upbeat. It was all quite refreshing, as I'd seen enough pained people to last me several more lifetimes.

"Hey, Sorn."

"Aye, lad?"

"You ever been to the capital before? I hear it's something to see."

"Once, when I was a lad, my old man took me along with him to work with my granddad over the winter. I'm guessing you haven't then?"

"No, I've just heard about it. Lots of stories."

"It's something. It'll be bigger than anything you've ever seen."

"Sounds like a sight." I had my doubts, this society only had so much population. I would be absolutely flabbergasted if it compared to something like a modern city.

About that time, I heard some shouting from over near one of the carts. They'd been formed in a half-circle with us up against a small cliff for protection. It looked like one was on fire. I could just see the flames licking up from the burning top.

"Sorn, fire."

He popped up, looking to the side. With a quiet *whoosh* followed by a thud, an arrow landed about five feet from us, sinking into the ground ominously.

"Bandits!" The alarm went up all throughout camp.

Sorn looked over at me. "After me, lad!" He turned and ran toward one of the carts right by the cliff. I followed after as fast as my legs could go, pounding along behind.

We ducked into the corner, trying to make sure no easy angles of attack were open. I unclipped my mace from my belt and looked about, hoping to stay well out of this fight. Sorn, for his part, pulled out a large knife, nearly a sword. The arrows were luckily all falling toward the middle of the wagons, giving us a bit of a reprieve from that.

"Stay down, lad, let the guards do the fighting." He moved like someone who'd seen a few fights. He probably had too. I assumed he'd been in the army to some extent, and the way he held himself seemed to confirm it.

"No argument here."

We were well away from the actual fight, situated as we were at any rate.

Then I saw them, a half dozen men were charging toward our position. It seemed they thought, quite accurately, that this area was less defended. Their leader was a good twenty feet in front of his men. He was much faster, and I could see his light aura shining a bit as he flew forward. His blade out as he beelined it toward Sorn.

He was upon us before I let out my scream. I hit him with the focused blast full on, laying right into his face. Physical magic or not, it hurt, and he dropped right in front of my friend. There was a satisfying crunch as I leaped forward, bringing my mace into his temple. Just as quickly I danced back, looking for his friends to sweep forward into us. I was already prepping another scream, hoping that Sorn could keep them off of me.

I was not disappointed as my cobbler friend stepped in front. He'd recovered his bearings and demonstrated how he could hold these men back. Between his front-line work and my supporting magic, two more bandits fell before the others turned and fled.

The two of us went back to huddling behind the wagon. We had nothing to do against an arrow or crossbow quarrel, so that seemed prudent.

"You're a wizard!?" Sorn almost yelled at me.

"Bard." It was a bit annoying to be mislabeled.

"Wizard, bard, whatever, can you toss a bit of fire into the tree line? Might spook them a bit."

"Uh . . . no, not really."

"Well, how about lightning? Or one of those water blasts some do?"

"Nope, my combat magic is fairly limited."

"How limited?"

"Fairly."

"Great, we just wait it out then."

I nodded; that seemed like a good idea to me.

I couldn't help but look at the body of the man I'd killed. He was decidedly dead, the strike to the skull had broken something and left a noticeable dent in the side of his head. I knew I might dream of this, but I didn't feel bad. I felt no guilt over him or any of the other bandits, they'd attacked us unprovoked and had been ready to kill. Taking them out was unfortunate, but the right course of action.

A few of the other passengers joined us not a minute or two later, seeking the same shelter from the ongoing battle.

"Do you think they'll come this way?" a woman asked.

"Hopefully not, they want the goods, not us," Sorn answered, his eyes scanning the nearby trees.

It didn't take long for the attack to stop completely, the bandits fleeing off into the nearby forest. Everyone looked confused at this. They'd taken us by surprise, had even killed a few of the guards. Why had they just retreated?

One of the guards came over to check on us passengers after a few minutes of quiet had passed.

"Why'd they run?" One of the men with us was just as curious as I was.

"Don't know, a couple of them were yelling that we had a wizard. Seems like they thought they might get their little hiding spots set on fire. Lucky for us at least. We don't have a wizard with the guards. Is one of you one by chance?"

I decided not to answer. Sorn gave me a hard look, enough that the guard quirked an eyebrow at me.

"Um . . . I'm not a wizard exactly."

The leader of the caravan was less than enthused when he learned that I was a spellcaster.

"Why exactly didn't you tell me you could sling magic!?" he roared as the sun came up, causing me to back down a bit.

"Because if I did, you'd want me to spend a lot of my time and effort helping your people, or one of the other passengers would. It would be a whole thing."

I could see the vein in his forehead bulging as he glared at me. "So what? You planned on just hiding it?"

"For the most part, yes. Unless there was an emergency, I planned on not casting anything anyone would notice."

He gritted his teeth. "I've got three dead men, and you could have taken those bandits down easy."

"No, I couldn't have. I know almost no offensive magic, and what I do know isn't particularly strong."

"You could have . . ." he began again, but I would have none of it.

"How much exactly do you know about magic?"

"Well, I've dealt with a few wizards and the like every now and . . ."

"So almost nothing. I've been studying for years, and I still only know a handful of spells, which I understand far better than you do. So *do not* tell me what I could and couldn't have done. If anyone is hurt, feel free to send them over to me. I can patch up most wounds. Attack magic though, is not something I can or will provide you with."

"What about those men on the side?" He was being annoyingly stubborn about this.

"I have a limited stunning spell, but because of how it works it's a last-ditch defense."

"Why is . . ."

"I have neither the time, nor the patience to explain that to you." I was probably being sharper with him than was proper, but I had no intention of going into details with a man who wanted to tell me what my abilities could do.

He rubbed his temple. "Very well then. I've got a few injured, nothing major. If you can, please fix them up."

I nodded and went to go fix up the injured. I could be charging for this, but they were either guards, who were in charge of protecting me, or passengers, who I honestly felt bad for.

When I finally got back to the wagon we were riding in, Sorn looked over at me with a grin. "So, let's talk about your future as a magic slinging cobbler lad."

CHAPTER 25

✦

BORDER CROSSINGS

I was correct in thinking that allowing others to know that I was a bard would lead to them pestering me. As soon as they found out that I was a spellcaster, the passengers and workers alike began to ask for a number of small favors, most of which I could not do. This was made all the worse by the fact that Sorn kept telling people about the things that I could do, every single one of which he made up.

For my part, I was intentionally vague about what exactly I could do. I saw no reason to explain my abilities in detail, it would only make people bother me for food or whatever. It also meant that I could shrug off things I might actually be able to do.

The average citizen had little understanding of magic. They knew that priests could heal, and that wizards could do all kinds of flashy stuff, but also knew bards had some weird abilities. They did have a slightly better understanding of physical magic: if a man can rip a tree out of the ground, that's easy enough to wrap your head around.

They continued to pester me anyway though. It eventually got to the point that I declared that the next person to ask me for magic in a non-emergency situation would be on the receiving end of a scream. This seemed to make them all back off.

Sorn was quite surprised when my response to being asked to summon a bunch of water was to drop him like a stone. It was one I could do, but he could go get his own bloody water. It was a few moments until he had recovered enough to yell at me. I liked to think it would do him good.

"Oy, what'd you do that for!?" The first words out of his mouth were not encouraging.

"Was I not unclear about what would happen to the next person to ask me for non-emergency magic?"

"Come on! It was just a bit of water!" He was yelling a bit; tinnitus will do that to you.

"Go get your own water if it's no big thing."

"Don't go talking like that, lad, it's the mark of a bad apprentice!"

"I will never be your apprentice."

"Now that's just being rude now, isn't it?"

"Like telling everyone I could instantly cook their food?"

"Yeah, like that."

I could feel my eye twitching and nearly screamed at him again. I couldn't bring myself to it; he was fun to hang around with. His laughing eventually brought me back out of my considerations. I joined him for a few moments before we headed back to the wagon. A guard had heard the scream and came to check things out. He left shaking his head and muttering about stupid clients and the like.

It was easy to tell that we had reached the border of the central duchies; the number of guards on the road increased dramatically. While the roads up to here may have been mostly dirt, these shifted over to cobbled as we joined the main road. The quality of everything increased dramatically as we went; I could even see some of the fields devoted to more cash crops than food.

I got my biggest shock as we approached the border between the two regions. There was an official border, with a border station and all. Leading up to it on both sides were corpses, hanged thirty or so feet back from the road, all clearly visible to those going to the station.

I froze as I saw them; most were long dead. Some might have been added only this morning.

"What are those, Sorn?" I pointed my head toward the dead bodies swinging in the wind.

"Smugglers mostly, if I had to guess."

"They kill smugglers? What is there even to smuggle?"

"Food, if I had to guess. It's not as bad as it was, but in times of crisis, it's illegal to take vital goods from the capital or central duchies. Most of them look older, a month or two perhaps. Shame, if they had waited a bit longer, then maybe they'd not have done something so foolish."

I was ready to vomit; this was insane and cruel. I'd heard that centuries ago the heads of criminals had been displayed, but there were too many here. It was also just smuggling, the punishment seemed too strict to me for such a crime. On some level, I knew that the society in which I now lived was brutally harsh, but it still hit me every now and then just how bad it was.

I was still stunned as we came up to the border station. They were doing individual checks, both on people and on goods. A group of guards at the station came out and had all the passengers come forward. I could see the caster that they had with them; he pointed to me as I approached the line.

"Come this way please." One of the men called me out of line and into a side area; a few more joined us. I was guessing that this was standard to look for dangerous spellcasters. After seeing how they dealt with those violating their rules though, the whole thing made me shake in fear.

We went into a room at the station. It was small with stone walls and a magic item in the center: an orb, covered in runes and sitting atop a small pedestal.

One of the guards took the spot in front of me. "Please put your hand on the orb, if you will."

When I did so, writing appeared along the pedestal. I could easily recognize a number of the stats it was spitting out.

"Thank you, let's see now, age eight, height, weight . . ." He narrowed his eyes at me. "Female?"

"You have less problems traveling if people think you're a boy. At least that's what my teacher said," I said with a shrug. I had my own reasons for wanting to not stand out too. What they didn't ask though wouldn't hurt me.

"I . . . see. What is your name?"

"Alana." I was unsure if this thing could tell if I was lying, so the truth seemed most prudent.

"The device indicates the presence of mana, but not your method of use?"

"I'm a bard, if that's what you're asking."

"It is. Do you currently have any intent to cause damage or chaos within the borders?"

"No, definitely not."

"Well, that's good to hear. What is your purpose?"

"Visiting a bard in the capital."

"Do you know healing magic?"

"Yes, is that important?"

"It is." I could hear the men behind me moving, but I didn't dare move. The guard in front of me pulled out his belt knife and made a small cut on the back of his hand. "Could you please?"

I healed it; the process took only a couple of seconds.

"Finally, could you demonstrate another spell for me? Anything not related to healing would do."

With a slow song, I made a small light over the table. "Like that?"

He nodded. "Well, that all seems in order. Can you support yourself resource wise? We are technically still under the rules for a crisis, so I have to ask."

"Um . . . I think I should be fine."

"I'll put that down as a yes then." He spent several minutes filling out paperwork before I was returned to the caravan. I looked at Sorn as I came back, standing near him.

"You look awful, lad. You okay?" I was apparently still a bit pale from the interview.

"Yeah, I'm fine."

He patted me on the shoulder. "Nothing to it, they don't give anybody problems as long as you've got legitimate business, and you're not a criminal or anything."

I looked over, several of the other travelers had been taken away from the group. My questioning gaze made Sorn give me a sad smile.

"Couple of the people here had no good way to take care of themselves. That kind of folk they don't let in. The leadership of the country doesn't want beggars in their areas. They don't want anybody who is likely to cause any kind of problem."

The restrictions on exporting vitals seemed to make a bit more sense now. The nobles and royals here took a dim view on anyone who might make it harder for those near them to have what they needed. Some kind of anti–French Revolution measure. The people in near the capital can't starve, because they might try to overthrow the king or his lackeys. With magic backing up the ruling class, I doubted they could, but perhaps something had happened in the past.

Sorn gave a light chuckle. "Tell you the truth, I was a bit worried before I learned you were a spellcaster, but anyone with mana can breeze through. There's always jobs for mages. Like making magical shoes."

I snorted at his last bit. "Never. Going. To. Happen." Then I gave an actual smile. It was amazing how well he managed to get rid of bad moods. I really needed to learn that skill.

* * *

That night, the caravan stopped in an actual city. This area of the country was much denser than I was used to. I suspected the fact that we were now very near our destination also helped. The city of High Rock was larger than Hazelwood by an order of magnitude. The inns here were a step above too. I managed to find one, The Mermaid's Rock, that even had small tubs and stoves in the room if you paid extra. I, of course, paid the extra, I hadn't had a proper bath for my entire second life, and I was eager to change that fact.

The tub itself was metal and situated near the stove for warmth and heating water. It was getting quite cold now, so that was a must. I had to heat water myself if I wanted it hot, which wasn't really possible for me to do. If I hadn't been able to make my own water, even filling my tub would have been a daunting prospect. I did try to make the magically created water warm, but the result was less than stellar. Still, a luke-warm bath in a toasty room after all that time on the road was almost dreamlike.

About fifteen minutes into my bath, I had an idea and tried to use my heating spell while in the bath, focusing as much mana as I reasonably could into the water around me. It was mana-intensive but brought the water up to just where I could call it hot. I nearly melted as I finished washing myself. Then I just lay there, enjoying it until it was too cooled for me to keep going.

I was perfectly relaxed when I fell into bed that night. Letting the covers embrace me and lull me down into sleep.

I awoke with a gasp, my heart pounding hard in my chest as images of myself hanging like one of the smugglers by the roadside jolted me back into consciousness. It was still early, but I would find no more sleep tonight.

If rest was impossible, at least I had time to beat my clothes as clean as they'd go and wipe myself down before joining back with the caravan. Doing that helped the images from my dreams fade at least, which was a blessing. I also had plenty of time to find and eat a breakfast, which contained neither bread nor cheese, something that I really wanted.

By the time we were set to leave, I was good and ready, greeting Sorn with a smile as the carts took us ever on, off to the capital and all that was there.

"When you think we'll be there, Sorn?" I asked, eager to be on with this trip.

"Oh, I reckon it'll be either today or tomorrow, lad, not much further."

I smiled peacefully as I rested against the side of our little wagon, content that soon I'd be somewhere I might actually relax a bit.

CHAPTER 26

◆

INTO THE CAPITAL AND ONWARD TOWARD LUCIEN

In the vicinity of the capital, the world looked completely different. It was almost at peace; the fields that had been poorly sown and harvested for years everywhere else looked manicured here. They grew a lot more of what one might call "luxury" crops, and far less grain. It was hard to tell exactly what they were growing, but the presence of things like beanpoles and vineyards was much higher than I was used to. All of the roads we traveled along were both paved and well maintained. The patrols between areas also increased significantly. This was a place where appearances mattered; that much was clear.

By evening, we reached the capital's lands. The city could be seen in the distance, but it was still hours away. We, of course, stopped at a way station. There was no camping out here like one might elsewhere; it would be unseemly.

As the sun set, I looked onto the city in the distance. It was dense, with three- and four-story buildings common, perhaps even a few six- and seven-story ones mixed in. The walls were white and quite tall, the area around them completely devoid of anything other than a field of grass, presumably to act as defense in case of attack. There was a small amount of smoke coming up from various places, but it was hard to see, particularly as the light faded.

Near the center of the capital was a huge building set upon a hill. I could make out few of the details, but based on its size and location I presumed it must be the royal palace. It was quite a bit taller than everything surrounding it and seemed to have its own private wall.

Off to one side, there was another large collection of buildings. These, too, stood well over their companions, reaching out into the sky. They were not nearly as organized from what I could tell, but were instead a variety of shapes and heights. I knew not what was here, but the design was certainly wild.

The way station where we were staying, too, was quite a change. Even the rooms for low-priority guests like ourselves were much more nicely furnished. It still featured a simple bed, desk, and chair, but they all properly matched, and had far better cushioning than those out in the countryside.

I ended up getting a room by myself that was a bit on the small side. There was no point in wasting money on getting something lavish, being that I had no clue how long my funds would need to last me. I'd already splurged on the bath, keeping it up would do no good at all.

The next morning, I opted to walk as we approached the city. The weather was clear, if nippy, and the road leading up to the main gate looked like something straight out of a fantasy game. There were small fences on either side, looking out onto an expanse of verdant grass. We managed to miss the morning rush so there were few coming and going as our caravan approached, plodding along the smooth stone of the causeway.

I was, of course, taken aside and interrogated again as I came to the gate, but I was sort of expecting that. They didn't even vary their questions that much and just waved me through.

I met Sorn at the other side of the gatehouse and gave him a small shrug.

"Well, I guess I'll see you later. Best of luck starting your shoemaking business."

"I'll be on the west side of the city. There's a district there for artisans. Come looking around where the other clothing shops are for Sorn's Shoes. I'll have something up by spring."

"Will do, I'm off to find my uncle then," I said as I turned to leave.

"Oy, lad, I never did get your name." He'd called me lad from the moment we met; I personally thought it was hilarious.

"It's Alana." I was going to get one last laugh out of him.

"Isn't that a girl's name though?"

"It is."

"Lad . . . are you a lass?"

Cackling, I turned and walked down the street; a few people looked as he yelled after me.

"Oh, come on now!"

This was, in retrospect not the best thought-out of plans. I knew the name of the man I was after, Lucien. I'd been regaled with enough stories of his and Mystien's adventures that I'd not easily forget it. I knew he owned a tavern too.

The problem came when I got to the entertainment district. There had to be at least a hundred taverns dotting the street up and down it. I was used to a dozen or so, tops in a city. Now I had to go try and figure out which one was his—a daunting task. I remembered that the name had something to do with the sky, but I was at a complete loss.

My first contender was a place called The Skyhook. It was a fairly ritzy establishment, near to where one might find nobles. It was a no-go, the man at the door didn't know a Lucien and looked at me like I was some kind of street trash. I worked my way down the main thoroughfare; there had to be fifteen different places that had names with birds, or flying, or something like that in their name. The doorman at each was either unhelpful or just downright rude.

I eventually found a guard to ask; it was getting late.

"Don't suppose you know of a tavern run by a man named Lucien? I think the name had to do with flying or the sky or something."

"No, kid, I don't. Where all have you checked?"

"All up and down the main thoroughfare, why?"

"You haven't checked the entertainment district?"

"Um?"

"First time in the capital, huh?"

I nodded, and he proceeded to give me directions to the actual region of the city that housed entertainment. Unlike most cities in the country, this one didn't just have it near to the nobles' section. The city was just too large for that. There were a number of establishments on the main road yes, but you needed to go down a side street to find the actual district.

I nearly wept when I got there. It was enormous, there were way too many places for me to check tonight.

I picked a side of the street and just started walking, trying any candidate that seemed to be likely. I went to The Silver Star, The Flying Fool, The Silent Soar, The Naughty Nimbus, and about half a dozen other places. Near the end of the road, I was ready to collapse.

I stumbled into the last of the candidates of the day. The slog was hard, and I was ready to rent a room until tomorrow. It was a seedy place, nestled between a bunch of brothels. There was no doorman here; the waitresses also seemed to be busy. So I found myself a stool near the bar, looking around. Half the customers had to be from said brothels; the number of women and their clothes gave that away as clear as day.

On one table sung a fat, balding, old bard. He was in the middle of some number about a man wandering the streets in search of his lost love. It was pretty good, and the lute he played to accompany his song was singing along as well. If nothing else, he had some serious chops when it came to music.

When the song finished, he let out the spell he'd been working on. A rather complex darkness spell spread across the ceiling, pinpoints of light sparkled, peeking out from it here and there. The crowd loved it, giving a great cheer as they downed their drinks. Having finished his number, he came back over to the bar and began slinging drinks. Eventually, he got to me.

"Welcome to the Starlit Sky. How is it I can help you today then?"

"I need a room, and I don't suppose you know a Lucien?"

His demeanor hardened a bit, and he looked me over.

"I don't know what you've been told, but Lucien's not your daddy, boy." He seemed oddly confident about that one.

"I'm aware," I deadpanned. "He's a friend of my teacher supposedly."

"Who's your teacher?"

"A wizard named Mystien." His eyes told me I'd found my target.

He began laughing. "How's the old codger doing then?"

"I was hoping you'd know. He disappeared a couple of years ago. Haven't heard or seen hide nor hair since."

He poured two mugs of ale and motioned me over to a small alcove. "Sounds like you've got a story. Why don't you go ahead and tell me."

It took well over an hour to relate the entirety of my adventure. He jumped in only a few times to ask for details as I wove the tale. I told him how his friend and my father had vanished like smoke on the wind. I delved into the confinement of our village and its eventual fall. Eventually, I got to the point where I made my way here, hanging around in the back of a cart with a cobbler.

"Hate to say it, but I've no clue where he is." The senior bard announced as I finished. "I wouldn't be worried though; he'll turn up eventually. So, what'll you do now?"

"Well . . . I was thinking about finding a new place to work. Somewhere the old man might eventually come . . ."

"Are you telling me you traveled halfway across the country to ask me for a job?"

"Pretty much, yeah. It's the best chance I can think of for finding my family, if you didn't know anything, that is."

Lucien blinked at me a few times. "If Mystien and Jackson trained you, I've no doubt you're not too bad at magic. I can see your aura, so I know you've practiced a good bit. You suck at planning though."

I puffed a bit at that one, glaring at him just a bit. "It seemed the best option."

"Not sure I'm the one who should be lecturing on making bad life choices . . ." he mumbled under his breath.

"Anyway," he continued at full volume. "I'll hire you for the winter. If you're any good, I'll keep you around. If not, I'll at least help you find somewhere else to go."

We hashed out the details of my employment then and there. I'd be working mostly mornings and afternoons. Two on one off, as I had back in Istlan. The pay was quite a bit lower, but it included room and board, so I was fine with that. I was also allowed to pick up some evening shifts if I wanted to earn a little extra cash. Pay for doing magic was separate, of course, and was about the same as I'd had in Istlan. There were more casters here in the capital, but there was also far, far more demand.

The room I was given as board was frankly spartan. There was a small stove in one corner, but other than that and the simple bed—nothing. I was told it was one of the cheapest rooms in the tavern, which was itself on the far lower end. The Starlit Sky didn't have many rooms to rent; it depended mostly on magic and alcohol sales.

My first day of work began the next morning. I was going to be cleaning up mostly. The place was nothing at all like Haven's. It was seedy-looking at night, tucked away in a corner between bordellos, but during the day it looked just like any restaurant you might expect. The tables were a bit worn, there was a constant war on incoming dirt, and half the staff was a bit cranky.

There were a handful of barmaids and cooks. When I was first introduced to them, they looked sour. Some kid butting into their work was most unwelcome. Lucien explained that I was a bard and would be mostly cleaning and helping out while doing magic stuff. It didn't really help matters, but he and I were casters. Having one bard working at your tavern was a good sign, two was excellent. It didn't really make many things go much smoother on the normal business side, but it was a point of pride for a lot of places, keeping a caster on staff could be quite expensive.

I wasn't too tired at the end of the day, but after an early dinner, I retreated to my room. Settling down to go over the past few weeks, one thing seemed obvious. I needed to up my magic game. How though? I knew that I'd about hit the limit on attack magic. Perhaps I should learn something defensive or to improve my stealth. I'd need to consider carefully where to go with this. If I worked on it at night, I could maybe get a few new spells up to a workable level before spring. That would be my goal.

As I looked out the little window in my room, a snowflake drifted past, the first soldier of the oncoming horde. While winter waged its yearly war on the world, I would prepare for mine . . . whatever that next fight would be.

CHAPTER 27

✦

TRAINING WITH LUCIEN

Step one on improving my magic was to talk to Lucien. I didn't know what all he could do, but he easily qualified as more experienced than I was when it came to magic. After one of my first shifts seemed as good a time as any.

"You're fighting an uphill battle there" was what he said when I explained that I wanted to add offense and defensive spells to my repertoire.

"How so?"

"Well, let's start with exactly how you're going to go about fighting with magic. What are your ideas?" He led me out back to the alley behind the Starlit Sky. It was fortunate that we had almost no customers in the early afternoon.

"What about something like a water or ice cannon? I already know the spells to make them and a movement spell."

"Try it." He pointed down the alleyway.

First I attempted my water spell, adding movement to launch it forward. The result was lackluster. A garden hose would have even been more powerful. The stream of water went perhaps five feet before burbling to the ground.

The ice spell was much the same. It lethargically threw the cubes, even a three-year-old could have done better. I was thoroughly disappointed.

"Before you continue to waste mana," Lucien broke in, "you should know that a wizard in their first month of training can generally knock a man off his feet if he focuses hard enough. What other ideas were you going for?"

"Could I summon something dangerous? Like . . . poison or something?"

"That's not a terrible thought, but it requires you to know that poison pretty well. If you've something safe enough in mind, go ahead and give it a try."

The easiest idea would be chlorine gas. It was nasty stuff on a good day. I knew a few things about it. It was a yellow gas that could be made by mixing bleach and ammonia. I even managed to picture its place on the periodic table. I think I got a bit of a yellow haze around one fingertip for about half a second. I couldn't even be sure of that.

"It didn't work. Not at all."

I was a bit dejected by that; I'd had real hopes on that after the water debacle.

"I'm guessing you tried something you'd read about, right? Perhaps you even knew a bit about making it?"

I nodded. I'd seen it in high school chem a few times, but there was no need to go into that with him.

"Not good enough, for a wizard maybe, but not a bard. What can you summon?"

"Bread, cheese, ice, and water. How does that matter?"

"These are all things you are intimately familiar with. You know them front to back because you've interacted with them for years. There's an instinct tied to them, you see? You need that to summon something; you have to know it in your bones. Now, if you were severely poisoned by something, or minorly poisoned many times, you might be able to manage it, but knowledge alone won't be enough for instinct-based magic."

"Why didn't the water and ice thing work then?"

"Because our magic just moves too slowly for putting that much force on something, at least most of the time. You could have built it up into something respectable, but it would be way too slow in a combat situation."

I pouted a bit and he flicked my forehead. Then pointed to a spot about five feet from himself. A small flame, about the size of my hand appeared, and spread to perhaps two or three feet in diameter over the course of a second or two.

"I use that daily to light the fireplaces in the main hall and rooms if I need to. Have done for years, and that's about as quick as I can make it spread. But it's not very useful in combat, huh?"

I shook my head. "Then what can we do? Am I doomed to forever be virtually helpless?"

He laughed, then whistled a quick tune.

The alley went black. I tried to look around and saw nothing, not anywhere. After around three seconds, it faded, and his hand came down lightly on my shoulder. It took me a few seconds to recover from almost peeing myself. That's when I saw the knife in his other hand.

"What!?" I hadn't heard him so much as move. The bare blade and quick change of place were enough to send my legs trembling.

"Not at all. Stealth will be your sword and shield. You already know how to stun someone, and how well that works. Work on developing a way to move unseen, and escape from bad situations. I'll teach you a few things later on, but think about what you can do now first. You can practice out here, or in your room. Just don't skimp out on your work." He glared a bit at the last sentence.

"No . . . no worries, I won't."

I had one last question as he turned to head back inside. "Why didn't Mystien or Jackson tell me this stuff?"

"Because while Mystien's a brilliant man, he's a wizard and doesn't understand it. Jackson , on the other hand, is not overly smart. He's a good skilled lad but just too interested in where he's going to get some next."

I paced around in the alley for a few minutes, trying to think of things that might fit into what I'd learned. On a whim, I tried to make some light like a laser. It was marginally better than a magnifying glass, even managed to set a little piece of wood to smoking . . . after about thirty seconds. Neat, but not combat effective.

That night in my room, I worked on another idea. I wanted to try invisibility; that would be the ultimate in stealth.

I knew that most of everything was just empty space. I also knew that light was waves, or particles, or something. I was a little unclear on how that worked, but it was enough. I needed the light to just go through me. If I could get it to just pass by without interacting with me, that *should* make me invisible, right?

I started casting, focusing first on my hand. I guess I was actually working on the light, not myself in this. I pictured the light just moving through, ignoring, bypassing, like wind moving a field of grass but not a stone at its center.

My hand got clearer. It was like slowly, very slowly, turning down the opacity. By the time I was out of mana, it looked like a projection. It wasn't invisible quite yet, but it was real progress.

Soon after, I went to sleep. It would not do to tick off the boss by being late to my morning shift.

A few weeks passed, and the snow started piling up. It was at least as bad here as it had been back in Orsken. I suspected it would be worse by the end of winter, but perhaps I was just being prissy about the cold.

Lucien did, in fact, keep his word and pulled me aside after work one chilly afternoon.

"All right then, Alana. I told you I'd show you some things. We'll start with darkness. It's an easy spell once you get used to it. What I want you to do is focus on keeping light out of an area. Imagine snuffing out candles and having shadows push in and deepen, until it becomes dark."

That sounded weird, but I found a quiet spot in the back of the tavern and pushed the shadows. I was trying to make each deeper and darker, letting them overtake the light. It sort of worked. The shadows did get a bit darker, not quite what we were going for though. After a few attempts that didn't really help much, I tried instead to think about the light being consumed. To me, light was a thing; it was in the air and could be taken out.

The area around me dimmed significantly, the lighting going from bright to something that one might see on the night with a full moon.

"Hey, look at you! Not bad, not bad at all, now keep pushing it harder and harder. Feel it out, that'll show you the way to go. Once you've got the basic picture, then work on making it feel right; that's the ticket."

I had to admit that Lucien was a completely different kind of teacher than any I'd had before. He didn't go into deep explanations; instead, he focused on the feel of the magic. He also let me practice ideas I had, not standing over me like Mystien had done.

Every instinct my first teacher had pounded into my head screamed. I wasn't supposed to be experimenting with magic. I was supposed to carefully, methodically work on one spell at a time, finding and making minute adjustments until it was perfect. At least that's what I had learned up until now.

Lucien, on the other hand, would show you something and let you try out whatever seemed best. Then he would tell you to go figure it out on your own. It was the difference between a college professor working in a lab and a baker. I personally had made enough bread that I felt more like a baker in every sense of the word. I would have to polish what I was doing for sure, but doing it, and things like it, felt like the right way for me to quickly learn what I wanted to know.

Every night, I began to practice the darkness spell, along with my invisibility spell. I had all winter and little else to do than that and my light tavern duties.

I got first my arm to disappear completely, then both arms. Once I had my arms, I worked on my legs. My torso was a tough bit, and it took a few weeks to push it up and along that until it went see-through too. When I finally got to my head, I experienced a real problem.

Making my eyes invisible rendered me blind. As soon as the spell pushed past them, I was in complete darkness.

"Well, shit."

Turned out that making light not interact with me would render me blind. I kept practicing moving it around other parts of my body; this spell was horridly mana-expensive while I thought about a solution.

Eventually, I kludged together an opening in the spell for my pupils, but that didn't work either. Even if the light could work with my pupils, it still didn't hit the back of my eyes. I thought and thought, and came up with the answer. I needed it not only to come in via my pupils, but to let all light hitting them in the right way actually interact with me.

Wrapping that concept up into the spell meant if I cast it, that was about it for a full mana charge. If I wanted to use this, it would take my everything, at least until I made it efficient or something. It also took several seconds to properly manifest. Still though, invisibility was a super-cool power to have gained.

The snows would be melting soon. I felt now would be the proper time to show the fruits of my labors to my new teacher. So I snuck down early one morning, before the rest of the staff had awakened. There I found the aged bard counting the previous night's take.

"Good morning, Alana. Not quite time to start up yet, but good on you for being early."

"I had something I wanted to show you. It's kind of mana-expensive." I was cheery and bright this morning. I really hoped I could surprise him.

"All right then, go ahead." He looked up from his work, giving me a sly smile.

I began to sing, letting the spell wash over me from toe to head, until only two black dots that were my pupils remained floating in the air.

"Invisibility, eh? Not a bad one. There is one fatal flaw to it though." He was moving quietly as he got up, slinking toward me. I didn't think a man that big, or that old would be able to move that quietly. "Renders you blind!"

I jumped back as he reached out to poke me where my forehead had been. He nearly tripped as I was not where I was supposed to be. For my part, I circled around, landing a number of pokes to the fleshy part just between his pelvis and ribs. Seeing the old bard jump and yelp was decidedly the highlight of my week.

"All right, how'd you manage that?" he asked after he stopped laughing, and I revealed myself.

"I let the light that came in through my eye interact with me. It's weird and clunky, but it works."

"That it does. I've heard of a few people making themselves invisible before, but it always ends with them unable to see too. Good way to hide though. How about the darkness? How's that going for you?"

"Honestly? Subpar, I can't get it going how I want it to quite yet."

"Eh, you'll get there, kid. Hammer out those two until they're easy. I would give them a few months of practice before I tried to gain too much more, but I'll let you decide on that."

I nodded. "Sounds like a plan to me."

"Good," he laughed again. "Now go get ready for the morning shift, no slacking."

"Yes boss-man!" I chirped as I ran off to my morning duties.

CHAPTER 28

SHOES, HOES, AND
A YOUNG MAGE

I smiled as the spring melted the snows, day after day driving back the signs of winter. As a celebration for being nine, and the freedom of winter ending, I decided to buy myself a new pair of shoes. On one of my days off, I slipped down to the artisans' district.

It took me a long time to find it, but Sorn's Shoes was here. It was tucked between two other stores, both of the clothing variety. The street here was not too close to the main street, but it was wide and paved. I'd give the location a 8/10 overall, good, but not great.

A small bell rang as I entered, tinkling lightly through the whole store. Sorn looked up from a bench in the back. Standing up from his workspace, he came forward to greet his new customer.

"Greetings, lass, how can I help you today?"

"I'd like to order a couple of pairs of shoes: one of light shoes for the city and a pair of medium-weight boots."

"All right then. Come on back and we'll measure you right up."

He took me over to a small stool where he proceeded to measure my feet. I had to put aside my current shoes, which were a disaster, for him to do so. Their soles were worn and thin from more walking than they'd ever actually been designed for.

"Here's what I suggest as materials." I'd never seen him in his element before. Sorn was an absolute professional. He laid out small patches of colored leather fit for both indoor slippers and boots, as well as a few sample designs.

I picked out sensible boots in a warm brown leather, and blue slippers for my work at the bar.

"It'll be ten silvers. Soon as your parents pay, I'll start on them. Both pairs will take around a week, but they'll be a fair bit better than you have now."

I laughed a bit as I put the money on the counter. "About a week then?"

He blinked for a second, scooping it up. "What name should I put these under? Also, be careful flashing money like that, kid; someone might try to rob you or something."

"Alana. And you know well as I do, Sorn, that anyone who tries to rob me will thoroughly regret it."

He squinted at me for a moment. As he did, I felt the corners of my mouth inching up.

"It's you!"

"Yup."

"You're actually a girl?"

"Yup."

He was rubbing his temples as I enjoyed my hearty laugh. It took him several moments to recover fully before he started smiling again.

"Come to be my apprentice then?"

"Not on your life."

"Ha, I suppose you found your uncle, didn't you?"

Oof, forgot I'd never actually told him the truth on that one. "He's not really my uncle, but yes. I'm up at the Starlit Sky now. You should come by sometime."

We said our goodbyes, and I meandered back to the tavern. The day was still young, and I had plenty of magic to practice.

Spring brought with it a number of changes to the Starlit Sky. There was a sharp uptick in business of all kinds, both drinking and the refilling of magical items.

One of the main jobs that I ended up doing was working on recharging the magical items that all of the brothels in the area used. These were two small orbs. The first one was to check for any diseases, important in that line of work. The second checked the age of anyone who touched it.

Prostitution was, in fact, legal in this kingdom. There were a few caveats. All of those working had to be checked weekly for any STDs, and they also had to be adults. There were periodic checks by the authorities, and the punishments for violating either of those ordinances were very heavy.

Society viewed working girls quite a bit differently than my previous world. They weren't considered respectable, but neither were they hated. Jealousy played a part in the hatred of them in any world, as most people don't like to share. At the same time, they tended to make good money, and there was less of a stress on sexual purity here. While prostitution was therefore viewed as a job that most men didn't really want their daughters going into, many still used the working girls' services at one point or another in their lives.

A very large number of orphans ended up working in a brothel as well. It was a sad fact that in this society without a support structure you really could die. Since most orphans also ended up with The Shield and were well educated (compared to a peasant), many times the women ran the businesses as absolute professionals. Of course, in the current state of things with the previous years of war, there was now an absolute profusion of women trying to break into the trade now. So competition between the various businesses was stiff.

This led to an interesting issue at the Starlit Sky. Since many of these women were customers when they were off the job, they tended to sit only with the others from their particular establishment. These groups held only a tenuous peace inside the tavern. They knew better than to irritate the proprietor, since he was instrumental in their businesses staying open. They also hated each other's guts; each time one got a customer, the others were losing that same man.

Fights were frequent, and quite a bit more violent than one might expect.

In my experience, men do not often actually want to fight. They posture, yell, and push; eventually, they'll punch each other for about ten seconds then go to wrestling on the ground. If the issue between them isn't deadly, they often leave friends afterward.

Women, on the other hand, do not do that. When they decide to fight, it goes from a handful of curses to hair ripping and nail scratching. There is no posturing, no buildup. It is an instant of rage followed by violence, and they aren't friends afterward.

It happened the night after I'd picked up my new footwear when I was carrying soups over to one of our larger tables. They'd ordered a frankly obscene amount of food, and I had a whole platter of the hot red stuff. I didn't hear how the argument began, but something certainly set it off.

As I was passing by the two tables, I heard "Fuck you, bitch!" That seemed to be the starting pistol.

I didn't really care about the details, because one of the stupid assholes knocked me over and the entire platter full of scalding hot soup landed on me, my dress, and importantly, my brand-new shoes.

I could see red on me, on my dress, on my fucking shoes. I let loose on the lot of fighting women. I had barely enough sense to not push as much mana as I could into the scream as I opened up on them.

The room went silent as the disoriented women tried to pick themselves up off the floor. A few particularly foolish ones tried to grab their opponents. A second blast served to straighten them out.

Nobody spoke or moved as the sprawled-out whores—I'd lost any and all respect for them at this point—tried to recover. There were scant few people who wanted to deal with an irate spellcaster, and almost all of those could use magic themselves. I could feel the eyes on me, waiting to see where this would go. Once I guessed that at least most of them could hear again, I decided to lay into them.

"Congratulations, you're all a bunch of stupid fucking cunts! Pay your tab and get the hell out!" I wasn't enamored with obscenities, but there was a time for everything. It probably sounded hilarious coming from a girl my age, but the representatives for each table quickly did so.

The room was dead silent as they left, except for one person. A boy of about twelve was sitting to one side of the room. Upon hearing me chew out the combatants, he had begun laughing so hard he had fallen out of his chair. I briefly considered tossing him a scream, too, but he clearly had some kind of aura, so I decided against it.

A hand came down on my shoulder. "Why don't you take the rest of the evening off to clean up and cool off?" Lucien had to have had ninja training somewhere at some point. It was absolutely obscene how he could move that quietly.

The boy was still laughing as I left. I could see him trying to pick himself up back into his chair.

I dreamed that night of seeing Rod's and Sandra's bodies. They were lying in the middle of a field, holding each other. As I looked up from where they were, I could see corpses all around. I recognized the mayor, several of the soldiers, many were villagers. There were others I didn't know.

When I looked around, I felt the first drop fall, landing on my cheek. Then drop by drop, it began to rain blood. I wept as the crimson tide fell upon the clearing soaking into everything.

I jolted awake, shaking and crying from the horror of it. For the rest of the night, I found no sleep. I curled up in my blankets wishing for the morning to come.

* * *

Lucien was there when I came downstairs.

"So . . . about last night . . ." I began.

"They were fighting; you threw them out. I would appreciate it if you didn't curse so much next time it happens."

He didn't seem mad at all, perhaps even a bit amused.

"You're not even going to yell at me?"

"For what? There was no permanent damage to them or the tavern, and I won't have people fighting like that here. It's bad for business. Having troublemakers tossed out by a spellcaster, on the other hand, tells people I can both hire one and keep you from turning them into paste."

"I couldn't have turned them into paste even if I wanted to . . ."

"They don't know that though. You forget that the average person knows about as much about magic as they do about . . . I don't know, blacksmithing. They know you can do stuff, but have no idea what."

"Oh yeah, I guess I have heard that."

"But do tone down the cursing. Having a foul-mouthed child is not as good for our image."

"I'll try."

"Good, now see what you can do about getting the tables set up before breakfast."

That evening as I was about to leave, the kid from last night showed up again. He walked up to me with a big smile. He had to be eleven or twelve, with sandy blond hair and a slight build. His robes were simple and screamed "Hey, look at me! I do magic!"

"Hey, I'm Dras." He seemed calm and collected, with a slight air of mischief.

"Hi . . ."

"So, if you don't mind me asking, how did you do that scream thing last night? That was cool."

"It's just a basic bard spell. You focus mana into your voice."

"Oh! You're a bard then. I'm a wizard. Been learning as much as I can so I can prep for school."

"I figured. The robes kind of say it for you."

"Yeah, suppose they do. Would you be interested in trading spells some time? I could teach you one of mine for one of yours?"

"We use different methods; that wouldn't work."

"Oh . . . well. That kind of sucks, I'd love to be able to yell people into the ground. Do you want to hang out? There's plenty of cool stuff around."

"Maybe another day, I've got stuff I need to do today. Like wash my stupid dress again."

He nodded. "Another time then, bye!"

I had no clue what to make of him. He didn't seem like a bad person, but my experience there was sort of lacking. As I went to leave, I passed by Lucien at the bar.

"What'd Dras want?"

"Asked about the scream. You know him?"

"Yeah, he's local. Decent kid, gets in a bit of trouble, but who doesn't? He does a lot of recharging for cash."

"Huh."

CHAPTER 29

✦

CITY SECRETS

Spring rolled round into summer, and news started to spread. There was rebellion in the countryside. It was unclear where, but many of the smaller villages had either stopped paying their taxes, or gone fully against the local nobles. This wasn't that big a problem from inside the capital; there were no food shortages in this region, but many of the smaller regions were having real issues. My understanding was that in places magic users were having to be dispatched to quell the rebels.

I idly wondered if the area around my former home was in flames, but I could only bring myself to care so much. I cared about my mom, my dad, and the brother I had left, and perhaps Sara, but that was about it. I didn't hate the people there, but I didn't know them anymore, and there was nothing I could do regardless. Lord Hazelwood was hopefully having problems though, because screw his whole family.

Someone plopped down at the bar, interrupting my musings.

"Hey, Alana."

"Afternoon, Dras, what can I get you?"

"Lunch, and some ale please."

Dras came by most days when it wasn't winter. He was involved in filling some magic item or the other. At first, I thought that this might make him competition for us, but it seemed that Lucien didn't mind. There was currently more business than he could handle, so shoving some off on the kid wasn't an issue for him at all. On some of my days off, I'd even end up doing some light practice with Dras in one of the open lots behind the Starlit Sky. It was good to have someone even relatively close to my own size to practice using my mace and spells with.

I pushed across his beef stew and bread, along with a mug of ale. That was the standard around here, though sometimes we'd have some other meat dish. It varied wildly by what was available in any given season. Today though was beef stew with veggies, thickened with barley. The bread was my old standard, good, but nothing particularly special.

"So, anything new?" I asked over the counter I could barely see over.

"Not particularly. More rumors about rebels in the country; they arrested one of the brothel owners for using underage girls . . . that's about it. By the way, you know any clothes vendors? I'm starting to grow and almost none of my stuff fits anymore."

"Underage? Hate to be that guy."

"Woman actually, and yeah. Word is that the Crown is taking all of her stuff and banishing her from the central duchies."

"That's basically a death sentence, yeah? No home, no money, no nothing."

"Maybe, I don't know her, but there are more than a few who could survive it. She'll be reduced to begging or something. I think I could make it through something like that, but I'm a caster . . . What about the clothes?"

"Don't know anyone in particular about clothes. I know a guy who makes pretty good shoes."

"Sweet, mind introducing me?"

"Sure, shift ends in a bit. I'll take you."

His question was a fairly normal one. Many people would have preferred shops, somewhere a friend or family member worked, or just somewhere they knew was good. If you weren't rich, knowing somebody was a good way to make sure you got the best deal or service, so asking those you knew was the best way for an in on that. Since I saved most of my money, I didn't know very many places, but I'd give Sorn a bit of business any time I could.

Ordering shoes for Dras was easy. Dealing with Sorn's teasing about when we'd be getting married was less so. Threats were made before it would stop. Eventually though, the order was placed. Dras, at Sorn's suggestion, even volunteered to walk me home.

As we were passing through one alley, what looked to be a manhole cover in the street opened up. Three men pulled themselves out. They looked a bit rough and turned when they saw us.

"Evening, lads," Dras spoke before they could say anything. He seemed completely unfazed by the situation.

"What're two kids doing out in the middle of the night?" one of the men, I'm guessing their leader, replied. He seemed a bit put off balance by Dras's confident attitude. I, of course, knew that in a fight the two of us would likely trounce these three, size difference or not. They, on the other hand, had no auras, and probably just saw two kids, aside from Dras's habit of dressing like a wizard.

"Heading home, and minding our own business."

"Well then, see that you keep doing so and have a good night."

The threat in his voice was real.

The other two didn't speak. They stood back, looking at us and around the alley. If I had to guess, these weren't street punks. For one, they were too old. While they looked rough, they were also too disciplined. Each knew where his place was and stood like he'd been thoroughly trained. In all likelihood, they had; most men in the country now had some level of military experience under their belt.

Dras took me by the arm and pulled me away, giving them wide berth as we passed. He walked so that he would be between me and them and quickly turned the nearest corner as we sped along.

"What was that?" I asked after we'd gone a block or two and made sure we weren't being followed.

"I don't know exactly, but not something we want to be involved in."

"Where did they even come from? The sewer?"

"Only sewers in the city run down the biggest streets. That was an Undercity opening. They're all over the place if you know where to look."

"Undercity?"

"Yeah, the city's really old right?"

I nodded as we kept walking.

"So there's a bunch of old parts that have kind of sunk, and people just built over them. Add to that cisterns that haven't been used in centuries, access tunnels for old businesses, some sealed-off basements, and a frankly insane amount of catacombs, and you have the Undercity. Over the years, it's all gotten connected here and there from collapsed walls and people digging."

"So they were exploring the Undercity? That sounds cool."

"No, probably not. Thieves and the like use those paths to escape sometimes. They might know one or two streets of the network, partially because it's huge, but it's also unstable and dangerous."

"It still sounds cool. I wonder if there are any openings near the Starlit Sky."

"Tons, and I mean that. Most of the businesses on the street have an entrance into it, but they keep them sealed up. There are a few minor monsters that live down there."

"Monsters!?"

"Just little ones mostly. A few big rats and the occasional slime or something. Anyone could deal with them, but they're still nasty. There's other things if you go really deep into the system, but smart people stick to the paths they know. Getting lost down there is no good. Jer's brother went down alone once to find a new path . . . Do you know Jer?"

I shook my head. "How do you even know all this?"

"Most everyone who lives in the city knows they're there. It's also a sort of thing for boys to go and explore the tunnels near their house. Older brothers and neighbors and stuff will take you down if you ask nice and show you the way around. I used to use them to sneak out with my friends at night, lots of fun."

"So did you like, fight the rats and slimes and stuff?" This was sounding like the city had a starter dungeon below it. Something out of an old MMO for sure.

"What? No, why would I? That stuff runs off if you've got a light with you. Anything that's aggressive and near the surface gets killed quick too. Nobody really talks about it, but ratcatchers and the like go down there and clean out anything they can."

"I thought maybe people would go down there and train or something . . ."

"That's weird. It's a maze, and really unsafe. What would you even train for? Who needs to practice on rats? They're too weak to act like real monsters, and nothing like fighting humans."

I pouted; my hopes for a starter dungeon were smashed. Reality seemed to not match up quite perfectly to games and books. I knew there were dungeons in this world, or at least its stories.

"I thought it might be like a dungeon or something . . ."

"Maybe if you went really deep, you'd find a dungeon-like area, but we're in the capital. If something like that got found, the army would just pour into it and tear it apart. There wouldn't be any big monsters, so thirty or so soldiers could move through and clean it in an afternoon."

"Yeah, I suppose they would huh . . ."

The rest of the way home, I asked Dras to point out some of the entrances. They really were everywhere, almost every alley had one of some level or another. Many were just a round cover over a spot in the road, but there were also a few doors that were sunk into low spots on buildings. Each was marked with a symbol to warn everyone away. By the time we'd made it back to the Starlit Sky, we'd made a game of it.

By fall, I'd bugged Dras about taking me down into the tunnels to the point that he was just ignoring it. Though he did tell Lucien because he was a spoilsport.

"You really shouldn't go down there, Alana."

"Because it's really unsafe?"

"Yes, quite unsafe."

"So you never did when you were young?"

"I am probably not the best role model."

"So Jackson didn't when he was young?"

"I knew him in his teens, but he's decidedly not the best role model."

"You knew Mystien when he was younger, right? He's a pretty good role model."

He stared at me for a few moments, then sighed. "Fine, will you at least please not go down there alone?"

"I'm not stupid, Lucien."

"You did trek halfway across the country to get here . . ."

"All right, all right, I have no plans on going into the Undercity alone." They were never going to let me live that down.

"Is there an entrance here by the way?" I felt I needed to ask.

"It's in the basement and quite well sealed. Do *not* try to unseal it." That got me a harsh glare.

"I won't without your permission. If all the businesses around here have them though, couldn't it act as a way to get around in the winter without having to go aboveground?"

He paused to think for a few moments. "That not the worst idea I've ever heard, but it would be a lot of work to seal up the edges around our street and clean them up enough to be a viable option."

"So why doesn't anyone?"

"You'd need all of the businesses to agree to it. They won't, because there are no incoming customers from the surrounding areas. Anyone using them would just be people who are already on this street, and those generally stay for the winter. That and all the work. Some of those tunnels are unstable, and many of them are weirdly designed. While you wouldn't need to deal with snow, you'd have to deal with lighting and the overall confusing setup."

I sighed; it would seem my idea for an underground walkway system was dead on arrival. These weren't caves either; they were buried streets. I'd made my mind up to avoid caves, due to a storied history of caves screwing me over. Well, two for two at least.

It was right at the end of fall that Dras showed up on one of my days off with about three other boys and one girl around my age in tow, along with one other older boy.

"You still want to go check out the Undercity? These four have been bugging everyone to take them as well, so Jer and I were going to show them one of the paths."

It took me only a few minutes to grab some boots and my mace. If there was going to be a monster to fight, I wanted to take it down.

CHAPTER 30

INTO THE "DEPTHS"

Our little group set off for the entrance to the tunnels, after I told Lucien where I was going. It was decided that we would gain access through a door at the end of the street. According to Jer, who would be leading this expedition, we'd come out one about halfway across the city, near the main road of the town. The entire trip would take an hour or two, so we needed to be ready for that too.

I quickly learned that Jer was something of a local expert on the tunnel system, at least among the children. His family had been ratcatchers and thieves for generations and had passed down intricate knowledge of the top layers. He, in particular, was well versed. He had often gone looking for his missing brother, who had disappeared into the tunnels a couple of years ago.

The other kids with us were from the neighborhood. None were directly related to either of the older boys, but I'd seen all of them around here and there. We were all on edge as we got near to the opening that we'd be using.

Dras turned to me and asked, "Hey, Alana, you got a fire spell or something?"

I knew he specialized in flame magic, so he always had a light.

"I've got light, but no fire."

"Mind taking up the middle then? We'll want a bit of extra light."

"Okay." I was super excited. I'd rather have been near the front, but I could deal with being just a bit back from it.

Jer took out a lantern. It was a small thing full of oil and quite a bit brighter than I might have expected. He looked around as we all got into position. It shocked me how large his eyes were: big, bright orbs of shocking blue. He had a small club, not unlike my mace, but only made of wood.

"All right, everyone, stick together after me. Do not go down any side tunnels or anything like that. If something happens, stay where you are. I've told my folks what route we're taking, and if I don't come back by later tonight, they'll come and get us. We're taking mostly the top layer, but we will have to dip down one to the second to get past some things. Any questions?"

Honestly, his little speech was like a safety briefing I might have gotten on a field trip on my old world. This kid might have been only a few years older than me, but it seemed he'd done this often enough. It was sincerely confidence inspiring. It also sounded like it had been learned word-for-word from his dad or something.

"You keep talking about layers. What's that mean?" I asked. I'd heard the term a few times, but was still unclear on it.

"Right, so there's a lot of tunnels, some are deeper. It's not like, exact or anything, but we're going down a little. Almost nobody goes down more than just a little bit." He gave a brief show of his hands, trying to indicate that some of the tunnels were below others.

"How deep do they go?"

That one got me a shrug. "Don't know, never been below three. Dad says he's been five deep. There aren't as many the further down you go, and they're way more dangerous. Gramps says he went eight down, but I think he's lying."

One of the kids with us piped up: "Will there be monsters?"

Jer shrugged again. "Maybe, but nothing that's a problem."

With no more questions, he turned and pulled open the door that was our passageway into the Undercity.

I tossed up a light behind me as I heard Dras closing the old, rickety door. The tunnel was about two people wide and looked a bit like a hallway at first. I could tell we were going down a bit, and eventually we came to a small room. It looked like a basement, but one thoroughly sealed off from the rest of whatever had been above it. We came in a doorway, then went out through a hole someone had made in the opposite wall, straight through the bricks.

From there, it just kept getting weirder. The size and shape of the path were constantly changing, from wide and regular, to cramped. Sometimes the ceiling even got really low. It was a mix of old roads, old buildings, and small dug-out ways, straight through the dirt and stone.

After a while, we had to go down a small ladder. Jer went first and was gentlemanly enough to let the girls come right after him. As we ventured down the tunnels, he pointed out different things.

"This is the second level, and we're about halfway through. Up ahead is a big chamber. Nobody's used it in forever as far as I know, but it's got some room, and it's cool."

Everything down here was, in fact, cool in multiple ways. The structures were in a layout that looked as if someone had just shoved them all together, giving them a dreamlike quality. It was also chilly; even though we weren't far down, the temperature was the same chilled level throughout. I'd almost forgotten that caves were like that, even unnatural ones.

As we moved into the large chamber, we all looked about in awe. The place was easily forty feet long and about half as wide. It seemed to have been built of stone or perhaps concrete blocks, domed in a half circle all around us. There wasn't much in the way of trash, which showed how well traveled these paths were.

We all spread out for a break, those who had snacks munched on them or drank a bit of water. I chatted with Dras and Jer, because these tunnels were everything I'd hoped for. Several of the other kids seemed to know one another and were having similar conversations. Most were astounded at how large the room was.

"Yeah, must have been part of a noble's house or something."

Jer turned to the other direction, toward the exit right as he spoke, looking a bit confused.

It was a few seconds later that I heard some noise coming from that way. It sounded like scratching, filled with some high-pitched squeaks and shuffling.

"Problem. Dras, can you cover me?" Jer slipped his club out, looking toward the exit. "Everyone who doesn't have a weapon, back to the tunnel, stay at the door."

"Heck, yeah. Alana, light us up." I saw my young wizard friend light his hands with flame as he moved into place behind the other boy. I tossed my light up toward the ceiling just above the entryway. I slipped up behind Dras as my mace came out, too, ready to back him up if needed.

Eight rats spilled out of the exit we were headed to. They were massive, each as big as a hunting dog. They took a few seconds to sniff around before turning and running at us, their tails flapping wildly behind as they did so, giant worms slapping the air.

"Big problem." Jer was refreshingly brief in his words.

Dras, for his part, had two small ribbons of flame shooting from his hands, whipping forward to slap a few of the first rats. The fiery tentacles engulfed them in light, making the whole group's charge stumble.

Once the charge reached our leader, he showed his muster. He was well trained in dealing with this kind of vermin, and his quick, fluid movements showed he knew exactly where and how to strike to take them down. There were a few moments that looked bad. But any time things got really out of hand, a ribbon of fire would lash forward, taking out the interloper.

I had the feeling that if Jer'd been without all the kids he just would have fallen back to a doorway and fought them one at a time. With a bunch of clumsy kids who didn't know how to fight and might get lost, that wasn't really an option. That said, he was still showing that he knew exactly what he was doing.

When just under half were down one slipped past, seeming to have found a new target. It dodged and wove, before jumping and latching onto Dras's arm, biting deep. He yelled and the fire faltered, until I stepped forward and got it right in the spine with my mace. The rat spasmed and let go, flopping around on the floor.

"Keep the fire up!" I yelled at the injured boy. He'd let his ribbons drop completely. He quickly remade one and set it back to work.

A few moments later, the battle ended. Jer was winded, panting as he bent over the burnt and bashed corpses around him. Dras looked like he was trying to keep himself from tearing up as his adrenaline faded and the pain came to the fore. The other kids looked scared from where they stood near the opening we had used to enter the room.

"We need to get him to a healer."

Jer hesitated, looking forward and back, seeming to weigh his options. Dras was just cursing.

"Here . . . I'll close it up." Dras summoned a bit of fire into his other palm, reaching for it.

"Stop that! I got it." I moved forward and worked on his arm, letting the magic slowly stream along the damaged muscle and skin. It was a nasty wound, and I took the time to just hit the cure disease on the area too. Fortunate, since I could feel something creeping in. Those things had disgusting stuff in their mouths.

"You don't burn wounds closed unless you're about to die." I bonked the dumb boy on the head once I'd finished. Doing it while he was in pain would have just been too much.

Dras flexed his arm, checking it out. "I didn't know you could do healing . . ."

"Cool."

Jer watched the whole thing until it was done, blinking a bit. A couple of the other kids made similar comments.

"Really? Huh, I guess it never came up."

We'd been hanging around for quite a while now, but I suppose he'd never been injured enough for me to actually do any healing on him. Now that I thought about it, I normally did any practice like that alone.

"So . . . what now?" I looked at our guide, who seemed to waffle on that decision.

"Well, I don't think there'll be any more . . . and going forward will be a bit faster."

After a bit, we did decide to proceed. Jer made sure of the rats' demise and then tied them all together. Dras would be dragging the corpses behind us, as they were all worth a fair amount. The vermin of unusual size, and number, would actually make a good deal of money when turned into the local authorities. Keeping even small monsters like those out of the city was worth a pretty penny . . . or copper I suppose.

Eight was also an extreme number. From what I was told, three was average, with five being considered a very large group. The boys would be letting the local ratcatchers know. That many might indicate something odd going on.

To my relief, the rest of our trip was widely uneventful. The other side thankfully had stairs leading up, as dresses and ladders were not a good mix. After about another half hour, we all made our way out.

I recognized the area, since it was just off the main market. The older boys slung the haul between them, and we began to walk home as a group. Everyone chatting about the fight and how exciting it was. I thought it was a bit weird that the kids who didn't do anything were all into it, but it was a fun little bout.

We were perhaps two streets away when a woman saw us and came over. She was a bit older, perhaps in her late thirties, and beelined it for our little group. Her blond hair was done up in a tight bun and she looked rather severe.

"Adraias, where have you . . . What the hell happened to your arm!?" She rushed forward, grabbing him and pulling the offending appendage close. It took her a few moments to realize it wasn't currently bleeding.

"Oh, Mom, I got bit when we got attacked . . ."

"Attacked! You were down there hunting rats, weren't you? And how am I supposed to pay for this healing, huh? Do you know how much that costs!?" She seemed determined to chew him out for everything all at once. There were a few passersby who stopped to watch the incoming discipline, snickering a bit.

"He was just showing us around. We really did get attacked." I decided to step into the line of fire for my friend. A mistake to be sure when his mother rounded on me.

"Which he shouldn't have been doing. Even if you were, the cost of the healing is going to be an issue."

I was doing a bit of mental math on that one. I knew how much I could make just filling items with mana. I also had a good feel for how much mana Dras had. Less than me, but not terrible. He could absolutely have paid for the healing without any problem. Conclusion: Dras was hiding money from his family, but I didn't know why.

"No, it isn't. I'm not charging for healing my friend."

That put a bit of a damper on her.

"Who are you? I don't think I've seen you around before."

"I'm Alana. I hang out with your son all the time . . ."

"Really? He hasn't mentioned you. You should come over and have tea some time. I'd love to get to know you."

Dras was mouthing "run" behind her, since she'd turned her head away from him. I wasn't sure if I was hurt because he hadn't told his parents about me, or curious as to why.

"Ah . . . another day then."

"Right, I'll have Adraias set something up. Speaking of . . ." She turned, grabbing her son by the ear. "Come along, we're going to get your clothes cleaned up and have a little talk about not introducing your friends to your parents."

I waved at him as he was being pulled by his mother . . . poor guy.

CHAPTER 31

✦

A MEETING OVER TEA

The next day, Dras came to see me after my afternoon shift. He looked thoroughly exhausted when he came in.

"So, my mom wants to meet you."

I narrowed my eyes at him. "Questions first. Why did you not tell her about me?"

"To avoid all of her questions, and because she'll try to sink claws into you too."

I didn't know what to say.

"My mom is nosy to an unbelievable degree. She also thinks that we're courting now, regardless of what I tell her. There's a lot that I keep from her, partially because I don't want her in my business, but also for other reasons."

"Like how much money you're making? She was worried about the cost of healing. With your amount of mana, it would be no problem to make that much. I know you well enough to know that you do already."

"Yeah, like that. Will you not tell her about that?" He seemed genuinely concerned that I would.

"Maybe, if you tell me why."

"You know that there's an academy for mages in the city, right?"

"I didn't, but I did kind of assume."

"Well, the tuition is expensive. I want to go when I'm old enough, but my family will want that money for their own expenses."

I was really familiar with my family taking the money I made. I hadn't minded at the time since I was so young, but now it would really grate if they did. "You should help them some at least, they are family."

"I do! When I first manifested my abilities, they took everything I made, all of it. Mom knows I'm making a bit more now, but not how much. If she knew how much she'd want more, and I can't afford that if I want to get into the academy. Right now, it'll be close as it is."

"Fine, I won't tell her." He was my friend, and that at least wasn't an unreasonable request. I did have another question though. "Does this academy take bards too?"

"Huh, yeah, any kind of caster. They start when you're fourteen. There's an entrance exam every fall, unless you're a noble or know someone who has a good in with the staff."

"Interesting, I'll have to look into that. So you're going . . . next year?"

"Year after, I was born in early winter."

"I'll have to think about all of that. That's a long time off though. When and where does your mom want to meet? I'm guessing not here, since she probably doesn't know that you spend so much time in a tavern."

"Yeah, maybe don't mention that, or explicitly where you work. Mom doesn't like this whole street."

"Don't you live like right down it?"

"We're two over. She wanted you to come by for tea on the next day you're off. If that's okay?"

"That's fine, mind taking me over then?"

"Yeah, yeah, but I won't be joining you two. She was real clear on that."

"All right then, come by around . . . late morning? Something like that. I'll be around all day anyway, so it's fine."

He looked relieved as we went off for our usual practice, running through several of our spells. I was still keeping the invisibility one secret though. It seemed like something special, and I wanted an ace up my sleeve to surprise him one day.

I woke early the day of and after a quick breakfast took my time getting ready. Getting truly clean was a pain, particularly at this time of year. I had no tub, nor large basin, so washing out of a couple of buckets was it. Using my improvised shower was also a bloody pain; there was water and soap everywhere. I was also thoroughly thankful for my heating spell, else I would have been freezing. My better clothes were luckily clean anyway, as I'd had plenty of time for laundry.

My hair was normally loose; but since this was as close to a formal event as I'd been to in the past nine years, I decided to go with something a bit fancier. I did a quick French braid, which I moved into a bun. In this world, I'd only seen something even a bit like this on Hazelwood's daughter. In my previous life, I'd done this and seen it done on a childhood friend's hair several times. It was a first for me in either life. I'd kept it short in my previous, and only done simple stuff before here.

I headed out to the common area of the tavern to sit down and wait for Dras. Lucien came over to look at me, looking like he wanted to say something.

"What?"

"All right, what are you up to?"

"Er . . . I'm going to tea with Dras's mom?"

"Tea with . . . okay." He skulked off, seeming to believe I was going to cause some mischief.

When Dras came in, he stopped and stared for a few moments before saying, "You did your hair different."

"Yup."

"It's . . . nice."

"Thank you."

I was getting the distinct impression that I might have overdone it. Sure, nobody in the village did much other than simple ponytails, but it wasn't that big of a deal. I mean, I was pretty sure I'd seen something like this before here. Racking my memory, I found only images of really wealthy women in the upper part of the entertainment district, or girls dressed super fancily with really done-up hair. Well, it had taken me too long, and I wasn't taking it down now, so whatever.

Dras's house was only a couple of streets away. The coward bolted as soon as I got to the door. It would appear he wanted nothing to do with this entire outing. Within only a few moments, his mother had appeared and brought me in, giving me a big smile.

"So, tell me about your family." She launched right in as soon as the drinks and small snacks were served.

Their house was not big, nor really fancy, but they were not terribly bad off either. It was two floors stuck between several other small homes right on the edge of the entertainment district, closer to the wall.

"We're from a village out east. Dad used to be a soldier. I have two . . ." I had to pause for a moment to compose myself. "One brother."

She raised an eyebrow, but didn't ask. "How long have you known Adraias?"

"Since spring I guess? Adraias?"

"My son dislikes his name for some reason I cannot comprehend. Something I'd rather him get over. It is a pretty name, isn't it?"

"It's nice." This seemed to be a sticking point between the two. I was beginning to understand some of his issues with her if she couldn't even call him by a nickname.

"How did the two of you meet by the way?"

"Oh, some people were fighting and spilled their food all over me. So I dropped them like a stone. Dras seemed to think it was hilarious and started to want to hang out after that."

"Really? What kinds of things do you do?" She leaned in, staring intently.

"Talk mostly, and practice. There aren't a lot of kids around here who're casters."

"Oh, that's true! What kind of things do you two practice?" I could feel where she wanted this to go already.

"Our magic is pretty different, so we each do our own. But it's fun to have someone to talk to while you're doing it."

"I see. What sort of things is he working on now? He's pretty shy about showing us that kind of thing." And there it was.

"What a caster can do is a very personal question. You should really ask him if you want to know." Her face went absolutely sour for about half a second before she recovered.

"Like I said, dear, he won't talk to me much about it. I really was hoping you might tell me."

"If he doesn't want to talk about it, then I shouldn't." It was clear that this was not at all the answer she wanted. Unfortunately for her, it was a super-personal question, and he'd made it clear he didn't want her to know anything at all.

"Well I am his mother, dear."

"If someone went to tell another about the magic I could do, I would be irritated, even if they were family. What you are asking is between him and whoever he wants to share it with." There came a time when you had to just be blunt, and we'd reached it. I did at least manage to keep my tone calm and polite, even if it was a hard no in a light tone with a smile, it was still a brutal turndown.

She huffed a bit, and changed over to some other mundane topic. Our little meeting ended shortly thereafter. I got the feeling that Dras's mom really, really did not like being told no, and I felt a hard pang of sympathy for him.

* * *

The next day, my friend came by to tell me how his mother had spent the better part of her evening railing against me, which he took to be the highest compliment on my personality he'd ever heard. He had, in fact, been told that he needed to not hang out with me, that I was a bad influence. So, of course, he was going to spend as much time as was possible hanging with me. I really worried about his family life; that couldn't be good.

Winter, on the other hand, quickly fell upon us. Dras did come by the Starlit Sky as much as he could during our snowy season, but that was limited to a couple of times a week. He could easily deal with the cold, but nobody really liked going out during the snowstorms that made up much of the winter.

As people returned to their travels with spring, the rumors of the rebellions continued. It wasn't one group either; details now seemed to speak of several. The empire was being slammed with them too. People were pissed at what the war had done to both countries, particularly the peasants. A few of the border baronies had already fallen, and while troops were moving, the peasants had taken to hit-and-run guerrilla-type fighting. There had even been a few assassinations of nobles.

Magic was a powerful weapon for war. The issue that the nobility was having was simple. Finding their opponents was proving nearly impossible. An army of only commoners could have been crushed, but there wasn't one.

None of that really concerned me. I'd managed to bring down my invisibility spell to a reasonable cost of mana due to a frankly insane amount of practice. Darkness was now easy, too, and while it wasn't at Lucien's level, it was still pretty good. With that, it was time for some new spells.

First I went for a cleaning spell. After some consultation with Lucien, I decided to combine something like the remove disease and remove poison spells. The trick was to imagine the grime and dirt, then pull away and dissolve it, leaving whatever you were working on squeaky clean.

On a whim, I tried to use it to bathe. It worked, sort of. It wasn't pleasant like a bath or shower, nor did it leave the nice soap smell; it felt more like being vacuumed. It also removed hair. My guess was that on some level I instinctively thought of body hair, and stray hairs as yucky. Which meant it was a no-go for washing my hair, unless I wanted to be bald.

I asked about a silencing spell as well. But according to Lucien, that would leave me unable to cast, unless I learned to dance or something. I put a pin in that one and went for an attempt at making sugar instead.

I had seen white sugar in the market once or twice, at insane prices, so I knew it existed in this world. I did not know enough chemistry to know what it looked like, but I was super familiar with it from my life on Earth. I knew how it melted, how it tasted, and how it smelled when it was hot. How to use it in foods and everything else. My experience was deep when it came to the delicious crystals. Thanks to one teacher who'd made us look at food under a microscope, I even had an idea of what the crystals looked like when you got close.

Making sugar was not nearly as easy as I might have hoped though. Even with all that I only got around a tablespoon full for what I needed to make several loaves of bread. I was not dissuaded; practice would make perfect in time, of that I could be sure. It could also be safely stored in a jar until I needed it for . . . research purposes.

Jer also started coming around every now and then with Dras. He seemed to think having a friend who was a healer might one day be a good idea. We would spend the spring evenings chatting and wandering the city, seeing what we could.

CHAPTER 32

✦

LIGHTNING STRIKES

I had a real issue as summer began to crest once again. My clothes were getting tight and short; I'd not bought any in a good while. I could make some adjustments, but the only solution that made sense was to go and get new ones.

Normally, I kept only one or two outfits at any one time, since they were quite expensive. This time though, I decided to buy an extra one that could be a bit more formal, in case I needed to make visits to anywhere fancy in the next year or two. To ensure that it would be used long enough to make it worthwhile, I had it made a bit big, with extra cloth in the seams that could be let out as needed to a fairly good degree. My hope was that it would last me at least until I was thirteen or so.

With new clothes also came new shoes. It had been a while since I'd seen Sorn; he came by the Starlit Sky every now and then, but we just moved in different areas of the city now. So I made a point to go see him.

"Hey there, Sorn!" I yelled out as the entrance bell to his shop rang announced my arrival.

"Oy, look at you!" We smiled at each other, even exchanging hugs. "So, I can guess why you're here. What are you looking for today?"

"Work shoes and boots of course. When have I ever needed something else?"

"I don't know, but if you're going to go out on the town, you'll need something, eh?"

"Nope, just the normal. How are things by the way? The shop looks good."

It really did. I could tell just from the look of things that he was getting plenty of customers.

"Been good, other than a scare last week."

"Huh?"

"Some noble got ambushed down the street. They locked down the whole area to talk to everyone and try to find the guys who did it."

"You're kidding me!? Did they get them?"

"Not that I know; the men who did it slipped into the Undercity and got away. There were guards going over every nook and cranny. They even ripped up half of my basement trying to find a way into whatever tunnels those idiots used."

"Attacking a noble is a pretty big deal. Were they from another group or something?"

He shook his head. "Rebels if I had to guess. You haven't heard about the goings-on outside the capital, have you?"

"No, I guess not . . ."

"Got a letter from a cousin a couple of weeks ago. Half the country is in some level of rebellion. They're trying to keep it quiet, since it's mostly bandits and the like, but there are still signs."

I blanched as I thought that over. "You don't think the Empire will attack us again, do you? We'd probably not be able to fight much right now."

Sorn snorted. "They've got it worse than us. Most of our stuff is just small unorganized groups. Some idiot calling himself the Lord of Shadows has started going after them, and he's taking huge swaths of their lands."

"What's the story on him?" If there was some rumors, particularly ones that weren't a threat to us, I wanted to hear them.

"Not sure honestly. There's not much anyone knows, save that some of his mages are pulling some terrifyingly powerful magic out of nowhere. Higher order stuff, at least that's what I've heard."

"Scary, I hope they stay over there."

"Me too, Alana. I've seen enough fighting to last me several lifetimes. On a happier note, I'm getting married come winter!"

"Huzzah! Someone I know?"

"Doubt it, but um . . . could I ask for a small favor?"

"Depends on what it is."

He moved behind the counter and pulled out a small box. Inside it, there was a little orb, covered in runes. "This is a little security device, but it requires a huge amount of mana. Stuff like this is also technically not something I should have, but . . . I want my Jana to be safe, you know? She got it from her father, but I don't know anybody who could fill it up for her, if you don't mind?"

It wasn't a big deal to me. I'd never seen this particular item before, but I had been recharging stuff for a good long while now.

Lucien had even taught me some new things about devices. For example, it was easy to put mana in, but it could also be drained. Draining mana from a device was much more difficult than putting it in, but it was possible. The only exception was your own mana, which could be pulled out with hard, but doable effort.

The runes themselves were some kind of language based on math. That wasn't overly surprising. It was interesting though that it could also represent concepts and was a full language. Many of these items could be made by a single caster, but advanced items required many, multiple types.

That said, books on the subject were expensive and hard to find, and Lucien refused outright to teach me the language. There were guilds and agreements and the like that specified who could do so, and he did not want to run afoul of those. He also explained that while he knew it, he was no expert and didn't craft items himself.

I nodded, placing a hand on it and letting my mana flow inside. I was nearly drained when I had to stop. "You weren't joking about it taking a lot of mana. It's just over half and I'm slammed."

He smiled as he saw the workings of it. "Tell you what, finish it off when you come to get your shoes, and there'll be no charge for them."

"Fine, fine, but this is your wedding present too. That really used too much mana."

About a week later, the shoes were ready. Sorn, for his part, had done a magnificent job on them. I finished recharging his item before I left, skipping out the door. It wasn't too bad, and both of us seemed to think we'd gotten the better end of the deal.

As fall arrived, I found myself with Dras, making our way deep into the upper part of the city. Both of us had worn our best, so as not to stand out too much among the crowd of rich folk and nobles, to limited effect. Ignoring the stares and the following eyes of the guards, we made our way forward.

The Academy of Mages was easy enough to find, being that it was the second-tallest building in the capital. It was also mercifully close to the edge of the nobles' district, rather than deep into it. On most days, the gates were shut and locked tight, but today was different. Today was the day that prospective students took the entrance exam.

Neither of us were nearly old enough to take it, but that mattered little. Our mission today was to go in and scout out what Dras needed to do to pass the exam. The arena where the practical portion took place was easy enough to find, but there was a small issue.

A man in midnight blue robes stood beside the door to the visitors' seating area. He was a lanky kind of guy, perhaps in his twenties. He gave us a deep and appraising look.

"I doubt you two are members of our student body. You're certainly not nobles here to scope out potential talent. What exactly are you two here for?"

"I want to see the tests and what they involve, sir," Dras stated, looking at the man straight in the eye. "It is my understanding that anyone can observe."

"That is technically true, but we generally do wish to know who is in our school and why."

It was clear that we weren't getting in without some explanation.

"I'm Dras; this is Alana." I waved to the man, observing his aura. He was strong, not nearly as strong as Lucien or Mystien, and he had nothing on the sheer terror my dad could give off. Dras's voice broke through my musings on that. "I want to join the academy when I come of age. So I'd like to see what is required."

"Ah, prospective students, I see. Observing the practical won't help you much, but it is permitted." He seemed a bit amused by that.

"Why won't it help us?" I asked. There seemed to be a hint of something truly important there.

"Because the practical is not really a series of tests. There are a few of those on basic mana handling, but judging by your auras, you two would easily pass those. It is primarily a demonstration of the abilities that you've learned before coming to us. The grading scale is based on their power and how you use them. Finesse is just as important as strength. Therefore, everyone's practical exam is different."

"Hmm, what about the written then? I don't suppose you'll tell me what it covers?"

Whoever this man was, and I was guessing a member of the staff, found that very amusing. "Generally speaking, it covers basic math, reading, and writing. On the wizard side, there is a slightly higher weighting toward math, needing a basic understanding of algebra and geometry.

There is a higher weight given to the ability to rhyme and craft prose on the bard side. For priests, there is a section dealing with common beliefs and practices of their order, should they belong to one. A current study guide can be found at any bookstore catering to casters."

I nodded along with what he was saying. Dras looked like he wanted to faint, but that wouldn't be helpful, so I just led him into the arena to watch after bidding the interloper a good day.

"How am I supposed to learn all of that? I can do basic adding and subtracting, and I can do a little bit of multiplication and division, but what even is geometry?"

"Math involving shapes, it's not too hard. We'll work on it together." I had frankly aced geometry when I'd taken it, trig too. I was not at all worried about that section, as long as the basic ideas held.

We found some seats in a visitors' section, well back from the actual action. It was difficult to see what was going on down there, but readily apparent why they'd put us so far away. There were perhaps a half-dozen students currently going through their practical, and the one who launched a bolt of fire into the stands by mistake was the first to go. It had hit well across from us, but the blaze was impressive. The extra space to react—and I was guessing some wards, based on how that fire had quickly gone out—were certainly welcome.

Several groups came and went for their practicals. Those who were obvious failures, like the kid with the firebolt, were removed once it was clear they wouldn't make muster. The others ended up spending quite some time before they were escorted out. Most of these took around half an hour to go.

Watching the proceedings was really close to useless. There were too many different techniques and too many different methods for us to truly understand what they were looking for. Seeing the utter failures didn't really help, either, because most of those were just out-of-control magic.

After two or three hours, we left, both thoroughly frustrated.

"That was a waste of time," Dras complained.

"Not at all. We learned that it would probably be best to focus on the practical. Let's go get one of those study guides!"

Dras grumbled but assented, and we made our way to a nearby bookshop. The girl manning the counter looked at us like we were some dirt on her shoes but got us the study guide, the cost of which we split. I was interested in it easily as much as Dras was, and his expression when she told him the cost made me decide I wanted to read it too.

The book itself was not huge. It was about as big as a textbook ought to be and dense. We'd gotten a small sealable case to go with it, leather with a watertight seal to keep it dry even in bad conditions. It fit over the book like a waxed box.

Dras had it in a small carry sack as we made our way toward home, going down a side street.

Suddenly, the world was bleached blue-white. A thunderous BOOM and the smell of ozone hinted as to what had happened, and it was nearby. We ducked as people started running, Dras pulling me into the nearest wall.

There was panic everywhere as everyone fled the area. I was still a bit stunned when I heard the shouting. Several men were pulling a boy, around fourteen and dressed in some of the nicest finery I'd ever seen, down the street. Behind them, arrows flew; every man had one or two bounce off armor with a few lodging themselves in flesh. On the other end of the street, another group was forming up, ten or twenty at the very least.

A shout went up from one of the groups quickly advancing down the street we were stuck on.

"Take them all down, boys; leave nobody alive." My blood froze, there was no way these men would leave us alive.

Dras, for his part, was thinking much more clearly. He ran to a grate in the street, quickly levering it up and out of its spot in the road.

"Alana! In!"

I didn't have to think. I ran, nearly jumping into the potential exit from the deathtrap of a road. Several of the guards and their charge followed us down the hole with haste. The others were stopped from doing so by another earth-shattering explosion just outside the opening. A few of the soldiers who were too close to the grate were cooked; the rest of us fled down the unknown corridor. Anything had to be better than what was behind us.

CHAPTER 33

✦

INTO THE DEPTHS

My heart was pounding as Dras pulled me through the tunnels. I didn't know these well, and I had a feeling he didn't know where we were either. We had no choice but to flee; after the last attack, I could hear people jumping down into our escape route.

The rich boy and his guards were following us. I was glad they had some kind of lights, so that I didn't need to waste any mana. It wasn't that they were friendly or anything, but we were all running from the same death. There were maybe ten left, mostly big-muscled men; a quick look confirmed that all of them had some kind of aura, and not pathetic weak ones. That honestly scared me a bit; whoever these guys were, they were not playing around. Each was dressed in heavy steel armor, perfectly matching the others of the group.

Eventually though, we had to stop. We ended up in a basement of some kind, all panting from the effort. There was clear delineation between Dras and me and the others.

One of the men, the one who'd been carrying the noble kid, moved forward. "Who are you two? How did you get involved in this?" He hadn't drawn his sword, but his hand was decidedly on it.

"Two prospective students to the academy, and we weren't involved more than running when the fighting started." Dras was a good guy, but I would be taking point on this. If he screwed up and got mouthy, we might be killed.

"How do I know you're not enemies?" The man didn't seem to consider us as such at the moment, and that was good. His interrogation was merely to make sure of things he already suspected.

"If we were your enemy, we wouldn't have led you to a safe location. One more of those lightning attacks would have killed your lot."

"How did you know it was lightning?"

"The sound, the color, the smell—it is obvious what it was."

"Wait, smell?" One of the other men stepped forward, quirking an eyebrow.

"Yes, lightning has a smell. It smells clean, like after a rainstorm."

Their leader seemed to think on that for a while before nodding. "Very well, I currently believe you are not enemies, do you know the way out?"

I looked at Dras, who shook his head. "I don't know this section at all, never been here."

"What about you men? Do you know a way out?"

Their leader, whose name I still didn't know, shook his head. "You two, stay where you are. The rest of you men, spread out, see what you can find."

Within a few minutes, they'd found that the only other way out of our little hidey hole was what looked like some kind of old pipe, drainage or something, that was in one corner of the room. It was far too small for the warrior types to fit through, but they convinced—ordered—Dras to put his head inside. He found that it was decidedly descending.

The noble kid didn't say a word to us. That seemed to be a thing here. For whatever reason, a lot of nobles wouldn't speak to commoners except through their guards unless they had to. I was unsure on exactly the rules and had hardly any experience with nobles, so I made a note to ask Lucien. That was assuming we made it through this.

That proposition seemed less likely when we heard the noise of many men coming down the hallway that had led us to this space. They weren't being quiet about it. That led to a few hasty decisions; most of the guards took up positions near the doorway and blocked it with anything they could find.

"So, Dras, pipe or lightning-wielding maniacs?" The answer seemed obvious to me as I whispered it over.

"Pipe, obviously."

We made our move. The soldiers were all a bit preoccupied with their impending doom and how best to make their final stand as Dras flitted in. I got spotted as I jumped in after him, but it was far too late for them to do anything about it as I hurried into the angled exit.

And angled steeply it was. As soon as I got in, I found myself being pulled down, like a water slide, minus the water. I half-crawled, half-slid down the metal tube. It was rough, each slide found little friction and ripped at both skin and clothes. The sound of whatever lightning weapon was being discharged sped me along with haste, as did what sounded like someone following. After two discharges of thunderous death, there were no others.

I gritted my teeth as we went. From both ahead and behind, I heard the occasional grunt or hiss of displeasure, but was thankful that nobody was stupid enough to speak in the echo chamber. I wasn't sure how long it took for us to make it through. Once we did, however, we came out into a massive cistern of some kind.

The room was massive, I couldn't count the columns that were supporting it as I pulled myself from the pipe and onto a ledge near Dras. He'd started up a small flame to light our way, and with that I could see dozens of columns, each one leading up to arches dozens of feet above us. There was a bit of water in the pool a couple of feet below us, but it seemed not much, less than two feet if I had to guess.

I motioned to my compatriot that we were followed, and we took up defensive positions. Sure enough, our fancy new friend had shuffled in after us. He looked a bit shocked when he saw the young wizard sizing him up for a firebolt to the face. The boy was maybe fourteen or fifteen, and the sword at his waist spoke to his vocation. Much like his guards, he, too, had an aura and a relatively powerful one.

We all stood fairly still for a few moments before Dras finally broke it and asked. "You going to stab us in the back?"

"I had not planned to, seeing as you're probably my best chance for getting out of here."

"Your guards?"

"Shoved me in the pipe after the first use of whatever that weapon was. I regret to say that they're likely dead." It was easy to tell that he was quite broken up by that and was struggling to maintain his composure.

"Sorry for your loss. We have more important matters at hand though. Do you know if you were followed?" I leaned forward as I talked. If we were still in danger of going up against those assassins, I wanted to know quickly.

He nodded. "I do not think so. It sounded as if there was a collapse behind me. I propose we work together to get out of this mess."

"All right then. I'm guessing you're a physical magic user?" Dras asked. I thought it was a fairly obvious thing.

"Of course, ah, but where are my manners, you may call me Pr . . . Lief."

"Dras."

"I'm Alana."

"Well then, do either of you know where we are?" Lief's question met to shaking heads. "Then I suppose we must find our own way out." He set off without further consultations. I wanted him as a vanguard anyway, but the fact that he was happy to lead us wherever we were going seemed promising, if a bit rash.

After exchanging a shrug with Dras, I followed. Our fearless leader produced a small stone from a pouch that lit up brightly, easily illuminating the room. Which gave a good scale as we moved along the ledge. This room was easily 250 feet wide, and nearly double that in length. We'd entered about halfway down one of the longer sides.

"This place is huge. Who even built it?" I couldn't help my curiosity as we trouped our way along.

Lief looked over briefly at one of the columns. "The kingdom, of course, or one of its predecessors. The stonework is around a thousand or so years old. There are a few pieces like it in the academy, and some of the areas in the nobles' section of the city. Though parts were likely added later, like that pipe."

"Okay, so, do you have any idea of where we're going?"

"First, away from that pipe. Then I suggest we go upward."

"Right, but we need to be careful. These tunnels are quite dangerous; there are even a few monsters."

He turned and gave me a rather charming smile for a teenager covered in filth. "Do not worry yourself. I will not allow you to come to harm." It was obvious he didn't know that I was a caster.

When we reached a doorway, we scanned the area. It seemed to be a maintenance tunnel of some kind that went neither up nor down, but rather led us along this level.

These tunnels, unlike most that I was familiar with, were both clean and matching. They seemed to be laid out so that someone could move along them to maintain a number of systems involving the cistern we'd found. Unfortunately, all of the exit shafts up were sealed.

After some hours, we came to a room off of a large pipe in the water transport system. It was small, and the pipeline was largely empty. At Dras's suggestion, we stopped to rest there. I summoned us up food and drink, much to the surprise of our erstwhile third.

"You're a bard?"

I smirked at him as I passed over a cheese sandwich. It wasn't much, but it was food and filling.

After we had all enjoyed a nice nap, we kept going. After a time, we'd worked our way past most of the likely candidates for openings back up to the street. We were near the end of one of the canal maintenance lines.

"I don't think there are any other areas down here, assuming the cistern hasn't seen a few of the people out to kill all of us. I suggest we see where one of these pipes go. If it's nothing, that's fine, but people run pipes to places."

Lief perked up, "Oh, that's quite the idea there." With that, he hopped into the large tube and offered me his hand.

The lack of any monsters was putting me on edge. Either there was something killing them, or this place was sealed so tight none could get in or out. I doubted the second, as there seemed to be at least one way in.

"There's nothing living down here, isn't that odd?"

"There was; it was in the cistern, and big." Dras laughed at the face I made.

"Why didn't you say anything!?"

"You didn't need to know. Besides I got the feeling that as long as we didn't go in, it wouldn't hurt us."

I pouted, even more so when our newest addition added his compliment to Dras's behavior and quick thinking.

Our new path led us into another area much like we'd just left. A notable exception though was a hole we found in one of the walls. It was small and hard to fit through, but we managed, ending up in a much more fancy-looking area. There were sculptures and engraving everywhere. It seemed to be a tomb complex of some kind.

A short amount of exploration led us to the large and circular main hall. It went up and down at least one level in each direction, not unlike a library. The hall was huge and open, with branches that led away all surrounding the platforms from which you could see up and down. Stairs linked all the levels. We happily climbed them, ending up on the top landing.

At the top level, there was clearly visible an arch as well as stairs leading upward. It was impossible to tell how far, but they did go decidedly up. Standing to one side of the arch was a large iron statue of a man at attention. The other side seemed creepily empty.

"If I had to guess, I'd say that is our way out." Dras smiled as he pointed toward the arch.

A slight shaking alerted me well before anything else. Slowly making its way around the circle toward us was the other statue. Its pace was far too fast for anything that big and its posture aggressive, each step moving it faster and faster.

The rich boy drew his sword and prepared to face the monstrosity.

"What are you doing!?" I didn't bother to hold back my scream as the thing barreled toward us. We were protected by the fact that it didn't start out fast, and the room was so large.

"We'll defeat this terror here and now!"

"You can't fight that! It's ten feet tall and made of iron, you idiot!"

That did not stop Lief from giving it a go. It wasn't far from watching a gnat try to fight a housecat. He dodged and weaved with ease around the lumbering giant as I indicated to Dras one of the nearby tombs. Its entrance was human-sized and far too small for the thing's shoulders to fit. I considered the stairs briefly, but they looked too sturdy; the iron thing would almost assuredly catch us before we could make it to safety.

The heroic idiot of a warrior was doing his best, but his sword couldn't really harm the giant. Lief would land a strike only for it to screech a bit off the surface of the golem, leaving at most a tiny line. He was fast enough to keep ahead, but it would only take one good blow. The giant got a glancing one on Lief's shoulder; it made a sickening thud, the sound of someone being struck with a tree.

Lief gasped and quickly backed off, one arm limp. We called out to him as we ran toward the doorway, hoping it would keep the titan back. The three of us flew into a room perhaps twenty feet long and ten wide, a few coffins here and there, but little else.

The golem did stop at the door. It shoved its arm in and then pulled its head down to look about, seeing us. It could not fit past the portal though, and it couldn't, or wouldn't damage the structure. Something I was deeply grateful for. The look of the giant peering in at us was enough to send chills down my spine. That thing could pulp a man in an instant; it would turn me into little more than a cute red stain on the ground.

Lief had managed to retain his sword. He did, however, find himself on the ground gasping in pain as the adrenaline wore off. I had Dras watch the door as I worked on his arm. It was certainly broken, and the flesh was pulp. Had it been more than a glancing blow, he would almost certainly be dead.

"I owe you a debt of gratitude, my lady." Lief sounded like something from a storybook. He even gave a sweeping bow as he got up. It took all of my self-control not to laugh.

"Yeah, well, then try not to get yourself killed."

"I will endeavor most assuredly not to. My honor would not allow me to leave such a debt unpaid." If this guy couldn't have caused me so much trouble if or when we got out, I would have been rolling my eyes upside down. He made a few comments at Dras before I told him to quit. There really was nothing an untrained fire wizard could have done to that nightmare.

Another quick meal and we all fell asleep, not sure if we could find a way safely around the golem. We did agree that after we'd rested up we'd take another hard look if possible.

When we did wake up, there was another lad, perhaps Lief's age sitting near us. He had a small lantern made of a box of barely glowing fungi. His skin was deathly pale and eyes huge. He, too, was a physical magic user, though the majority of his aura seemed focused around his eyes, as if to strengthen them in the bleak darkness.

"So, mind telling me how you three got down here? 'Cause I'd really like to leave."

CHAPTER 34

✦

FLESH VS. IRON

I nearly screamed at the newcomer, his appearance shocking me.

Lief in fact leaped to his feet and drew his sword. "Identify yourself!"

Dras jumped up, too, the tiny flame he'd made jumping back to his hand and roaring to life.

"Name's Charles. You still haven't answered my question." He seemed utterly unconcerned with their apparent hostility.

"Wait, Charles? Like Jer's brother?" Dras blurted that out in shock, earning him an appraising look from the new guy.

"You know Jer? Oh, are you that fire-mage kid he was hanging out with? Look how big you got, good on you. I'd love to hear more about that in a bit. Anyway, a way out, do you have one?"

"Um, we came in through a pipe in a big cistern room. We might be able to get out through there."

"And the thing in there didn't eat you?"

"We didn't see it."

"Yeah, weird thing that. It doesn't mind things coming in, but as soon as you try to go back out that way, munch."

"What about through the stairs near here?" Lief spoke up this time around.

"Good idea, wish I'd thought of that a few years ago. So, how do you plan on passing the golem at the door?"

Lief took the cue to think about what he was saying. "Any ideas on how to go about that?"

"Not really, I was thinking I might try dropping part of the ceiling on the wanderer, see how that goes."

"What can you tell us about them? Are they solid or hollow? Is there any indication on them or the rest of the area on how to turn them off?" I smacked him with a barrage of questions about our enemies.

"Oh, now you're asking the real questions. Come on, I'll show you what I've got." He turned toward the exit to our little hidey hole.

"Um, what about the wandering golem?"

"Two floors down. As long as we keep well away from him, he won't come after us."

Charles was right, and our friend the killer iron monster was nowhere around. I could hear him walking about far off, but we saw nothing.

He led us to his little lair, one of the larger tombs, still with a very small entrance, that had several rooms. Glowing moss and lichen had been gathered and was all along the walls, providing a small amount of light. In the middle was a little carving from some kind of clay. It was a golem in extreme detail, every rune and line on it standing out.

"As far as I can tell, they're solid or mostly solid. They don't ring if you hit them with something big. I've got no clue on the runes. I copied them here as you can see, but I don't know anything about what does what. There isn't anything else around quite like them."

Lief jumped into looking at the model, even asked for an extra light. While he was doing that, I looked back toward our host.

"What about sight, how do they see?"

"With their eyes, I guess?"

"No, do they need light to see? Or can they operate in perfect darkness?"

"Oh, not sure, but they seem to do fine in the dark. I haven't tried to get close to one in pitch-black, but I don't care to die either."

"Do they have to recharge or something? They've got to be using a lot of mana."

"They're drawing it from the ambient mana down here. There may be some form of storage, but I wouldn't know if I couldn't get one apart." Lief had looked around as he spoke. "See here, this group of runes is for doing that. It's a bit strange and I'm not completely familiar with the arrangement. Probably explains why there isn't much down here though, between them killing it, or just eating the mana most bigger things won't move in."

"Can we just break that sequence then?"

Lief shook his head. "Not unless you've got a siege engine, no."

I sighed, looking back toward Charles. "Do we even need to fight them? What if we just distract them and get past? Do you know what's up those stairs?"

"The wanderer can be avoided, but the one at the stairs can't. He never moves from his spot unless you get really close. He also won't chase, so no leading him away. As for what's up there, there's a door, the stairs guy will follow you up to it."

"Can we at least do something about the wanderer? Maybe lead him over to the cistern and let him and the monster there fight it out?"

"Wanderer won't leave the tomb area."

I sighed, really wishing for something like a machine gun, or someone more experienced. While Lief and I both thought out plans, Dras caught Charles up on his little brother. It was several hours of me trying to put together an idea for a cannon or something before Lief spoke back up.

"Hey, I figured out how they see."

He instantly got all of our attention.

"It's some form of sound sight. Their movements bounce off of the walls and back to them, letting them see what's around them."

"What would happen if we overloaded it with noise?" That might be a key to at least distracting these things for a while.

"I don't know."

We decided to set up an experiment. Waiting until the golem was on the top floor of the tomb, I positioned myself on the opposite side of the open hole that was the center. I got the boys to sing with me for support and let loose on our friend the wanderer. I'd never hit a scream quite that hard, and it was painful even from where I stood.

The golem turned and charged straight at me. It would appear that it couldn't see anything else, because it ran right into the big hole in the middle of the room. I stopped as it fell, and the enormous crash could be felt by all of us.

"So . . . is it down?"

Charles leaned over the edge. "Looks like one of its legs is bent all weird."

"It seriously cannot be that easy, can it?"

"I mean, it's still moving, barely."

There was a loud snap and a crack ran up across the ceiling. "Oh, oh, that's bad."

More cracks started spiderwebbing out from the main one, running all down through the tomb. As they expanded one by one a few small pieces of ceiling began to fall. I could feel the blood draining from my face as I turned to the others.

"The time for planning is over! We need to go now!" Lief declared and he turned toward the second golem and started running. "I'll distract it; get that door open!"

He'd learned his lesson last time and didn't even bother drawing his sword, instead he charged and dipped to dodge the monster. Charles and Dras slipped past quickly, easily pulling ahead of me as rumbles filled the hall. They had no issue passing as the golem did its very best to squish Lief.

"It's stuck," yelled Dras.

I managed to get up the stairs and start pulling along with them, but it was no use. The door adamantly refused to budge, and none of us had the strength to change its mind.

Having an idea, I yelled to Lief. "Bring the monster in here. I think I've got something."

Lief obliged; as he led it in, I put myself right in front of the door, looking down the stairs. The tomb was falling apart. Even the floor near our area was starting to break near the center of the main room, tossing hunks of stone into the abyss. We'd have only one shot.

As the golem followed its target up the steps, I motioned the noble out of the way and let loose the loudest scream I could. The giant stopped turning toward Lief and came at me full-on. With my back pressed to the door I needed removed, the monster pulled back its leg for a mighty kick as it flew forward.

I cut off my scream and dove for cover as the golem came in. I was not quite fast enough though, and part of the uncompromising limb rammed my left leg. I heard the sound of metal breaking and the door flying off of its hinges. Someone had me, pulling me up and past the broken portal. I could hardly see, the pain was immense as I was dragged before finally being put down on the floor. I didn't scream; it was too much for that. All I could do was gasp for breath as my body flopped like a fish.

"Alana! Alana, look at me!" Dras shouted. He was kneeling beside me, pulling my face to look as him as I shook in agony. "It's your leg. You have to heal it; you're bleeding. We can't get you up like this, and you'll die if we can't stop it."

A quick look down at my leg revealed a bloody disaster with bones sticking out here and there. I tried to sing, to push my magic into it, but it was so hard, so hard to keep a tune going.

"You need to cast, now." Dras was leaning over me still. The other two looked pale, in Charles's case even more than usual. "Here, I'll sing with you." He hummed a lullaby to me. I knew it; every child in the region probably did. It was this world's version of "Twinkle, Twinkle, Little Star." I managed a few notes here and there, each pushing the healing spell I was focused on into my leg.

I had enough in me to realize I needed to stop the bleeding fast, the growing pool of blood around my mangled limb a constant reminder. I sealed up the wounds, reconnecting the broken blood vessels as best I could. The bones I just sort of shoved back in. There was no time for more since I was bleeding so badly. If I survived, I could worry about that later.

There was a loud booming sound and a rush of air and dirt as I closed up the wound. The bones were still looking like a broken window, just little shards everywhere, but I was no longer bleeding in a manner that would surely mean death down here. My mana was gone, down to just the last dregs.

"It's sealed up. Just need more mana. Don't move me."

My vision blurred and closed off as I lost consciousness. The worried faces of my friends the last thing I saw.

I awoke sometime later in profound pain. Gasping as a few tears streaked down my cheeks. Everything hurt; my body was complaining on all fronts. My head was pounding like someone had taken a hammer to it, and let us not forget that my leg was sending waves of torment, one after the other, but I was alive.

"Water." My voice was hoarse as I called out for aid.

Charles brought over a skin, a literal skin, and brought it to my lips. It was foul and warm, but the water there was enough to sate my thirst. I made a mental note to get him more when I had the option.

"Can everyone sing with me again?"

A few nods and we all went into a halting version of the same children's song. The gestalt effect was a lifesaver here, potentially literally. With the extra power, I managed to get my leg back into a workable state. I was still in a lot of pain, but I was fairly sure I could walk on it. Magic sure was great.

Looking down at my leg again gave me an idea of what it must have been. My dress was soaked with blood, staining it a darkening burgundy. The ground near me was also sticky with the drying stuff that had leaked all around it. My now whole-ish leg was dark purple with bruises. I didn't have enough juice to fix that, even with the gestalt.

Dras sat beside me in a place that was clean enough. "You going to be okay?"

"Yeah, yeah, give me a few minutes and I'll be ready to start moving again." I said, patting him on the shoulder.

"Take all the time you need; we don't seem in immediate danger." Lief turned and looked down at me kindly as he spoke. He seemed a good guy.

"It would be nice to get on the way though, when you're ready." Charles was practically bouncing. The years alone had really messed with his social skills and potentially his brain.

After a few more moments of break, I got Dras to help me shakily stand up. "Okay, let's go home."

CHAPTER 35

✦

THE ASCENT

Trying to make my way down the tunnel was a bit rough. I needed to heal my leg as soon as possible, since it was slowing me considerably. I was also going to have to maintain a light and start making food and water here soon. Charles had a bit, but the rest of us were right out.

"Can we stop for a moment when we find a good place?" I asked. Lief was leading, with lots of advice from Charles.

"Sure, soon as we find a spot."

It was perhaps fifteen minutes later when we did find something. A small section of carved-out rock, it had moss and fungi growing along the walls. Some gave off a light glow, meaning I could at least drop my light and rest a tiny bit.

Charles went around, picking several off the different types. "Some of these are quite yummy. These mushrooms here go well with rat; make it a little spicy."

"That's . . . good to know I suppose. Here, bring your water over; I'll top you off." As soon as I had the water, I drank it all, then refilled it with fresh, cool stuff. We passed it around after that, filling it a couple more times.

"Nice trick, could have used that."

"Where were you getting water anyway?" Dras set a little flame to hovering as he spoke.

"Oh, there was a drip in one of the cistern's pipes. Came down onto a bit of stone that'd worn down into a bowl."

"Yeah, I like the magic stuff better than the funky old cistern water." Since I was planning on running it for us until we got out I could be picky.

There was a good little alcove outside the mushrooms and moss cave where we took turns relieving ourselves. I was thankful that it went back far enough that nobody could see when someone did so.

A couple of hours later, we found what might have at one point been remains. A few pieces of cloth, some scattered buttons and buckles, and a club. After saying a few prayers for the dead man, asking him to rest and thanking him for leaving his weapon for others, Charles took the club and gave it a few swings.

"Whoever he was died a good long time ago, not as old as some of the bodies in the tomb, but old. Looks like rats got to him too."

"Did you actually open the coffins!?" Lief looked scandalized.

"Yes, I was hoping to find something to stop the golems. I never did; there were a few rings and the like, but I left them all alone. I've no desire to disturb the dead, nor to desecrate them for money."

Lief still looked miffed and a bit put off.

"Look, there's plenty of old tombs down here. Most lacking murderous golems. And sometimes those tombs get infested with rats or other small monsters. It is a ratcatcher's job to clean those out, and all the best know the proper prayers to say before and after disturbing their graves, and not to take of the dead for financial gain. I took this because I needed a weapon, not out of greed, but out of the hope that I may return home. Do you think this dead man would begrudge me that?"

"Well, no, I suppose not . . ."

"Of course not. Also I didn't, and won't go through his corpse for coins, or rings, or anything like that. Just too damn disrespectful."

While I might not have had as much of an issue because of my previous life, it seemed this was a strong taboo here, strong enough even to discourage those that had been stuck for years, not that gold would have helped Charles. Either that or Jer's brother had raided that place and just didn't tell us. Whatever the answer was, I couldn't bring myself to care too terribly much about it.

"So, we don't really have anywhere to bury him . . ."

"No, we'll leave him here." Charles looked down at the fallen man once more, and thanked him for the club again, then we passed onward.

We had to rest again, this time to sleep in an old destroyed basement. I made us dinner and thought Charles would weep when he saw me make food out of thin air. He ate his portion and another, declaring how magnificent my food was. Dras and Lief both told him to chill just short of him making marriage proposals.

We had nothing to sleep on save a bit of rubble. Any other time, the boys might have rolled up a jacket for a pillow, but it was chilly, and laying on the stone and dirt floor sucked the heat from you. I considered using my heating spell, but with all the mana for healing, lighting, and food, I was much lower than I'd like to be. If I used it and there was some emergency, I might run out, and that was unacceptable. So I just shivered on the ground. We did keep a rotating watch, though with this many of us, there were few creatures that would attack.

I woke up in a sorry state. It felt like I'd aged forty years in the last three days and had a hard time stretching my cold, sore joints. Lucky I was a child and bounced back easily. Lief and Charles both seemed all right. I was fairly sure their damn physical magic had done something to keep them in top shape, the pricks.

We kept moving, taking a few more breaks. It was clear that we were moving in the right direction at least. Every now and then, we'd find a ladder or slope that led upward, and we'd cheer. Sometimes though our paths seemed to lead us down. Some amount of backtracking was needed. All of the tunnels so far seemed lifeless and uninhabited, save for the occasional giant rat or slime, which we avoided.

We might have been healthy, but all of us were a bit frayed, save Charles. He was practically giddy. We were caked in sweat, blood, and dirt, barely functional clothing, and confusion from the constant change of direction. I wondered what I looked like, before I looked at the current state of my clothing, then I dreaded what I might see in a mirror, had I had one.

We had to rest again before continuing, and as I went to lay down after my watch, Lief offered me his outer coat. I blinked a bit, it was an extraordinarily nice piece, even ruined.

"You looked horridly cold last night. I'll get it back later."

"Are you sure?"

"It is the duty of the higher classes to protect those lower than themselves."

I stared at hearing that, causing Lief to quirk an eyebrow at me.

"What?"

"That has most decidedly not been my experience with the nobility."

"That . . . pains me to hear, but some have allowed their power to overtake their sense of duty. I hope nothing too bad happened?"

"I don't really care to talk about it." He nodded as I told him that, looking quite concerned.

I thanked him for his kindness and curled up to rest again, deep in thought about how this young man was so very different from other members of the nobility I'd known. It was still bloody cold, but the extra layer really did help, and I wasn't nearly as exhausted the next morning. I returned the nobleman's coat as Dras frowned a bit at the exchange.

"So anyone got any ideas on how deep we are? Or how long till we make it back to the surface?" I asked the boys.

"Well," began Charles, "we can't be too much further from the surface, two or three layers if we're lucky. Only issue is finding the way up and out. I don't know any of these tunnels. It's been years since I really got a chance to be in the ones near the surface, but I used to know the ones in town pretty well down to two. So I think we're still below that."

As we kept moving, we eventually came to another ladder leading up. It brought us into a small little tunnel, after some squeezing and another rip to my dress, we made it into a larger space. After a few rooms, Charles looked around a bit, leading us on a different path and nodding to himself. Only a few minutes later, we came to a big round room, with a small drainage hole in the middle; he gave a big smile and looked around at us.

"I know this place. We're close to the surface, follow me."

He hurriedly moved along tunnels, going this way and that. We all struggled a bit to keep up as he came to another ladder leading upward. Charles's grin was huge as he peered up to the tunnel above us, one hand on a rung. As he looked like he had something to say, I heard voices drift down from up above.

"Anyone find the brat's body yet?"

"No, not yet, but we kind of know where he went."

"What do you mean kind of?"

"Some pipe, had to go find someone small enough to fit in after him. That guy didn't come back so we think he ended up monster food. Boss says no body no proof though, so until we find him . . ."

"Can't we send someone to, you know, kaboom whatever's down there?"

"Used all those in the fighting, won't get more for a few weeks at least."

"That's a shame."

I turned to see Lief beginning to draw his sword. His face looked like a mask of rage. I looked over at him, making a calming gesture, then toward Charles. I held up two fingers with a questioning look. He listened for a few more moments before shaking his head, holding up three.

We took another few moments to decide on a basic plan, shared through gestures and a few mouthed words. That done Charles led the way, with Lief right on his heels. I didn't know who these guys were, or what they were about, but they had tried to kill me. With that in mind, I could wait to get answers to my questions until after we'd beaten them into the dust.

CHAPTER 36

✦

CONFESSION

I heard it when the two older boys got up to the top. It would appear that they saw Charles and started talking.

"Oy, kid, what are you doing down here?"

"Hey, who's that . . . ? They're armed!"

I heard the crash as the groups met when Dras made it to the top of the ladder and moved toward the fight. I was scrambling up as quickly as I could, in case something went wrong. There was still fighting when I got there. Charles was very nearly as fast as Lief was, but the three men were in some amount of armor. They were being pushed back, but it was hard for either boy to land a killing blow.

The appearance of Dras changed that. His flame-ribbon spell worked around the sides, jabbing at the men and cutting off their escape routes. With that, and the boys jabbing in, there was no hope. Within only a few moments, two of our enemies fell to the ground, the blows that had hit them fatal. Charles had taken a hit to the side and had to fall back.

Lief caught the last man under his right arm, causing him to drop his weapon and fall. The boy stepped forward, with hate in his eyes, raising his sword.

"Stop, he's beaten." I spoke calmly from behind as I approached.

"Men like him deserve to die." He hesitated but did not lower his weapon.

"Perhaps, but not like this. If you kill him, you will regret it."

He snorted and asked, "What would you know about putting down garbage like this? Nothing. Hold your tongue."

"I know enough about this sort of killing and I know you will regret it. Do not go down that path."

That caused a pause in the room. Lief didn't look away from the man he was standing over, but I could sense his hesitation. I could feel Dras's eyes boring into me as well, even Charles seemed a bit put off. Lief allowed his eyes to flick to Dras. "See if his friends have some rope or chains or something and bind him." Then he looked back to the man where he lay on the ground and said, "If you try anything, I will kill you."

I moved to Charles's side and began to heal him. The wound was luckily not very deep. If there'd been organ damage, it might have been a real drain on my mana, but the long gash only went into his muscle at one or two places. A quick patch job would be enough to deal with this for now.

Dras had bound the man using some rope from one of his companions; he stripped off most of the armor and all of the weapons, tossing it all to the side.

"We'll take him with us and hand him over to the guards," Lief declared.

"We need to go up there and see what's what before we do that. I'd rather know what our situation is." It seemed I would have to be the voice of reason here.

"Oh, I'll go and scout!" Charles offered.

"No, I should go with Lief. I have some stealth abilities, and if we do find some guards, having the son of a noble house will get them to actually do something."

Almost nobody seemed to like that idea. Dras was having trust issues because of my recent declaration. Charles wanted any chance to get out of these bloody caves. He would have been a good choice, except that I wasn't really sure if he'd come back to the group if he went scouting. Lief seemed to understand that I didn't want to leave him with the man he'd been about to kill, and that irked him a bit. It took them a few minutes, but eventually they all did agree, only after giving me a few glares though. Charles pointed us in the direction of the nearest exit; it was an easy straight shot.

For once, Lief had me in front. He was tense, like he no longer trusted me. I knew what was coming and was thankful that he waited until we were out of earshot to begin asking his questions.

"You've killed a man before?"

"Yes, are you planning on handing me over to the guards when we're done down here?"

"Without the help of all of us, I would have died down there. Whatever happened, if I can't make it right, I'll keep your secret, but I need to know what happened."

I quirked an eyebrow up at him. Even with what I'd already said, I might have signed my death warrant. I couldn't help but trust him here though. I knew to tell him everything could kill me, but I was so tired of carrying all of it. If I died, at least I could die with a clean conscience.

"I'm sure you had a good reason for it, whatever it was."

"I wish I was as sure as you are." I took a few moments to think, then looked at him. "What do you know of the villages throughout the kingdom? About how the people live there?"

"They farm, giving some of their products as taxes, the rest they keep to live off of."

"The war with the empire, it shattered that. Without men to help with the fieldwork, it just couldn't get done fast enough."

"Well, that's bad, but I don't see where this is going."

"Because of a series of events that would take far too long to tell you, the village I was from was dying."

"Certainly, it couldn't have been . . ."

"Starvation. My ability to make food is limited, Lief. For years, I pumped as much bread as was reasonable out just to keep us afloat, and it just kept getting worse. Disaster after disaster struck, and as winter approached, all of us could look at the numbers and see it. Most of us would be dead by spring."

He looked shocked; his eyes were wide as he listened to my story. "But the local lord should have done something, or the mayor at the very least."

"Our lord didn't care, Lief. You have not seen things from any side but your own, so let me tell you something you don't know. Most of the nobility seems to regard those not close to them as disposable. It was the lord's proclamation that led to the final disaster that doomed us and our mayor. Our bastard of a mayor didn't do anything; he went along with what he had to have known would be our destruction. He turned his back on all of us and assured we would die."

"And so you killed him for it?"

"No, no, I killed him because after all of that he showed up on my doorstep with his men demanding healing while standing over the corpse of my brother. I don't know why, but they'd cut his head off, and then had the gall to come to me to patch them up." I was shaking, there were tears forming in my eyes as I stared him down. "It wasn't self-defense, or justice, or anything like that. It was rage and hate. Just like that man you were going to kill back there, and it haunts me, Lief. When I sleep, I dream of bodies and blood on my hands. I don't want you to understand that, to do anything like I did that day."

Lief slumped, he let his eyes fall for a moment. "I . . . understand. I understand why you stopped me, thank you."

I turned and walked on in silence. I could feel how close to the verge of tears I was, but I couldn't cry now. I had to make it just a bit more, just a little bit longer.

When we got to the exit, it was thankfully just a door, a small mercy that I wouldn't have to climb a ladder out of here. I took a few moments to compose myself before I turned to my companion. It was hard, but it was enough to get me back to where I could speak to him without tearing up.

"I've got an invisibility spell. I'll go out and see what I can find out. Will you wait here for a few moments?"

"Yeah . . . I'll do that. Hey, don't mention my name. If you find someone, just bring them back here and I'll talk to them, all right?"

"Okay, sure."

I sang for a few moments and cloaked myself. It was still a ton of mana but manageable now. I slowly opened the door and slipped out onto the streets.

It was late afternoon and overcast. The roads were strangely empty. I took a few moments to mark my location and set off to find what information I could. I didn't see a soul as I made my way toward the nearest guardhouse. We'd come up in the nobles' section of the city, and they were fairly common here, so it didn't take me long to find it.

What I found there though was alarming. The whole place was abuzz, like someone had kicked a hornet's nest. Men were coming and going at speed. I did note that all of them were in standard guard uniform.

Falling back a block, I found a secluded corner and dropped my spell. That done, I went back to the street and began walking toward the guardhouse. As soon as I got to the street, several of the men came over, looking a mix of surprised and deadly serious.

"What in the world happened to you!?" one of them remarked. I had been so distracted by everything that I'd nearly forgotten that I looked like I'd been beaten, cut up, and left in a mud puddle.

"I got stuck in the tunnels with a couple of my friends a few days ago. What happened? Where is everyone?"

"There was a major attack by some rebels. Several were killed; the king has locked the city down for the moment."

"I think that we might have run into a couple of them as we were trying to get out. The boys took them down and captured one. Could you send some help?"

A number of guards were brought, and they seemed leery of both me and my story. Regardless, they came along. They really wanted to catch the people who'd done all this damage. I was made to lead the way, and several of the men had crossbows, keeping an eye all around them as they went.

I opened the door to find Lief standing there looking at the guardsmen. His face was almost like it had been when we'd first met. Those first few hours when he wasn't a friend or companion and still the high-born noble boy ruling all that he saw.

"Do you know who I am?" he asked the man who appeared to be leading this unit.

"I-I do." The guardsman looked shocked.

"Good, send two of your men straight down this tunnel. There are two boys down there keeping an eye on a prisoner. Send another for additional guards."

I was taken back to the guardhouse and allowed to rest while a whole new bevy of activity exploded. Soon enough, Charles and Dras joined me. The former was a bit overwhelmed with all that was going on and all the people. The latter however was much better at reading me and came and sat beside me, wrapping one arm around my shoulder.

"Hey, we're out now. It's all going to be all right."

"Yeah, yeah, it will."

It didn't take too long before a group of guards in much nicer uniforms came over to us. They seemed to be from a much higher-ranked unit than those in the guardhouse.

"Come with us please. There are a number of things that need to be taken care of."

The three of us rose as one and let them lead us out.

CHAPTER 37

✦

RESULTS

There was a small carriage waiting for us. It was functional, not overly decorated, but neither was it uncomfortable, with plenty of room for both us and the three soldiers. They did not speak as we rattled along down the streets. The vehicle had windows, of course, but nobody seemed much interested in looking out of them.

I was nearly trembling as we slowed to a halt and were led out of the carriage. Where we were was obvious in an instant. The large gleaming building standing above us was one all of us knew quite well. The guardsmen who'd brought us led us inside what could only have been an entrance for servants and low visitors, as we were joined by several more, two women and another man moved into our party as we passed through the doors.

"Come with us please." Our little group was broken into three. Two guards led each of us off into rooms. The women, of course, came with me, the men splitting themselves between Charles and Dras.

The room I was led into was rather spartan: a table and two chairs. The guards took up spots beside the door as another woman bustled in. She quickly and quietly took all of my measurements, a small tape being pressed against me again and again. I counted myself lucky at least that they'd allowed me some dignity by not having male guards watching as this woman worked. She had an aura, which was offputting; it hung on her like a shroud.

"Excuse me." I began to try to start up a conversation with the strange lady.

"Not now, dear, I'm working."

She was noting down a number of measurements on a small piece of paper. She took numbers on several places along both legs, even the upper thigh, somewhere that made me stiffen and turn red, along with arm length and diameter, neck, and all along my torso. In the end, she shuffled off, exiting without giving me even the slightest bit of information.

I considered trying to talk to the guards, but one look at their disciplined posture dissuaded that. They stood like statues by the door, watching my every move. It was unnerving. I stood there, tiny and covered in filth and dry blood before the two in their pristine armor, looking down from high above at what must have seemed to them like a beggar.

The awkwardness was "mercifully" ended by the entrance of a slim man dressed in dark gray. He slithered into the room, and even through their discipline I could sense the guards recoil a bit. He had no aura that I could see as he gestured to one of the chairs beside the table.

"Would you please sit?" His tone was smooth and businesslike, but made clear this was an order, not a request.

I sat where he'd indicated, the chair was a plain wooden affair, well made save for the fact that one of the legs was a bit off. No matter how I shifted, I was constantly off balance. From my angle, I also could not see the guards, the whole setup was like it was meant to unnerve. Even knowing that, I could still feel shivers running up my back.

"Good evening, Alana, my name is Emil. We're going to have a little conversation, and you're going to answer me truthfully. Am I understood?"

I nodded.

"Good, good. Now, I'd like you to tell me exactly what happened."

I began my story, detailing how Dras and I had gone to watch the entrance exams, and how we were headed home after visiting a bookstore. When I got to the part of the attack, he interrupted me.

"Did you purchase the book you so desired?"

"Um . . . yes."

"Do you have it with you?"

"Yes." I took it out and showed it to him, he briefly flipped through as he continued asking questions.

"Did you know there was going to be an attack?"

"No."

"How much did the book cost?"

"What?" The sudden jump back was a bit jarring.

"The book you bought. How much was it?"

"Um, ten silvers with the leather case and everything. I split the cost with Dras, since we both wanted to read it."

He raised an eyebrow at that.

"He mostly wanted to read it . . . I cared a bit less."

He chuckled a bit. "I see. That's quite a bit of money. Wherever did you get it."

"I work as a bard."

Another nod and he had me continue. There were a few points here and there where he asked for details on what transpired, but nothing too deep. Eventually, I finished, and he gave me a slight smile. I had pointedly left out the part where I had confessed to murder to a young man who was seemingly far more important than I'd previously gathered.

"Now, I believe you left out the part where you confessed to killing the mayor of your village to His Highness, but that is a rather minor matter."

I felt myself stiffen and my breathing hitch as he spoke.

"Relax, with what you told him, no court would convict you. There's no name that I know of, no place, all that. Not that it matters anyway, if His Majesty has so deemed it, you would still be convicted."

At this point, I was visibly shaking. This man, Emil, sat there with a light smile on his face. He was enjoying himself watching me panic.

"I told you to relax, didn't I? You really must learn to listen, Alana. It's an important skill. The fact is, that nobody cares if you killed some man, well, nobody important. The king did seem a little concerned for a bit, but I'm told our dear queen declared that she didn't care if you'd killed a hundred men and mounted their heads on spikes, for you'd returned her dear son to her. You didn't do that by the way, did you?"

I shook my head, trying to parse out everything he'd just said. Apparently, I'd been casually conversing with a royal for the last few days. The implications of that were a bit staggering.

"Now, your two young friends are being rewarded with a nice little sack of gold each, but you, I think you'll find this more to your liking."

He pulled a piece of parchment from a belt pouch and laid it down. The writing was significantly more complex than what I generally dealt with, but it was clearly rather official. A brief read-through showed that was a royal pardon for all crimes I'd previously committed. All of the worry about that melted away. I'd put everything forward, and at least as far as the law was concerned, I had been forgiven. I knew I'd still feel bad about it, but that mercy was a potent salve. I froze where I was, only barely holding back the tears.

Emil read my face easily. "Ah, I see you understand, good. Now, as it's late you'll be staying as a guest here. There are a few more things." His face darkened, and I felt like a mouse staring up at a snake. "Listen, and listen well. As far as anyone is concerned, His Highness was rescued by several apprentices to his guard. They did an excellent job and are getting a public commendation. You and your friends are unimportant. You are to speak of what happened to no one. You are also not to try to contact Prince Lief. You and he live in different worlds. I suggest you make sure to keep that close in your mind."

"I . . . understand."

"Make sure that you do." The smile returned in an instant. "Well, you've given me everything that I need for now. If all goes well, we'll never speak again."

"I certainly hope all goes well."

"As do I, young miss Alana, for your sake." He looked over to the guards. "Please show our guest to her room."

After he swept out, I was led off to a guest room. The door opened to an opulent little suite. A servant girl stood by and after one look at me set the table with food and began to prepare a bath. The tub in the corner was certainly on the larger side, and the many soaps beside it nearly made me jump for joy.

The food was amazing. It was not like the food of Earth. The methods and ingredients just weren't there, but it was so fresh. Every bit had been made with exacting care, and there was tons of it. The meat was, of course, the best part. I seldom got much in the way of meat, and the excess here nearly put me into a food coma.

The servant who'd been assigned to me saw to it that I did not pass out at the table and instead pulled me over to the bath. She expertly helped me undress and wash. It was a bit weird to have someone else washing you, particularly a stranger, but the warmth of the water and sweet, clean smell of the soaps helped ease me.

"So, how did you end up as a guest? Particularly one covered in dirt and, what I'm assuming is blood. I should hope not yours." The girl hadn't spoken much, only doing so after I'd been soothed into the calming water.

"It's not important. Simply a kindness as it's late." This was an obvious test, and based on what I'd been told, one I certainly did not want to fail.

She nodded, and once I was finally clean, helped me into a rather nice chemise. It was of quite a bit higher quality than what I'd owned before, but didn't quite look like something a noble might wear. This was this world's undergarments and a bit long, but they did at least keep your clothes cleaner, something needed if you didn't change every day.

As I finally lay down in bed, it all hit me. I was safe, really, truly safe. After everything, I no longer worried about someone finding out about the village, about what had happened there. There was nobody coming to kill me. No monsters were hiding in the corner of the room, waiting to eat me. All the tenseness fled from my body and a few tears streaked down my cheeks.

"Finally," I muttered as exhaustion overtook me.

That night I found my dreams were, for the first time in a long time, peaceful. I couldn't remember the details, but I felt as if I'd been held and protected.

I was given another excellent meal the next morning, along with a dress to replace the one that had been destroyed. It slipped over the one I'd had as nightwear and fit magnificently. There were even places where it could be let out when I grew a bit, so I could probably keep it for a good long while. The cloth was a cool midnight blue, and it was easily now my nicest garment. I spun with joy as I checked it out.

The boys met up with me in the hall as the three of us were being taken back home. It was a short trip to another plain carriage, which we were told would take us right to our respective streets.

"Nice dress," remarked Dras, who was suitably impressed. He, too, looked quite good in a brand-new set of clothes, his in a deep red. Charles was similarly dressed, in his case in a pale yellow.

"Thanks! You two look good too. You'll have to figure out how to explain everything to your families though."

"Oh, that's simple. We got lost in the Undercity, stumbled upon Charles trapped deep in it, and escaped with a magical item, which we sold. Charles came up with it, even ran it by the . . . man we met yesterday afternoon. It's now the official explanation."

"Well, you could have included me in your planning for all of that."

"By the time we got together to come up with it, you were asleep. At least that's what the person we sent to check on you said," Charles explained.

"Dras's mom isn't going to believe that for a second." I looked over at the lad in question as we pulled up near the Starlit Sky. "Have fun with that, and leave me out of it. I don't need her accusing me of running off and stealing her son." I fled before he could come up with a good response.

MEANWHILE IN THE EMPIRE

Suzanne shivered as the late fall rain fell on her and the others. Everything about her hurt: her feet where her sandals were wearing through, her hands as they pushed on the bar in front of her, her wrists and throat where the chains hung, binding her in place.

This whole thing was odd; their whole construction operation had been evacuated in too much of a rush. The masters had come in and hurried them all along, lashing them to pull carts full of goods. They were supposed to be building a new fort for some merchant, at least that's what they had been doing.

Suzanne worried about where they were being taken. The building crew hadn't been too bad; she was mostly assigned to cooking and cleaning, which was easy enough work, and the overseers hadn't been cruel. Thankfully, none of them were handsy with her either; they had their own women for that. If they were being taken to a city and sold . . . who knows where she would end up? The thought of being sold to one of the perverts she knew dwelt there made her tremble in fear.

For now, she could at least count her blessings that the thrown-together cart to which she and the other girls were tied wasn't that heavy. She could even see up ahead some, which was a real blessing. Since they were likely to be the slowest, the makeshift wagon drawn by the girls had been put out front to pace the rest of the convoy. The roads of the empire were safe from monsters, so there was that too.

"Faster, don't slow down!" The sound of a whip cracking nearby caused her to yelp, then quickly speed her pace whimpering in fear, a few strands of black hair falling in front of her face.

Suzanne had been sold into slavery at eight, so her parents could pay off some debt. Now fourteen, she'd only been whipped three times and those not badly. Even then, it was a horrid pain, the rough brown tunic she'd been given to wear wouldn't do much to protect against it either. If they were snapping the whips, then soon they'd find someone who wasn't working hard enough as an example, and she was going to make sure that it wouldn't be her.

They began to pass through a large gully. It shifted and turned here and there. As they came around a corner, there was something surprising to the overseers. A huge hunk of ice had appeared in the roadway, blocking it completely; the outriders were supposed to find and report anything like that, so as to avoid exactly this. They were already too close to it, and she heard the yells from behind as something barred their way back up the road.

As the trap was sprung, she heard rustling from the sides, even saw a few flashes of movement. Bandits were the only explanation. Was this good or bad for her? Well, that would depend on the bandits. Some were known to free slaves to join them. Others . . . well, they wouldn't kill her; nobody would throw away perfectly good merchandise without a reason.

"Throw down your weapons and surrender, and your lives will be spared." A shout echoed across the caravan.

For her part, Suzanne tried to stay still and look unimportant. She resigned herself to the fact that there was nothing she could do except potentially get herself hurt or killed, neither of which sounded like something she'd want.

A few of the guards tried to take up positions; they were quickly filled with arrows from the unseen bandits. Suzanne wanted to drop to her knees and cover her head, but chained as she was, that was impossible. Instead, she huddled in toward the crossbar, trying to make herself as small as possible as arrows whistled around, thunking into the wood behind her. She hated it, hated being powerless and at the mercy of those around her, unable to do anything to even keep herself safe. It burned in her, the fear and desire to do something.

There was nothing she could do though. She could hear screaming as the men fought, a few stray arrows lodging here and there hitting those that weren't their targets. Soon, the guards stopped returning fire. They were not warriors prepared for a major fight against an armed force, but men hired to keep an eye on slaves and goods.

Asking this was too much for them. They called out in surrender to their assailants.

The defeated overseers were ordered to vacate the caravan, marching forward to where they would be captured. Suzanne heard men moving through after they left, presumably the bandits deciding on what they wanted. A man near her slid down the side of the gully, coming to a stop right beside where she stood.

She couldn't help but look at him; he was young, just out of boyhood, with short golden hair cropped close. She stared, whoever this was, he was no bandit. He, along with all of the men coming down to the caravan, had on fitted jet-black armor, dyed metal plates attached to mail. There were two short swords hanging by his sides as he smiled over both the caravan and herself. His eyes were deep blue and set in a pale face; she met them briefly. Remembering who she was, she looked down as fast as she could. Whoever this was, he was of a much higher station than her, and irritating him would be very bad.

"Are you injured?" he asked, his voice was a bit rough, but didn't hold any anger.

"No, Master."

"Don't call me that."

"Master?"

"Yeah, that."

"I . . . then what shall I call you? 'Sir' or 'my lord'?"

"Nah, just call me John."

"I understand, may I ask a question?" The other girls nearby were clenching their fists so hard in fear that their knuckles had gone white.

"Go ahead."

"If you know . . . what will you have me doing after I'm taken by your band? I-I would rather know so I can be prepared."

"Have you . . . nothing in particular. We can find you some work if you need it, or you can go home, that's up to you. Soon as we get the keys off those guards we'll get all your chains off, just hold tight."

"Please don't tease me so." This was a game some people liked to play with their slaves, promise them freedom only to laugh as it was snatched away.

A hand reached out and gently pulled up her chin.

"Look at me." As soon as her eyes rose to meet his, he continued. "Lord Durin has declared that all slaves are to be freed. You may believe it or not, but it is so. The Lord of Shadows is going to lead this world into a new era, just you wait and see."

She believed him, it still pained her to do so, but she did. The way the young man spoke was as if he were telling her about a hero. As he left, she silently prayed that he wasn't toying with her.

Three days had passed since Suzanne had been rescued. True to his word, John had gotten the keys and even personally released the collar and shackles that had been fixed on her.

The camp of this army was sizable, and she understood why the overseers had fled after she saw it. Such a group moving into an area would cause upheaval. They were indeed freeing every slave they found. Many of the men, soon as their chains fell away begged to join the host, which was all too happy to have them.

Suzanne herself had asked for work. She wasn't going to return to a family that had sold her and she really had nowhere else to go. The men who freed her had been kind enough to give her a place cooking for the army. This many soldiers required a staggering quantity of food, and preparing it all was a herculean task, attended by a horde of freed women, those who had nowhere else to go.

The work was good. She spent her days happily making huge dishes of food. None of the men here were the slightest bit rude to her at all; they even gave her proper clothes. She'd wept when she was handed a second-hand dress. It was then that she realized it really wasn't a trick or a dream: her nightmare was truly over.

She did manage to keep an eye on her personal hero too. John was apparently sent out with different units, still in training for whatever job they had assigned him. She once caught a look at him sparring on a slow day, he and another man blurring as they fought at a speed she couldn't even follow. Watching it had made her heart flutter and had been enough of a distraction from her work that she'd been reprimanded when she got back.

After all of that, and all she'd been through, Suzanne made her decision. She wanted to be as close to this young man as she could. She harbored no delusions about him taking her as a wife, but perhaps a mistress, or even a maid. One of the other girls working in the kitchen told her she shouldn't when she spoke her desire. She was just latching on to the first person to help her, and it was massively unhealthy. She ignored the older girl who was obviously jealous.

GOINGS ON IN
THE ROYAL PALACE

The marble halls echoed my footsteps as I quickly walked down them, two guards hovering behind. As I came to my room, they settled beside the door, several servants moving forward to assist me. I was filthy and they'd already prepared a bath for me.

I was washed and given clean clothing as fast as was functionally possible. The sheer amount of filth was amazing; it came off in layers, much of the water even had to be changed. It was as the last of my buttons were being done up that the head servant for my chambers spoke.

"Your Highness, Their Majesties wish to speak with you as soon as feasible."

"Yes, I assumed as much. Please let them know I'm on my way."

It was a bit exhausting, sending servants to and fro to ask to see someone then more to confirm. The strict formality of it all was tiring. That was one thing that the commoners I'd spent the last few days with had done well. If they wanted to say something, they just did so. Sadly, that was not what one would call an enjoyable time because of the situation.

The doors to my parents' room were opened as I approached. If my room had been busy with servants, then their rooms were an absolute riot. Beside them stood Emil. I didn't really like the man, he felt like a snake. Nobody else really liked him either. That said, he was the best spymaster according to anyone in the kingdom. He seemed to know and be quite proficient with every technique of the job, from ferreting out lies to torture. He also seemed to have a contact for almost everyone; he could even track the histories of a given commoner in a day or two at most.

I sat opposite my mother and father, then looked to them. "Could we have a bit of privacy?" With a flick from mother's hand, a small dome appeared around the four of us, opaque and able to muffle any noises from outside. Mom was a rather skilled wizard, controlling both sight and sound at once, and shaping it all was no easy feat.

Once it was in place, we three royals could finally relax a bit.

"I'm glad you're unharmed, son," Father said, giving me a kind smile. Mom actually came over and hugged me, a bit embarrassing as I wasn't a kid anymore.

"I'm glad too. It was a bit of a mess there."

"You just got lost in the Undercity, right? A few encounters with those damned rebels?"

"No, quite a bit more than that." I proceeded to give them a basic run-over of our encounter with the golems; both were quite surprised at that.

"Emil, did you know such things were living down under our city?" Father turned to look at the man in question.

"Not those specifically, Your Majesty, but I knew there were a number of things down there. Removing them isn't really feasible, and if we did, something else would just take their place. The only long-term solution would be to have soldiers stationed in the Undercity all the time. Regardless of that, we should try to find those golems. Items like that are rather rare, and they could be useful." He scratched down a few notes on a pad as he spoke, notes on what I'd said and plans obviously.

"Well, we'll need to reward those three commoners. You said they were all magic users, son. Could we elevate them to the nobility?" With that, he looked at Emil again.

"I would recommend against it, Your Majesty."

"Is saving my son not enough for that even in your opinion?"

"That is not the issue at all, my king. Of the three, I've almost no information on two. The older boy claims he was lost in the Undercity for years. If he's still completely sane, which I'd be worried about, there is no way to verify that story completely. The girl is also unusual. I've received a handful of reports about her before. She's been on my watch list for quite some time."

"A rebel?"

"I doubt it, sire. There is some evidence of contact with suspected rebel elements, but no more than anyone living in the lower parts of the city might have. And I have no indication that she's sympathetic to them either."

"Then what about it?"

"She's powerful, not world-shakingly so. But even at this point, her aura indicates she has far more mana than even most fully trained casters. She's also connected to one of the more potent bards in the city, albeit I don't know how."

"The main question though is where she came from. She's decidedly not from the capital, that much I'm fairly sure of. There was a report filed of a girl posing as a boy years ago who entered the city and had a strong aura. I do not know where she lived before that though, the merchant caravan she came in with stopped in a number of places."

"You've been keeping an eye on her for years?" I turned to Emil, the surprise I'm sure was written on my face.

"Of course, a skilled unknown caster is someone to keep tabs on. There are a few hundred casters in the capital, most of them not really of note. Keeping files on all of them is an important part of my job."

"You spy on all of them!?"

"Most of those files are rather sparse, Your Highness. Unless there's something odd, it's generally enough to know who they are and where they're from. This girl is decidedly a bit odd."

"That is beside the point. With those two, you're right, Emil; elevating their status is not viable for the time being. We'll give them some money or something and keep an eye on them for future raising to the nobility, from afar." Father looked at me pointedly on that last bit. It was clear he wanted me not to get too involved with these unknown elements.

"There is a reward one of them would likely want more than that, Father, one that would be easy enough to give and might even win us loyalty in the future." All three adults raised an eyebrow at me at that.

"What would that be, son?"

"Can I ask that what I will tell you not be pursued if you decide not to grant the reward I ask?"

Father waved his hand in assent. "Very well."

"One of them admitted to killing a man. A royal pardon for all past crimes would be a fine reward, no?"

"A man? Are we talking a noble or a commoner? If one of them is responsible for the death of a noble or their child, pardoning that might be difficult."

"A commoner it would seem, a minor official for the kingdom."

Father hesitated. "That could be construed as rebellion, son, or being part of one."

"I don't care if a hundred men were killed and had their heads mounted on pikes, they brought my son back to me." Mother seldom spoke in exchanges like this, but her words always carried weight.

"Dearest . . ."

"Don't you dearest me," she continued. "Issue the pardon and be done with it. If the youth continues on any path of rebellion, let it fall upon their head. For now though, let it go. It would be no different than giving a general pardon to a village that rebelled then surrendered."

Father looked toward Emil. "Your thoughts?"

"I support Her Majesty. From the sound of it, the cost would be negligible, and if the one in question is a rebel, we might well turn them, or I'll at least know to keep a closer eye on them."

"Very well then, I'll issue it. Which of them is it?"

"The girl, apparently she killed a mayor in a fit of rage. He'd killed her brother or something."

Emil chuckled a bit.

"What?" I asked.

"I was wondering which of the two it was. The boy hiding for years in the Undercity, or the girl who seemed determined to hide her origins. I guessed wrong, not something that happens often."

I shook my head at the spymaster, before turning back to my parents.

"We'll have them treated as guests for the night, give them their rewards, then send them home. Emil, I'd like you to speak with them to see if they know anything useful personally. I'll have the steward arrange some gold and the house seamstress to make them new clothing. They should like that if they were half as filthy as I'm told you were."

I nodded at his commands; they made good sense. After all was settled, we bid our farewells and went back to the various tasks that needed doing. For me, that mainly meant going to get food. I was quite hungry and had only had bread, cheese, and wild plants from the tunnels in the past few days.

The house seamstress was a bit of an odd woman. She was a bard who'd specialized in making clothing for some reason. With the spells she'd developed and put her all into, she could turn out a full outfit in astounding time. More complex pieces would take her a day or so, but simpler ones she could push through in an hour or less. Very simple things like undergarments, she'd toss out in around ten minutes. I loved watching her work; it was like seeing things just jump into place, cutting themselves and sewing as she moved hands across them. After my meal, I went to watch her in her workshop, if for nothing else then the simple joy of watching a master at work.

Eventually though, my tutors and trainers came to pester me. There was always more to be done here in the castle, and sitting to enjoy something idly would only be allowed for so long. I looked back at the work the seamstress had finished so far. My friends would look quite good in their new outfits; it was a true shame I wouldn't get to see them.

On my way back to my chambers, I passed my sister in the hall. She raised an eyebrow as I came near. Her friend, some noble girl from a back-woods barony stood back while we spoke.

"Oh, dear brother, I'm so glad you survived. Are you feeling quite well?" I doubted that she'd fallen in order of succession when it was found that I had more potential for mana than her.

"Yes, sister, quite well, and yourself?"

"Oh, I've no complaints; we were just on our way to enjoy a bit of tea. You've met Lady Gwenna, have you not?"

I explained to my dearest sister. "Only in passing I believe, a pleasure." I nodded to the girl. "Well then, don't let me keep you." With that, I excused myself, I'd no desire to deal with her right now.

CHAPTER 38

✦

WINTER CELEBRATION
AND BASIC ILLUSION

I yawned and blinked. I'd had the strangest dream, and it had told me to write it down. Unfortunately, as I woke up, I couldn't remember it at all. Something involving a cave or something like it? I shrugged, looking around at my room.

Then I sat up straight; it was midwinter. We'd gotten together several days ago and talked, and both Dras and Charles were coming by today. Hopping up and tossing on clothes, I was going to have some things ready before they arrived. The now full jar of sugar joined me as I made my way to the kitchen.

Lucien had kindly allowed me to try out some recipes in exchange for some of my failed sweets, something I could happily give up. Today would be the day for a simple cake with proper icing and some sugar-glazed pastry stuffed with a bit of jam I'd secured. It had taken a good amount of practice and a few total failures to manage the sweets, but I had a fair idea of how to make such things from my previous life, so it was mostly dialing it in to match the local ingredients.

The pastry I had put together the night before, so that was easy enough to prep this morning. The cake was fairly straightforward too. The Swiss buttercream, on the other hand, was an absolute monster to make, taking the better part of the morning. The lack of power mixers was a big hindrance, and without a spell to move things around, I'd have been in a really bad state. The kitchen work was too hard to do normally without magic; even with modern tools, this would have been a bit much.

There were no plastic bags for doing something like cake decoration. Waxed linen was a crude substitute for something like plastic wrap, but the cost was such that it wasn't really viable to cut a hole in it just to make a cake fancy. I had wanted to do roses and the like for the cake, but had to just pout that it would only be tasty, not pretty and tasty. Not that the boys would care much, but I hadn't been able to bake much in the way of sweets since coming to this world, and going a little over the top now would be fun.

The end result wouldn't have looked like much of a spread back on Earth, one small cake and less than a dozen jam pastries. Here though, it was quite different; the sheer amount of sugar pumped into this would have been enough to break a family of farmers. That was not counting the other ingredients.

Soon enough, the boys did indeed show up. They shivered as they came in the door, trying to warm themselves. Dras could easily clear a path, but it was still chilly. I quickly waved them over to a booth in the back corner and they all piled in as I brought out the sweets.

"I've been baking!"

"So we can see, what is all of this?" Charles looked at the cake a bit dubiously. It did look like a mound of white cream to the uninitiated.

"Cake and pastry," I spoke as I distributed the goodies, cutting the tiny little cake into three slices.

"Whoa." Dras's eyes went wide as he took his first bite.

"Mmm, cake is yummy." I dug in, it was a decent cake, but not great. The sweetness though . . .

"Can you make this more often?" Dras asked as he dove into one of the pastries.

"The cost of the ingredients would make you puke if you tried to buy them in a store. The sugar alone . . ."

"How much did you spend on this?" Charles leaned over, speaking as he finished his first bite.

"Not much in coin, but a lot of time to get it. It's miserable outside, and I wanted to celebrate with my friends."

"Why?" both of them asked in unison.

"Because it's nice to sometimes and . . ." It should be roughly my birthday and Christmas. "And I just wanted to try something new out."

I couldn't tell them the truth, that I'd missed holidays. There were few here, and most of those were rather plain affairs, an extra-large meal and no work that day for most people. Perhaps nobles or the wealthy did something more, but farmers didn't, and I'd been working for them since I'd moved to a city. Birthdays weren't even a thing; it was based on the season you were born in and the day was considered unimportant. I didn't even know mine for sure, just that it was in winter.

"Well, it's great, very, very sweet." Dras was slowly working his way through the slice he had.

"So, how are your winters going?"

"Good enough. I don't know that I want to join the family business of being a ratcatcher or the like. Reckon I've had enough of being underground to last me for the rest of my life. I've also forgotten a lot of the tunnels that I used to know, so I'd have to go and learn them again. Hey, Alana, I meant to ask before. Dras was telling me I had an aura. I think it's physical, but neither of us know jack about that, you know about it?"

"Not much to be honest; my dad was like that. I could teach you to hide it, but you should ask Lucien if he knows anyone who could train you how to use it. Yours seems to be mostly around your eyes."

Charles nodded. "Yeah, I noticed that I was seeing way better. Didn't really occur to me back when we were down below. I thought I'd just gotten used to not having much light. Now that I'm out . . . if I try I can see even in the middle of the night, or things that are kind of far away. It's hard to describe."

"Right, you can probably move faster and hit harder, too, but I don't know. Like I said, talk to Lucien. What about you, Dras?"

"My family doesn't believe me about finding an artifact and selling it. Mom's being a real pain about it. She thinks you got me involved in something criminal."

I snorted. "I would get you involved if I was interested in committing any crimes, but I'm not. How's the studying going?"

"Right, about that, I've got a few questions . . ." The rest of our meal fell into me and Dras going over basic algebra and geometry. Charles decided to follow my advice and go speak to my boss, who I was sure knew someone. Lucien seemed to know just about everyone in this section of the city. It was weird, useful, but weird.

As our afternoon of fun came to an end, Dras looked over to me. He seemed a bit nervous.

"What is it?"

"What you said back in the tunnels . . ."

"About killing a man?" That was said rather more quietly.

"Yeah . . . so you've . . ."

"Yes, and I don't care to go into it."

"Oh . . . okay then."

I sighed. "He was at least partially responsible for the death of my oldest brother."

"I-I didn't know you had a brother."

"Two, I don't know where my other one is. It doesn't matter though."

"You don't talk about your family much."

"No, I do not. Please let it be."

He nodded, catching on finally. He seemed uncomfortable about the whole thing, so I led him back to the studying. There was quite a bit he needed to learn, and if it kept him from making me uncomfortable, I was happy to use it as an excuse.

The rest of my winter, I whiled away rather happily. Work during the winter was always light. Lucien asked about getting the recipe for the cake, which I happily sold him for a few silvers in pocket money. I thought he was going to smack me when I told him just how much sugar he was going to need.

At this point, I did need to consider if I wanted to keep working at the Starlit Sky or if it would be better to just sell sugar. I decided to stay at the tavern, if for no other reason than to keep close to a man who knew enough about my kind of magic to keep me learning for years.

I went to my local resource and asked him about interesting new spells he might care to share with the rest of us. Lucien took a few moments to run me through my current list, laughed at both the sugar spell and how I could now reasonably cast the invisibility one, and sat back to think for a few moments.

"Let's add a bit of illusion to your repertoire. You're already pretty good and on your way to being a little monster of a support caster, and a sneaky one at that, so I think that's for the best."

I nodded at his comments. "Okay, what kind should we go with?"

"We'll start with something simple. You've already got light and darkness, so let's do some inanimate shapes. Try visualizing making a cube, not shining and bright, but having light coming off of it to match what's around it; form it in your mind and try to make it in the world before you."

I did as he said and imagined it. It took a long while to get it to manifest properly, but in time it did, a small gray cube hovering between us. Lucien took some minutes to examine it from different angles, even passing his hand through once. After a few moments, he nodded and patted my head.

"Not bad, not bad for a first try at all. You do need to work on the shadows around the cube; it's not interacting with light as it should. Also it's glowing ever so slightly. Work on those on your own. Illusions are powerful, but learning to make them look good is a long process. After getting the shapes, shade, and light correct, we'll move on to textures and the like. Then we can add more and more complexity."

Magic homework still felt like homework. The upside was that it was a ton of fun if you could just lose yourself in it. Lucien had suggested that I keep to simple shapes for the time being. Since he had more experience than I did, and all his advice had worked out in the past, I was all too happy to follow it. I came to realize that learning this wasn't nearly as exhausting as other spells I'd worked on. Useful since making even simple shapes that looked right to the world around them was a massive headache.

As spring rolled in and I could officially and really call myself eleven, I got to see Charles and his new mentor. She was a woman about Lucien's age with a sharp, hard look to her. Based on how often he came to the Starlit Sky to get healed, I could guess that she was running him ragged as well.

Dras ended up spending a lot more time hanging around too. With his newfound wealth, he no longer had to worry so much about being able to pay for school. For that reason, he ended up coming by almost every evening after work to study with me. He really had no mind for numbers or reading; still we powered through. He kept practicing his fire-ribbon spell too, it was his favorite and signature attack.

It was near to summer when Dras's mother came to the tavern herself to retrieve her son. I saw her approaching the doors with an irate look on her face and tried to wave him to flee, but the poor lad thought I was trying to get his attention and perked up right as she walked in the door. I briefly considered beating my head on the counter as she waltzed up to her unsuspecting victim, rage written on her face.

CHAPTER 39

✦

AN ANGRY MOTHER

She looked pissed, absolutely, positively furious. I waved to one of the other girls near the kitchen to go for Lucien; there was no telling why exactly she was here and what made her so mad. I could only watch from across the room as Dras's mother grabbed him by the arm.

"I told you not to come here. We're going home!"

"Mom . . ."

"Don't 'Mom' me. I told you, in no uncertain terms that you were forbidden from coming back here or seeing that girl again. I won't have you getting involved with criminals and whores!"

The Starlit Sky went silent as she yelled. Dras was a regular by this point and well known for his work and study. A number of the people were now glaring at this woman who'd interrupted their food or drinks. Several of the prostitutes who'd come in for an afternoon breakfast looked particularly peeved at being compared to criminals.

As she tried to drag her son from the booth, I saw the burst of flames. If I had to guess, it wasn't strong enough to actually hurt her, but she did fall over and back from Dras, who was now standing and looking monumentally angry.

"Do not insult my friends. There is so much you just don't understand. You're so hardheaded about all of this, why won't you just listen?"

I approached just a bit to see if he'd actually managed to hurt her. Like her or not, she was still my friend's mom, and I'd still be willing to clear up any burns his little show had caused. I realized my mistake as she turned to me, rage on her face.

"This is your fault! You dragged my son into this place, pulling him into whatever mess you're involved in. You should be ashamed of yourself!"

I looked down at her where she sat on the floor. "Let's get a few things straight, lady. Your son was coming here well before he met me. He's the one who approached me to make friends. Finally, as far as I know, he hasn't done anything illegal. You're crazy and controlling, and it's going to lose you more than you understand."

"Oh? And you expect me to believe the little story about your adventure in the Undercity? Just finding something like that? And that Charles boy, too, no doubt he's in on whatever scheme you came up with!"

"I don't care what you believe honestly, but we did get lost during an attack, we did find some neat things, and we did help Charles escape the Undercity in the process. Your opinion on that doesn't matter." I managed to keep my voice low and calm for that, though I was monumentally pissed that she was going around blaming me for all that nonsense.

She stood up and began advancing toward me, right as a hand came down on her shoulder.

"You are bothering my patrons and staff. It is time to leave." I'd never seen Lucien angry before, but something about him now felt a bit dangerous. The happy-go-lucky look he normally kept was replaced with dark eyes and a low, barely audible voice.

Dras's mother seemed to catch on as to how badly she'd messed up, and with one last look at her son, allowed herself to be quietly led to the door. After she left, the talking quietly resumed. It took a few minutes for Lucien to come back over and look at the two of us; he still looked rather irritated.

"Care to explain what all that was about?"

"My mom told me not to come around here, or hang out with Alana. Guess she found out I was . . ."

"I like you, kid. You're decent enough and you don't make a mess, but I can't have that kind of thing happening. Handle whatever business is going on with your family, because I do not want to have to intervene in a mess like that again."

The older bard turned his eyes to me, looking down quite severely. "You surely have somewhere to be, do you not?"

I nodded quickly and made my escape. Lucien had been rather good to me and while I didn't think he was mad at me specifically, it was best to stay out of his way.

After my shift, I went over to where Dras was still sitting. He'd gotten a bit of food and another drink while I'd finished up and looked up as I came to sit down. It took him a few moments for his eyes to meet mine, even then he seemed a bit put off by the whole incident.

"Sorry about that."

"You didn't do anything to me, so there's no need to apologize."

"I don't know what to do about it. My mom did tell me she didn't want me hanging around here or you anymore . . ."

"I can't tell you what to do, but I can make a suggestion if you want."

"Go for it."

"Try to make up with your family."

"After all that? After I've done so much for them, and she treats me like that? I was honestly thinking of trying to rent a room . . ."

"You'll regret that if you do. Give your mom a little time to cool off maybe, but try to patch things together."

"What would you know about . . . uh, sorry."

"My family is gone to who knows where, if they're even still alive. So, for me, at least try to make up with them, try to do something. Will you at least do that much? Please?"

"I . . . in the morning, I'll get a room here for . . ."

I had to cut him off there, "No, go across the street or something. Lucien's a good guy, but if he rents you one now, it'll look bad, like he's trying to keep you from your family. He might do it anyway, but if you're going to rent a room for tonight, it shouldn't be here."

Dras looked a bit hurt by that. "I thought we could hang out a bit."

"I like you, Dras, but me being here might already irritate somebody, Lucien isn't blood to me, nor is he that close to my family. I could probably play it off, as could he, but it would already be a bit of an ask. Adding you to that could cause real problems, make him look like he's gathering up kids from their families."

"I guess . . . well, I'll see to it tomorrow."

The two of us talked and went over some of the study materials from the book a bit more. To me, it wasn't too much. I'd done all of this either in school back home or under Mystien, but for Dras a lot of it was new. As night fell, he rushed off across the street to get a room, and I headed over to talk to my boss.

"Um, Lucien, about earlier . . ."

"I know it wasn't your fault, kid, but if your boyfriend doesn't take care of his family I'll have to ban him from the Starlit Sky. I don't want to, but I will."

"His mom is the problem, not him."

"True, but she's going to come after him wherever he is. I can't much blame her for that. Because not even I believe that pile of garbage you told everyone as to where you lot got all that money."

"I really wish you wouldn't pry into that."

"I'd be one heck of a hypocrite to do so. I didn't get all the money to build this tavern by being the most upstanding of men, and I doubt Mystien told you how much of a little group of ne'er-do-wells we were back in our day. That said, do not get involved in anything you can't handle."

"We didn't do anything wrong. Will you at least believe that much?"

He gave me a rather deep look, taking a few seconds to rub his chin. "Aye, I'll believe that much."

"Thank you."

"Now, off with you, before you give me another headache."

The next morning right before breakfast, a new problem arrived. The man strode through the doors in his priest robes, eyes scanning the Starlit Sky before they finally landed on me. Both of us recognized each other immediately, and he strode over.

"Hello, Alana. It's been a long time hasn't it."

"Hello, Rosk, it has indeed."

"We need to talk."

It only took a second to arrange for us to have a word in the back room. As the two of us settled down, the priest looked at me with a deep frown.

"I'm quite surprised you're here. You've caused more of a stir than I think you know."

"Oh?"

"Yes, I ended up in Istlan after leaving Hazelwood land, did you know that?"

"Nope . . ."

"I gather that I arrived a few months after you left. To find that you had run away from the orphanage there. The father was quite concerned for you. Did you know that?"

"I . . . left a note."

He frowned at my words. "Highly irresponsible. You could have been kidnapped or killed."

"And I suppose you know where my family is? You arrived just after I left to tell me then?"

He sighed. "No, I can tell you that they're alive and very worried about you. After several weeks of searching, your brother took your mom and uncle off somewhere. He refused to tell even me where he was headed."

"Great."

"Not great. You are a child, currently working in a tavern with no supervision from a guardian. It's completely unacceptable."

"Lucien is a friend. It is likely that my family, or other close friends, will contact him in time. More than that, he's trustworthy; this is the best place for me to be."

"The best place for you to be, young lady, is at the temple. The Shield will happily look after you."

"Not going to happen."

"Is that so? You are not the first problematic child who has needed to be shown that they should respect both their elders and the law."

"If you try to press this, it will be a fight, and not one I'll hold back on."

Both of us were tensed, ready to unleash magic on each other in what would be a giant waste of time.

"What are you even doing here, Rosk? Shouldn't you be back at the temple, helping people rather than harassing girls who are perfectly fine?"

"We received a report about a girl being forced to work in a tavern and potentially to commit crimes. An orphan at that. I was sent to investigate. It is quite surprising that I found said girl was you."

"Oh, talking to Dras's mom then? She's a bitch, and one who thinks I'm manipulating her son."

"Language."

"Fuck you, you're not my father, my mother, or any relation. You're just someone who thinks he knows best. And if my language bothers you that much, you can just screw right off. I am not going back to your temple."

"I cannot leave you to the devices of someone who might not even have your best interests in mind."

"Lucien has done more for me than you ever have. He's taught me plenty and done what he can to keep me out of trouble."

"And I . . ."

"Sat by while those men caused my home to starve almost to death. Everything got worse and worse until it all just fell apart. Now it's all gone, and you don't even know where my family went."

"What happened there was horrible, and the destruction was . . . I hated to see it."

"It's not your fault, it's Lord Hazelwood's. He and his men, and his daughter and her men, in particular, can all go jump off a cliff."

"Alana, I do not expect you to understand why we can't get involved with wars and the like. Why even if it pains us we must remain neutral."

"Then remain neutral here, and get out."

Surprisingly, he obeyed.

CHAPTER 40

✦

A WAGER AND SILENCE

Something about the old priest just leaving surprised me to my very core. Perhaps it was shame on his part for what had happened to my home. Perhaps it was that he knew that I'd hold strong to my position. Perhaps he was just biding his time. I didn't know, nor did I really care. So long as he was gone, I was happy.

I didn't tell Dras what his mother had done. She might have thought it best for her to act that way and try to protect him. Personally, I just choose to believe that she was a bit of a controlling bitch; that idea worked best for me. I didn't really have to though; he and his family had a fairly explosive meeting.

Dras ended up spending very little of his time at home after that; he also decided to avoid the Starlit Sky for a while. Instead, we ended up studying while walking around the city. It was quite a bit more free, and the market was a good place to practice basic math; there were plenty of examples for problems to be had.

So Dras and I spent our summer and autumn taking light walks along the main streets. As it got colder, we ended up taking shorter walks, but there was a nice little place on the city's main street that sold a form of spiced fruit juice; it came hot in a little cup. It was not unlike hot cider, but it had no cinnamon and wasn't quite as sweet. There was a note to it something like licorice, but much milder with a vanilla aftertaste.

"How are we going to study over the winter?" Dras asked over his drink.

"Just work at home when you can't come to the Starlit Sky, and make sure to practice your magic. Try to come by once or twice a week to go over stuff with me."

"Yeah . . . I suppose that'll work." He seemed a bit dejected.

"What's wrong?"

"The winter is always awful."

"I like it; it's peaceful. It's a time where we can rest and prepare for the coming year."

"Yeah, but it's cold."

"Okay, fair enough. I'm not really fond of the cold, but I have spells for that and I suspect you do too."

Dras laughed and nodded. "Suppose I do. Too bad I can't make a spell that makes it quiet."

"Why not?"

"Why not what?"

"Why can't you make a spell that makes it quiet? I mean, it doesn't really work for me since I use noise for my casting, but you don't. There's no reason why you couldn't make a spell that would make it quieter."

"Hmm . . . how would I do that though?"

"Why don't you try to figure it out over winter, and then we'll see what you came up with in the spring, and how it works. It'll be a fun challenge."

"Not really a challenge if I'm the only one doing it." He was getting all mopey about this.

"Fine, I'll work on a spell to keep sound out of an area too. We'll see whose works better at the end of the season." I already had a few ideas on how to go about this, but it would be neat to see what he came up with.

"If I win, you have to make me another cake."

"Fine, fine. And if I win, you have to buy me a new outfit."

"Clothes are super-expensive!"

"So is sugar."

He grumbled but finally accepted my terms. I had every plan on winning our little game now; clothes were a huge part of my budget, saving even a little would be a big deal. The simple amount of work involved in making even a plain outfit was staggering.

As for my current wardrobe, I was having to take out and adjust the seams as it was. At my age, I was already hitting the beginnings of puberty. The increase in growth speed meant I was having to replace stuff far too fast for my liking. I looked forward to hitting my full height, so I could at the very least slow down that financial disaster. If I hadn't spent a large part of my formative years eating little more than bread, I imagine that I might be growing even more than I was.

My work on illusion was coming along much as Lucien had said, quite slowly. I could manage something simple and non-moving now, like a plain cup. It even looked mostly real. Light and shadow got more and more complex to deal with even with the simplest of shapes and textures. People were also shockingly good at spotting things that didn't quite fit right. Humans have a real knack for finding those bits that stick out as different.

So I added a silencing spell to my list of things to work on. I hadn't picked up many new ones recently, instead ironing out what I had to perfection. I liked having everything I knew work really well, but having more tricks was never bad.

As I sat on my bed a few nights after we began our contest, I began to focus on the spell I wanted: a dome that would stop vibrations around the hearing range of humans. I wanted to extend that out just a bit to make sure it covered all sounds, but not too much. Missing a shaking of the floor or wind or something might be a real issue. I'd make it about as big as a booth at the Starlit Sky for now, and work on fine-tuning the size later.

I hummed as I began to extend out my magic. First I formed the dome that would act as the structure of the spell, folding it over the area I wanted like laying a cloth over a solid object. Once it was in place, I pumped mana into it to filter out the noise. I started with high pitches and worked my way toward the lower ones. It was weird trying to imagine something you couldn't hear, but not too bad. The room got quieter and quieter as I reached toward the lowest pitch I could hear, then just beyond.

As the spell finished and I quit humming it into existence, the room was creepily, deathly quiet. It was a bit unnerving since I'd never thought about how much sound was roaming through the city at any given time. The simple absence of the noise of things on the street or downstairs was just weird.

I was also on the verge of fainting from mana loss, so I had to quickly end the spell before it dropped me on my bed regardless of what I wanted. It was huge, and I got the feeling that my magic really didn't like perfect silence. That was weird, but it was magic. I also considered that it might be something mental with me, some tick that just made me not want to do it.

As I lay there, waiting for my mana to return so I could practice more, I laughed. I was going to win, hardcore. I could feel bad for the money I was going to get from Dras, but he was the one who wanted to make it an expensive wager, so he could eat the cost. Perhaps I'd make a small cake or something for him anyway. Boys could get pouty when they lost something like that, and I liked sweets too.

I spent my time making up and solving a few basic math problems. It wasn't really my normal cup of tea, but it was a thing that would help me in the long run. As was practicing with words and letters, I didn't get much of a chance to read, but being extremely well versed in all the subjects in our little study guide would be good for me too. Particularly, if I was planning on attending the academy, something I was feeling more and more confident I would do.

I wanted to learn more and more about magic. It was powerful, and I would need power for me to keep up with the world around me. I never ever wanted to be left with nothing and alone again. I wanted to find my family, to have a good life, and to not be crushed by the powers that be again.

That winter was rather quiet. I loved winter for that. We had a handful of people every day, and easy work combined with the peace and quiet of snow and a crackling fire was always welcome. The Starlit Sky stayed warm and toasty throughout, with alcoves that were cheery and inviting. By the end of it, I could officially call myself twelve, one step closer to being truly considered an adult, not something I really wanted, but it would help keep me out of a lot of the trouble I'd been in.

As the first of the snows melted, Dras came by to settle our bet. We'd even roped Lucien in as the judge the competition; he was curious to see what the two of us devised.

"I'll go first; be prepared to be amazed." Dras was sure feeling sure of himself as he began to cast.

Lucien nodded as the sounds around us faded into a low buzz; you could still hear things, but it was indistinct and much, much quieter.

"Not bad, Dras. Let's see what Alana has brought for us."

I smiled across the table at my friend as I sang a quick tune. As the final note sounded, dead silence reigned over the table where we sat. No sound from outside could make it in, and practice had indeed lowered the mana cost to something just barely manageable.

"She beat you, lad." Lucien patted Dras on the shoulder; he was trying not to laugh as he shook his head.

"How did you . . . what were you picturing?" Dras asked.

"It's a dome around us that excludes all the sounds that we can hear. The mana cost is too high for it to be very useful, but it's a neat little spell."

"That's a neat way of picturing it, limited, but useful. Why didn't you just exclude everything?"

"Seemed like I should let breezes and the floor shaking through. That kind of thing can be really useful to feel."

"What's feeling got to do with sound?" Dras asked.

"They're the same thing?"

"Explain please, Alana." Lucien seemed a bit put off by my answer too.

"So you ever been near something loud and felt it, like in the ground or on your skin?"

I got sort of confused nods.

"Well, sound is just vibration, right? It's just the air moving in a way our ears feel it."

Lucien blinked. "That's an interesting way of thinking about that, that things shaking is sound. Not sure if it's right, but it seems to be working well for you."

It was weird to me that they didn't think of it that way. Perhaps this world had weird views on how things worked. Or perhaps they didn't work that way here. I decided the first was far more likely; what I knew of physics and stuff had seemed to work pretty well if I knew and experienced it.

Dras and I arranged to meet up in a few days for me to claim my prize. We'd had a fair bet after all, and I really did need new clothes. The fact that I'd roped him into helping me pick them out and pay for them was a big bonus. I had no real girlfriends and shopping on your own for clothing was a bit depressing.

Lucien seemed to find our whole arrangement to be hilarious. He laughed the whole way back to the tavern after we'd informed him of what I'd won. I saw him laugh and make a few comments to another one of the workers, of course the barrier kept me from knowing exactly what he said. Her apparent giggle and covering of her mouth led me to believe it was something terrible though.

As I watched Dras sulk off into the night, I sighed a bit. He was going to be sulky. Sure, he'd lost a good bit of money, but not enough to break him, and it wasn't like spending time shopping was going to be that much of a chore, was it? I was personally really looking forward to it.

CHAPTER 41

✦

CLOTHES AND MARKS

The day before, I took a bit of time to bake some simple sugar cookies. A quick wrap in waxed linen made a pleasant little package, and they were easy to make, if a bit expensive. As a final touch, I took a small ribbon and tied it up with a pretty bow. People around here didn't normally do things like that for presents, but it looked good to me.

Dras came by early in the morning to pick me up. I had the day off and was bouncy with excitement as he came through the door looking like he was going for his least favorite chore. We met near the door, and I took him by the hand.

"Come on, let's go!" I dragged him right back out and into the busy morning street.

"So, where are we going? Do you have a favorite shop?"

"There are a few good places. Let's go by some stores and see what they're displaying, and then we can make a decision."

"That'll take hours."

"Yup, yup, let's go!" I knew that he wasn't really enjoying this, but . . . Well, I hoped if I stayed upbeat enough, he'd start to like it.

The first place we went by was somewhere I'd been to a few times. I looked at their current displays and was rather disappointed; there were a few nicely made pieces, but they just weren't what I was looking for.

This process repeated itself twice more before I found something that I rather liked.

"Hey, Dras, what do you think of this?" I looked back at my companion, who'd seemed completely disinterested up until now.

"It's fine, I guess."

"That's not an answer, look at it." I pouted, trying to pull him over.

"Alana, I don't really know anything about girl's clothes."

"Dras, you wear robes. Which is similar enough in design to a dress. Now, at least make some comments on the cut and the matching of the fabrics."

"Fine, the grommets they used here don't look quite right with the color of the fabric."

"Yeah, you're right. Let's go to the next place."

Two more shops later, and he was actually giving me good constructive information.

"This fabric with that cut would look better on you, I think." He pointed out two pieces on display, and I had to agree.

"You're right, let's get something here. Are you getting new clothes too?" I asked him as we approached the shopkeeper.

"Huh?" He blinked at my words.

"Your robes are getting a bit older, and kind of short. You should think about getting something fresh. Here, let's take a look." With that, I turned away from the salesman and pulled Dras over toward the men's displays.

There were a number of different styles on display here, including some rather nice robes. There were a few different colors, and he seemed a bit offput by my sudden change in subject.

"Here, I think you should look at something like red or dark orange. It'll match your fire theme better, or do you want something else?"

"Hmm, I don't know . . ."

"Personally I think you'd look best in a dark red or something similar. Definitely darker warmer colors to go with your look."

"Warmer?" He looked over a couple of the display pieces as he spoke, seeming to judge how each was cut.

"Yeah, reds, oranges, yellows, and browns. As opposed to blues and greens."

"I didn't know those had words . . ."

"Many things have words, Dras. Now, what do you think?"

"I think another set of good robes would be nice. Some of these are a bit pricey though."

"Yeah, don't go too expensive; you're still growing. Something you don't mind getting a bit dirty and can work in would be good though, for day-to-day wear."

It was cute how much more animated he could be when talking about something he would use. It occurred to me that I should have had him looking at things for himself the whole time, but what was past was past. After comparing a few more things and me steering him more toward something that would be less formal, we made our orders and he paid. The clothes themselves would take some time to make, but that was normal. Not everyone could just push out three brand-new outfits in an evening. I was still wondering how exactly that had been done.

The shopkeeper looked at us like we were the most adorable couple he'd ever seen. His young assistant had to put her hand over her mouth to hide her smile a few times as we were measured. I don't know if Dras even noticed, but I found it personally quite annoying.

Dras was elated when I gave him the little package of cookies upon our return. His mood had been going steadily up from its low point earlier in the day. He thanked me as he turned to head home; it was getting a bit late.

A couple of weeks later, we picked up our new outfits, and as I returned to the Starlit Sky, Lucien pulled me aside.

"Hey, Alana, I've been called away for the next few days. The notice is a bit short, and I haven't had time to work out some of my more regular appointments. Could you handle those for me?"

"Is it any different from what I normally do?"

"Yes, I don't believe you've dealt with Lovers' Marks before, have you?"

I could easily tell that was a proper noun, but not exactly what it did. "Erm, no, I don't think so."

"Yeah . . . normally, adults take care of those. I know it's short notice and all, but it's easy enough. I'll show you."

With that, he motioned over one of our regulars, one of the girls who worked at a nearby brothel, by the name of Inga. We all then went upstairs.

"Thanks for assisting me, Inga, it's a big help."

"Oh, no thanks needed, four weeks for free is payment enough." She gave him a soft chuckle as we entered one of the back rooms that I knew Lucien used on a regular basis.

"Regardless, if you would please, Inga dear."

At his words, she began to remove her skirt. There were a few moments when I worried what exactly I'd gotten myself into before she had it pulled down, exposing herself to us.

"Um . . ."

Lucien pulled my attention to a small tattoo on her abdomen, just above the pubic mound. It was quite familiar, but I couldn't quite place it.

"This is a Lovers' Mark; they are made by the Order of the Lovers. It functions to keep someone from having children should they not desire to. There are variations for both men and women, though they are, by far, more used by women who do not wish to get pregnant."

It clicked as I looked at the mark for a few more moments. I'd seen these twice before. One on Mystien's "friend" and another time on my brother's . . . well, I didn't really want to know about my deceased brother's sex life, but I suppose he had one.

"I . . . I think I've seen one of these once or twice. I didn't know what it did though."

"Yes, it can store enough mana to operate for up to a year; a month or two at a time is rather more common, since mana is a bit pricey. To recharge it, just place your hand or finger on the tattoo and do exactly as you would with any other item. You're fairly experienced in that by now."

He demonstrated, pushing a bit of mana into the mark. I'd gotten quite a bit more used to the subtle color changes that some of these went through and that did seem to be about two weeks for a functioning item.

"Now you try, roughly the same amount."

I worked slowly, not knowing how much mana this would need. Turns out not very much. Judging by what I had done before, I was very sure that my mana capacity had increased dramatically in the last couple of years.

"Thank you." Inga smiled as I pulled away my finger. She bent a little to keep an eye on the mark, judging for herself how much mana had gone in.

"Lucien, how many of these do you do?"

"About twenty a day, it's one of our main sources of income here at the Starlit Sky. Though generally only older casters charge them. It is a bit . . . rude of me to push this on you, and if I had another option, I would use it."

"That's a good few. The amount of mana shouldn't be an issue, but I won't be able to do as much of the other work as I normally do."

"That's fine, Alana, most of that we can handle. If working girls don't get these recharged regularly, they can't work, and that's not good for any-one. I'll give you a little bit of a bonus for my having to push this onto you, and all the marks have been prepaid, so that's taken care of. It'll be two weeks on each girl, that's our normal pace."

"Lucien . . . I know roughly how many brothels there are in town, and roughly how many girls at each. There's no way they can recharge all of these that easily; it'd take at least a thirty of me to keep that up if I ran myself ragged. Only twenty a day? Where are all the others getting their mana?"

"Well, my dear, mana is expensive. How do you think many of the poorer students at the academy pay their tuition? The boys are also known to trade mana for . . . time with the ladies."

I tried and failed to hide my disdain. "Does Dras . . ." I didn't quite get to finish that one.

"Sixteen is the normal minimum age most women will let a man charge their marks, even prostitutes. The fact that you're a girl means they're not so bothered."

That wasn't a no, but I suppose that Lucien might not have known. I wasn't sure if I even had any right to feel a bit . . . put off by the idea of Dras dealing with lots of naked women, but it still rankled a bit.

"Okay, I'll take care of it then, Lucien. Leave it to me."

Inga had excused herself after getting redressed and seeing how the conversation was leaning toward more personal subjects. I was quite glad that she had done so, but I suppose that it was smart on her part; she surely didn't want to get involved if it could influence her getting what she needed to work. Not that either of us would have done anything that bad to her. Did she know that though?

"Oh? Well if you need help I'm sure Dras will . . ." He didn't finish that comment when he saw my glare. I might be young, but I could still be awfully mean. "Just kidding, just kidding."

Lucien was gone for nearly a week. That was an enormous amount of time for him to not be at the Starlit Sky. He might be gone for a day or two every now and then, but an extended leave was new. He didn't tell me where he was going, and based on his actions, I chose not to ask. He'd not pried too deeply into my private life, so it was only proper for me not to pry into his.

There was an absolute line of girls daily while he was gone. I hadn't really noticed it before since most of them came by after I left my shift. There was some sort of rotating schedule, and it had very little wiggle room in it. Of the girls I saw, most of them had only a day or two left in their marks. It seemed that although they could hold an impressive amount of mana, actually doing that was really rare.

The tattoos themselves could be placed anywhere it seemed. Most people liked to place them somewhere they could easily see them. They were also invariably covered by clothing. I asked one of the madams in charge when she brought her girls by and was informed that displaying one, particularly if it was charged, was seen as an invitation. While the girls might want to do that at work while trying to attract customers, doing so while walking down the street was bad taste. It also was thought to lead to assaults, an even bigger reason to keep them covered.

By the time Lucien had returned, I had made the decision that I wanted one of these. The pure importance of having birth control coupled with the chance that I might end up someplace where I couldn't get one in the future made me bump it up to rather high on my priority list. I just had to consider where to get one. And if the Order of the Lovers would even give me one was still a question too.

CHAPTER 42

✦

THE TEMPLE OF LOVERS

I considered my options for around a week; if I was going to go about getting inked up; I wanted it to at least be a good one. I also heavily considered not getting it at all, at least not for a couple more years, but remembering the sudden exit from my last home killed that thought. I probably wouldn't be cast out of the capital in the near future, but it was best to be prepared.

After much consideration, I decided that an outer thigh was the best place. Nobody would see it except me, and I could easily recharge it myself. Anywhere that might be publicly visible was, of course, out, as was anywhere where anyone not seeing me absolutely naked. Clothes here were quite a bit more covering than those back on Earth, and a woman's upper thighs were normally only seen by a lover.

Most prostitutes went for someplace similar; my guess was that they didn't want someone to have to get too personal to recharge it. From what I'd seen, the side or bottom of breasts was quite popular, as was the outer thigh or armpit. The lower parts of the belly were also popular, for all of the connotations that were there. That was something that I had no concern for at all, since I would be the only person I'd have filling the tattoo with mana.

So as early fall came around, I headed off in the general direction of the Temple of the Lovers. It would be my first time going there, so I was not exactly sure where it was. As a matter of course, I tended to avoid the area of town where all of the temples were situated, mostly out of concern that I might run into someone from the Istlan branch of the Order of the Shield.

It was near enough to the areas frequented by nobles, so the streets were clean and safe. That said, it was still a bit weird to go and explore a part of the city I had little experience with; it was so unfamiliar compared to the markets and the entertainment district. Even the Undercity felt more familiar to me than this area; there were a handful of large temples, each a few blocks from the other, dominating the streets and all around them.

The first temple I recognized belonged to the Order of the Shield, stark and white, it stood enormous, much larger than the one in Istlan. A man stood nearby taking information and directing those visiting the complex to where they needed to go. I nodded as I passed, and he smiled in return.

I passed another enclosed area. It wasn't really a complex in the same fashion, in that it seemed to be walled off by shaped vines. From the gate, I could see a number of plants growing within, along with a handful of animals wandering around. I wasn't sure whose place this was, but it was not a group I had knowingly met.

There were a number of other buildings along the streets: shops selling trinkets whose use I didn't know and a few more mundane doctors, for minor injury or those who couldn't afford a priest's healing. There were also those selling minor magical items produced by the temples near to their complexes. Those shops were well guarded and looked to be too expensive for me to reasonably purchase anything in, not that I needed anything they had.

It took me a few blocks of wandering, because I was completely unwilling to ask anyone where this particular establishment was, but I eventually found it. I was beginning to get a bit concerned that I might have to actually publicly embarrass myself by requesting its location before I saw the temple where the Order of the Lovers made their business.

This place had to be correct, if I was any judge. There was an open gateway that led into a columned entry, wide and open with pale white stone walls on either side. They were smooth and on the roof over the entry was a mark, a man and woman face-to-face, lowered hands held. Beneath them a pair of red banners fluttered gently in the wind.

There were a few people in the small yard before the temple, tending to various plants in the garden. They gave me a once-over as I passed. I gathered that those as young as I was were not particularly common here, but no one stopped me. By the time I got to the top of the stairs though, there was someone waiting for me.

"Greetings, my name is Kiana. Please come in." The woman was obviously a priestess, the pale blue glow surrounding her gave no misunderstanding to that.

"Oh, hello, thank you." I was a bit at a loss at her quick appearance, and a tad nervous about my business here.

She led me down a corridor to a small room, letting us both take a seat on well cushioned couches before she began the conversation in earnest.

"Now, you're quite a bit younger than most who come here, my dear. Though some come with their mothers . . ."

"Oh, my mother is . . . not in the city as of right now."

"Ah, I see. You are about that age, and I'm sure you have a lot of questions about the things you're going through. I'm quite happy to explain." I could see her winding up her puberty talk and nearly turned purple. "No need to be embarrassed dear; it's perfectly normal."

"Um, no, actually, I'm not concerned about that. I'm actually here because I wanted to get a mark."

That stopped her in her tracks, and her eyes turned suddenly more serious. Her brows climbed up into her bangs as she began to speak. "You are very young. Are you involved with anything that would make it necessary? If so, that is quite the serious matter."

"I'm not, and it isn't because I think I'll need it now, or any time in the near future. Rather so that I have it covered in case I do need it later in life."

"Is there some reason to not simply get it when that time comes?" She seemed unconvinced as to my explanation.

"Things are not stable in my experience. It is best to be prepared as early as possible to keep things from getting out of hand."

"That's . . . an unusual view of things."

"During the war, my village was destroyed. Because my teachers showed me how best to prepare for even the worst, I managed to survive. So . . . I don't think, or want anything to happen, but if it does, and I can't get a Lovers' Mark in the future, I want to be prepared."

The priestess made a quick movement of her hand, and a blue light flashed over me ever so briefly. In a second, I'd jumped from my seat and was glaring at her. I was unsure what exactly she'd done, but casting something on me without my permission or consent like that was unbelievably rude.

"My apologies. I had to make a quick check on some things, just to be sure." She held up a placating hand as she spoke.

"You checked to see if I'd . . ." I didn't manage to finish the question completely before she cut me off.

"No, there is no spell that can determine with complete surety if someone is a virgin, at least not to my knowledge. I can, however, check for signs of abuse, and for a girl your age to come here seeking a mark, you must understand my suspicions that they would be present."

"Look at my aura. If anyone tried something improper, I'd bury him." I glared at Kiana, my teeth clenched. I really wanted to scream her into the floor, but that would probably end with me failing this mission.

"I would like to believe that, but what can be done and what is done are often not the same. As it stands though, I found nothing of concern, so if you still want a Lovers' Mark, I will arrange it. Will the fee be any issue?"

"It will not, and thank you." I had enough silver coins saved up to easily cover the cost. I wasn't sure on exactly how high it was, but I was sure that I'd brought more than enough.

After informing me of the cost and taking it, Kiana left me there in the comfy little room to remain irritated and returned a few minutes later with a small box. Upon opening it, I saw a number of tools, including a hammer-and-needle tattooing instrument and some rather fancy-looking bottles of ink. She closed and locked the door behind her.

"Now, please show me where you want the tattoo, and we'll begin. If you need to undress, you may do so."

I did as she indicated and pointed to a place high up on my right thigh. Kiana gave me another look before she began. The ink was literally beaten in; it was an old type of tattooing I'd seen talked about once or twice, and nothing really prepared me for how painful it was.

By the halfway point, I was really regretting my decision and thinking about all the stupid things I'd done in my life. It wasn't singularly painful, not a harsh stab, but a growing throbbing agony. It wasn't enough damage for adrenaline to kick in and block out the pain, nor slight enough to ignore. It was instead constant, like a stabbing and ripping.

My teeth were clenched as she finally put away the tools and turned back to the work itself. It was red and raw, the skin angry at its punishment. There she put her finger upon it, and I could feel her working some kind of spell. The magic was invasive, moving through my body along various routes. I squirmed as the spell wormed its way into me, like something living wriggling through every inch. Then it faded; even the pain was gone as everything finished and I felt strangely normal.

A look down showed the mark standing bright against my skin, with a tiny amount of mana in it. The skin itself appeared to have been healed by the spell that was added to it, as well as any and all of the little imperfections in the tattoo worked out.

"Thank you."

"My dear, I am quite discomforted by this. I do hope you speak the truth about your situation, but if something ever does happen, please do seek shelter either here or with the Order of the Shield. The only reason I did agree was that the possibility of something horrid happening to you would only increase had I refused."

It was weird leaving. I'd done what I came for, but it was still a major thing, a hurdle I had wanted to and succeeded in passing. The walk back to the Starlit Sky was far shorter than the one out this morning, though it was already late afternoon as I strolled home. I took my time, letting the sights and sounds wash over me. I'd wanted safety for a long, long time, and today I'd managed one step closer to it.

As I entered the tavern, I saw Dras, huddled in a corner. I went over to join him and plopped down on the opposite side of the table.

"Hey, I came by to study, only a few weeks till entrance exams. Everything all right?"

"Yeah, I just had an errand to run. How goes things?"

"I think I've got everything I need down. Can we go over some of the geometry again though?"

We spent the rest of the evening working on problems. If I was any judge, he was going to ace the math and reading. He should with how hard he'd put his nose to the grindstone for the last couple of years. I couldn't help but be proud; his hard work had really paid off.

CHAPTER 43

✦

THE EXAM

I spent more and more time studying with Dras as the day approached for his exams. I was assured that he was going to ace the math and reading parts at least if the book we bought was good. It was all we had at any rate, but he knew it back to front, as did I. I still remembered a bit of trig from my past life; I'd even run a few of them myself to keep up my skills. Sharing those seemed to go against Mystien's advice of not adding new or unknown knowledge though, so I held off for now.

The night before, Dras wanted to come and go over everything one more time, but after a very quick review, I told him to go rest. He knew everything he needed to, and trying to force any more would just make him tired for his exam. He briefly argued, but eventually he did head to go sleep. I kept our study guide to discourage any late-night work on his part.

Dras and I would be traveling separately. His parents were going to come to watch and cheer him on, and my issues with his mother did not need any further prodding. It also meant that I could sleep in a bit, since there really was nothing I could do for the written part. I was planning to come to the practical though, to cheer him on from the stands.

I put on one of my nicer outfits, the one Dras had paid for, and headed out to the academy. There was far less wandering around as I'd been there once before, and finding the testing area was rather straightforward. I could see the line of people headed for the entrance, those dressed as nobles skipped the line naturally and went straight to the front. I wondered if they were here to watch their children, or perhaps for some other reason.

"Why hello there, young lady." A voice interrupted me as I came up to the entrance.

I turned to see a man who was vaguely familiar. He was lanky and tall, somewhere in his mid- or late-twenties. His pitch-black hair was falling straight to his ears, and he had a pair of spider-like hands woven in a scholar's cradle in front of him. Even his robes were a bit unusual, nicer than what Dras normally wore, and in a deep, almost black purple. I gave him a once over and tried to place him, but couldn't quite. He stood beside the entrance with an amused expression.

"You're the girl who came with your friend a couple of years ago, are you not?"

"I . . . you remember that?" I finally remembered who he was. This was the same man who'd led us to the study guide.

"My dear, it is not often that we get people seeking to watch the practical who aren't family of the tested. Even more rare that they should be here to examine our examinations. I suppose the lad who was with you is taking his test today?"

"He is." I nodded. "I've come to cheer him on."

"How kind, do you think he'll pass? He looked a bit confused when I explained what was needed."

"His math and reading have improved greatly over the past two years. I've no worries about that at all."

"I hope he does. I suppose you'll be joining him in a year or two?"

"Two, and I think I will. I've learned most of the basics so far, at least as far as I can tell."

"You seem sure, would you consent to showing me one of your spells? I'm always eager to see what those from outside formal institutions come up with. It's rather more original than some of the rote things nobles learn, at least sometimes. Some people come up only with truly bland magic."

I thought for a few moments on what I might show him. Eventually, I settled on the spell I had come up with for the competition with Dras. I sang a few notes, and it was like a bell jar had fallen over us, locking out all sound from outside.

"This is something I came up with for a competition with my friend."

"Oh-ho, a dome of privacy. Not bad, and it doesn't just muffle or distort, but complete negation. Is it both ways?"

"It should be, but I've never actually stood outside and tried to listen or anything."

"Did you win?"

"I did."

"Well, I'll have to look forward to seeing what else you've come up with when you do join us. For now though, you'd best hurry along. Wouldn't want to miss your companion's examination now, would you?"

At his urging, I hurried off; it turned out that the dome did block sound both ways. I saw him laughing from the inside before I cut the spell. I'd made quite the mistake not figuring that out before and was quite glad he'd pointed out my oversight.

My spot today was quite a bit closer than the last time I'd been here. I saw Dras's mother, and who I assumed was his father; they were just behind the nobles watching the students being led out. As they came into the arena-like area, I saw Dras scan the crowd, his parents waving to him first. I gave him a happy wave, too, as he moved his eyes past my spot and saw his smile in return before they began.

I watched on as Dras demonstrated first what I guessed was his muffling spell, followed by a lot of fire magic. Other than a light spell, everything seemed to be fire actually, and not even a large variety of it. He showed his fire ribbon, but while it was powerful, it was his go-to. I realized our mistake too late: we had drilled over and over on the bookwork, but his variety of magic was lacking. His exam was over soon, too soon. He just ran out of things he could show to the proctor.

He was at least not the first to be led out of the arena, but decidedly not far up that list. As I sat in the stands, I buried my face in my hands, cursing that we had not covered at least a few basic elements for his spells. I saw his parents get up and head to the exit; they looked so excited. I could only hope that he'd managed to scrape by with a pass.

Dras did not come by that evening, and I didn't see him for a full day. When he did, he looked broken, coming in and slumping down in a booth.

"How bad?" I asked.

"Failed by a sliver. I aced the written, but when I got to the practical, they said I just didn't have it, not enough control, not enough finesse, not enough variety. Guess I'll just take up a job like I have; it's no big deal."

"It is, and what you're going to do is go in next year and pass."

"No, didn't you hear me? I'm just not . . ."

"Quiet. We spent all of our time focusing on the written portion. That's my fault, I should have known you'd need to work more on your practicals. You're in luck though. I need to as well, so we can do that together. What we'll do is get you hitting several different elements, then combining them into some really cool stuff. By next year, you'll be so strong, they'll not even recognize you."

"Did you not hear me!?" He almost stood up before I brought a fist down on his head.

"I did; you're the one who's not listening. I'm going to make you a little magical monster. We'll do reviews, and I'll help you come up with new spells, and Dras"—I leaned forward as he kept rubbing his skull—"don't you ever even pretend to give up that easily again."

Lucien was at the bar and had apparently heard enough to send him laughing as I took the boy by the scruff of his neck and pulled him out the exit into our back alley. A not quite so easy feat as he seemed to be gaining height by the day.

I raised my voice as we made our exit and stood there in the empty street. "All right, quitter, listen up. Your new training starts today, first is water. My first teacher was an expert in water, and I know enough to get you started. What water-type spells do you know?"

"Er . . . none."

"Basics it is then. First, water starts in the shape of a triangle." I drew one like Mystien had used in the dirt. "Focus on this symbol as you try to summon some."

It took him a few minutes as I walked him through the basic summoning of the easiest liquid. His spell was much like mine, in that he had not imparted any force into it. The water just fell to the stones.

"Good, now, try to make a stream and give it direction." I demonstrated, though for me it was kind of like a weak water pistol, even then it was horridly mana inefficient. Being a bard had its limits. Dras, on the other hand, was able to quickly get it into something like a rather powerful hose, though he ran out of mana shortly thereafter.

We continued like that until it was too dark to see. I'd push him to try and make a stronger and stronger water cannon until he ran out of mana. Then while we waited for some to come back, I ran him through basic math and grammar. Progress was slow, as it always was with new magic, but by the end of the day he could at least make something.

We spent weeks working on that alone. He complained that his water stream was strong enough only for me to counter and he needed to bring the cost of it down through practice. I was practicing fire magic as he did so. It wasn't something I'd bothered much with before, but I figured if I was going to drag him into learning water I could at least set a good example by learning some of what he did. It was a bit pathetic when compared to his, but that was sort of the way of things. I knew my magic would never be stronger in some areas, but learning how to do fire would at least be useful.

After about a month, we each had something that was, if not very good in comparison to what we knew before, at least workable. I could make small fires, and he could make something just short of a fire hose, easily able to power wash the alley clean, something Lucien was thankful for and amused by. There were a few issues; both of us had to work, and that meant that practice time was limited. We also didn't often start with our full mana and quickly ran out, but it was unavoidable, so there was no point complaining.

It was starting to get colder, and I thought now was a good time to teach Dras about ice. This was one I'd learned years ago, and while there wasn't much use for it in winter, having ice all around us seemed to me a good way to have ready examples. I explained that ice came in hexagons, something Mystien was surprised I'd known, and we set off. I was still working on making fire and moving water as Dras struggled his way through conjuring up the cold stuff. He outshone me in all of these things; in speed and force, wizard magic was just better. We set up a target so that he could hurl chunks of ice and streams of snow at something.

I'd been using ice to keep food for longer since working at the Starlit Sky. It was one of my occasional and helpful uses of magic. It was also something that everyone understood already. Larger estates and businesses had an ice room, normally in the basement. The tavern had a very small one for meats and cheeses, surrounded by a wall in the basement.

While Dras was learning ice and hammering out some of the roughness of water, I worked on illusions. I could now make a few objects move believably so long as I kept them rather simple. Furniture that moved on its own or walls that did the same were a go-to for me. I felt like I still had a ways to go before I could make something that looked like a person, but I was making progress. Dras, for his part, had no head for the subtlety involved and didn't bother with those after a few rather poor attempts.

We each practiced together on our chosen magics until spring came and we felt that we'd gotten close enough for us to progress to something else. Dras suggested we move on far more quickly than I'd like, but nodded when I told him about Mystien's insistence on hammering fundamentals before learning too many different things.

I was glad to work with Dras. It took a bit of effort at first, but I saw my friend brighten and rekindle his hope, letting it grow into a blaze like it had before his first attempt at the exam. I was sure that he would pass both written and practical exams this time around. If they failed him after what he was learning now, they were the ones who had the problem.

CHAPTER 44

✦

STALKER

As summer slammed into us, Dras and I were surprised by a visitor who joined us in the tavern one night.

"Good evening, bookworms," Charles said as he flopped down beside us.

It took me a few moments to realize who it was. His skin had started to take on a bit of color, and his whole body had filled out. He was still pale and had huge eyes, but no longer looked like a cave-dwelling lost kid.

"Hey, Charles, long time no see." Dras looked up from where he was working, giving our friend a light punch on the shoulder.

"There somewhere we can talk? You know, without people overhearing us."

Dras blinked a bit and I put up my sound barrier, before turning back to the young man. For now, he was certainly a man, lean muscle all over his wiry frame.

"Okay, that's a neat one. Love to be able to do that on command. Anyway, we've got a problem."

"Um . . . okay? What kind of a problem?" Dras asked before I had a chance.

"You two are being followed."

"How do you know?" It was my turn to speak up this round.

"Because I've been following you every now and then."

"So . . . you're here to tell us that you've been following us?"

"Yes and no. I've been following you as part of my training, and not for very long at a time. The issue is that somebody else has been following you."

I narrowed my eyes. "I'm so very glad that you've been stalking us. Who is our other stalker?" I felt like I needed to put in just a bit of sarcasm there.

"I don't know, haven't gotten a look at his face. He's also significantly harder to follow than you two."

"We should tell Lucien," Dras pointed out.

"He knows, or will shortly. My teacher is going to go over it with him. She wants us to handle it if we can though, think of it as a test she said."

"We could probably take them, but what if it's a noble or you know . . ."

"Fringe of the law . . . if you catch them, they'll be in trouble. If you'd caught me and been mad, I would have been. The two of you are a bit oblivious, just so that you know. So if we catch them, there'll be no big issue. Assuming they're not from . . . you know."

It went without saying that it would be trouble if we attacked someone the royal palace had sent to spy on us. I couldn't think of a reason for them to do that though, or to send someone who Charles could catch.

"What are your opinions?" I was fully at a loss of what to do here.

"Catch and stomp them." Dras was direct, if nothing else.

"Capture, then see where it goes." Charles was only slightly less so.

"Are we sure we can? Do we know if this person is stronger than us?"

"Should be possible. Teacher looked in on them a few times and seemed only mildly concerned. She's a friend of Lucien, so if she thought they were a serious threat, she probably wouldn't have told me to handle it."

"I would like to ask Lucien his opinion before we do anything. Let's come up with a plan to take them down nevertheless."

We spent the rest of the night going over ideas and things we might be able to pull off. The boys knew the city much better than I did, and so having them pick out places for an ambush was a lot better than asking me.

The next morning, I went to ask the most trustworthy adult caster I knew, well, at least the one who was in the capital. It was really telling how screwed up that the caster was an aging bard who had, for all tellings, been an absolute womanizer in his youth. Though maybe his hard won experience would be useful here, and he'd certainly calmed as he'd aged.

"So, I'm guessing you already know what's going on?"

"Yup."

"Do you know who it is?"

"Not exactly, but I've got a pretty good idea."

"Are you going to do anything?"

"I think letting you kids handle it will work out best."

"Any advice?"

"Don't aim to kill, capture only."

"Wow, thanks for all the help."

"Cut the sass. If I thought it was any real issue, I'd do something, most likely let the city guard know. As it stands though, I think you can handle this on your own, and the three of you need experience that will only come from fieldwork. So take care of this, or don't, the results will be educational for you whatever you do."

The boys and I took several days to get a real thorough idea of how exactly our stalker was following us. Habits, how far behind, where they'd be if we went down an alley, things like that. It was exhausting to go and walk around the city every day for no real reason, but needed. I suspected that if our little friend was a pro, they'd have figured out that they'd been made, but it didn't appear so.

Charles, for his part, stalked the stalker, flitting between buildings and roofs like a shadow. Even knowing he was there, I didn't see him, not unless he wanted me to at least. His teacher, and I hadn't been given a name, had certainly taught him well. I wondered what else he was learning, then decided not to ask. There were only so many reasons to learn a skill set of stalking and hiding. Of course, I wasn't really one to speak on that account.

We met at night after our daily work to go over what we had and to plan. This part was fairly simple; we all knew about what we could do. The question was what could the stalker do. In a few brief glimpses I'd stolen, I'd confirmed that our follower had an aura, though not strong. I suspected that they were suppressing it to avoid attention, but perhaps I was being paranoid. The reason for that suspicion was that it flicked in and out, also making it hard to get a good feel for it.

All auras I'd come across so far had a unique feel or taste to them. Often something about the person who had one was reflected into their aura; sometimes not, but it was always very unique. The weaker it was though, the harder it was to get a feel for it. For particularly weak ones, like the girl I'd seen at a noble's house so long ago in Istlan, it took a lot of time and close inspection to figure it out.

When the day to strike rolled around, it was perfect. I had the day off, our stalker had shown up early, and a thick fog had rolled in with the early morning, Dras had even come for an all-day magic study session. Charles insisted that we leave early, to make the most of the fortunate weather, something I concurred with fervently.

Ten minutes in, we made it to the agreed-upon point. Dras and I turned into the alley and saw a green bottle laying against one of the side walls. It was a cheap piece of pottery and our sign that as of a couple of minutes ago that our tail was still in place, something Charles had suggested. I made a mental note of that being a really good one as we passed.

I moved behind a bin, humming out two spells in quick succession. The first was my invisibility, the best I could do for remaining unseen, along with pushing down my own aura. After that, I sent something that looked rather like a shadow version of myself walking along with Dras. It wouldn't fool anyone who got even relatively close, but the fog helped a lot, and our tail was keeping well back.

If something failed here, it would be the illusion. It bobbed as if walking, but the colors were all wrong; it didn't move quite right either. Again, the fog was a great help, as was the fact that many people just see what they want to see. I hoped that it would work long enough that our pursuer didn't realize it didn't have an aura.

Dras and the shadow Alana walked to the end of the alley and into a door that was one of the lesser-known and used entrances to the Undercity, not that they were actually going in.

I heard the quick footsteps as someone marched down the alley, a fast *tap-tap-tap* of shoes on stone. As she passed, and I was now sure it was a she, I could hear the muttering. Her dark cloak with hood pulled up not managing to hide the distinctly feminine voice.

"Of all the stupid . . . Where are they even going? Isn't that building a store? Basement? Don't tell me they're going into . . ."

At this point, she was far enough past the bin I'd pressed myself behind that I could get a clear shot at her back. It was oddly enjoyable to smash her with the scream I let loose. I hadn't had much a chance to really let go in a while and I was absolutely going to take it. I'd even brought out my old mace.

The scream was the sign for go, and Charles dropped down from above, running forward with a net to try and catch the woman. Dras almost literally exploded out of the door he'd just gone in, water swirling around one hand. He'd chosen it because it was far easier to keep it nonlethal than fire or ice.

The woman was a far quicker to recover than I'd have anticipated.

Before Charles could get to her, she'd already come up to one knee and loosed a spell of some kind at him, strong enough to drop him to the ground, curling in pain. It was about that time that Dras's water cannon hit her and threw her across the stones, sprawled out in a quite undignified way.

She sent something headed his way, which he dodged, and I saw red. As she got to her feet again, I sang the wet ground below her into ice, one of Jackson's tricks. She stumbled and slid a bit but kept her feet as I closed in with the mace, a powerful swing at her thigh, enough to drop her to the ground, and keep her there.

A swing and a miss, truly my lack of practice with that was coming back to bite me. She yelped at the attack and pushed herself against the wall as a brace. Her eyes flicked to me and another spell flew forth, catching me square in the stomach.

My whole body went numb, like someone had given me Novocain just everywhere. Like a puppet with my strings cut, I fell to the ground, unable to move as the muscles just wouldn't respond. It didn't hurt but was quite disconcerting. Moreover, it was clear what we were up against now, not that I could do anything about it.

Dras's roar of rage as he saw me fall could have shaken the buildings. I wanted to tell him not to do anything stupid, to keep his head, to keep to the plan, to not kill the priestess. Unfortunately, I couldn't feel much of anything, or move at all.

A powerful jet of water whipped over me, catching the woman again. A few drops splashed on me, and even I could feel that it was ice cold; the little bits of slush coming off of it were strong confirmation. In moments, the girl was down, unable to move from her quickly onsetting hypothermia.

Marching toward her was an enraged young wizard.

CHAPTER 45

✦

THE BISHOP

Whatever you've done, undo it. Now!" Ice had been replaced with flames, now licking up and down Dras's arms as he looked over the shivering priestess.

I, for my part, was trying to find a way to do magic, but having a bit of a time at it. I was trying to hum or speak, but it was going nowhere fast. I knew that eventually I'd manage to get a tune going, but the question was, would it be too late?

For her part, the now sopping wet and freezing woman was still trying to pick herself up. I had no idea if she needed to do that to undo her magic, or if she had any foolish notions about fighting Dras in the current state. If she did, she'd have to hit him with something truly terrifying, or he'd turn her into baked caster.

"B-b-b-b-be f-f-ine," stuttered the woman, speaking seemed to be giving her a hard time. "J-just . . . d-dis . . ."

"I don't care, undo it." I'd never heard Dras actually angry, and his voice was trying its hardest to fall into a growl.

I could still see from where I was, in a skewed sort of way. Our would-be follower pointed at me first, and I could feel the feeling start to creep back into my limbs. It moved in a prickling sort of way, rather like when your leg was asleep and coming back.

"Calm," I slurred out as it hit my face, making me shiver a bit as the unpleasant sensation passed over me. It was slow to pull out the numbness, and I had to wonder if it was a poison or if she'd done something to my nerves.

Charles groaned as she pointed to him next. I couldn't see him from my position, nor was I totally confident in picking myself up off the ground quite yet. After her hand pointed to him again, she fell back down, shivering overtaking her once more. I wasn't sure she had a way to counter that.

From what I knew of priests and their manner of magic, they could only work on living things. I guessed she might be able to pull up her body temp with a spell, but if she didn't have one she knew, that might be quite difficult. I also didn't know how long until she suffered real damage from being soaked in what was effectively slush, but surely her falling back onto the ground wasn't going to help at all.

A few individuals had heard the commotion—mostly Dras yelling—and were now peeking down the alley we were in, leading to a general look of panic at what seemed to be casters going at each other. That was something we'd have to deal with shortly as well. There was no really good answer to that issue however. For now, we needed to get everyone to calm down and talk.

"Dras, enough, she's done. Remember that we're supposed to not hurt her too bad," I offered up as I got up off the ground.

"She hurt you too . . ."

"I'm fine, little numb, but fine."

"Ugh, I hurt." Charles was not being helpful here.

"What'd she hit you with?" I looked over at our older friend as he struggled to pull himself up.

"Like a full-body cramp, couldn't hardly move."

"Effective, not nice, but you'll be fine soon enough."

"C-c-c-old." The voice from the only person still on the ground brought me back to my senses quickly enough.

"What order?" I asked as I looked over to her.

"Sh-sh-sh . . ."

"Got it. Dras can you see about drying her off a bit? Cold can do some nasty stuff to a person." He furrowed his brows at me as I hummed up my warming spell, trying to wrap it around the priestess. That was a bit difficult. I'd used it on myself quite a bit, and on my surroundings, too, but never on someone else like this.

I was more than a bit irritated at the whole situation. The Order of the Shield seemed determined to be overprotective busybodies, inserting themselves into my life even after they'd been told to shove off. If this was going to continue, I hoped we could at least avoid violence in the future, without me giving into their obtuse demands as well, because I wasn't going to go back to their temple.

At this point, a few guardsmen did show up. City guards were not something you saw all that much, being that they mostly kept to their barracks and the upper parts of town. For an incident not in the section of the city frequented by nobles, someone would run to the local guardhouse and grab one. It was easy to identify them by their distinctive armor. Each wore chain mail with a crest on their shoulder and on their shields. They commonly carried a shield, a truncheon, and a sword, in case lethal force was needed.

"Care to explain?" The one who seemed to be their leader looked at the lot of us. He seemed on edge, certainly knowing that magic was involved. The sheer amount of slush on the ground midsummer was an obvious sign.

"Case of mistaken identity," I offered him, hoping he'd jump on it. The boys looked at me a bit askance at that one.

"How so?" The guardsman raised an eyebrow.

"We thought she was following us with bad intent, but it seems she's from one of the priest orders. I've got an old acquaintance there who likes to check up on me from time to time. He's just a jerk and can't bring himself to do it by stopping by to see me."

That actually got a few snorts from the crowd. I really was hoping the guards would accept it.

"That true?" The guardsman looked down toward the priestess. She was an adult, but not by much, and was easily a head and a half shorter than him.

"Cl-close enough." She was finally managing to get back to her feet, even if she was still shivering a bit. I noticed that Dras had done all of squat to help warm her up, but I couldn't actually blame him.

"Which order?"

"The Shield."

"Fair enough then. We'll head down to the temple, if they confirm and there's no other issues, we'll leave it at that." I could feel my heart sink as the guard spoke, knowing that this would be unpleasant.

There wasn't even any grumbling from the boys, which surprised me. They allowed themselves to be herded toward the temple district without any issues at all. I noticed while we walked that the guards kept well behind our group, hands on their weapons as they directed us. Charles, for his part, seemed completely unbothered, like he knew he could get away or take one out regardless of where they stood. That put them a bit more on edge around him.

For my part, I quite disliked having armed men behind me. I severely disliked not being in control in situations like this, and it had me on edge, which was apparently the normal response, because it didn't really get much attention at all.

Dras just looked pissed: at me for not explaining everything, at the guards for driving us toward the temple, and really, severely pissed at the priestess. I was fairly certain I'd be getting an earful at some point, not that there was really anything here that was—completely—my fault.

It wasn't too long before we stood before the gates of the temple of the Order of the Shield. They were quickly opened, and we were all hurried in and into a side hall. A rather unhappy-looking old man came down to meet us shortly after we arrived.

"Greetings, what seems to be the issue?" He looked over the lot of us and I almost shrank back.

Whoever this man was, he was potent; his aura flowed over us in a wave; it looked bright and hard as steel, forming a protective wall around him. I could see Dras looking pale too; this was someone we could not win against in a fight.

"This lot claims there was a bit of a case of mistaken identity. Seems they thought this young woman was following them with ill intent, but she's one of yours, sir?" the guardsman who'd taken charge asked, keeping his tone quite polite.

"Indeed, one of our trainees. I'd rather prefer to handle this internally, if you don't mind?" It was worded as a question, but everyone understood it was more an order.

"Of course, sir, have a good day." The guards and priest nodded toward each other, and we were left alone in the temple.

As soon as they were gone, the old man waved off the priestess. "I'd rather like to have words with the three of you. If you don't mind?" With that, he began walking, expecting us to follow.

He led us to what I could only assume was his office. It was well made, but not fancily so. It seemed everything here was for function, the desk and chairs sturdy and comfortable, but not ostentatious, the shelves lined with various materials and files for whatever work this man did.

"Now, I believe that introductions are in order. I am Bishop Theodore. I'm in charge of the training of our more advanced priests here, including the young woman who it would seem the three of you decided to get in an altercation with. I'm guessing that would make you miss Alana? And the boy there would be young Adraias?"

"Dras, if you don't mind." I had to respect his guts on that.

"I do. Now, as for the third member of your little group. Who might you be young man?"

"Charles, nice to meet you, sir."

"So, am I to understand that the three of you noticed your tail and decided to incapacitate her?"

There were nods all around.

"Interesting, and you succeeded?"

Again, the three of us bobbed our heads.

"That's mildly impressive."

"I would prefer it if you didn't have someone follow us in the future." I spoke up, having the man's eyes settle on me.

"I will not promise anything on that, but perhaps it would not be an issue if you would agree to stay with us instead of wandering around the city without a proper guardian."

"No, thank you. I've already explained my opinion on that to Rosk in detail."

"I'm aware. He was quite displeased with your attitude and asked that we keep an eye on you periodically. Which is why I've had our trainees take turns tailing you every now and then. It's good training and makes sure you have someone looking out for your interests."

"I do not need anyone to look after me. I've plenty of friends who are quite capable of helping me, should I have any issues."

"My dear girl, what were we supposed to think when you got a Lovers' Mark? That all was well and you were quite safe?"

I felt both Dras and Charles turn toward me a bit as my face went beet red. This was his version of punishing me. He didn't have to lift a finger to do it, no paddle or belt was needed. I'd pissed him off by defying his little order, and his response was to shame me in front of those I called friends. It was a contest of emotions for control, between profound embarrassment and absolute rage.

"That is none of your business," I hissed out.

"Everything concerning unattended minors is our business, young miss, even more so when they are capable of magic. The simple fact is that we've allowed you to remain outside of our direct supervision so far. That allowance can be revoked."

"If you try, you will find me an enemy for the rest of time." I wanted to punch this bastard, but that would only end poorly. We were in his fortress, and he was at his strongest here, fighting was a losing proposition.

"Which is why I will not revoke it for now. Understand though, that should I come to believe it must be done, it will be. If you should hate us afterward, that is a problem for the future. The three of you may show yourselves out."

CHAPTER 46

✦

CONFERENCE AND STUDY

I was fuming as we left the temple, hands clenched so tightly that my nails bit into the soft skin of my palms. None of us talked as we walked out, the bishop having dismissed us. For a brief moment, I thought Dras might argue with him as I got up to leave, but he seemed to take my lead and follow. Charles was hard to read; he looked irritated, but also as if he had a lot of questions.

"So, what are you going to do about that guy?" Charles asked once we'd made it about half a block away.

"Nothing."

"Nothing? We can't do nothing, we could . . ." Dras seemed a bit unhappy with my decision.

"Lose, we could lose. He wants an excuse to do something and he has a lot more power than we do. Half of that was probably him poking us to see if we'd strike at him. If we do, we lose." That was the worst part of it, there really was nothing to do. I could have come up with some way to cause him issues, but if I did, he'd have all the reason he needed to come after me.

"So that whole thing about you getting a mar—" I heard Dras's hand come down hard on Charles's shoulder as he spoke. I turned around to glare angrily at him as I saw the younger boy pull him in.

"Charles, I know you spent literally years underground, so I'm going to give you some solid advice. Shut up." I was thankful for Dras's correction. I had no desire at all to get into that conversation.

The rest of our walk back to the Starlit Sky was quite silent. The boys looked like they didn't quite know how to restart the conversation in a direction that wouldn't cause an argument. I was busy keeping my jaw clenched so that I didn't start hurling obscenities, or some other ridiculous emotional outburst.

When we arrived, we found Lucien and Charles's teacher sitting at a table waiting for us. I was more than a bit surprised at that development as they waved us over.

"I'm glad to see you three made it back safely. Alana, Dras, I don't know if you've met Meg."

Lucien motioned for us to take some of the extra seats around the table then spun up his own version of a quieting spell. I suspected it was based on mine, but he worked in some kind of illusion that made everything around us look like frosted glass. That was a neat little add-on, I would have to think about stealing it for some purposes.

"So, how would you say things went?" he asked.

"Well, the fight wasn't too bad . . ." I began, before Meg cut me off.

"You three took her by surprise then got your arses handed to you. Only the fact that you outnumbered her so badly helped at all." Meg finally spoke, the first time I'd heard her say anything.

Meg was as old as Lucien or Mystien if I was any judge. Her graying hair was tied back in a rather tight bun, and she looked like someone's very angry aunt. Sharp features and hard eyes. She was also quite solidly built, and for a change wore some kind of loose pants rather than a skirt. The last part was of great note as almost no women wore anything but a dress or skirt unless it was part of some specialized work clothing, even that was really rare.

"We didn't do too badly . . ." I tried.

"Arses handed to you. You, lad, you went down too fast. No worries though, we'll be solving that issue soon enough." Charles paled as she fixed him with a rather hard look. I did not envy whatever she had planned for him.

"Meg here kept an eye on things as you might have guessed. I'm assuming you met Theodore? How is he, still a bit of an ass?" Lucien seemed downright amused by the whole situation.

"That might be the understatement of the century. You know him?" I asked.

"We've met. My own personal history is long, and we'll not be covering it today. I'm assuming that since you're here he let you go, or did you just come back to get your things?"

"Did you know what he was up to?" I now fixed my erstwhile employer with a cold gaze.

"I suspected he was watching. The Order of the Shield are known for wanting to keep all orphans under their purview. That said, as a caster and someone who's shown she's quite capable of taking care of herself, I thought you'd be fine."

"You could have told me."

"Sure, but letting you see for yourself is better for learning. You also got the experience of fighting a priest, which isn't something that's easy to come by, at least not under normal circumstances."

"That could have gone wrong in a lot of ways." Dras seemed peeved that they'd let us blunder into that mess too.

"Which is why I kept an eye on you as you did it, didn't I?" Meg growled out from her spot. "Make sure you didn't get hurt, or cook your-selves a priestess. Nearly had to stop you though, lad. The ice spell was a nice touch. I liked that."

"Er . . . thanks?"

"You're welcome. Anyway, come on, Charles, let's go have a word about where all you screwed up." With that, she grabbed and pulled the young man after her and out of the dome. It was impressive, being that he was quite a bit larger than the older lady.

Lucien looked over toward Dras, "I'd like a private word." He took the hint and bid his farewells, promising to return tomorrow for more studying.

"You could have at least told me the bishop was going to be that much of a jerk." I looked over to him once we were alone.

"No, if he'd thought I'd coached you on how to deal with him, he might have used that as evidence against you." It was sour, but I hadn't thought of that.

"I see."

"They're going to make a few more passes at bringing you into their fold. I doubt it will be anything as hostile, but they will want you some-where you're kept an eye on, The Order of the Shield is rather like that. You may not like it, but it may be important for you to compromise with them on that at some point."

"Compromise!? After they stalked and threatened me? You've lost your mind if you think I want anything to do with them!" I was still pissed about how much they'd dug into what I considered private business, and no way was I going back to their orphanage.

"Listen to me." Lucien let his voice get hard; he was seldom serious, but when he was he meant it. "They've got the law on their side, and enough

CHAPTER 47

✦

EXAM ROUND TWO

The sun rose early on our last morning of study, and I rose to meet it. That in itself was rather normal, having lived on a farm and then working a morning shift, I was used to waking up at the crack of dawn, if not a bit earlier. Breakfast was a bit of a hurried affair, where Dras joined me looking quite a bit less like a morning person. I wondered if he'd stayed up studying all night, but that didn't really matter that much. Today was a day for prepping.

As we finished a rather tasty meal of soup and bread, we looked at each other and began to talk over the important points of his studies. His having taken the test before was a big help here, since he already knew the basics of what was on it.

After breakfast, we decided to take a walk down the merchants' district, then up to the academy gates. There was no real reasoning for this, just a good way to get outside a bit and go enjoy the autumn air. The gates were closed, but he'd registered for the test weeks ago, so there were no worries there.

After lunch, we went for a bit of magic practice through the afternoon, going over each and every spell he planned to show them during the practical. I was satisfied that he had a good variety now, and some of them really did show off more of his control than his fire-ribbon spell ever had. He planned to make a few small ice sculptures, just to show he could, and even made me a small cat that fit well in my hand as practice. Add to that, the various water and fire tricks, and I was confident about how far he'd come.

Unlike the last few days, we went slowly through all of this. The point was to bring confidence, he had the material down, all he had to do was show it. My only fear was that he would get too nervous or something, and that might cause him problems. That was the whole purpose of today, to make sure he didn't.

We went out for dinner, something I almost never did. I liked to think of my life as frugal, though in the opinions of others it might be considered spartan. For that reason, I'd only ever been to a few of the various eating establishments throughout the city. Dras claimed to know a place though and led us on, right up to the edge of the noble's district of the city.

The place he led me to was rather taller than the rest of the buildings around it, though significantly less fancy from the outside. As we entered, I could see small wisps of aura around the hostess, one of the weak, barely there kinds that signified those who'd never developed far, or were suppressing their power.

"Welcome to The Tower, do you have a reservation?" she asked as we came up, this place was far, far more than I was used to.

Dras replied, "Yes, we do. Is there a table on the top level?"

"Indeed there is, right this way please." She turned and led us over to a spiral staircase, taking the steps up slowly and with the grace of someone who did it every day.

Our table was on what might have otherwise been the roof, and it looked out over most of the city. It was even possible to see over the wall in places. From here, I could tell why they had built this place as they had: there was a clear view to watch both sunrise and sunset on either side, a rather well-thought-out gimmick.

"My parents brought me here when my magic first manifested. They were so happy to see that I had a real chance that they spent the coin we normally wouldn't. Since then I've loved it and tried to come back a few times. It's too expensive to do often though."

"Thank you for sharing this with me. It's certainly lovely."

"The food's amazing too. I would have preferred to bring you in the morning, but . . . well, I couldn't afford, or get reservations. Too many couples . . ."

I didn't really follow that, but I'd ask later. I seriously wondered how great the sunrise here would be. While it would be a great view, it would also mean waking up so very early that I would probably pass.

"Morning would mean waking up early though, night is better."

"Yeah, I guess you're right." Dras passed me over a menu, an actual small paper one.

We decided to have fish. It was brought in daily from a local river and slowly baked. The light greens and citrus it was served with worked with the flaky pale meat. It was also one of the cheapest things they had. I worried about how much Dras was spending on this outing, and while I appreciated it, I didn't want to break his bank. Also, I hadn't eaten decent fish in some time, so it was a nice change.

"So, are you excited?" I asked between bites, making a note that Dras's table manners really needed some work.

"A bit, I know that things will be very different tomorrow. That I'll take one more step toward being who I want to be. Thank you, for everything."

I looked at him as he gazed toward the slowly setting sun. "You're welcome. You did the work though, how far have we come since we met?"

"Well, I don't see any groups of angry women around here for you to put to the ground," he said with a smirk.

"I'm sure we can find someone, just have to look hard."

He was chuckling as the waitress came by and asked us if we wanted dessert.

"Yeah, what do you have for it tonight?" Dras answered for us.

"Oh, we have a new product coming out of the eastern part of the country. It's called ice cream, and it's quite wonderful. We have three flavors, strawberry, roasted cinnamon apple, and honey walnut."

I nearly died. Both at hearing that it had spread this far, and at the flavors. Some of those were a bit . . . original, where was the chocolate? The vanilla? The mint? On second thought, honey walnut didn't sound all that bad though.

"Honey walnut please." I tried to keep my face from breaking as I asked.

"Then I'll go with the roasted cinnamon apple." Dras seemed to be weighing the options as I choose mine.

"Okay, what's with the face?" he asked after she left.

"I wasn't really expecting it here."

"You have ice cream where you're from? I've never even heard of it before, but if it's from here, I'll trust it's good."

"Um . . . yeah, I think our village was the first to make it, though we just used honey for sweetener, I imagine they will have some amount of sugar in it here in the capital."

"You and your sugar, that stuff's too expensive." He shook his head with a good-natured smile.

When it came, I thought Dras's eyes would pop out of his head. He was obviously keeping himself from just digging in all crazily. I was glad to see he liked it.

"You know, you could make this stuff pretty easily, Dras; you can make the ice for it. You'd have to get a churn and all, but it's fairly straightforward to do."

"Really!?" he coughed. "I . . . I mean, that's great; you'll have to show me sometime. I can see why people like it."

We laughed and tried each other's flavor as the sun set. The view from up here did not disappoint at all. Dras paid the bill without letting me even see it, said it was a thank-you for teaching him so much.

As I waited for him, I could hear the hostess from the back room talking to one of her coworkers.

"They're so cute, and her manners, she's got to be related to a noble family."

"A daughter, here?"

"Nah, cousin or something like me. The boy has an aura too. I think he might be first generation, if only he were a few years older . . ."

"Are they?"

"Casters? I think so, maybe physical, but I'm betting casters."

"Oh, that's good, if we get more casters or hopefully even nobles for business . . . But I meant a couple."

"Most definitely. I'd wager their families set them up or something, trying to get them together to improve everyone's standing."

"Yeah."

At this point, the door to the back was opened by another passing waitstaff, and I got to see the hostess pale as our eyes met. I wanted to go collapse in a corner or something, but she was probably having a minor heart attack at the idea I might cause a scene. I wouldn't, the food was good and her assumptions were not that far outside of the average.

I decided not to share their thoughts as we walked back to the Starlit Sky. It was still early but we both turned in. Tomorrow was Dras's big day, and he needed his rest. I looked at my sugar jar and considered making him something sweet, but decided against it. I was sure there would be celebrations afterward for his inevitable success.

Our morning was fast. Dras's parents came to pick him up and take him over to his exam early. His father and I exchanged a nod and smile while his mom scowled in the background. He seemed like a nice-enough guy on that short meeting. I was planning on leaving a bit later as I did last year; they needed their time together after all.

Upon arriving at the practical, I met the same guy again. He stood there as he always did, giving me an amused smile as I came over. I knew by this point where to go, but it was tradition to speak to him, so I did.

"Ah, I'm glad to see you returned. I did notice that your friend didn't quite make it last year, but registered to retake the exams today."

"Yup, we neglected the practical too much, but I've no worries this time."

"Oh? I took the liberty of going over his exam results. On the written, he got top marks; it was only by a small margin that he didn't make it before. Had he been the child of a noble, or even a close relative . . ."

"That's a lot of favoritism."

"Of course, not showing how much we prefer the higher classes would be unthinkable." He said it as if giving nobles an easier pass was the right and proper course.

"Are you telling me that I'll have to struggle hard to make it in then?"

"That depends. If you're truly skilled, you'll have no issues. I would say that if your little spell from last year wasn't just a one-off fluke, then you'll do well."

"It wasn't, and thank you."

"You're quite welcome, would you by chance be willing to show me another?" Now we got to the meat of it. He wanted to see what I could do.

"I'm planning on taking the exam next year. Why not run my practical if you're so interested?"

"Oh-ho! It isn't often that people come to me so snippishly. Very well, I will."

"I mean, I don't even know your name . . ."

"Ah, well. I must wait until next year to learn more about you, so I see no reason to tell you more about myself until then."

I wasn't sure how much I liked that this guy was a teacher, but he was fun conversations every now and then at least.

"Fair, see you next year."

"Indeed you will, and best of luck with your friend young Adraias."

"Dras doesn't need luck; he worked hard."

The laughter as I left was a bit irritating. I'd have to come up with something quite fun to show him next year. I had an idea or two on that, and it seemed well within the realm of possibility.

As I sat in the stands and watched, I knew that Dras was on the right track. I saw all that we'd worked on pulled out and displayed for the tester, and cheered to myself for my friend. Unlike last year, his test went on and on, well after those who had been canned early were ousted.

He made it, of course, and that night the party we threw at the Starlit Sky was amazing. I pulled out the sugar, and we tossed out a few caramel apples for the table. Dras's dad got a bit drunk and sang several songs with Lucien; sadly, he had no skill at it. Even his mother was friendly. We still didn't like each other, but there would be plenty of time for that later.

Dras had less than a week to prep for school, and prep he needed to. I saw the list of things he needed to get ready and nearly fell over. He'd been debating but ended up going with living in the dorms. The walk in every morning from where we lived would be too much. Preparing for that was an effort though, and I only saw him a few times in the evenings.

The evening of his first day of classes, I sat at a table, enjoying a meal. It was strangely lonely. I had gotten so used to sharing my evenings studying with Dras that his not coming by felt sad, like there was just something missing from that part of the day. I really needed to make new friends or find a hobby.

It was as I considered this that a beleaguered-looking man stumbled in. His jaunty hat was to one side, and he looked like he'd been traveling hard for days. Even his normally colorful clothes seemed a bit more sedate. Then again I'd known him for . . . Wow, about a decade, and he was pushing into his late twenties, maybe early thirties at this point.

"Well, well, well, look what the cat dragged in," I said as he drew near.

"If it isn't the traveling troubadour of trouble," Lucien added, having appeared by my side in his characteristically silent way.

"Alana!? Good grief, how did you get . . . You know, never mind, I don't want to know."

"So, is it a father, a spouse, or the law you're running from?"

"Oh, come now, Lucien, when is the last time I . . ." He cut himself off as he saw both of our smirks.

"To tell the truth, I just wanted to get away from the borders."

"Don't tell me we're going to have another war with the Empire?" That was a thought I truly dreaded.

"No, we won't. Mostly because the Empire no longer exists." The silence that greeted that statement spread through the whole room. "I see news hasn't made it this far yet."

FOOL'S FOLLY

I smiled at my generals as they stood around me, "We've won, men. Tonight, we celebrate the end of this miserable uprising."

I was, of course, greeted with cheers. I could see from top of the hill where we'd put our command camp atop how far the enemy army had been driven. It had taken days for us to press and chase this lot of slaves down. They'd run like rats as we followed, eventually being maneuvered into the valley where my regulars had chased them.

I had to give it to them, for a collection of slaves they'd done marvelously. They'd harried caravans with impunity, razed a few small towns and industrial operations, even destroyed a couple of bridges. I had personally had to gather the full army to come deal with them. The first three generals I'd sent to clean up the rabble had failed to even locate their camp. Such failures were unacceptable.

But I'd done my duty as emperor, gathered an enormous host of one hundred thousand men, and we'd scoured the countryside. When we found them, they numbered only perhaps ten thousand, barely half of what my least cautious advisers had believed. A few had had the audacity to suggest that they'd managed to get nearly eighty thousand men, but that was impossible. They would have to be found and supply themselves, and we had seen no way they could have done either. An army of any size left a footprint and had to have a supply train. They had almost none.

My own army was comprised of professional soldiers, armed and armored properly. We had ten thousand cavalry, thirty thousand heavy infantry, twenty thousand light infantry, twenty thousand archers, and around ten thousand specialists. Most of the rest were support staff. They could wield a weapon in a pinch, but a host of this magnitude required great organization. I'd even pulled a fair number of my combat-ready mages, as we'd had reports of casters in their army, nearly a hundred of them.

It was painful to deploy magic users. They were like siege weapons, each capable of great destruction, but needing special treatment. Few had training as soldiers, and their magic was often quite varied. Taking on special roles, they did amazingly well, but whole units would have to be built to optimize the results. Armies had tried to do without them before, but magic was too potent a weapon, they'd just run into someone who could hide from their arrows and rain death upon them. Killing a unit is not particularly difficult for an army, but without a mage to counter, chasing down one wizard who knew the area was a monstrous pain.

My own guard had nearly twenty mages in it. They had been trained as both casters and soldiers, and worked together like folded steel, stronger than any of those that could take the field against them. Most of them had gone down to the field to win glory for me today; my men would whoop and cheer as they saw such heroes among them.

I looked back to the rebels, coming out of my thoughts. They'd fled up to a small rock shelf, hardly big enough for them to even stand on, they didn't even have any cover from the sides or above. They would die on that rock. There was even a lake on one side; they had nowhere to go.

"We should give that valley a new name, or . . . maybe the little rock they've tried to hide themselves on, any suggestions."

There were snickers from some of my advisors, a few even handed out some ideas.

"Slave Rock."

"Dead Man's Valley."

"Rebel's End."

Not bad ones, but not great. I looked to some of the guards standing around, indicating they could speak. Such men often had a good sense of humor.

"Fool's Folly."

"Oh, that one's good. Who are you?" I turned to the man in question, he seemed to be a unit leader, older, and grizzled.

"Verren, Your Imperial Majesty."

"I like that, Verren, very good indeed. Perhaps when this is all over, I'll give you some lands nearby."

"My emperor, something's happening!" I turned toward the man who'd broken my conversation, few had that kind of audacity.

As I watched, the lake began to move, not a bit of water, not a stream or the like. The. Entire. Lake. My eyes went wide as it circled behind slamming first into the flank, then the rear of the soldiers, smashing them like children's toys. It flowed and flowed, and then it moved through my whole army, picking them up and pulling them along. It smashed into the edge of the little rise the rebels had been standing on, then flowed back into the lake bed.

I felt numb as I watched so many of my men pulled into that bed along with the water, unable to find anything to even hold on to as it swept them to their dooms. As the rebels flew down to slaughter the survivors, I realized it had been a trap.

"That's . . . that's not possible, the mana to . . . It would have taken months, years maybe of . . ." My head adviser on magic was just as flabbergasted as I was. The man couldn't do anything but stand there and spew nonsense.

I put my hand to my head. How many had just died? Seventy thousand? Eighty? Most of the army was in that valley; most of them were dead. I steeled myself as I took in a breath, preparing to call for a retreat.

It was so fast I hardly felt it. The spearhead bloomed from my chest like a silver flower bursting from the ground. The breath caught, and I could hardly make a noise as the other guards moved against their companions and my advisers. I turned to look at the man who'd gotten me, shocked as I saw the hate in his eyes.

"This is where a Fool's Folly ended his empire." I fell as he withdrew the blade, unable to move to aid my men as my lifeblood soaked into the ground, a Fool's Folly indeed.

BISHOP'S MEETING

Theodore closed the door to his office, locking it tightly in place before turning back to his desk. This room had always been the office for the bishop, the highest authority for his order in the central area of the kingdom. The reason for that was unknown to most. But as he passed back behind his desk and pressed a certain place in the wall, the doorway that opened before him made the reason clear.

He stepped in; it was nearly the appointed time. He went down a narrow stairwell into a room slightly smaller than his own. It seemed plain as well; a single stone chair lay before a small table. A small magically powered lamp providing calm bright light. The real magic was hidden within the stone in a technique unknown to him. As he sat down, it activated, connecting his eyes and ears to other such devices.

There was a much brighter light hovering the bare room, showing a number of priests and priestesses sitting around a large table. At its head an old man sat in a plain off-white robe, his bearing fatherly. The others were still arriving, the bishops and leaders from the orders in the surrounding countries came one by one, until nearly three dozen sat waiting.

"Allow us to begin," the Elder intoned, bringing all eyes to him. "What is the current situation in the . . . former Ermathi Empire?"

There was a brief look between the different heads of the empire, then their representative finally spoke. "Surprisingly stable. Normally, I would expect more problems, but the Lord of Shadows has for his part done what he can to keep the peace. There have been a number of changes to the law, but no wholesale slaughter or destruction. At least not after what happened to the emperor and some of the other leaders of the government."

"That is unusual, but good to hear. How has his relationship with our various orders been?"

"He has respected the various orders, allowing civilians to seek shelter under their respective shields, and those in his army who have been found to have preyed on civilians against both his orders and those of the Order of the Lovers have been handed over for punishment." He took a deep breath. "I will say that the Order of the Vine has some issues with his actions at what is now being called Fool's Folly, but he's making a few concessions to apologize for such a disturbance."

Theodore did not pity those men given to the Order of the Lovers; they surely would suffer for such foolish viciousness. As for the Order of the Vine, they tended to be prickly about any large-scale disturbance of nature, so their irritation was no surprise.

"Do we know how he did that by the way?" The elder looked over toward the representative with a questioning look.

"It would seem he has a unit of water mages of unusual power. The head of it is alarmingly strong as I told you all in our previous meeting. I'm not sure if this is the maximum of their collective ability or not."

"Based on the actions of the Lord of Shadows so far, I worry some about that. How go our attempts at building relations and control measures?"

"I would say they go well, neither Lord Durin nor his generals seem to want overmuch. In comparison to most governments, I worry little. We've done what we can to ingratiate them to us. There is the matter in the kingdom of Bergond."

"The child is safe, if uncooperative. We are keeping an eye on her welfare from afar." Theodore frowned; it was not exactly the thing he would want to tell his companions.

"Forgive me, my absence from our last meeting must have caused me to miss this. What exactly is this about a child?" The Order of the Vine's bishop from the northeastern part of Bergond turned to the others. That was not unusual, with limited communication over such distances and infrequency of these meetings such things sometimes got lost.

"One of Durin's generals and the aforementioned head of his water mage unit have been making some inquiries as to the location of the general's daughter. The issue is that if they find it, they may go to retrieve her and start a war, and if any harm should come to her . . ." the elder allowed his explanation to fade off.

"They could try to use it as *casus belli*? What is the general's ranking?" The bishop of Vine furrowed his brow as he considered.

"The hierarchy of the Lord of Shadows is a bit unusual, but I feel we should treat him as something equivalent to a highly respected noble," the earlier representative explained. "He's at the least high in their rankings. Our reports also indicate that he was the one who killed the emperor a few months back."

"Ah, I see."

"Do we have any other news of note?" The elder looked around the table getting a few nods here and there.

The meeting went on for hours after that. One of the Elven nations across the Eastern Sea was trying to increase relations, not unwelcome but highly unusual. Some strong monsters had been sighted in the far north, and more trained priests were being requested to aid in their destruction and the cleanup of the mess they'd made. The rebels throughout Bergond were being a right pain in the neck, disrupting large swaths of the country, though the government was trying to keep that quiet.

These meetings were like that though. The various orders had a working, if sometimes a bit strained relationship, and communication between them was an absolute must to keep the peace. Theodore sighed as it finally ended, exhausted from the long conversations. It had nearly drained the artifacts of all the mana needed to maintain contact and would take weeks to refill. At least he only had to attend one of these once a season.

ABOUT THE AUTHOR

Wandering Agent is the North Carolina–based author of the Melody of Mana series as well as other fantasy and isekai stories.

Podium
DISCOVER
STORIES UNBOUND
PodiumAudio.com